Romantic Suspense

Danger. Passion. Drama.

Stalker In The Storm
Carla Cassidy

Undercover Heist
Rachel Astor

MILLS & BOON

STALKER IN THE STORM
© 2024 by Carla Bracale
Philippine Copyright 2024
Australian Copyright 2024
New Zealand Copyright 2024

First Published 2024
First Australian Paperback Edition 2024
ISBN 978 1 038 91047 9

UNDERCOVER HEIST
© 2024 by Rachel Astor
Philippine Copyright 2024
Australian Copyright 2024
New Zealand Copyright 2024

First Published 2024
First Australian Paperback Edition 2024
ISBN 978 1 038 91047 9

This is a work of fiction. Names, characters, places, and incidents are either the
product of the author's imagination or are used fictitiously, and any resemblance to
actual persons, living or dead, business establishments, events, or locales is entirely
coincidental.

MIX
Paper | Supporting
responsible forestry
FSC® C001695

Published by
Harlequin Mills & Boon
An imprint of Harlequin Enterprises (Australia) Pty Limited
(ABN 47 001 180 918), a subsidiary of HarperCollins
Publishers Australia Pty Limited
(ABN 36 009 913 517)
Level 19, 201 Elizabeth Street
SYDNEY NSW 2000 AUSTRALIA

Cover art used by arrangement with Harlequin Books S.A.. All rights reserved.

Printed and bound in Australia by McPherson's Printing Group

Stalker In The Storm

Carla Cassidy

MILLS & BOON

Carla Cassidy is an award-winning, *New York Times* bestselling author who has written over 170 books, including 150 for Harlequin. She has won the Centennial Award from Romance Writers of America. Most recently she won the 2019 Write Touch Readers' Award for her Harlequin Intrigue title *Desperate Strangers*. Carla believes the only thing better than curling up with a good book is sitting down at the computer with a good story to write.

Visit the Author Profile page
at millsandboon.com.au for more titles.

Dear Reader,

Growing up in the Midwest, thunderstorms are just a force of nature to be dealt with. Sometimes they can be nothing more than distant rumblings in the sky and a patter of welcomed rain at the window. Other times they are tornado-breeding monsters that put people and property in imminent danger.

I've always wondered, in my sick little writer's mind, how frightening it would be to wake up during a thunderstorm and realise there's a stranger in your home. How horrible would it be to only see the intruder during the lightning flashes and not be able to hear them due to the thunder overhead.

Stalker in the Storm is about a woman who is being stalked by an unknown person. There was a time in my life when I was stalked by an ex-boyfriend. Wherever I went, I would see his car and I knew he was watching me. Even when I went out on dates, when my date took me home, I would see my ex-boyfriend's car parked just down the street. Thankfully, it only lasted for a little while and then he stopped.

Still, it was a creepy feeling that hopefully I brought to this book. Storms...stalkers...and secrets—I hope you enjoy reading *Stalker in the Storm*.

Happy reading!

Carla Cassidy

DEDICATION

This book is dedicated to my friend and inspiration—
my mother.

Chapter 1

Bailey Troy roared down Main Street, aware of the minutes ticking by far too quickly. She was late to open her business, the Sassy Nail Salon. One of her first customers of the day was Letta Lee, head of the women's gardening club and number-one gossip and mean witch of Millsville, Kansas.

She and some of her cronies would make Bailey's life an absolute living hell if Letta had to wait ten minutes or so to get her butt into the salon chair to get her nails done. With this thought in mind, Bailey stepped on the gas.

The late September air caressed her face, reminding her of how much she loved her sporty red convertible. Her big, round sunglasses reduced the bright sun's glare and it was nearly impossible for the breeze to mess up her short, spiky hair.

She was almost to the salon when she heard a siren coming from someplace behind her. Looking in her rear-view mirror, she couldn't see what kind of an emergency vehicle it might be. She should pull over to the curb, but instead she hit the gas once again, thinking she could stay well ahead of it.

The Sassy Nail Salon was just to her left and she whirled into the lot and parked, pleased to see that Letta Lee's car wasn't there yet. Hopefully, Bailey would have time to get inside and set things up for the older woman before she showed up.

Her pleasure was short-lived as a patrol car pulled in just behind her, the siren blaring and the lights on top swirling in a red-and-blue blur.

"Crap," she murmured under her breath. She couldn't tell who was in the patrol car, but she hoped it wasn't Officer Joel Penn. He could be a real jerk, and she knew she'd never be able to talk him out of a speeding ticket. The siren stopped its shrieking and the lights quit spinning.

She watched in her side-view mirror as the door opened and Officer Benjamin Cooper stepped out. Her heart immediately took on an accelerated beat. His blond hair sparkled in the sunshine as he approached her car.

She'd had a mad crush on the man forever, but he'd never made a move for her to think he might want to date her. He'd certainly dated most of the other women in town and rumor had it he was now seeing Celeste Winthrop, a very thirsty, attractive divorcée.

His blue uniform shirt stretched taut across his broad shoulders and his dark blue slacks fit nicely on his long legs. His holster was slung around his narrow hips and Bailey felt half-breathless just looking at him.

"Bailey," he said, his deep voice somber as he reached her driver window. He pulled down his sunglasses, exposing his beautiful, long-lashed blue eyes. He glared at her sternly. "You want to tell me what's the hurry?"

"Oh, Officer Cooper, was I speeding?" she asked innocently. "I'm sorry, I guess I might have been going a little bit over the speed limit."

"Nineteen miles over the speed limit isn't a little bit," he replied.

She looked at him in genuine surprise. Jeez, she hadn't realized just how fast she'd been going. "License and registration," he said.

"Are you really going to give me a ticket?" she asked miserably, and to make her misery worse, at that moment Letta Lee pulled in and parked.

"Bailey, this isn't the first time I've seen you speeding down Main Street. One of these days you're going to kill yourself or somebody else," Benjamin said.

"Please—please don't ticket me. I'm so sorry and I'll definitely do better in the future. I was running late this morning. I overslept and then I forgot to put a pod in my coffee machine, so I got nothing but a cup of hot water, and I had Letta Lee as my first client of the day and she can be such a pain and…" She was babbling and she couldn't seem to help herself. Not only did she not want a ticket, but she also always felt ridiculously nervous around him.

"I got it," he replied with a hint of sympathy in his voice. "Okay, Bailey, I'll let you go this time, but the next time I see you roaring down the street, I promise you're going to get a ticket." He pushed his sunglasses back up. "Now, go tend to Letta Lee before she calls 911 for having to wait on you."

"Thank you, thank you," she replied with relief. "I swear I'll do better in the future."

"I'll be watching you, Bailey," he replied. "Now, have a good day."

As he headed back to his car, she got out of hers. She'd never had much actual contact with Benjamin and it upset her that the brief exchange she'd had with him had been about her speeding. Why couldn't he have pulled her over to ask her out on a date?

What made things even worse was Letta Lee was standing by the salon's front door, tapping her foot with obvious impatience. The thin, older woman was clad in a light blue pantsuit and her short white hair was perfectly coiffed. She looked like a sweet old lady, but her personality was anything but sweet.

"I must say, it's quite an embarrassment for me to be doing business where the police show up," Letta said as Bailey unlocked the front door. "I hope that isn't going to be a regular thing here."

"The police were here because I was speeding to get here on time so you wouldn't have to wait on me," Bailey replied.

"And yet here I am, waiting on you," Letta said with an audible indignant sniff.

Bailey swallowed a deep sigh and ushered the older woman inside. Ten minutes later Letta had her feet soaking in a bowl of warm, scented water and Bailey began to take off her old maroon fingernail polish.

"How are things going with the gardening club?" Bailey asked in an attempt to make some pleasant small talk.

"Really well. We're getting things all ready to have a nice display at the fall festival," Letta replied.

The fall festival in Millsville was a big deal. All the businesses closed for two days and there were booths to buy goods, cooking contests and a full carnival for everyone to enjoy. The festival was in a week and already there was a thrum of excitement in the town.

Lord knew they all needed something to look forward to after the two heinous murders that had taken place recently. Bailey didn't even want to think about them, but thoughts of the murders now played in her mind. The first one had occurred almost two months ago. The victim, a nice young woman named Cindy Perry had been stabbed to death and then made into a human scarecrow and stood up in a corn field.

The second victim had been Sandy Blackstone. She had also been stabbed and made into a scarecrow then stood up in the backyard of the bakery. Thinking about the murders always gave Bailey the shivers.

As she painted first Letta's fingernails and then gave her a pedicure and painted her toenails, the two continued to talk about the festival. By the time she was finished with Letta, Jaime Davenport and Naomi Crawford came into the shop. The two women worked for Bailey. Naomi worked full-time and Jaime part-time. Within minutes of their arrival, the busy Saturday began.

It was just after seven that evening when she finally closed up shop. She was exhausted and grateful that the salon was closed the next day and on Monday. She intended to use her "weekend" to thoroughly clean her house. She had a feeling the next week would be crazy busy as most of the women would want their nails all done for the festival next Friday and Saturday.

She got into her car and once inside she headed home. Home was a two-story house just off Main Street. She'd bought the place two years before and loved being a homeowner.

Before that she had been living with her mother in the small ranch house where she was born. As much as she loved her mother, they often butted heads. It had been important to Bailey to build her own life and live by her own rules. She'd wanted to set down roots and live on her own terms, so owning a house had been important to her.

As she drove, she kept her speed within the legal limit and continued to look in her rearview mirror to make sure she wasn't followed by anyone.

When she reached the attractive Wedgwood blue house with the white shutters, she parked in the driveway. Her garage was filled with salon supplies and was completely disorganized, making it impossible for her to park inside there right now.

She entered by the front door and beelined into the kitchen, where she set her purse on the counter and then opened the fridge to see what she was going to eat for dinner.

Her kitchen was painted a bright yellow and she had large colorful roosters hanging on one wall. She loved the airy, cheerful room. She'd chosen a round glass-topped table and red accents popped around the room.

She pulled out a bowl of chicken salad she'd made the night before and made a sandwich with it, then added potato chips to the plate and grabbed a soda.

She had just sat down to eat when her cell phone rang. She looked at the caller identification, swallowed a deep sigh and then answered. "Hi, Mom."

"Bailey, I'd like you to come over tomorrow and help me clean out the spare room." Angela Troy was a strong woman who had raised Bailey as a single parent. Bailey had spent most of her life trying to win her mother's love and approval, and at thirty-four years old she felt as if she had yet to gain it.

"What time do you have in mind?" Bailey asked, even though the last thing she wanted to do on her day off was work in her mother's spare room.

"Around noon, but don't expect me to make lunch for you. Eat before you come," Angela instructed. "I heard that the police were at your place of business this morning." There was more than a touch of displeasure in her tone.

"Don't worry, Mom, it was nothing serious," Bailey assured her.

"I do worry about you, Bailey. You do realize you are the physical type for the Scarecrow Killer. I would feel so much better if you were married or at least had a serious boyfriend and you didn't live all alone."

Bailey rolled her eyes. This was a common diatribe from her mother. "Mom, it's hard to get married or have a serious boyfriend when you aren't even dating anyone."

"What was wrong with Howard Kendall? He's a nice-looking man who has a good job at the bank and he was absolutely crazy about you."

"But I wasn't crazy about him," Bailey replied. Howard Kendall was a nice man she'd dated several times, but he hadn't given her butterflies or sparks. Even if he had, Bailey had a rule—she only dated a man three times or so and then she was done with him.

"You aren't getting any younger, Bailey. Surely you do realize your biological clock is definitely ticking faster now," Angela continued. "I'm ready for some grandchildren."

"Okay, Mom. On that note, I'll just see you tomorrow," Bailey replied.

The two said their goodbyes, and as Bailey ate, her thoughts weren't on her mother, but focused on Officer Benjamin Cooper. He definitely gave her butterflies in the pit of her stomach each time she was around him. If she was anyplace that she might talk to him, she became a tongue-twisted fool. It was no wonder he'd never asked her out.

She finished eating, then put her plate in the dishwasher

and headed to her bedroom upstairs. Her bedroom was definitely her safe haven. Decorated in hot pink and black, it was both contemporary and stylish.

Not only did the room boast a king-size bed and a large smart television, but it also had an en suite bathroom done in the same pink-and-black color scheme.

After a quick shower, she pulled on her comfy nightgown and then crawled into bed. She turned on her television and found a program she enjoyed watching, but her thoughts were scattered and made concentrating on the show difficult.

As much as she would love to date Benjamin, she knew marriage was probably not in her future. And she'd made peace with that. But there were times when she got lonely and wished she had a special man in her life. There were times when she wished she could be normal.

When she thought about her conversation with her mother, there was one thing that threatened to walk shivers up and down her spine. The Scarecrow Killer. The man had already killed two women, but the worst part was what he had done to their bodies.

He'd dressed up each of them in frayed jeans and a flannel shirt, then put them on poles as if they were scarecrows. Their mouths had been sewn shut with thick black thread and their eyes had been missing.

The whole town had been on edge since the murders had occurred. It was obvious there was a sick, vicious serial killer at work in the small town of Millsville, Kansas. And her mother had been right: with Bailey's blond hair and blue eyes, she fit the Scarecrow Killer's victim profile.

The next day at precisely noon, Bailey pulled up to the farmhouse where she'd been raised. It was a small, two-bedroom place painted white with black shutters. Her mother rented out ten acres to the farmer next door, since she had never been interested in farming and it had been an easy way for her to make a little extra money.

Rather, Angela had worked as a secretary for the mayor, Buddy Lyons, for years and had finally retired from that position last year.

"Mom," Bailey yelled as she stepped through the front door and into the living room. The living room had a burgundy sofa and a matching floral chair. Bailey didn't remember there ever being different furniture in the room. New furniture had never been in her single mother's budget.

"I'm back here." Her mother's voice rang out from down the hallway.

Bailey headed back to the bedroom that had been hers while growing up, but the minute Bailey had gotten her own place, the bedroom had become the catch-all spare storage room.

Angela was in the process of pulling boxes off the closet shelf and placing them on the twin bed. "Bailey, I'm glad you're here. A lot of this is your stuff and I want you to take it all with you today. I'm not a storage unit and I'm going to need this space for my own things."

Angela Troy was an attractive woman with short ash-blond hair and pale blue eyes. Even though it had only been her and Bailey, her mother had never really fostered a close relationship with her daughter. Of course, she'd had to work hard to support the two of them, and then when she was home from work, she was often too tired to have time for Bailey.

For the next few hours, Bailey carried boxes and bags to her car, and then helped her mother get the room reorganized with new craft items Angela had bought for herself.

"I think I'll really enjoy getting to know how to make jewelry," Angela said.

"That's great, Mom," Bailey replied. "I'd be proud to wear anything you made."

Angela looked pointedly at Bailey's oversize, dangling bright yellow earrings. "I don't think you'll be interested in wearing any of my jewelry. It's going to be quite subdued and tasteful."

Bailey stifled a deep sigh. This was Angela at her best, throwing out little jabs to undermine Bailey's confidence. But Bailey was used to it and it quickly rolled off her back.

It was nearly four o'clock when the two sat at the kitchen table and her mother poured them each a glass of iced tea. "Thank you for all your help today," Angela said. "How are things going at the salon?"

"Good. I'm expecting a really busy week ahead as most of the ladies in town will want their nails done before the festival," Bailey replied.

"Yes, I have an appointment on Thursday to come in and see Jaime," Angela responded.

"Mom, I've told you a million times just to call me and I'll come over and do your nails." Bailey took a big drink of the cold tea.

"It's all right, dear. I know how busy you stay and I would much rather you spend your spare time dating. So has anyone asked you out lately?"

"Howard is still calling me, although I've been firm in telling him that I'm not going out with him again. Then last night after I talked to you, Ethan Dourty called to see if I wanted to grab a cup of coffee with him tomorrow morning at the café."

"I certainly hope you're going. Ethan seems like a fine

man, and with him owning his own insurance company I'm sure he's solid financially," Angela replied.

"I'm going," Bailey said. Ethan wasn't the man she was most interested in, but Benjamin certainly wasn't making any moves on her.

The truth of the matter was that Bailey was lonely. She'd been particularly lonely since her best friend, Lizzy Maxwell, had hooked up with the love of her life, Joe Masterson. While she was thrilled that Lizzy had found her one true love, that left Bailey uncomfortable playing the role of third wheel whenever she visited with Lizzy.

"You know, Bailey, you're very picky when it comes to men. You only see them a few times and then you find something wrong with them," Angela said.

"I can't help it that they aren't right for me," Bailey answered.

"You have to compromise, Bailey. You're never going to find a husband that way."

"Then maybe I'll never find a husband," Bailey replied airily.

"Don't be ridiculous," Angela said. "You need a husband. You don't want to go through life all alone like I have. If your father had been a real man and had stepped up to the plate when I found out I was pregnant with you, then my life would have been much better and so much easier. I should have married one of the nice men who dated me when you were young."

"But from what you've told me in the past, you weren't in love with any of them."

Angela made a scoffing noise. "I've come to believe love isn't all that important. If you're compatible and share common goals and respect each other, then that's enough to make a good marriage and you should remember that, Bailey."

"I'll keep that in mind," Bailey replied. "And now, if you're finished with me, I think I'll head on home."

"All right, dear. I'll see you in the salon on Thursday." The two women stood up from the table and headed for the front door.

"Then I'll see you Thursday," Bailey said, and minutes later she was in her car and headed home.

She always found spending time with her mother completely exhausting and today had been no different. She realized Angela expected her to get married and pop out a couple of kids, but Bailey knew that wasn't in her future.

The next morning at ten o'clock, she walked into the café to meet Ethan. The Millsville Café was a popular place in town. Inside, the walls were vibrant with color, and three of them were decorated with huge paintings. The first held golden bales of hay with bright red roosters. The second was a yellow cornfield with three silos and the final wall was farmland in patterns of browns, greens and golds.

It was definitely a place for friends and families to meet neighbors and enjoy a good, reasonably priced meal. There were booths along both walls and a row of tables and chairs down the middle. The place was packed with the Monday morning crowd. Ethan rose and waved to her from one of the two-tops.

He was a nice-looking guy with light brown hair and hazel eyes. She knew he was well-liked and respected in the town, and she wished he gave her butterflies like Benjamin did. But even if he did, she knew there would be no future for them.

Most men her age would be looking to start a family, and Bailey just wasn't ready for that.

You're not right. You're the most selfish woman I've ever met. You're not normal.

The deep male voice echoed in her head, a voice from her distant past. She quickly shoved away the memory. The last thing she wanted was for that voice to start playing around and around in her mind.

"Hi, Bailey," Ethan said with a wide smile as she joined him at the table. He was dressed in a pair of jeans and a short-sleeved white button-down shirt.

"Hi, Ethan." She sat in the chair across from his. "Thank you so much for asking me out for this morning." It would be nice if she and Ethan could just be friends. It would be nice to have a male friend who just wanted to spend time with her and wanted nothing more.

"No problem." He sank back down in his chair. "I know I said we'd meet for coffee, but if you'd like some breakfast or an early lunch, feel free to order whatever you want."

"Thanks, but coffee is fine," she replied.

"I just thought it would be nice to get to know you a little better. We sometimes run into each other on the street or at a town function, but I've never really gotten an opportunity to sit down and talk with you."

At that moment, Regina Waltz, a waitress, appeared next to the table to take their orders.

"I'd just like a coffee," Bailey said.

"I'll take the same, but I'd also like one of those big cinnamon rolls," Ethan said and then looked at Bailey. "Are you sure you don't want something else?"

She smiled at him. "No thanks, coffee is good for me."

Within minutes they had been served and Regina left

their table. "I figured with both of us being business owners, we'd have a lot in common," Ethan said.

"I'm sure we do," she agreed. "I don't know about you, but my business keeps me very busy."

"Yeah, I have to hustle quite a bit to keep mine growing." He smiled at her once again. "So tell me about Bailey Troy. Why isn't a beautiful, smart woman like you not married yet?"

"I guess I just haven't found that special man yet," she replied. "And I could ask the same thing about you. Why isn't a handsome, smart man like you not married?"

"I guess I haven't found the right woman yet," he replied with another smile. "I've been so focused on my business that I've neglected my love life, but I'm ready now to relax some on the business end of things and get more social."

For the next forty-five minutes or so, the two visited and got to know each other a little better. He seemed like a nice man and she found him easy to talk to. They talked about the difficulties and joys of owning a business and how much they enjoyed living in the small town.

"I was wondering if you'd like to go with me to the festival next Saturday," he said as she got ready to leave.

"Oh, I'm so sorry, Ethan, but I'm working at the festival. I'm offering all the kids under sixteen a free nail painting," she replied.

"Wow, that's really nice, Bailey," he said.

"I just thought it would be fun. We're also doing five-dollar face paintings, too, however Naomi Crawford is in charge of that."

"Maybe we could get together sometime after the festival," he suggested.

"Sure, just give me a call," Bailey replied. "And now,

it's time for me to get out of here. Thank you so much for the coffee and good conversation and I'll talk to you soon."

Minutes later, as Bailey drove home, a wave of depression swept over her. There was no question that she was often lonely, and she filled that loneliness by dating men who really meant nothing to her.

Even though her mother thought it was because she was too picky, that simply wasn't the case. Bailey was just trying to protect herself and anyone she might date. She didn't want feelings to get too deep on either end because she knew she was a bad choice as a wife and mother.

You're not right. You're the most selfish woman I've ever met. Again, those words from her past haunted her. As much as she didn't want to believe them, she knew Adam had been correct about her, and that was why she would never have a serious relationship after him.

It had been ten years since she'd dated Adam Merriweather, and still, he had a profound effect on her. When she'd told him what she saw as her future, he'd told her how selfish and sick she was.

Thankfully, it was soon after they broke up that he had moved out of town. It was nice that she didn't have to worry about bumping into him around town. Even though she'd put that relationship far behind her, his parting words to her still haunted her and stabbed her in her very soul.

The rest of her evening she cleaned house and did laundry to prepare for the busy workweek ahead. Tuesday morning, she got up and dressed in a pink dress that was one of her favorites with its cinched waist and flirty skirt. She added pink-and-white polka-dotted earrings and white sandals.

By the time she left her house, she felt ready to take on

the world. It was a beautiful sunny day without a cloud in the sky. She was careful to watch her speed as she drove and then she pulled up and parked in front of the salon.

Ten years ago, right after her relationship with Adam was finished, she had decided to go to nail school and she had opened the business eight years ago.

She had begged, borrowed and tapped into every credit line she could get to buy the building, all the equipment and then get the business up and running. There had been no other nail salon in town and almost immediately the place had been a huge success. That very first year she had turned a profit and she was very proud of what she'd built here.

The building was the perfect size for the salon. She had five pedicure chairs and four manicure stations. There was a nice restroom for the guests and a back room for the employees to take their breaks or eat lunch.

The outside was painted black with hot pink trim. Large pink lettering announced it to be the Sassy Nail Salon. She loved every inch of it.

She got out of her car and walked up to the front door. She frowned as the doorknob turned easily in her hand. Had she been in such a hurry to leave on Saturday night that she'd forgotten to lock it up when she'd left? If so, it wasn't the first time it had happened. She reminded herself she had to be more careful in the future as she pushed open the front door.

Bailey took a step inside, flipped on all the lights and then she saw her. "She" sat in one of the salon chairs. She was clad in frayed blue jeans and a red plaid shirt.

A straw hat rode her head at a cocky angle. Her mouth was sewn shut with thick black thread and her eyes were missing. Even with everything that had been done to her,

Bailey immediately recognized her as Megan Lathrop, a young blonde who worked as a nurse at the hospital.

She was a horrific sight. As Bailey stared at her, the back of her throat closed up as cold chills raced up and down her spine.

Help. Oh, God, Bailey needed to get help. As her mind worked to process the fact that the Scarecrow Killer had struck again and there was a dead woman in her salon, her hand fumbled in her purse to grab her cell phone. As she punched in the emergency number, she tried desperately to stifle her screams.

Chapter 2

Officer Benjamin Cooper sped up to the nail shop, parked and then jumped out of his car. He shoved open the door to the salon and Bailey immediately flew into his arms. She sobbed into the front of his chest as her entire body shook with deep tremors.

He stared over Bailey's shoulder and gazed at the life-less body that sat in one of her pedicure chairs. It... She was a terrible sight. Dammit, he'd hoped there wouldn't be another one. He'd hoped like hell they would be able to catch the killer before he could take another victim.

Despite what had been done to her, he recognized her as Megan Lathrop, a cute blonde with big blue eyes—eyes that were now missing. The whole salon smelled of death and he hoped like hell they would be able to get some clues with this one that would lead them to the killer.

"D-do you s-see her?" Bailey asked between choked sobs. "Oh B-Benjamin, why wa-was she left here? Wh-why is she here?"

Benjamin guided the sobbing woman outside the salon and to the bench that sat in front of the place. The last thing he wanted was for her to contaminate the scene any more than she already had. As she sank down, he sat next to her and put an arm around her slender shoulders. He'd stay with her until other officers showed up. She weakly leaned into his side.

"Wh-why here?" she asked again. "Wh-why was she l-left in my salon?"

"Bailey, we don't know why they are left where they are," he said softly. As sorry as he was for Megan, he was just grateful that Bailey hadn't been the victim.

This murder confirmed for sure that the killer had a penchant for blondes with blue eyes. Bailey was highly visible whether she was racing around in her red convertible or walking down the street in one of her stylish outfits. Benjamin was incredibly drawn to her and that was why he had always stayed away from her.

Now that they were outside and he was sitting so close to her, he could smell her scent. It was the very attractive fragrance of fresh florals and mysterious spices.

"Wh-who is this m-monster?" Bailey continued to cry as her entire body trembled against his.

"I wish we knew. Can I ask you some questions, Bailey? Can you tell me exactly what happened when you arrived here this morning? Did you see anyone lingering around the salon?"

She shook her head. "No...nobody, but the front door was unlocked this morning when I got here. But sometimes I forget to lock up after myself. I just assumed I'd forgotten to lock up when I finished up here on Saturday night." She released a deep sigh and melted farther into the side of him.

"So you didn't see anything or anyone unusual before you walked into the salon?" Benjamin asked.

"No...nothing. It was just a normal day," she replied and then began to cry once again. "I can't b-believe she was just—just sitting there. It's so—so horrible. She looked so h-horrible."

At that moment, Chief of Police Dallas Calloway pulled in with his sirens blaring and his lights whirling. He turned off both the sirens and the lights and then quickly got out of his car. He was followed by two more police vehicles, which held officers Joel Penn and Darryl O'Conner.

"You good out here?" Dallas asked Benjamin.

Benjamin nodded, and Dallas and the other men entered the building. "I—I just can't believe this is happening," Bailey said. She looked up at him with her big, beautiful blue eyes. "Who would do this to poor Megan? She was such a sweet young woman. And what does he do with their eyes? Oh, God, why does he take their eyes?"

"I wish we had all the answers," he replied.

She began to weep all over again and Benjamin pulled her closer and awkwardly patted her back in an effort to comfort her. Under ordinary circumstances, he would have enjoyed having her in his arms. She was petite and fit perfectly against him. But these weren't ordinary circumstances. Another heinous murder had occurred and he was sure it had been horrendous for Bailey to walk into her salon and find a dead woman in one of her chairs.

They remained sitting there for several long moments and once again she got herself under control. Dallas stepped out of the door and greeted her softly.

"You might as well go on home, Bailey. Your salon is going to be closed for the next day or two while we process the crime scene," he said.

They all paused as the coroner pulled up in his black hearse. Josiah Mills was probably ten years past retirement age, but according to him, he had no desire to retire anytime soon.

He got out of the hearse along with Gary Walters, his

thirtysomething assistant. "Bastard got another one, eh?" Josiah said as he approached them.

"That's right, although this one is a little different in that she's sitting rather than standing somewhere outside," Dallas replied.

"Let's go see what we've got," Josiah said somberly.

Dallas ushered in Josiah and Gary, and then indicated to Benjamin that he wanted him inside, as well. Benjamin stood and cast a sympathetic smile toward Bailey. "Go home, Bailey. Or better yet, go to your mother's place or go sit with a friend. I know you've been through a terrible shock and right now you need to be with somebody who can comfort you."

"I was finding you very comforting," she replied with a shuddering sigh.

"I'm sorry, but I need to get to work now. I need to help process the scene, so hopefully we can catch this guy."

"Okay, maybe you could check in on me later today?" she asked anxiously as she stood.

A faint breeze caught the bottom of her pretty pink dress and sent it ruffling all around her shapely legs. "Sure, I'll try to stop by your place later tonight," he replied. "Now, get home or get someplace safe."

At thirty-seven years old, he wasn't looking for marriage or even a long-term relationship and that's exactly why he kept his distance from Bailey, because he suspected if he had a little bit of her, he'd want way more.

It was just after nine that night when he pulled into Bailey's driveway. He was absolutely exhausted, with more work to come before the night was over. Dallas had given some of the men thirty minutes or so to get something to eat and then return to the salon, as they intended on working through the night.

Instead of getting anything to eat, Benjamin had first headed directly to Bailey's house. He'd kind of promised he'd check in on her this evening. He got out of his car and walked toward her house, where light spilled out of several of her windows, letting him know she was still up.

He knocked on her door and she immediately answered. She was dressed in a pair of gray jogging pants and a gray-and-turquoise T-shirt. Her makeup was minimal and her eyes were slightly red and swollen as if she'd spent most of the day crying.

"Oh, Benjamin, I'm so glad you came by," she said as she opened the door wider to allow him entry. She gestured him toward the sofa and he sat down. The room looked exactly like he'd expected it to—contemporary and colorful with bright pink and yellow throw pillows on the sleek black sofa. There was also a bookcase holding books and knick-knacks. "Would you like something to drink?" she asked.

"No thanks, I'm fine. The real question is how are you doing?"

She sank down in the chair facing the sofa and shook her head. "To be honest, I don't know how I'm doing. One minute I think I'm doing just fine and then I think about poor Megan again and I totally lose it."

Even now her beautiful blue eyes filled with the shimmer of impending tears. "I mean, I'd heard about the women who were killed before, but hearing about it and seeing it up close and personal are two very different things." She swiped at her eyes.

"I'm so sorry you had to see that, Bailey," he replied. "But keep in mind that it had nothing to do with you."

"It's hard not to think that it has something to do with me. I mean, out of all the places in town, why did the killer choose my salon? Is the killer somebody I know? Did I somehow make him mad at me?" She searched his face.

"Bailey, you shouldn't be thinking that way at all. If we've learned anything from the first two murders, it was that the places where the bodies were found were totally random and we're sure that's the case with this last one."

"I just wish he would have randomed someplace else," she replied dryly.

"The bad news is that we'll have your salon closed for tomorrow, but the good news is hopefully on Thursday you'll be able to open up for business again," he said. "We're working as long and as fast as we can to see that will happen. And now, I need to get out of here. I need to grab a burger and then get back to work at the salon." He stood from the sofa.

She rose, as well. "I really appreciate you stopping by to check on me," she said as they walked toward her front door.

"Just take tomorrow to rest up because I'm sure you'll be really busy on Thursday," he said as they reached the front door.

"Or I won't be busy at all because nobody will want to get their nails done in a place where a scarecrow body was found."

Benjamin released a small burst of laughter. "Surely you know the women in this town better than that. They'll be beating each other over the head with their purses in order to get a chair in the infamous salon."

She offered him a small smile. "You're probably right about that," she agreed. She then leaned forward and into his arms. It was unexpected and he had no other choice than to put his arms around her.

Once again, he noticed her scent, one that drew him in. Her body fit perfectly against his own, and for a moment he wanted to hold on to her forever. Which is exactly why he stepped back away from her.

"Take care, Bailey, and I'm sure we'll see each other around town."

"Thank you again for stopping by to check on me," she replied.

As he walked back toward his car, he tried not to think too much about the woman he had just left. She'd always appeared so strong and full of a zest for life as she went about her business in town.

But the woman he had just left had appeared anything but strong. She'd been achingly vulnerable and all alone. He knew she'd been dating Howard Kendall for a while, but that lately she hadn't been seeing anyone.

So who held Bailey Troy when she was afraid? Who comforted her through a long night? Why was she still alone? She was beyond pretty and appeared very successful, so why was she not married with kids?

And why in the hell was he sitting in her driveway and contemplating these things about her?

Benjamin was back in the salon at six thirty the next morning despite the fact that they had worked until after one the night before. The only officer there before him was Dallas. Not only was Dallas Benjamin's boss, but the two men were also close friends.

With his dark, curly hair and gray eyes, Dallas had always been a favorite among the ladies in town. But since the first murder had occurred, it had been obvious his love life was the very last thing on his mind.

"Hey, man," he greeted Dallas as he stepped inside the salon.

"Hey, Benjamin," Dallas replied and sighed heavily.

"That sigh sounded very tired," Benjamin observed.

"Yeah, I'm sure all the men are going to be tired today, but I want to get this all processed so we can give it back to Bailey as soon as possible. I also had trouble going to sleep when I finally did get home," Dallas admitted. "I was really so hoping we wouldn't have another murder and then I was hoping we'd get more than a damned button as potential evidence."

The day before, when they had been collecting evidence, they'd found a button at the foot of the chair where Megan's body had been sitting.

But they weren't sure if the small light blue button had come off their killer or off one of the many women who visited the salon. However, it looked like a man's shirt button and it had a bit of Megan's blood on it. So it had either been there before, or they were all hoping it had been accidentally lost by the killer during the placement of Megan's body.

"That's more than we've gotten at any of the other murder scenes," Benjamin replied.

The first woman who had been murdered was Cindy Perry, who had worked as a waitress at the café. The second had been Sandy Blackstone, who had worked as a teller at the bank.

There had been no clues left behind at either of those scenes, nothing to present any kind of a lead in those two cases. However, both women had been blond with blue eyes.

"He's stayed with the same pattern of picking blond-haired women with blue eyes," Benjamin observed.

"Yeah, that definitely seems to be his go-to for a victim," Dallas replied. "So far, this bastard isn't making any mistakes and I have a sick feeling that he isn't just going to go away. This is the most public place that he's left a body, which to me means he's getting far more brazen, and I feel so damned helpless."

Cindy's body had been found in Lucas Maddox's cornfield. Lucas was a local farmer and he had been quickly cleared of the crime. Sandy Blackstone's body had been found standing in the backyard of the Sweet Tooth Bakery. They didn't have a clue as to why those two places were chosen to leave the bodies.

"Dallas, everyone knows how hard you've been working on these murder cases," Benjamin said.

"All of us have been working hard," Dallas replied. "I swear I don't know what we're missing," he said in obvious frustration. "But we have to be missing something."

"I can't imagine what it is. We've interviewed everyone close to the victims several times and we've gone over the crime scenes with a fine-tooth comb. We just don't have anything to go on in identifying a suspect."

"And it doesn't look like this one is going to give us anything to go on, either, except a damn button that is too ordinary to give us much at all. Still, like I said to all the men yesterday, I want that button kept from the public."

"I agree. It's the one thing we have that might identify the killer. But if he finds out we have it, he'll sew on another button or get rid of the shirt it might have come off of," Benjamin said.

"I wish we knew what kind of a time line this creep is on."

If the Scarecrow Killer wasn't enough, three weeks ago they had dealt with a serial killer the press in New York City had dubbed the Nighttime Creeper.

It had been discovered that a new ranch owner, Clint Kincaid, was actually in the witness protection program. His real name was Joe Masterson and he had been the star witness against Wayne Lee Gossage, a man who had raped and killed at least six women, including Masterson's wife, in New York City. Joe had walked in while the crime against his wife was being committed and was able to identify the killer and see that he was put away for the rest of Gossage's life.

Because Gossage had made vile threats to Joe and his little daughter when he'd been sentenced, it was agreed that it was best if Joe entered the program and disappeared. He'd moved here to start a new life, but it was a life interrupted as Gossage had escaped from prison and had come after Joe by kidnapping Joe's young daughter and Lizzy Maxwell, the neighbor he'd fallen in love with.

Thankfully, in the end Gossage had been rearrested and sent back to prison, and Joe, Lizzy and little Emily were safe to resume their normal lives.

For several days, the Nighttime Creeper had been in the headlines of the local paper and had used up all the resources of the police department, but now it was over with a happy ending.

In fact, Lizzy and Joe were now planning their wedding and the paper was running stories about the upcoming fall festival. But this morning, once again the headlines had been all about the Scarecrow Killer and this latest murder.

At that moment two other officers arrived, and close on their heels were two more, and the work in the salon began again. They reswept the floors, paying special attention around the chair where the victim had been found.

The actual entry had been through the back door, where the cheap lock had been jimmied open. They checked the parking lot in the back of the building, around the back doorway and down the hallway where they assumed Megan had been carried inside.

They fingerprinted every surface they could and tried to ignore the lookie-loos who stood at the large front window staring in.

As they worked, they threw out different scenarios about motive. It was one of the things that was completely missing with regard to these murders. Maybe if they could figure out the motive, a potential suspect would surface.

"Maybe a blond-haired, blue-eyed woman broke his heart and so now he's killing her over and over again," Joel Penn said.

"That doesn't explain his trussing them up like scarecrows," Darryl O'Conner replied.

"There is absolutely nothing in my wheelhouse to figure out a motive for that," Ross Davenport said with disgust. "I mean, why sew their mouths closed and what in the hell does he do with their eyes?"

"It's so damned creepy," Darryl replied.

Benjamin listened to the others discussing the case and the only thing he kept thinking about was Bailey's sparkling blond hair and bright blue eyes.

She would make a perfect victim. She lived alone and was often out and about on her own. She didn't appear to have many friends, and even if she did, they weren't joining her when she was out shopping or whatever.

It had been after the second murder that Dallas had

called for a town meeting, where he'd warned all the women to travel in pairs. Most of them had taken his advice for a week or two after that murder, but many of them had now gone back to their usual ways. Hopefully, this murder would remind them of just how deadly it could be to be out by themselves.

They had no idea why the killer picked his victims and they didn't know how he got them into his control. It appeared he just picked them up off the street, as there was nothing at the victims' houses that indicated a struggle of any kind. They also didn't know where he actually killed them and dressed them up. It was someplace different from where he staged them as scarecrows.

They also had been unable to find the source of the frayed jeans and straw hats and flannel shirts. Where was the man getting them all from? There were so many things they just didn't know about this killer.

What they did know was the cause of death in each case was knife wounds to the chest. There had also been a high level of valium in the victims' systems and needle marks in Cindy's arm and Sandy's thigh. Thank God, according to the coroner, the women were dead before their mouths were sewn shut and their eyes were taken out. Josiah believed that a sharp, delicate scalpel had been used to remove the eyes.

Toward the end of the day, the talk turned more personal among the men. "How's Amelia?" Joel asked Ross. "The wedding is only a few weeks away, right? Are you starting to get the jitters yet?"

Ross laughed. "No—no jitters—but I've never been so happy that my fiancée has black hair and dark brown eyes."

"Don't think that keeps her safe from this creep," Dallas

warned. "At any time in the future, this guy could change the victimology and start going after dark-haired women."

"That's a scary thought," Darryl replied.

"It's something we all need to keep in mind," Dallas replied.

"Hey, Benjamin, are you still seeing Celeste?" Joel asked.

"Yeah, but not for too much longer," Benjamin replied.

"You breaking it off with her?" Darryl asked.

"Nah, she's going to break if off with me," Benjamin responded. "The next time I see her I intend to tell her that I'm not the marrying type and we all know more than anything Celeste wants to be married again. She'll drop me like a hot potato and move on to the next available man."

"Don't you want to keep dating her?" Joel asked.

"I'm over it. To be honest, I find her rather, uh—"

"Shallow," Dallas said, interrupting Benjamin as the others laughed. "Personally, I don't know why you started dating her in the first place."

Benjamin knew the answer. It had been loneliness and she had just happened to be in the right place at the right time. But he was ready to stop seeing her. It was the best thing to do. He never intended to get married and so it was wrong of him to keep seeing her and leading her on.

Besides, lately he couldn't get a certain woman off his mind. He had a feeling that Bailey would be a lot of fun on a date. Lord knew with everything that was going on in his professional life, he could use a little fun in his personal life.

The officers continued with small talk for a few more minutes, but then it was back to business. It was around four o'clock when Bailey showed up at the front door.

As usual, she looked stylish in a neon green blouse and a pair of black slacks that hugged her shapely legs perfectly.

Big neon green-and-black earrings hung from her ears and accented her gamin features.

Dallas opened the door and allowed her to step inside. Benjamin saw her gaze shoot directly to the chair where Megan had been found and her beautiful eyes darkened. "Uh, I was just wondering if I'm going to be able to open in the morning," she said.

"Yeah, we're pretty much done in here," Dallas said. "We'll finish up the last of things by this evening and it should be fine for you to open back up again in the morning."

"Okay, thanks," she replied. She turned to go back out and Benjamin quickly walked out with her.

"Bailey, how are you doing today?" he asked.

She offered him a small smile. "A little better than yesterday. It will be good to get back to work, although it's going to be hard at the same time."

"I understand," he replied. "You'll be just fine and the more distance you get from all this, the better you'll be. You're a strong woman, Bailey."

"Maybe not as strong as some people think I am," she admitted.

"No matter how strong you appear, you definitely worry me," he replied.

She looked up at him in surprise. "How do I worry you?"

"Bailey, you're always alone when you're out running the streets," he said. "And you have to know by now that you're the killer's type."

"I do know that, but there isn't much I can do about it."

"I just hope you stay aware of your surroundings whenever you're out. Don't let anyone get too close to you. Remember that this killer is somebody we probably all know, somebody you might think is perfectly harmless."

"If you're trying to freak me out, it's definitely working," she replied dryly.

"I want you to be freaked out if that's what it takes to keep you safe."

She smiled at him once again. "Thanks, Benjamin."

"I was also wondering if Friday night after the fair closes up if you'd like to have a quick drink with me at the Farmer's Club."

Once again, she looked at him in surprise. He felt a bit of surprise himself, as he hadn't intended to ask her out... until he just had.

"I would love to," she replied. "Thanks so much for asking."

"How about I give you a call sometime tomorrow and we can firm up the plans."

"Sounds great to me," she agreed. "Then I'll talk to you tomorrow." He watched her as she headed back down the sidewalk. What had he just done and why was he suddenly looking forward to Friday night?

Chapter 3

It felt so wrong that Bailey could feel this kind of hard-core giddiness, especially given the fact that she was still traumatized by finding Megan's body in her salon. That trauma still weighed heavy in her heart and probably would for some time to come. But she couldn't help the happiness that danced inside her and filled her heart as she raced down the highway toward her best friend's house. Only Lizzy would know how absolutely monumental it was that Benjamin had finally asked her out.

The fall festival closed at ten on Friday night and then on Saturday it was open until midnight. There were two bars in Millsville.

Murphy's was a large place that was popular with the singles in town. It was loud and raucous and the bar to go to for a night of drinking and dancing.

The Farmer's Club was much smaller and more popular with the older people in town. It was more conducive to conversations and she was thrilled to be going there with Benjamin. She couldn't wait to get the opportunity to get to know him a little better.

When she reached Lizzy's farmhouse, she went past it to the place next door. It always shocked her a little to see the

For Sale sign in front of Lizzy's place, but Lizzy now lived next door with Joe and his five-year-old daughter, Emily.

She pulled up in front of Joe's place, parked and then raced for the front door. She knocked and Joe answered. He was a nice-looking guy with dark hair and blue eyes. "Hey, Bailey," he said with a warm smile.

"Hi, Joe. I was wondering if I could grab Lizzy for a quick little girl talk."

He opened the door wider to allow her inside. "She's in the kitchen."

"Thanks." Bailey beelined to the kitchen, where Lizzy stood at the island cutting up vegetables. Little Emily was on a step stool next to her.

Lizzy was a pretty woman with shoulder-length blond hair and blue eyes. She and Bailey had been best friends since their early high school days. While Lizzy was also the Scarecrow Killer's type, Bailey didn't worry about her friend too much as she had Joe to protect her.

"Well, doesn't this look like fun," Bailey said.

"What a nice surprise," Lizzy said with a big grin. "I wasn't expecting to see you today."

Bailey had spent some time here with Lizzy the afternoon that Megan had been found in the salon. Lizzy had cried with her and consoled her the way a good friend would.

"Yeah, I'm not staying for long," Bailey replied.

"Hey, Emily, why don't you come on into the living room with me and we'll color a picture together," Joe said.

Bailey flashed him a grateful look as the little girl got down from her step stool. "Okay, Daddy. I love to color with you. 'Bye, Bailey."

"Goodbye, sweetie," Bailey replied.

A moment later the two women were all alone in the

kitchen. "How are you doing?" Lizzy asked as she put down her knife and looked closely at Bailey.

"To be honest, I'm kind of all over the place," Bailey admitted. "I'm still freaked out and sad over Megan's death and her body being in the salon. At least tomorrow I can open the salon again, but it somehow doesn't seem right to continue business as usual."

"It will be good for the entire town to get back to business as usual," Lizzy replied. "We can't give this killer any more oxygen than he's already getting."

"Easier said than done," Bailey said. "However, I came to share some good news for a change."

"Share away." Lizzy offered her another smile.

"Guess who asked me out to the Farmer's Club Friday night after the festival closes."

"I can't imagine."

"Officer Benjamin Cooper," Bailey replied.

"For real?" Lizzy's eyes widened. Only Lizzy had known what a mad crush Bailey had had on Benjamin.

"For real," Bailey confirmed as another wave of joy swept through her.

"Oh, Bailey, I'm so happy for you." Lizzy gave her a quick hug.

"Thanks, I can't wait to spend a little quality time with him and get to know him better."

"So, is he going to be like all the others you've dated?"

Bailey looked at Lizzy curiously. "What do you mean?"

"Does he get the same three-date maximum that everyone else you've dated has gotten?" Lizzy eyed her pointedly.

Bailey released a slightly uncomfortable laugh. "I don't have a maximum number of times I see somebody. I can't help it if after two or three dates I realize the person I'm seeing isn't right for me. Anyway, I can't wait until Friday night."

"I'm so happy for you, Bailey, and I hope he turns out to be the man you've always imagined him to be. I hope he meets all your expectations."

"Thanks, Lizzy. I just had to come by and tell you that he asked me out. And now I'll get out of your hair so you can finish up your dinner preparations."

"You want to stay and eat with us?" Lizzy offered. "You know I always make plenty."

"Thanks for the offer, but I think I'll just head on back home with a quick stop at Big Jolly's. I've been yearning for a double cheeseburger from there." Big Jolly's was a hamburger drive-through joint on Main Street that, as far as Bailey was concerned, made the best burgers and fries in the world.

"Bailey, I hope you're being safe," Lizzy said somberly.

"I try to be," Bailey replied, knowing Lizzy was talking about the Scarecrow Killer. "Hopefully Dallas and Benjamin and the rest of law enforcement will catch him before he can strike again."

"We can all pray that will happen, but in the meantime, I worry about you."

"Don't worry. I can take good care of myself," Bailey assured her. That made three people who were worried about her. "And on that note, I'm out of here."

The next day flew by as the salon was packed with women who had appointments along with plenty of walk-ins who had missed their appointments on the two days that the salon had been closed.

All of them wanted to know what chair Megan had been found in and exactly what she'd looked like. Bailey refused to give out any information about the dead woman, making some of the women get a little testy with her, but she didn't want to talk about the murder and she certainly didn't want to point out the murder chair.

She and Jaime and Naomi stayed until a little after nine that night to make sure all the clients were taken care of. She fell into bed almost as soon as she got home, exhausted by the long day she'd had.

It was just after ten o'clock on Friday morning when she headed to the fairgrounds. The big festival was taking place in what had once been a rodeo area. However, the big rodeos no longer came to Millsville, so the massive grounds with an old grandstand were dormant and unused except for special events like this.

She was dressed in a good pair of jeans and a bright royal blue blouse that hugged her body and showed off the blueness of her eyes. She had to dress knowing that there would probably be no time to change between working the fair and going out with Benjamin after the fair.

A nervous flutter shot off in the pit of her stomach as she thought of her date that night with the very hot police officer. She couldn't even believe it was really happening. She'd wanted to go out with him for what felt like years. It was just too bad it had taken a terrible tragedy like a horrendous murder for it to finally happen.

The fairgrounds came into sight. The carnival had already set up with a Ferris wheel rising up in the sky, along with a variety of other rides.

It was a perfect day to spend outside. The sun was bright overhead and there wasn't a cloud in the sky. The temperature forecast was for a pleasant eighty to eighty-four degrees, with just a faint breeze that was refreshing.

As she entered the actual grounds, she drove up and down the aisles of tents that the town provided, looking for the one she'd been assigned to. She finally found it and pulled behind it to park. Her location was absolutely perfect.

She was smack-dab in the center of the aisle and across from her was a hot-dog stand next to a fried-ice-cream-and-dessert place. Those two places would draw a lot of traffic and hopefully some of that would trickle over to her tent.

She was not only offering free nail painting to anyone under sixteen years old, but she had also brought plenty of new products to sell to any adults who needed polish and such.

For the next twenty minutes or so, she worked to unload her car. Folding tables and chairs were set up inside. She walked back outside to get a table for her display of nail bottles for sale. She finally leaned against the side of her car for a moment to take a break.

RJ Morgan popped out of his tent next door. RJ was the tattoo artist in town. He was a big bald man and his muscled arms were covered in bold tattoos. He carried himself rather aggressively and most people in town steered clear of him.

"Hey, baby doll, need any help?" he hollered over to her.

"Thanks, but I think I've got it all," she replied. "Are you actually going to be tattooing people today?"

"That's the plan. Why don't you come on over here and let me give you that sweet little butterfly tattoo we talked about doing on your neck?"

She laughed. "You talked about that, not me."

"You definitely have a beautiful neck, Bailey."

She laughed again. "And you, RJ, have a gift for flirting." She pushed herself off her car. "Now I've got to get back busy."

"You know, Bailey, I wouldn't mind us going out to-gether again," RJ said.

"We had our time dating, RJ, and things just didn't work out between us. I just think it's best if we remain good friends."

"I suppose you're right," he replied. "But you'll call me if you ever change your mind and want to go out with me again?"

She laughed yet again. "I promise you'll be the first per-son I call." She opened her trunk to retrieve the last of her items.

As she worked to arrange things inside the tent, her thoughts remained on the buff, bald man next door. She had gone out on a couple of dates with him and had dis-covered that beneath his big muscles and wild tattoos, he was really a sweet guy. However, the minute he started talking about wanting to get married and have a houseful of children, she was out.

By that time, Naomi had arrived. She was a pretty woman with long dark hair that cascaded down past her shoulders and brown eyes that snapped with liveliness. She was petite like Bailey, and had been married for five years to her high school sweetheart. "Are you ready for this?" Bailey asked as Naomi dragged in two chairs.

"Actually, I'm really looking forward to it. It should be lots of fun," she replied.

For the next half an hour, they got things in place and Bailey decorated the interior with pink-and-white boas and gold-and-silver crowns, turning it from a mere tent to a magical place for little girls.

Naomi had rented a canister of helium so they blew up dozens of pink and white balloons that now danced across the ceiling, adding to the fanciful aura. They also hung a bouquet of the balloons at their tent's entrance to catch peoples' eyes.

When they were finished, they each set up a chair in the front of the tent and watched others scurrying around to get ready for the noon opening.

The air now smelled of cooking hot dogs and hearty chili. There were also the scents of popcorn and cotton candy, and of fried Twinkies and funnel cake. It all smelled absolutely delicious. Colorful flags and banners hung on many of the tents, announcing the business being offered inside.

They knew when the festival officially opened, as people began to surge down the aisles. Children screamed with enthusiasm and parents urged them to slow down. The air of excitement grew, and within minutes Naomi was painting the face of a six-year-old while Bailey painted the nails of her seven-year-old sister.

The afternoon flew by. Their tent stayed busy with girls coming in and out. It was about six that evening when there was a lull in the traffic.

"You want to get us something to eat?" Bailey asked Naomi.

"Definitely, I'm starving," she replied.

Bailey pulled some money out of her purse and handed it to Naomi. "Dinner is on me. If you could just get me a hot dog and some funnel cake, then I'll be a happy camper."

"Okay, what do you want on your hot dog?"

"Mustard and relish," Bailey replied.

A moment later Bailey was once again alone in the tent. She sat out front. The crowd seemed to be a younger one now, with lots of teens and fewer little kids in the mix. However, she would remain open until the very end of closing in case a young girl came along and wanted her fingernails painted. After all, they were all future clients.

She saw him coming up the aisle and her heart began to beat a quickened rhythm. Officer Benjamin Cooper. He looked tall and handsome in his police uniform. He also looked like a man who owned the space around him. There was a command to him that definitely drew her in.

A slow grin curved his lips as he approached her—a grin that made her heart speed up even more. "Hey, handsome. Want your fingernails painted?" she said to him when he stopped in front of her tent.

He laughed. "No thanks, I doubt if you have my color. Are we still on for tonight?"

"As far as I'm concerned, we are," she replied.

"Great. Why don't I show up here at ten and I can help you load up for the night," he offered.

"Oh, you don't need to do that. All we're loading up is the nail polish and face paint. We're leaving the chairs and tables here."

"You do realize the security overnight is going to be pretty minimal," he said.

She smiled up at him. "If somebody wants to steal a card table or folding chairs, then they must need them more than me. Besides, I'm really not too worried about a theft."

"Then why don't I just meet you at the Farmer's Club as soon as you can get away after closing time."

"That sounds good," she agreed. "I'll see you then."

As he ambled away, her heart continued to beat wildly in her chest. Lordy, he looked as good going as he had coming. His broad back tapered down to what appeared to be a nice, firm bottom. Physically, he appeared to be the perfect specimen of a man.

She couldn't wait until ten o'clock. It would be so great if he really did live up to the kind of man she thought he was, aside from his physical attributes. Hopefully, she discovered they both wanted the same out of life.

Oh, it would be wonderful if he turned out to be the one for her. She could easily imagine their life together. He would continue his job and she would continue to work the salon. But there would be time for traveling and exploring new things together. There would be years of laughter and love with him. Yes, it would be absolutely wonderful if he turned out to be the special man for her. At that moment, Naomi returned with their food, pulling her out of her wistfulness. They ate and then sat in front of the tent once again.

Within an hour, the sun had begun to set and the lights on the rides pierced the encroaching darkness. Everything looked magical with the colorful illumination. There were only a few girls who came in for nail work and face painting.

It was a few minutes before ten when they began to pack up everything. Once again, her heartbeat had picked up speed in the sweet anticipation of spending some quality time with Benjamin.

It was then she found it—a single red rose. It was on the ground just inside the entrance and there was a small note attached to it. She stared at it for a long moment before picking it up. She wasn't sure why, but she didn't have a good feeling about this.

She finally reached down and picked it up off the ground. "'Bailey, I love you,'" she said, reading the note aloud.

"Oh, Bailey, that's so romantic," Naomi said as she tucked a strand of her long dark hair behind her ear. "Do you know who it's from?"

Benjamin certainly didn't seem like the type of man to leave this for her before their very first date. This also wasn't the kind of thing RJ would do.

"I don't have any idea," she replied. It didn't feel romantic. It felt creepy and the creepiness continued when minutes later she headed from the tent to her car.

As she unlocked the car door, she looked all around. The hairs on the nape of her neck stood up as she couldn't shake the feeling that somebody was watching her. Still, she didn't see anyone to give her pause, or to explain the creepy feeling.

She couldn't help the fear that filled her and chilled her blood. A dead person had been left in her salon and now she'd gotten a creepy gift from somebody. Who had left the rose for her? She just hoped she wasn't being sized up to be the next Scarecrow victim.

Benjamin arrived first at the small bar. Before he'd left the fairgrounds, he had dipped into one of the restrooms and had changed out of his uniform. He now wore a pair of jeans and a light blue pullover.

He went inside the bar and grabbed a booth, and fought against a wave of nerves. He sat down and wondered what in the hell he was doing here.

He'd always stayed his distance from Bailey because instinctively he knew he would like her. Whenever he saw her, aside from her tears over Megan, she was always smiling. There was a pep in her step that spoke of gusto for life and he found it very attractive.

He'd broken things off with Celeste on Thursday night and she had not taken it well. She'd cried and called him every name in the book and then had finally hung up on him.

The one thing that had pushed him into asking Bailey out was the fact that she seemed so all alone. She'd gone through a terrible trauma with seemingly nobody by her side. He knew she had a mother, but he suspected the two weren't very close. He found himself wanting to help her through these dark days.

He figured if she wanted, he'd see her a couple of times and by then the trauma in the nail salon would be behind her. When the time felt right and she appeared strong enough to not need anyone anymore, then he'd break things off with her.

Then he saw her. She stood just inside the front door of the fairly busy bar and looked around. Even after working all day, she appeared refreshed and beautiful.

He stood and waved to her. He could tell the moment he saw him—a wide smile curved her lips and she hurried toward him. A deep warmth filled his chest. God, she had such a beautiful smile.

"Hi," she greeted him and slid into the booth seat facing his.

"Hi yourself," he said in return and sank back into his seat. "Did you get everything squared away at the fair?"

"I did—it's all ready to unload once again in the morning," she replied.

Bright blue was definitely a good color on her and the blouse showcased her slender waist and full breasts. Her jeans hugged her long legs and slender hips and big blue earrings danced from her ears.

"Tomorrow is definitely going to be a long and crazy day, especially with all the contests going on in the afternoon," he said.

She smiled. "All I know is Letta Lee better win the best-apple-pie baking contest or there will be hell to pay."

He laughed. "You've got that right. I don't think she's ever lost."

"I don't remember her ever losing," Bailey replied.

At that moment, Ranger Simmons, the owner of the Farmer's Club, stepped up to the side of their booth. "Hey, Benjamin... Bailey. I see the two of you survived the first day of the fair." Ranger was an older man who was liked by everyone in town.

"Yeah, we live to fight another day," Benjamin replied.

"What can I get you two to drink?" Ranger looked at Bailey first.

"I'll take a gin and tonic with a couple of twists of lime," she said. "Light on the gin," she added.

"And I'll just take a beer. Whatever you have on tap is fine with me," Benjamin said.

"Got it. I'll be right back with those." Ranger moved away from them.

"Bailey, how are you really doing?" Benjamin asked her when the two of them were alone once again.

"I have my good moments and I still have some bad ones," she admitted.

"Do you have a good support system? Is your mother there for you?" he asked curiously.

She released what sounded like a dry laugh. "Angela Troy is a tough cookie and I'm not sure she knows how to be there for me."

"I'm so sorry to hear that," he replied.

"Are you close to your parents?" she asked.

"Very. In fact, I usually have dinner with them and my sister and her family every Sunday, which is one of my days off." He almost felt bad saying this, given her position with her mother.

"Your sister comes into the salon from time to time to get her nails done. She's always been very nice."

Benjamin smiled. "Yeah, Lori is all-around a great person, although there was a time I would have gladly paid somebody to kidnap her." He laughed as Bailey widened her eyes. "She was the definition of a pesky little sister, always bugging me and wanting to hang out with me and my friends. I love her dearly, but there were times growing up when she was definitely a pain in my side."

Bailey smiled. "You don't know how lucky you are to have a sibling. I would have loved to have a brother or a sister. In fact, for about a year when I was around eight years old, I pretended I had a twin sister. I made my mother set a place for her at every meal and kiss her good-night when we went to bed."

"Here we go," Ranger said as he came back to their booth. He placed the gin and tonic in front of Bailey and a cold mug of beer before Benjamin.

"Thanks, Ranger," Benjamin said.

"Enjoy." He once again left the side of the booth.

"So what happened to your sister?" he asked, picking up the conversation where it had left off.

"Oh, it was all very tragic. She was struck by a speeding car going by our house. The driver of the car didn't even stop." Her blue eyes were lively as she spun her tale and he found himself drawn toward her.

"And I'm sure her funeral was completely over-the-top," he said.

"Totally," she replied. "I decorated the whole backyard with everything black I could find in the house and I wrote a long eulogy about how much she was loved, and then poof, she was gone."

"To be replaced by more present friends, I hope." He took a drink of his beer.

"Definitely, but it was in high school when I met my very best friend for life, Lizzy Maxwell."

"I got to know her and Joe when she was kidnapped by the creep who came after Joe," he said.

"I've never been so afraid for anyone as I was for her and little Emily when they were missing." Bailey took a drink of her gin and tonic and then continued, "Thankfully it all ended on a happy note."

"Thankfully," he agreed.

For the next hour, they got to know each other better. He was surprised by how many things they had in common. They both liked old rock and roll and crime suspense shows. Their favorite type of food was burgers and fries with an occasional steak or pizza thrown in.

She had a terrific sense of humor—one that vibed with his own—and the more time he spent with her, the more he liked her. Then there was the fact that he found her very physically attractive.

He could lose himself in the depths of her bright blue eyes. As she talked, he found himself wondering how she would kiss and what her lips would taste like.

Despite his overall attraction to her, he just wanted to see her a few times, until she got some distance from the horror in her nail shop. At least that was what he kept telling himself.

"This has been really nice," she said when their drinks were almost gone.

"It has been," he agreed.

Her eyes darkened a bit. "It's nice to talk to somebody who understands what I've been through, somebody who is a bit sympathetic."

He couldn't help himself. He reached across the table and covered one of her small hands with his bigger one. "It will pass, Bailey. It will eventually get better." He withdrew his hand as she smiled warmly at him.

"I know. It helps to keep busy. The festival couldn't have come at a better time. And speaking of the festival, I'd better get out of here before it gets any later."

"Yeah, the day starts early tomorrow and it's going to be a long one," he agreed. He waved to Ranger for the tab and once he'd paid, he and Bailey walked out of the bar together.

The moon was high up in the sky and spilled down silvery strands that caressed her pretty features. He could once again smell the enticing fragrance of her perfume as he walked her to her car.

They reached the driver side of her vehicle and she turned and smiled up at him. "Thank you, Benjamin. I really enjoyed spending this time with you and getting to know you a little better."

"I enjoyed it, too. In fact, I was wondering if you'd like to have dinner with me at the café on Sunday—that's given nothing comes up with work to stop me."

"I'd love to have dinner with you," she replied. "And, of course, I would understand if your work interferes. But don't you usually eat with your family on Sundays?"

He smiled. "I'm allowed to skip a Sunday with them to have dinner with a pretty woman. How about I pick you up around five on Sunday?"

"That sounds perfect and, in the meantime, I'll probably see you at the fair tomorrow," she said. "Can I ask you one question about the Scarecrow Killer?"

He looked at her in surprise. "Sure, but I'll warn you there are some things I can't talk about."

"I was just wondering if he left little gifts for the women he intended to kill." Her eyes were now somber and filled with what looked like a touch of apprehension.

"Not that I'm aware of," he replied. "Is there something I need to know about, Bailey?"

She hesitated a moment and then shook her head. "No, it's fine. I'll just see you tomorrow."

He watched her drive away from the parking lot and then headed toward his car, which was parked nearby. He couldn't imagine why she had asked him about gifts from the Scarecrow Killer, but it certainly made him wonder what was going on in her life?

He'd definitely ask her more questions about it on Sunday and he didn't even want to think about how much he anticipated spending more time with her even though he knew there would be no happy ending for him with her.

He was back in the headlines again and he couldn't be prouder. Scarecrow Killer Strikes Again, the headline of the paper had read. For the last couple of days, he'd dominated the news.

How many nightmares was he in? Whose dreams did he haunt at night? All the people in town who had never paid any attention to him before were definitely paying attention to him now.

He leaned back in his chair and looked around his basement with a sense of contentment. He still had plenty of the frayed jeans and flannel shirts in all sizes. He had the poles for when he wanted to use them to tie the victims to in order to stand them up wherever he decided to leave them.

It was amazing what could be bought on the internet and he'd planned this for years, ordering the supplies here and there that would make his dreams come true.

Scarecrows.

He definitely knew what it felt like to be one and there had been nobody to save him when he was young. He remembered it all—standing in a hot field...thirsty and with legs aching. He remembered begging for it to stop, but it hadn't. Oh, yes, he remembered.

His gaze finally landed on the shelf that held three large jugs with the eyeballs floating inside. They weren't right. They'd looked right before he'd taken them, but he realized now they weren't quite right. They weren't *hers*.

He tore his gaze away from them and instead looked again at all the supplies he had. Even though it had only been a couple of days since his last scarecrow, the hunger was back inside him. The hunger was back and the crows cawed loudly in his head.

It all roared inside him and he knew it wouldn't be long before he made the headlines once again and inspired more fear in the hearts of every single person in town.

Chapter 4

"What color would you like me to paint on your pretty little nails?" Bailey asked a nine-year-old girl the next morning. "As you can see, I have lots of colors to pick from."

The girl frowned and looked at all the nail polishes on display. It was as if this was the most important decision she would ever make in her life. She then smiled up at Bailey. "I want pink."

Of course, she wanted pink. Almost all the little girls who had come in for nail polish had chosen pink. Thankfully, Bailey had brought extra bottles of that color, suspecting this would be the case.

"Are you having fun so far? Have you ridden any of the rides yet?" Bailey asked.

"We rode the carousel. I sat on a big white horse with flowers painted all over it. It was beautiful," the girl replied. "I wanna ride the Ferris wheel but my mom is scared of heights so I don't know if we'll ride it or not. I'm gonna try to talk her into it."

So went the day…pink polish and carnival rides. Both Bailey and Naomi were kept busy until about two o'clock in the afternoon, when there was a lull in traffic and Bailey knew the winners of the various contests were being announced at the grandstand.

It was during the lull when Benjamin walked up to their tent. "Bailey... Naomi, how's your day going?" he asked with the smile that threatened to melt Bailey's insides.

He was so handsome with his strong brow and straight nose. His lower jaw was also strong and well-defined and his lips held just enough curl to make them sensual and very kissable. Despite the light blond of his hair, his blue eyes were surrounded by thick, dark lashes. He rocked the police uniform he wore and as far as she was concerned, he was easily the best-looking guy in town.

"Very busy. This is the first real break we've had all day. What about you? How is your day going?" she asked.

"Not too bad. I've had to arrest two men for drunk and disorderly and then I chased after a teenager who stole an older woman's purse and that's been the highlights of my day so far."

"Sounds way more exciting than listening to young girls gossiping about their schoolmates," she replied.

He laughed. "Ah, future women of Millsville in the making."

"Yes, and I already know who is likely to become mini Letta Lees in the future. By the way, have you heard—did she win the apple-pie contest?"

"No, she didn't. Mabel Treadway won and Letta came in second."

"Oh, there will definitely be hell to pay over that. Even though Mabel is Letta's best friend, Letta is going to find a way to punish Mabel for a while," Bailey said with a small laugh. "If I was Mabel, I would not want to be at the next gardening club meeting."

He returned her laugh. "You've got that right."

"Any other wins from the grandstand that were surprising?" she asked.

"Not really, but I was glad to see that our mayor presented an honorary award to Elijah Simpson for running the food bank out of his basement," he replied.

"Oh, I'm so happy to hear that. Elijah is a wonderfully kind man and he makes sure the people who are in need in town get the ingredients they need to have a home-cooked meal." Elijah was an older man who ran his food bank on donations. As the economy had gotten tighter, there were more and more families than ever depending on him and his kindness and hard work.

"Well, I'd better get back to my beat," Benjamin said. "I just thought I'd stop by to check in on you."

"Thanks, I appreciate it," Bailey said.

"Have a good rest of the day," Naomi said to him.

"Thanks, Naomi," he replied and then looked at Bailey once again. "And I'll see you tomorrow evening."

She smiled. "I'm looking forward to it."

"That man is totally crazy about you," Naomi said once Benjamin was out of earshot.

"How do you know that?" Bailey asked as she worked to suppress happy shivers.

"Just the way he looks at you. I'm telling you he likes you a lot."

"So far I like him a lot, too," Bailey admitted.

Minutes later Bailey was once again painting little nails and talking about the carnival with bright-eyed little girls. By the end of the day, she was absolutely exhausted. It was after one when she finally got home and crashed into bed.

She slept sinfully late the next morning and then spent the day cleaning up her house and unpacking the fair items from her car. At four, she took a shower and got ready for her date with Benjamin.

Forty-five minutes later she looked at herself in the floor-length mirror that was on the back of her closet door. Her skinny black jeans fit her perfectly and the red blouse was one of her favorites. Big black-and-red earrings completed her outfit. Her makeup was light and she looked casually chic—perfect for dinner at the café.

At four forty-five she sank down on her sofa to await Benjamin's arrival. Nerves jumped around in the pit of her stomach and her chest was tight with anticipation.

Aside from the time spent patrolling the fair, she knew he and the other law-enforcement officers had been working hard to identify and catch the Scarecrow Killer. A shiver walked up her back as she thought about the person who had now killed three women.

What in God's name went on in his head when he made them into human scarecrows? Why was he doing it? She couldn't imagine what darkness must be inside him, a darkness that sane people couldn't begin to understand. She just hoped he got arrested soon, before another woman was murdered. She really hoped that the rose left in her tent at the fair hadn't been left by the Scarecrow Killer.

She jumped as a knock sounded at her door. She got up and answered. It was Benjamin, looking totally hot in a pair of jeans and a blue button-up shirt that enhanced the blond of his hair and the gorgeous blue color of his eyes.

"Hi," she greeted him.

"Hi, yourself," he replied with a smile. "Are you ready to go?"

"Just let me grab my purse and I'm ready."

A few moments later she was in the passenger seat of his car. His personal car was a nice dark blue sedan.

"Are you hungry?" he asked as he backed out of her driveway.

"Definitely," she replied.

"How has your day been?" He turned onto the road that would take them to the café on Main Street.

"Quiet. I slept obscenely late this morning and then did some chores and unloaded my car, and now I'm here."

He slid a quick glance toward her. "And I'm glad you're here."

A warm glow filled her. "I'm glad I'm here, too." She drew in the scent in his car. It was a fragrance of leather cleaner mixed with his spicy cologne, and it was more than appealing.

"So what did you do today?" she asked.

"I reinterviewed Megan's parents to see if there was anything else they could tell us about her and her life, then I went back into the station, where our little task force went over everything we have so far concerning the killer."

"What a hard day it must have been for you," she replied sympathetically.

"They've all been pretty hard since the first victim was found," he confessed.

"Well, tonight over dinner, anything to do with the Scarecrow Killer as conversation is strictly off-limits," she said firmly. "Besides, I thought Sunday was your day off."

"Normally they are, but I decided to go in for a while this morning."

By that time, they had arrived at the café. He found a parking space down the street and together they got out of the car.

"Beautiful night," he said as they walked toward the front door.

"Yes, it is." The sun was still bright overhead, but there was a slight chill in the air that whispered of autumn's fast approach.

When they reached the café door, he opened it and ushered her inside. On Sunday evenings, the place wasn't too busy, as most people were at home preparing for the new week ahead.

He led her to a booth and they sat. Almost immediately, Lauren Kane, one of the waitresses, appeared to take their orders.

"I'd like the cheeseburger with fries and a cola to drink," Bailey said.

"And I'll take the big bacon burger with fries," Benjamin said. "And a cola, too."

Minutes later, their orders were in front of them and their conversation was light and easy. "Autumn is my favorite time of year," she said as she squeezed a pool of ketchup on the side of her plate for dipping her fries.

"It's my favorite, too," he replied. "I enjoy the cool nights, when there is a bit of woodsmoke in the air and you can sleep with your windows open."

"Exactly, and you can cuddle up on the sofa with warm fuzzy blankets and drink apple cider or hot chocolate." She would so love to cuddle up with him. His big strong arms would surround her and his scent would infuse her head. Oh, it would be wonderful.

Their talk moved on to shows they had seen on television, and what sign they each were—she was a Libra and he was a Cancer. He talked a little about his work as a police officer. She found everything about his work interesting.

She then began to share stories about the antics of some of the women who came into her shop. She didn't mention any of them by name, but she did do some pretty fair impressions of them that had him laughing.

She loved the sound of his deep laughter and she had a feeling that he hadn't had much to laugh about lately. With his job so heavy and stressful right now with the Scarecrow Killer, she wanted to be his light and soft place to fall.

"Oh, Bailey, this has been so good for me," he said once she'd finished one of her tales and they had finished eating. "How about some dessert?"

"Not for me," she replied. "But you go ahead, I'm just too full to want anything else. As you can see, I ate almost all of my fries—they were my dessert."

"Yeah, I don't need any dessert, either. Shall we get out of here, then?"

Even though she hated to have the evening with him come to an end, she also knew his time right now was limited and he was probably exhausted from all the extra hours he was having to put in. She would just gladly take whatever time he had for her.

He paid the tab and then they left the café. Evening had fallen and the sky overhead was filled with bright, sparkling stars. "This is one of the things I love about being in small-town Millsville. There are no bright city lights to interfere with us being able to see the complete beauty of the stars," she said.

"I love it here. I've never wanted to live anyplace else," he replied.

"Me, neither," she agreed. "But I wouldn't mind doing a little traveling sometime in the future."

"I agree—there are several places I'd love to see."

They reached his car and got inside. As he drove her home, they made small talk about the little town they both loved. From the unique shops on Main to the new gazebo in the town square, Millsville had never tried to be anything bigger than a nice quaint town that wanted the best for its residents.

Before she knew it, he was pulling into her driveway. They both got out of the car. She saw it before they even reached her front porch. A rather large white teddy bear holding some sort of a sign was sitting right in front of her door.

You Belong to Me, the sign said.

"Ah, it looks like I have a little competition," Benjamin said with a touch of amusement.

She didn't pick up the bear. She didn't even want to touch it. It creeped her out, just like the rose at the fair had. Chills rushed up her spine as the back of her throat threatened to close up. First it had been a dead woman in her salon, then the rose and now this. What was going on? Who on earth was leaving these things for her?

"I don't know who it's from," she finally said. "I can't imagine who left this for me, but could you please take it away for me? I don't want it. I don't want anything to do with it."

"Sure, I'll be glad to if that's what you want," he replied.

"That's definitely what I want," she replied as tears pressed hot in her eye.

She turned to unlock her door and when she turned back around to face him, he stood just mere inches away from her. "Hey, are you okay?" he asked softly. It must have been obvious to him that she wasn't. "Come here," he said and pulled her into his arms.

"This is why I asked you if the Scarecrow Killer left gifts for his victims before he killed them," she said against his broad chest.

"Bailey, look at me."

She raised her head to meet his gaze with hers. "We have absolutely no evidence to show that the killer leaves items for his victims. Have you received anything else?"

"On the first night of the carnival when we were closing up, I found a rose on the tent floor with a note that said 'I love you,'" she replied.

"These things have the earmark of a secret admirer, not the killer."

His words lessened the fear inside her. She still found it creepy. But being in his strong arms definitely comforted her.

His eyes shone as bright as the stars overhead and before she could guess his intent, his lips claimed hers.

The kiss started out as a light one, but then he deepened it by dipping his tongue in to swirl with hers. Immediately, she was lost in the sweet, hot sensations that rushed through her.

However, all too quickly he released her and smiled. "That's just to let you know that I intend to be an active participant in this competition." He leaned down and picked up the teddy bear. "Are you sure you want me to take this with me?"

"Positive, and, Benjamin, trust me. There is no competition. There are no other men in my life," she replied.

"That's a good thing to know," he replied. "On that note,

what would you think about coming over to my place on Thursday night for a steak dinner?"

"I think it sounds absolutely wonderful," she answered, once again a warmth swirling inside her at the thought of another date with him.

"Then why don't I pick you up about five thirty on Thursday evening and I'll cook you dinner," he said.

"I'll be ready and thank you so much for tonight. I had a wonderful time," she said.

"Yeah, so did I." A small frown appeared across his forehead. "Bailey, with the fact that somebody you don't know is leaving you these uh…gifts, it's all the more important that you watch when you're out and around. Make sure you don't let anybody get too close to you. You know the drill."

"I do," she replied somberly.

"Good, so I'll see you on Thursday evening." He waited on the porch until she was safely in her house.

She stepped in, then closed and locked the door. Her lips were still warm with the imprint of Benjamin's. The kiss, although far too brief, had absolutely lit her up inside.

He was exactly the kind of man she'd always imagined him to be. So far, she'd found him kind and intelligent, and he had a great sense of humor. And that kiss they'd shared had been absolutely toe-tingling amazing.

The vision of the teddy bear suddenly intruded into her happy thoughts, making her frown. *You Belong to Me.* Who was behind these "gifts"? First the rose and now the teddy bear. She moved over to her front window and peered outside.

Was somebody out there right now? Watching her? Why? What did they want from her? Seeing nothing out of place and nobody lurking about, she let the curtain fall back in front of the window and fought against the shiver of apprehension that threatened to creep up her spine.

Benjamin followed Dallas's patrol car down Main Street. They were headed to the motel, where apparently another fight between two men who lived there was in progress.

It was just after ten and it was another beautiful day— far too beautiful for two men to be fighting and definitely not the way to start a new week.

This wasn't the first time they'd been called to the motel to settle a fight between Burt Ramsey, an alcoholic who worked as a handyman around town, and Rocky Landow, a vet who was in a wheelchair after losing a leg.

Even though Rocky was in a wheelchair, the man was strong with upper body muscles, and if Burt got too close to him, Rocky could pull himself up and out of the chair to do a lot of damage to the weaker and much thinner Burt.

The Millsville Motel was mostly populated by drug addicts and people who'd fallen on hard times. It was a low gray building that breathed of failure and hopelessness. A couple of the units sported broken windows covered over with thick cardboard. Several people lived there permanently, as was the case with the two men who were going at each other this morning.

Benjamin couldn't remember anyone passing through town choosing to stay there. Millsville definitely wasn't a destination location.

They now whirled into the motel parking lot and immediately saw Burt standing in front of Rocky, who had a gun in his hand. Benjamin's chest immediately tightened.

This was the first time a gun had been present in one of the many squabbles the men had and that instantly raised the stakes.

Dallas got out of his car, as did Benjamin. They both drew their own weapons, but they didn't move any closer.

"Rocky, put the damned gun down," Dallas demanded.

"No, I won't. I'm going to shoot this lying bastard through his black heart," Rocky replied, his voice deep with anger.

"He's crazy," Burt whined. It was obvious the man was already sloshed. "All I said to him was 'good morning' and he went off like a rocket."

"That's not what you said to me, you damned liar," Rocky yelled and lifted the gun higher. "You called me a dirty cripple and said I needed to die and save the taxpayers having to pay for my disability checks. Damn you, I lost a leg defending the likes of you."

"And thank you for your service, Rocky, but you need to put the gun down now," Dallas said.

"All I did was come outside for a little breath of fresh air and you started flapping your mouth at me," Rocky said to Burt.

"Rocky, you're a good man. You know you don't want to shoot Burt. For God's sakes, man, don't destroy your life because of him," Benjamin said.

"He needs to not talk to me. He's a damn drunk who talks way too much," Rocky said. Benjamin saw Rocky's hand on the gun start to relax.

"Hey, I can't help it that I drink a little bit," Burt said, his voice slightly slurred. "You know I love you, man," he said to Rocky. "I'm sorry if I ran my mouth at you."

Rocky stared at Burt for several long moments and then

he finally set the gun down in his lap. "Apology accepted," he replied gruffly.

Dallas holstered his gun, then approached Rocky and grabbed the gun away from him. Meanwhile, Benjamin walked over to Burt and grabbed the man by his arm. He reeked like a brewery and was unsteady on his feet. He'd obviously had a lot to drink despite the early hour of the day.

"Listen, you two are close neighbors here and you both need to be good neighbors for each other," Dallas said. "The next time I'm called out here for a fight between you two, somebody is definitely going to go to jail. I'm not even kidding, I'm dead serious about that. I've had it with you two and your petty fights that take up my time and resources."

He turned and looked at Burt. "Go get into your place and don't speak to Rocky again for the rest of the day." He then looked at Rocky. "And the same for you. Do you have a permit for this thing?" He held up Rocky's gun. Then he broke it open to check if it was loaded.

"Yeah, I've got it inside. Do you want me to go get it for you?" Rocky asked.

"No, I trust you, but if I see you brandishing it again, we'll be having another kind of conversation and it won't be so pleasant," Dallas said and handed the gun back to him.

Minutes later, the two lawmen were on their way back to the station. As Benjamin drove, his thoughts turned to Bailey and his date with her the night before.

He had found her absolutely delightful. From her intelligence to her quick wit, he couldn't remember ever enjoying being with a woman as much as her. She'd made him laugh and it had felt wonderful after his long days of dealing with law-enforcement issues and a vicious murderer.

She'd looked beautiful in the jeans that hugged her slender waist and legs and the red blouse that complemented her blond hair and bright blue eyes.

Kissing her had been beyond wonderful. Her lips had been so soft and so inviting. He could have kissed her forever. He couldn't wait until Thursday night to see her again.

However, apparently another man wanted her attention, too, even though Bailey had professed that she didn't know who he was. Who had left her a teddy bear?

Benjamin had never understood the whole secret-admirer deal. If someone really wanted to tell a woman they admired or cared about her, why not just tell her to her face? Why play games?

Certainly, he and Bailey weren't anywhere near exclusive with each other, but he was surprised to feel just a little bit of jealousy when he thought about her going out with another man.

This was what he'd been afraid of, that he would love spending time with her and that he would not want it to end. But eventually it would have to end. He just hoped nobody got hurt when that happened.

He reached the station and went inside, where he found Dallas seated in the break room with a bag of peanuts and a soda before him. Benjamin fed the vending machine enough money for a soda and then he sat next to his boss.

"I'm so sick of those two taking up our time," Dallas said, his irritation rife in his voice.

"It would help if Burt wasn't drinking so much or so often," Benjamin replied and cracked open his soda can. "The man definitely needs treatment for his alcoholism."

"Yeah, and it would also help if Rocky wasn't so damned sensitive," Dallas added. "I swear, I was really tempted to throw them both in jail today."

"I get it, as if we don't have more important things to focus on right now. Too bad all the criminals and fools in Millsville couldn't take a break for a month or so and let us focus strictly on the Scarecrow Killer crimes."

"Ha, yeah, that would be nice." Dallas finished off his peanuts and chased them with a drink. "And speaking of the Scarecrow Killer, I want us to start from the very beginning with the first murder and go through everything we have again."

They'd already done this half a dozen times, but there was always a chance that they'd somehow missed something. Benjamin finished the last of his soda and then the two men left the break room together.

They headed down the hallway to a room where the murder books were spread out on a table. On a whiteboard there were pictures of the victims in life and in death, with their names written next to the photos. There were also enlarged photos of the button that had been found at the last scene.

Benjamin took a seat at the table and Dallas sat across from him. "You start with the Cindy Perry file and I'll start on Sandy Blackstone."

"Got it." Benjamin grabbed the file and opened it in front of him. There had to be something…some clue they were somehow missing. Surely no killer was this organized…this utterly clean.

As the two men began to read, Benjamin was aware that there was already a clock ticking. It beat in his head, reminding him that if they couldn't solve these murders quickly, then there would be another victim.

They had to catch this man before he struck again, before he made up his mind that the pretty blond-haired, blue-eyed Bailey was perfect as his next victim.

Chapter 5

"And then Robin threw down her plate. I mean, she literally threw the whole plate down to the floor. Pieces of china and food flew everywhere," Liza Settle said. "Thank goodness my dining room floor isn't carpeted or it would have been a real nightmare to clean up."

"I always knew she had a temper, but I never dreamed it could explode like that," Sharon Burke replied. "Knowing this, I certainly don't intend to invite her into my home anytime soon."

"I will never have her back in my house," Liza replied. "And I told her that after her fit."

Bailey tried to ignore the gossip as she worked on Liza's nails. Poor Robin, whoever she was—she didn't know she was being gossiped about in the public nail salon by these two women.

That was part of Bailey's job, to do nails and ignore the gossip she heard…and she heard a lot. She knew who was mad at whom, who was having financial issues and who was sleeping with whom. However, she had never heard any gossip, good or bad, about Benjamin.

It was just after noon on Wednesday when Celeste Winthrop swept into the salon. Celeste was a striking blonde with big, doe-like brown eyes and a fashion sense to rival

Bailey's. Today she was clad in brown slacks and a tiger-striped blouse. A gold belt and earrings finished the attractive ensemble.

"I don't have an appointment today, but I was hoping you could work me in," she said.

"Naomi can take you in about five minutes," Bailey replied.

"Bailey, I would really much prefer you take care of me today," Celeste replied with a thin smile.

"Then it will be fifteen to twenty minutes," Bailey said. She still needed to finish up with Sharon's fingernails and she wasn't going to rush it just because Celeste was waiting.

"That's fine, I'll wait." Celeste sat in one of the chairs in front of the window that were for the waiting clients. She picked up one of the magazines Bailey kept on an end table and began flipping through the pages.

A small ball of dread formed in the pit of Bailey's stomach. If Celeste just wanted to have her nails done, she would have allowed Naomi to serve her. Celeste liked her nails dipped and Naomi had often dipped Celeste's nails in the past.

Celeste must have an ulterior motive for wanting Bailey, and Bailey had a feeling it had something to do with Benjamin. He'd obviously broken up with her before he'd started seeing Bailey. The dread increased inside her. She knew the conversation with Celeste probably wasn't going to be a pleasant one.

Fifteen minutes later, Celeste sat in a chair at one of the nail stations and Bailey began to give her a manicure. Celeste had already chosen her dipping color—a bright red with sparkles.

"So I hear through the grapevine that lately you and

Benjamin have been seeing each other," Celeste said, wasting no time in getting to what she wanted to discuss.

"We've been hanging out a bit together," Bailey replied as she began taking the old polish off Celeste's long, pointy nails.

"I just want to give you a little friendly advice because you seem like a very nice woman. I know Benjamin is quite a catch, but you better hang on to your heart where he is concerned. He'll only hang out with you for a little while and then he'll be back together with me."

Bailey looked up to meet the woman's narrowed gaze. "I guess only time will tell," Bailey replied, keeping her tone even and calm.

"Trust me on this. He'll give you the three- or four-date treatment and then he'll break it off with you. I know he'll come back to me. Benjamin and I shared a very special relationship. We had a little spat, but once he gets over being upset with me, he'll come back to me." There was a brazen confidence in Celeste's voice.

Bailey looked back down at Celeste's nails. "If that happens, then it happens. I don't intend to lose any sleep worrying about it."

"I just figured, you know, woman to woman, I needed to give you a heads-up so you don't get hurt in the process," Celeste said.

"I appreciate that. Who knows, maybe I'll be the one to stop seeing him," Bailey said, knowing that was probably what was going to happen, anyway.

"Oh, are you already tired of his company?" Celeste asked with a raised, perfectly plucked eyebrow.

"No, I just mean nobody can say what might happen in the future," Bailey replied.

Celeste spent the rest of her time in the chair in a sullen silence. Forty-five minutes later, she left the salon with her new fancy red nails and snide smiles.

"I'm surprised you didn't pull all her nails clean out," Naomi said with disgust. The two of them were momentarily alone in the place. "She is one nasty piece of work. It's no wonder she's been single for as long as she's been."

"I'm not sure why she thought it was necessary to have that conversation with me," Bailey said.

"She was just trying to stir up doubts in your head about Benjamin. Celeste has always been a brazen witch. Honestly, Bailey, I've never seen you as happy as you've been lately. I know how long you crushed on Benjamin from afar and I think it's wonderful that the two of you are now together," Naomi said.

"We're not exactly together. We've only gone out on one official date," Bailey replied. "Well, two if I count the drink after the carnival. Although he did ask me to his place on Thursday night. He's going to cook steaks for us."

"Oh, you are so definitely together," Naomi exclaimed. "When a man takes you to his house and cooks for you, it's definitely serious."

Hours later, as Bailey drove home, she thought about what Naomi had said. It wasn't serious with Benjamin… It couldn't be, because the moment things got too serious between them, then she'd have to bounce.

You're not right.

You're not a normal woman. You're selfish.

Those hateful words shot through her head with a stabbing pain—pain, because she knew Adam had been right about her. She wasn't normal and she would never seek out a long-term relationship again.

It had been a late night at the salon and the shadows of darkness were creeping in by the time she parked in her driveway. Before winter hit, she had to arrange everything in her double garage so that she could use half of it to park inside.

She got out of her car and before she even took one step, she felt it. The hairs on the nape of her neck rose up and she had the distinct creepy-crawly feeling of somebody watching her.

She looked all around. There were no strange cars parked on the street. Nothing appeared out of the ordinary and yet the feeling was strong enough to make her feel more than a little afraid.

She hurried to her front door, unlocked it and went inside. She locked the door after her and then went directly to the window and moved the curtains aside just enough so she could see outside.

Her heart beat a quickened rhythm as she peered out. There was nobody lurking around on her property. Maybe it had just been some sort of a false signal from her over-worked brain.

She was about to release the edge of the curtain when she saw him. Across the street in her neighbor's yard, a man looked out from behind a large tree.

The curtain dropped from her hand as she slammed her back against her door. Her heart pounded so loud in her head that for a moment she could hear nothing else.

There was no question that the man had been looking directly at her and her house. The shadows had been too deep and the distance too far for her to see exactly who it was.

With her heart still beating a million beats a minute,

she peeked out the window once again. She stared at the big tree across the street.

Seconds ticked by, then minutes passed and she saw no more movement. He was gone. Or maybe he hadn't really been there after all. It could have been a trick of the light or her overactive imagination.

She walked across the room and sank down on her sofa, waiting for her breathing to return to normal and her thoughts to become clear from the panic that had momentarily gripped her.

She was sure somebody had been there. Who had been out there? Who had been watching her and why? Who had left the rose and the teddy bear for her?

Somebody was stalking her and she needed to find out why. She wanted to know who it was. Should she call the police? If the man was already gone, then what could law enforcement do about it?

Her biggest fear was that it might be the Scarecrow Killer. Benjamin had told her there was no evidence to indicate that the man had left gifts for his victims before he'd killed them, but how did anyone know that for sure? Was he the one watching her? Was he trying to decide if she would be his next victim?

It took her a very long time to fall asleep that night. The next morning, she got ready for work and as she opened the door to leave her house, she nearly stumbled over a vase filled with bright, colorful flowers. She grabbed the note that was in an envelope and opened it.

You are mine.

She read the words and looked around, wondering if the bearer of the gifts was watching her now. In case he was, she kicked over the plastic vase and then tore the card into little pieces.

Was that what the man behind the tree had done? Waited until she was at home and in bed to leave the flowers? She'd had enough of this secret-admirer stuff. The day before she'd found a box of chocolates waiting for her at the salon door. She'd immediately thrown the box in the trash. There was only one person she could think of that might possibly be behind it all.

She stewed about it all the way to work and once she got to the salon, she sat in one of the chairs and pulled her phone out of her purse.

She hadn't heard from him for about two weeks and so she thought things had been ironed out between them. She found him in her contacts and hit the button to call him. Enough was enough and nothing was going to change her mind about him. If he was behind all the gifts, then she needed to tell him to stop it all now. He answered on the third ring:

"Bailey, it's so good to hear from you," Howard Kendall said warmly.

"Howard, this isn't exactly a social call," she said tersely. "I just need to know, are you leaving things for me? Like a teddy bear and flowers and candy?"

"No, but if I do, will you go out with me again?"

"Howard, we weren't right for each other and, no, I wouldn't go out with you again no matter how many gifts you left for me. Howard, this is really important to me, so please don't lie to me. So have you been leaving gifts for me?" she asked again.

"No, it's not me. I've pretty much moved on, Bailey. You've made it very clear to me that there's no way forward for the two of us. Besides, from the sound of things, you now have another man besotted with you," he replied.

She believed him. She didn't believe he would lie to her. He wasn't her secret admirer. Then who was it? Who was skulking around her house and leaving love notes and items for her?

She couldn't imagine who it was. She spent so much of her time in the salon with women. Was it possible it was Ethan Dourty? She didn't believe so. He hadn't even called her since they'd had coffee together at the café. So who? Who was possibly "besotted" with her?

Was she in danger from this person? She just didn't know what to think, but the whole thing definitely had her on edge. The good thing was that Thursday night she had a date with a cop. She was definitely going to bring it up with him and get his thoughts on the whole thing. Maybe he could tell her how often stalkers turned dangerous.

Thursday morning, the Scarecrow Killer task force was officially together again in the small room they worked out of. The task force consisted of Dallas, Benjamin and Officers Trent Lawrence and Ross Davenport.

If they had a bigger police force there would be far more people on the task force, but this was Millsville, Kansas, and manpower and resources were very tight.

So there were only four men completely dedicated to this case while the rest of the officers dealt with most of the petty crimes in town. Although with the investigation at a standstill when they weren't working on the case, they were all back to patrolling and dealing with various petty crimes that occurred.

"I got a tip this morning over the tip line," Dallas said. "And I think it's something we need to check out."

"What was the tip?" Trent asked. He was a middle-aged man who had been with the department for about ten years. He was sharp and dedicated, and Benjamin had always liked and trusted him.

"Somebody called in and said that George Albertson keeps a lot of straw hats in his barn," Dallas replied.

"He's got a pretty big barn on his property," Benjamin said thoughtfully.

"And he's isolated on all that farmland, too," Trent added. "Isolated enough that nobody would hear a woman if she screamed."

"He's always been kind of an odd duck. He keeps to himself and doesn't seem to have any friends or family," Benjamin said.

"I think this definitely warrants a visit from law enforcement," Dallas said. "What do you all say?"

"I say we don't have anything to lose in checking it out." Benjamin rose from the table where the four of them had been sitting.

"Benjamin, you can ride with me. Trent, take Ross and follow us in your car," Dallas said and also stood.

Minutes later, they were on their way to the large spread on the western outskirts of town where Alberton lived. "It would be nice if this tip panned out," Dallas said.

"Yeah, it would be good for the town if we could finally get this madman off the streets and into jail," Benjamin replied.

"If we could get him behind bars, maybe I'd start sleeping again. On another, more pleasant note, are you ready for your big date with Bailey tonight?" Dallas asked.

"As ready as I can be. The apartment is clean and the food is all ready to be cooked."

Dallas shot him a quick, amused glance. "Tell me the most important thing of all… Did you put clean sheets on the bed?"

Benjamin laughed. "A gentleman never tells." He sobered. "Seriously, man, we're not at that place in our relationship. In fact, I'm just trying to be a friend to her because I think she needs one right now."

"I'm sure she's probably still having a rough time with everything that's happened. It had to be horrible for her to walk into her salon and see our victim seated in one of her chairs," Dallas said.

"Yeah, it was horrible for her and she doesn't really have much of a support system." Benjamin hadn't seen Bailey all week and he was really looking forward to seeing her that night.

No matter what he'd told Dallas about the relationship with Bailey, it was beginning to feel like he didn't just want to see her to support her, but he wanted to get together with her because he really wanted to spend time with her.

He'd run into Celeste in the grocery store the night before. She'd been quite flirtatious with him, as if she'd never had words with him. But he had no interest in picking things back up with her again, especially not with Bailey now in his life.

Celeste had been so desperate to get married and have babies, and that's all she'd talked about when they'd been together. Her desperation had been exhausting to him. With Bailey, things were so much lighter and easier, and right now he was completely enjoying his time with her.

All thoughts of his dating life fell from his head as they

approached the Alberton place. The home was a relatively small one. It had once been white, but had weathered to a dirty gray.

The barn was set to the right of the house and was a huge structure that was also weathered and gray. The doors to the barn were closed as they pulled up in front of the house and parked behind George's beat-up black pickup.

The four officers left their vehicles and approached the front door of the house. Hopefully, George wasn't somewhere in his fields working. If he was, the odds of him hearing them were minimal.

Dallas knocked on the door. There was no reply. He knocked again, this time harder and louder. George had to be around somewhere since his truck was here. Hopefully, he was close enough for him to hear them.

"George," Dallas yelled. "George, are you here?" he yelled again.

They all turned in unison at the sound of a door screeching open in the barn. George Albertson was in his late fifties or so. He was a tall man with the shoulders and thighs of a linebacker. He was certainly in good enough physical shape to manipulate and move a dead woman's body.

"Chief Calloway...what's up?" George said as he approached them. He was wearing overalls and a straw hat rode the top of his head. He swept off his hat, exposing his thinning salt-and-pepper hair, as he reached where they were.

"I'll be honest with you, George. We need to see inside your barn," Dallas replied.

George's eyes narrowed as he frowned. "And why would that be?"

"We got a tip this morning and we need to check it out," Dallas replied.

"A tip, huh. I'm sure it was that bastard Sturgis Devons." George's gaze shot across his property and he glared at his neighbor's house in the distance. He looked back at Dallas. "That man's been trying to break me down for years. He wants my land, but as long as I'm alive he'll never get it."

"I really don't know who called in the tip," Dallas said. "We just need to check out a few things in your barn."

"You got a search warrant?" George asked, his blunt features radiating his intense displeasure at this whole thing.

"No, but if necessary, I can go get one. I just figured we could do this the easy, friendly way," Dallas replied.

George released a deep sigh. "All right. I got nothing to hide, so let's go to the barn."

Dallas walked alongside George while Trent, Ross and Benjamin brought up the rear. Would they find something in the barn to point to George as their killer?

Benjamin desperately hoped so, but the fact that George was now fully cooperating with them gave him little hope that they would find a den of evil inside the big, weather-beaten structure.

What they did find inside were neat stacks of hay, a clean floor and four straw hats hanging off nails in one wall. There was absolutely nothing to indicate that any women had been killed and dressed up like scarecrows in the barn.

Benjamin walked over to get a closer look at the hanging straw hats. They were in various conditions—one was neat and clean while the others were sweat- and dirt-stained around the headbands. The ones found on the victims had been brand-new and completely clean.

He turned to look at George. "Why four hats?"

"One is my go-to town hat and the rest of them are field

hats. The sun gets really hot if you're bare-headed out there all day. Why? Is it against the law to have more than one hat?" George asked rather sarcastically.

"Of course not. I was just curious," Benjamin replied evenly.

"Okay, I think we're finished here," Dallas said.

A few minutes later they were in their cars and headed back to the station. "I'm so disappointed that this didn't pan out," Dallas said, his frustration rife in his voice.

"Yeah, me, too," Benjamin agreed.

"At least you have something to look forward to," Dallas replied. "You have your date with Bailey tonight to take your mind off all this."

"But I also worry about her," Benjamin replied. "You know she fits the profile to become a victim of this guy. As long as he's out on the streets I believe she's in potential danger."

"After this latest murder, I think I need to have another town hall meeting to remind all the women in town to stay in pairs or a group when they're out and about. In fact, I think I'll set something up in the next week or so."

"Sounds like a plan to me," Benjamin agreed. "It never hurts to remind the women that they could potentially be in danger every time they leave their houses."

Dallas turned the car into the lot and parked behind the station in his official parking space.

The afternoon flew by and at four o'clock Dallas told Benjamin to take off for the day. Benjamin didn't argue about getting off early, then headed for the exit and quickly left.

He made one quick stop on the way home, and once there, he took a quick shower and shaved, then changed into a pair of jeans and a royal blue polo. He then went into his kitchen and turned on the oven to bake the potatoes.

He didn't particularly enjoy cooking, but it was ridiculous how much he was looking forward to cooking for Bailey. There was something about her that stirred something deep inside him. It was something he'd never felt before and it both excited and frightened him a little bit.

He enjoyed looking into her bright blue eyes and seeing her wide smile. He loved the sound of her full-bodied laughter. He even enjoyed the big colorful earrings she wore that seemed to be her trademark.

For the first time in his life, he really wished things could be different. But they weren't and they never would be, and so the odds were good he'd spend the rest of his life all alone.

He knew he couldn't get in too deep with her, but surely, they could continue seeing each other for a little while longer as long as things remained light and easy between them.

Chapter 6

Bailey stood at her front door and awaited Benjamin's arrival to pick her up for the evening at his place. She was excited. Her heart beat a little faster than normal and a delicious sweet energy swirled around in the pit of her stomach.

She hadn't seen him all week long and was eager to spend more time with him and to get to know him on an even deeper level. She was especially excited to see the place he called home. Surely, it would be a peek into what was important to him and what he surrounded himself with.

Once again, she'd dressed casually in a pair of jeans and a pink blouse. Her makeup was light, her hair in its usual spiked-up style, and large pink-and-denim-colored earrings hung from her ears.

Since she had gotten the flowers in the vase, there had been no more "gifts" left for her. She hoped whoever was responsible for them would either stop or simply reveal themselves to her. She still intended to talk to Benjamin about it.

For the past week, each day after work she'd gone into her garage and moved the boxes and bags of salon supplies to one side of the double garage. Thankfully, she was now able to pull her car into the garage and park there each night. She'd realized just how vulnerable she'd been walking from the car to her front door each evening and now that problem had been solved. She could go into her garage and enter into her kitchen without having to walk outside.

Her heart lifted up as his car pulled into her driveway. Before he could get out, she pulled her door shut behind her and practically danced out to his car.

She slid into the passenger seat and shot him a wide smile. "Hi," she said.

"Hi, yourself," he replied in what had become a pattern of greeting every time they saw each other. He offered her a wide smile of his own. "You look absolutely beautiful this evening, as usual."

"Well, thank you, kind sir. You cut quite a dashing figure yourself," she replied.

"Pink is definitely a good color on you," he said.

"Thank you, it's my favorite color. And I would guess that your favorite color is blue."

"You'd be right. Are you hungry?" he asked as he backed out of the driveway.

"Starving and I can't wait to taste your expert culinary skills."

"Ha, don't expect too much," he said with a laugh.

"It's another beautiful night," she said. The sky was clear and the temperature was a bit cooler than it had been. Outside, it smelled like autumn, but inside the car all she could smell was the delicious scent of Benjamin. It was a combination of shaving cream, his slightly spicy cologne and wonderful male that enticed her.

"It is a beautiful night," he agreed. "In fact, it's so pleasant out I decided it might be nice if we'd eat outside on my patio, if that's okay with you."

"That sounds lovely," she replied. "I didn't even think about you having a patio at the apartments."

"My place is on the ground floor so I have a very nice patio. Have you ever been to the apartments before?"

"No, I haven't," she replied. The Downhome Apartment Complex was the only one of its kind in Millsville. It was a two-story structure that she guessed had about fifteen units. It was only a couple of years old and she'd heard it was very nice.

"Living there works for me right now. With all the hours I work, I'm rarely at home, anyway. Maybe eventually I'll buy a house, but up to now I've never really felt the need," he explained.

"Home ownership isn't for everyone, especially in this day and age," she replied. "But it was important to me. I dreamed of having my own house since I was little." Still, she wouldn't have cared if Benjamin lived in a dark, dank cave. She was interested in the man, not his dwelling.

They reached the apartment complex, which was painted an attractive tan with darker brown trim. He turned in and parked in one of the covered spaces provided to the tenants. They got out of the car and he gestured toward one of the doors. "I'm in apartment 106," he said.

She followed him to the door, which he unlocked and then opened. "Welcome to my humble abode," he said as he gestured her inside before him.

She walked in and looked around the place with interest. The furniture indicated it was a typical bachelor pad. A glass-topped coffee table set before a black sofa. There was also a recliner chair and a huge flat-screen television hung on the wall.

What really drew her attention was an array of photos

hanging on another wall. She stepped closer to gaze at them. It was obvious they were photos of Benjamin's family. There was one of the family all together and then there were photos of Benjamin with his sister and her family. There was also one of the two siblings together and several of him alone with his niece and nephew.

"These are so nice," she said.

He came up to stand behind her. His body heat engulfed her at the same time his scent dizzied her senses. She turned and he took a step back from her, but not before she thought she saw a fevered blaze of desire in his eyes. It was there only a moment and then gone, but it was enough to light a small fire in the pit of her stomach.

"I only have one regret about photos," she said in an attempt to fill the sudden awkwardness between them.

"And what's that?" he asked.

"I never managed to get a good photo of my sister," she replied.

He laughed. "You should have used an imaginary camera," he returned, making her laugh. "Are you ready to head into the kitchen?"

"Just lead the way," she said.

She followed him through the living room and into a kitchen that had a small table and a long island with three stools in front of it. Bailey sat on one of the stools as Benjamin went to the refrigerator.

"The potatoes are already cooking in the oven and should be ready in about fifteen minutes or so," he said as he pulled out two beautiful steaks marinating in something that smelled wonderful. He opened a drawer and withdrew a torch lighter. "I'm just going to step out and start the grill. I'll be right back."

He disappeared out the sliding glass door that obviously led to his deck. She took the moments while he was gone to tamp down the wild physical desire that had gripped her the minute she had slid into his car.

She wasn't anywhere close to wanting to make love to Benjamin…was she? Only rarely did she sleep with the men she was dating. She always broke things off with them before that point came. She tossed the very thought of making love with Benjamin out of her head. Tonight, she was just looking forward to some good companionship and a delicious meal.

Benjamin came back inside. "We'll let that warm up for a couple of minutes and then we'll move outside so I can cook the steaks."

"Sounds like a plan to me," she replied. "So how was your week?"

He leaned with his back against the refrigerator. "Frustrating," he admitted. "We thought we had a good lead on the Scarecrow Killer from the tip line, but it didn't pan out."

"I'm sure the tip line is going to fill up with a bunch of foolish nonsense. Mad at your neighbor…call the tip line. Ticked off at a relative…call the tip line."

"I'm afraid you're right," Benjamin replied. "Dallas is doing his best to vet the calls that come in, but that's time-consuming in and of itself. He's also planning on having another town-hall meeting. It's going to be this Wednesday night."

"That's probably a good idea," Bailey replied.

"I hope every woman in town attends and that's including you."

"I'll plan to go," she replied.

"Ah, I've been remiss… What can I get you to drink?" he asked.

"What are you offering?" she asked.

"I've got soda, ice tea and beer. I'm going to have a beer."

"Make that two, bartender," she replied.

He grinned at her and then pulled two bottles out of the refrigerator. "Now, shall we move outside?" He grabbed the platter of steaks and his beer while she picked up her beer and followed him out the door.

The patio was a pleasant area. There was an umbrella table and the yellow-and-white-striped umbrella looked beautiful against the deep blue of the sky. He had set it with black plates and yellow napkins. He looked incredibly hot with the sunshine sparking in his blond hair as he grabbed a large pair of tongs off the grill.

"This is really nice," she said as she sank down in one of the yellow cushioned chairs at the table.

The grill was on one side of the patio, far enough away from where she sat that she couldn't really feel the heat from it. However, it was obviously hot, since the steaks immediately began to sizzle when he put them on to cook.

"Do you spend a lot of time out here?" she asked curiously.

"Not as much as I'd like to. To be honest, it's not much fun sitting out here all alone."

"I'm sure if you called Celeste, she would be more than happy to come over and spend some time with you here," Bailey replied.

He frowned. "Why would I call her? I don't want to spend any time with her."

"Not according to her. According to her you two will be

back together very soon." She told him about Celeste coming into the nail shop and having a conversation with her.

"That woman has a lot of damned nerve trying to interfere with my life," Benjamin said when she was finished. "I'm so sorry you had to deal with that... With her."

"Don't worry, she didn't bother me at all," Bailey assured him. "I found her to be more than a little bit desperate."

"She's definitely desperate to find a new husband," he replied. "But it's certainly not going to be me."

He turned the steaks, which had filled the air with their mouth-watering scent. "How do you like your steak?"

"Medium," she replied. "How do you like yours?"

"Medium." He smiled at her, that smile that melted her insides and made her want to fall into his arms.

It didn't take long for the steaks to cook and then they sat down to eat. The salad he'd made was crispy and fresh, the baked potatoes were perfectly cooked and the steak was seasoned and grilled to perfection.

As they ate, they talked about the week that had passed. He shared what they had done in an effort to find the elusive killer and she told him about what had happened in the nail salon.

In a perfect world, they were perfect together. He shared the darkness of his work with her while she tempered that darkness with the lightness of silly gossip and the latest in nail news.

But it wasn't perfect because she wasn't perfect. She wasn't normal and if she could help it, she would never be put in a position again for another man to tell her that.

"How about some dessert," he said once they had finished eating. "I stopped by the Sweet Tooth Bakery on my way home from work today and picked up a few things."

"Did you know the way to a woman's heart is anything from the Sweet Tooth Bakery?"

He laughed. "I didn't know that, but it's good information to know. Sit tight and I'll bring them out." He picked up their two dinner plates, then went into the house and returned a moment later with a pink-and-white-striped box from the bakery and two small plates.

He gave her one of the plates and then opened the bakery box. Inside was an array of sweets. There were cinnamon and cream-cheese bars, little chocolate fudge squares and bite-size raspberry fritters.

"Hmm," she said as she helped herself to one of each. "Now this is what I call a real dessert."

"I wasn't sure what you would like, but I figured cinnamon, chocolate and fruit was a good combination," he said as he took a couple of the cinnamon bites for himself.

"Definitely a good combination," she agreed. "I've never had anything bad from the bakery. I'm so glad the place is up and running again after the fire."

Harper Brennan owned the bakery, and several months ago one of her customers had tried to kill her by trapping her inside and starting the place on fire.

Thankfully, Sam Bravano, the man who Harper had been dating, had managed to save her. Sam and his brothers, all carpenters, had worked hard to rebuild the place after the fire. The man who had set the fire had been a regular customer and had developed an obsession with Harper. Thinking about all this made her remember that she wanted to talk to Benjamin about her "secret admirer."

She waited until after dinner, when they'd cleaned up

the dishes and were seated in his living room and having coffee. "Benjamin, I want to talk with you about something serious," she said.

"Okay." He moved a little closer to her on the sofa. "What is it?" He looked at her with concern.

"I might be overreacting, but you were there when the teddy bear was left for me and since then there's been a couple more things left for me."

"Things like what?"

"A box of candy and a vase full of flowers, and each one has a note attached that says something like 'you belong to me' or 'you're mine forever.' I think this person might be stalking me."

"And you don't have any idea who it might be?" he asked.

She frowned. "I thought it might be Howard Kendall. We went out a few times and then I broke it off with him and he tried for weeks after that to get me back. But I called and asked him point-blank if it was him. He denied it all and I've never known Howard to be a liar, so I believe him."

"Is there anyone else you might have dated in your past or anyone who has indicated an interest in you recently?" he asked.

"I had coffee with Ethan Dourty not too long ago, but it was just a friendly cup of coffee at the café and nothing more. And before I dated Howard, I also went out a few times with RJ from the tattoo shop, but this isn't RJ's style. RJ would be all up in my face. My main question for you is should I be afraid? How often do stalkers get dangerous?" She searched his beautiful blue eyes.

"To be honest, I don't know. But my first instinct is to tell you not to worry too much. I really believe this man is going to reveal himself to you very soon. He's just hoping to win you over before that happens." He looked at her intently. "Is it working?"

"God, no. I'm finding it all very creepy and irritating. So you don't think I need to be afraid?"

"I think you need to be very cautious," he replied. "It's the same thing about the Scarecrow Killer. You need to watch your surroundings and be aware of who is around you." He reached out and slowly slid a finger down her cheek. "Bailey, if you are ever afraid, call me and I'll be at your place immediately."

He dropped his hand, but his eyes suddenly burned with a light that made her breath catch in her throat. "Bailey, I really want to kiss you right now."

Her heart fluttered as she held his gaze. "Oh, Benjamin. I would really like for you to kiss me right now."

He leaned forward, gathered her into his arms and then his lips took hers in a kiss that shot fire through her veins and made her realize just how difficult it was going to be to stop seeing him.

Chapter 7

Kissing Bailey was like taking a powerful drug. Benjamin's head dizzied and his heartbeat accelerated the moment his lips met hers. She tasted of a hint of cinnamon and warm coffee and sweet hot desire.

He deepened the kiss by dipping his tongue in to dance with hers. She tightened her arms around his neck and pressed herself closer to him, making him half-mad with his own heightened desire for her.

He reminded himself that he didn't want to get in too deep with her, but it was hard to remember that when she filled his arms and her mouth was so hot and so hungry against his own.

What he wanted to do right now was to take her into his bedroom. He wanted to strip her naked and then make slow, sweet love to her. However, he still had his wits to-gether enough to know he couldn't let that happen. That definitely wouldn't be fair to her.

He cared about her enough not to sleep with her and then dump her. With that thought in mind, he finally pulled away from her. She dropped her arms from around his neck and sat back with a sigh.

"I could kiss you all night long, Bailey," he said.

"And I would let you kiss me all night long," she replied softly.

"Unfortunately, I have an early morning at work tomorrow, so I think it's time for me to take you home."

"Of course. I would never want you to be too tired at work because of me. That could be very dangerous for you."

He smiled at her. "Thank you for being so understanding."

"I've really enjoyed tonight," she said minutes later when they were in his car and headed back to her house.

"I have, too," he agreed. "But I always enjoy spending time with you. You're very easy to talk to, Bailey."

"And I find you very easy to talk to," she replied. "I don't know what I would have done without you after… you know… Megan and everything."

"You've impressed me with your strength. Bailey, you're far stronger than you think you are."

She laughed. "You keep telling me that, but maybe I just have you fooled."

"Sorry, I'm a police officer and that means you can't fool me," he replied.

She laughed once again. "So you're telling me you're like a human lie detector?"

"That's me," he answered lightly. "Don't you know that officially I'm a detective and so I can detect lies?"

He pulled up in her driveway and parked. "Maybe Saturday night you could come over here and we could get pizza?" she said.

"Better yet, why don't I pick you up and we go to the pizza place to eat?" he suggested. With the physical-attraction level so wild between them, he thought it was better if they spent their time together in public places.

If he had his way, he'd package her in bubble wrap to keep her safe from harm, but he couldn't exactly do that. He also didn't want to parade her out in public too much, but the pizza parlor was a small place off the beaten path and so he thought it would be safe to take her out there.

"Okay, we can do that, but only on one condition," she said.

He looked at her curiously. With darkness having fallen outside, the only illumination came from his dash lights and they painted her face in a lovely way. "And what's that?"

"I pay for the pizza."

"That's not necessary," he immediately protested.

"Yes, it is," she replied firmly. "And really, I insist, so don't argue with me now and don't argue with me at the pizza place."

"Well, okay then. I don't want to argue with you. How about I pick you up around six."

"Sounds good to me," she concurred. She looked so beautiful in the faint lighting that stroked her features in a soft aura and it made him want to kiss her all over again.

Instead, he unbuckled his seat belt, and she did the same, and together they got out of the car. When they reached her porch, her gaze shot all around, including across the street. Initially, he could feel her tension, but it faded away quickly and she smiled up at him.

"You okay?" he asked.

"Fine. I'm just happy there's no new gifts left for me and there doesn't appear to be anyone hiding behind the tree across the street."

"Whoa, you didn't tell me anything about a man across the street," he replied with surprise.

"It was on the night before I found the vase of flowers on my doorstep. I was sure I saw a man lurking behind that big tree over there, but honestly, now I'm not sure if I really saw somebody or if it was just a figment of my over-active imagination. If he was real, all he did was leave me the flowers on my porch."

"If you think you see something like that again, you call me and I'll come check it out immediately," he insisted. He would hope that if she really saw somebody lurking around her house or across the street, she would call him and he could get out here fast enough to catch the creep.

"I'm so glad I have a personal lie-detector detective bodyguard to keep me safe."

He laughed. "That's a pretty heavy title for me to wear."

"But you do it with such grace and style," she murmured, her beautiful eyes sparking in the moonlight.

"On that note, I think it's time I make my exit." He kissed her on the cheek and then took a step back. "I'll see you Saturday night."

"Thanks again for the great food and conversation to-night," she said and then moved to unlock her door. When that was done, she turned back to face him. "Good night, Benjamin."

"Good night, Bailey." He waited until she was safely inside her house and then he walked back to his car. God, he'd wanted to kiss her again and not just on her cheek. He'd wanted to take her in his arms and kiss her properly. Still, it was a good thing he hadn't.

For a few minutes, he merely sat in his car and gazed all around the area. It bothered him that she'd thought she'd seen a man across the street watching her. When she'd asked him about stalkers turning dangerous, he'd tried to downplay the threat.

However, the whole gifts thing coupled with the possibility of somebody watching her, stalking her, did trouble him. There was no way to know if the person was a threat to her or not. He was certainly hoping whoever was leaving the things for her wasn't dangerous.

At this point there wasn't much he could do about the situation except be there for Bailey. He could definitely ask Dallas for more nightly patrols down her street.

He finally pulled out of her driveway and headed back home. His mind shifted to when he'd held her so close and had kissed her so deeply.

In those moments, he had wanted her badly. But making love to Bailey wouldn't be fair to her. He had no intention of having a long-term relationship with her. She was a beautiful, bright young woman and deserved a man who wanted to be married and have a family. And that wasn't him, and it would never—could never—be him.

He should stop seeing her now, but with a potential stalker in her life, it wasn't the right time for him to just walk away from her.

"Is it a possibility to get a couple of extra night patrols down Bailey's street?" he asked Dallas the next morning. Dallas was in his office and Benjamin stood just inside the door.

"I'm sure I could arrange for that," Dallas replied. He gestured to the chair in front of his desk. "Want to sit and tell me exactly what's going on?"

"It seems that Bailey might have picked up a stalker," Benjamin revealed as he sat in front of his boss. "She's been getting anonymous gifts and love notes from somebody and she thought she saw a person hiding behind her neighbor's tree a couple of nights ago."

"And she has no idea who is behind it?" Dallas asked with a frown.

"None," Benjamin replied. "I'd just feel better if some officers had eyes on her place throughout the night."

"Got it, and I'll arrange for extra patrols down her street." Dallas leaned back in his chair and his frown deepened. "I think we can write off this being the Scarecrow Killer. None of the family members or friends of our victims mentioned anything about them receiving anonymous gifts or notes before their deaths. I just hope this doesn't blow up into anything serious. That's the last thing we would need right now."

"I completely agree," Benjamin offered.

"Do you have any of the notes she's received?" Dallas asked.

"No."

"That's too bad," Dallas mused with a shake of his head. "At least if we had one of the notes, we could fingerprint it and possibly get an identity off it."

"I'll tell her the next time she gets one to give it to me," Benjamin replied, irritated with himself that he hadn't thought about it before now.

"In the meantime, I've got you on street patrol today since we're stalled out on the Scarecrow Killer investigation," Dallas said.

"Fine with me." Benjamin stood. "You know I never mind patrol. I just came in to talk to you about the extra patrols for Bailey, so now I'll head on out and hit the streets."

"I'll see you sometime before the end of the day," Dallas said.

Minutes later Benjamin was in his patrol car and headed down Main Street. He parked and got out to walk. He always enjoyed being on foot and talking to not only pedestrians who were out shopping, but also the people who owned the shops. It was especially important now that law enforcement was seen out and about. With the Scarecrow Killer on most everyone's mind, it was imperative that the people of Millsville saw the presence of law enforcement.

One of the first things he saw just up ahead of him was Fred Stanley following closely behind Annie Cook. Annie was an attractive mother of two young children and Fred was known as the town's lech.

Benjamin sighed and hurried toward the two. "Hey, Annie," he called out.

She stopped and turned to face him and he saw the relief that quickly flashed across her pretty features. He reached the two and stopped Fred, as well. "Annie, is Fred bothering you?" he asked and turned a stern look at the old man.

"Yes... I mean, no, it's fine," she replied, her cheeks flushed with color. "Fred was just, uh, giving me some suggestions of things we could do if I came to visit him at his house."

"Like what kinds of things?" Benjamin asked, easily able to imagine what sorts of things the old widower had suggested.

"Oh, that's not important now," Fred interjected hurriedly. "Annie looked kind of sad so I was just trying to be friendly and cheer her up." Fred offered Benjamin his most innocent smile.

"Annie, I'm sure you have more important things to do than listen to Fred's suggestions. So why don't you go on about your day and I'm going to stay here and have a little chat with Fred."

"Thank you." She looked at him gratefully and then turned and hurried on down the sidewalk. Benjamin turned to look at the old man who smelled of an ancient cologne and a menthol muscle cream. "Fred, you have got to stop accosting women on the street," Benjamin said sternly.

"I wasn't accosting nobody. I was just trying to be a little friendly," he protested. "The poor woman looked a bit lonely and sad and I was just trying to cheer her up some."

"You definitely need to be a little less friendly with the women. If you aren't careful, you're going to end up in jail," Benjamin replied. "I know Dallas has warned you over and over again about this."

"I hear you," Fred responded grumpily. "Now can I go?"

"Where are you headed now?"

"I suppose I'm going home."

"That sounds like a very good idea," Benjamin replied. He watched as the old man ambled away. Fred had been warned a million times about speaking inappropriately to the women in town. He was a problem, but at least he was a fairly harmless problem.

Benjamin spent the morning walking the streets and visiting with the people he came across. The day was fairly cool and everyone he encountered was pleasant. Much of the conversations were about how much fun people had had at the fall-festival celebration and the upcoming town meeting. As he passed the salon, he shot a quick gaze inside and saw Bailey seated at one of the workstations painting a woman's nails.

At noon he got back into his car to continue patrolling the streets. By midafternoon, a thick layer of clouds had diminished the sunlight overhead, turning the day a miserable gray.

He stopped two people going too fast and gave out a warning to one and a ticket to the other, who was a teenage chronic speeder. The rest of his day passed uneventfully.

It was about six thirty when he decided to knock off for the night. He called and checked in with Dallas then did a final drive-by of the nail salon. It was closed up and Bailey's car was gone.

It was ridiculous how much he'd wanted to pop in to see her today... Just to see her beautiful face...just to enjoy her beautiful smile for a minute or two.

Before heading home for the night, he decided to do a quick pass by her house. In the preternatural darkness of the evening, the streets were fairly deserted.

He turned down Bailey's street. Her car must have been parked in her garage, since it wasn't in her driveway, but lights flooded out of her front window, letting him know she was probably home. His gaze shot across the street and all his muscles tensed as he saw a figure attempting to hide behind the big tree there.

He stomped on the brakes, shut off his car and locked it as he bolted from it. The figure took off running and Benjamin raced after him. The person looked relatively thin and appeared to have a ski mask on to hide his identity. He was clad all in black—black pants and a black sweatshirt.

He left the yard and ran down the side of the street. Dogs barked in alarm as the man passed each of their territories. Who in the hell was he and what did he want from Bailey? Why in the hell was he watching her home?

Benjamin followed as fast as possible, desperately wanting to catch the person. His breaths became deep pants as he tried to shorten the distance between him and the man he now believed for sure was stalking Bailey.

However, the masked person ran across the street and disappeared into a dark backyard. Benjamin chased after him, but when he reached the yard, he saw no sign of the man and he had no idea which direction he might have run.

He searched the area as he fought to catch his breath. Damn, he'd lost him. He stood for several long moments, but he saw and heard no movements anywhere. Whoever it was, he was definitely gone or hiding so well that Benjamin couldn't find him. And the odds that he would be behind that same tree on another night were slim to none.

"Dammit," Benjamin said aloud as he finally headed back to his car. This had probably been his best opportunity to find out who Bailey's stalker was and he'd totally blown it.

He clicked on his flashlight and headed for the tree across the street from her place. Maybe the person had dropped something there that could identify him. The only thing he found there was a box of candy. He went across the street to his car and opened his trunk. He was thankful that even in his personal car he carried things for an emergency.

He grabbed a pair of latex gloves and a brown evidence envelope big enough to hold the box of candy. Once he'd taken care of that, he did a check around her house before getting back into his car and heading toward home. What bothered him was the possibility her stalker could be the Scarecrow Killer.

Despite what Dallas had said on the matter of gifts, they really didn't know what might have happened to the women before they'd been murdered.

They didn't know anything about what the murderer did before ultimately leaving his victims to be found. Was it possible he left them little gifts and notes? Absolutely, although none had been found when they checked the victims' homes. That didn't mean the killer hadn't gathered them up at some point before the victims had been found.

The fact that Bailey had a stalker worried him, but the possibility that it could be the Scarecrow Killer scared him half to death for her.

There was no question Bailey was a little bit disappointed that her date with Benjamin was going to be at the pizza parlor and not at her house. That meant there would be no hot kisses or hugs or physical interaction between them at all.

Still, she was looking forward to spending more time with him. In fact, she couldn't remember enjoying a man like she enjoyed him. He was warm and witty and so very easy to talk to. She felt safe when she was with him and loved the way he seemed to really listen to her.

This was about the time in most dating situations when she walked away from whomever she was seeing, but she wasn't quite ready to do that with him. She didn't want to stop seeing him yet. He stimulated her intellectually. Their shared laughter moved her and his mere presence comforted her. Surely, she could see him a few more times without any harm.

It was now just a few minutes before six and she stood at her front door waiting for him to arrive. As always, her heart beat a little faster at the thought of being with him again.

When he pulled up in her driveway, she flew out of her

door. She reached his car and slid into the passenger seat, then offered him a big smile.

"If you aren't careful with your running out to my car like this, you'll make me think you actually like me," he said teasingly.

"Oh, no, I'm just really looking forward to the pizza," she replied.

He laughed. "Then I better get you to the pizza place as quickly as possible." He backed out of her driveway and headed toward Main Street, where the pizzeria was on the other side of town from the café. "How was your day?" he asked.

"Fairly boring as nail days go," she replied. "It was a slow day and I'd much rather be busy than slow. What about you? What was your day like?"

"Fairly boring as police days go, but in my line of work you definitely want slow days," he replied. "However, I did have a rather eventful evening last night."

"Really? How so?" She looked at him curiously. He had such a nice profile. As usual, this evening he looked hot as hell. He wore blue jeans and a navy blue polo shirt. His short, neatly trimmed blond hair looked clean and shiny, and he smelled of his delicious scent. She would never, ever get tired of looking at him.

"I decided to drive by your place on my way home from work last night and guess what I saw behind the tree across the street from you?"

She straightened up in the seat and looked at him intently. "You saw somebody?"

"I not only saw him, but I got out of my car and chased after him. Unfortunately, I lost him in a backyard down the street from you." His regret was heavy in his voice.

"At least I know now that I'm not crazy and imagining things. I'm assuming you didn't get a good look at him."

"He definitely doesn't want to be identified. He was wearing all dark clothes and a ski mask." He pulled into the pizzeria parking lot. He parked, unfastened his seat belt and then turned to look at her. "We really need to work on trying to figure out who this guy is. We can talk about it more while we eat."

Gino's Pizza was a quaint little place just off Main Street, with red-and-white checkered cloths on the booths and tabletops, and an overweight Gino wearing a sauce-splashed white apron that made him appear as if he'd just walked away from a crime scene.

He greeted them at the door and gestured them to seat themselves. There were two couples already there, one settled in at a booth and the other at a table.

She was glad Benjamin guided her to a booth. She always found a booth more intimate and conducive to more cozy conversations. And from the sounds of things, she and Benjamin had a lot to talk about.

They had just seated themselves and agreed on a pizza when Gino approached their table. "Officer Cooper, it's nice to see you here…and Bailey, it's always good to see you."

"Thanks, Gino," Benjamin replied as Bailey smiled at the older man.

"Have you two decided on what you want?" Gino asked.

"We have," Benjamin answered. He ordered a large pizza, one side filled with meats for himself and the other side with mostly vegetables for her. He also ordered sodas for them both.

The drinks were quickly delivered and then they were

left alone to wait for the pizza. "Shall we talk about the elephant in the room now?" she asked.

He frowned. "How about we eat first and then talk about it after."

"That's fine with me. I hate talking about negative things while I'm eating."

"Me, too. I'm assuming since Gino knew you that you've eaten here before."

"Yes. Occasionally, I'll order over the phone and pick up a small pizza for dinner on the way home from work," she replied. "I think there's going to be plenty of leftovers with you ordering a large pie."

He grinned at her. "Ah, but you've never seen me eat pizza before."

She laughed. "No, I haven't, but I'm looking forward to it. Do you fold it or eat it as is?"

"As is. I've never really understood the whole fold thing. Why smoosh all that goodness together?"

"You have a point." She took a sip of her soda.

"By the way, you look quite lovely tonight." His gaze on her was warm across the table.

"Thank you." Her body heated from head to toe. Drat him. Why did he have to affect her on such a visceral level? Why did he have to affect her on every single level she had?

She wanted to hear his every word, whether he was talking about silly things or heavy, important topics. She loved the way he looked at her, as if she was beautiful and every single thing she said to him was equally as important as whatever he said to her. She wanted to kiss him and feel his touch all over her body.

Thankfully, before those kinds of things began to play

too much in her mind, their pizza arrived. As they ate, they talked about the different kinds of pizza they would eat.

"I would never eat it if it had any kind of fish on it," she said and made a face. "That sounds absolutely disgusting to me."

"For me it's fruit," he added. "I prefer my pineapple separate from my pizza."

Their talk continued to stay light and fun as they ate. It was so easy with him. There were never any awkward silences or stuttering around for something to say.

A few more couples came in, along with a family of five, raising the noise level in the small restaurant. Still, they had no problem hearing each other as the children in the group were well-behaved.

"Your sister has a couple of kids, right?" she asked.

"Yeah, she has two. She has a three-year-old little boy and a five-year-old girl," he said.

"And are you a good uncle to them?"

"Apparently so because they seem to love their Uncle Benjy."

"That's what they call you? Uncle Benjy? Oh, that's so cute," she said.

He laughed. "I don't know about that, but I find them really cute and very entertaining." He leaned back against the booth and looked at the leftover pizza. He had a piece left of his and she had three pieces remaining of hers. "Do you eat leftover pizza?"

She nodded. "As far as I'm concerned there's nothing better in the morning than a warm cup of coffee and a cold piece of pizza."

"Then I'll make sure you get home with your leftovers. Would you like some dessert?"

"Heavens no, I'm absolutely stuffed," she replied. "I should have stopped eating a piece ago."

"Then shall we go?" He dug in his back pocket for his wallet.

"Put that away," she said sternly. "Don't even go there with me, mister. Have you forgotten our deal for tonight? I'm paying and that's the end of it." She reached into her purse and pulled out her credit card.

"I don't like this," he replied with a frown.

"Well, deal with it, macho man," she said jokingly. When Gino came to their table, Benjamin instructed him to box up her leftovers and she handed the man her card.

A few minutes after that they were back in his car and headed to her house. "Thank you for dinner," he said.

"You're more than welcome. Why don't you come in for a nightcap and we can talk about the elephant in the room," she suggested.

"Yeah, we definitely need to have a talk about it," he concurred.

The evening had been so pleasant and she dreaded ruining it by talking about stressful things like her stalker. But she couldn't exactly hide from what was going on in her own life.

When they reached her house, she was grateful to see nothing had been left on her porch, although she was aware of Benjamin's gaze shooting all around the area.

"What's your poison?" she asked once they were inside. "I think I'm going to have a small whiskey and cola."

"That sounds good to me," he replied.

"Sit tight and I'll be right back." She went into the kitchen and fixed their drinks, then carried them back into the living room, where she placed both of them on the coffee table and then sank down on the sofa next to him.

She picked up her glass. "Cheers," she said.

He lifted his glass and clinked it with hers. "Cheers."

They both took a drink and she could only hope the warmth of the alcohol as it filled her could keep away the chills she knew their conversation might produce.

"Okay." He set his glass back on the coaster on the coffee table and gazed at her soberly. "There's no question that you have a stalker. So far, he's been harmless and I'd say that's a good sign and he might stay that way or he might eventually turn his attention to somebody else. Are you sure none of the three men you mentioned to me before is the person?"

"I'm as positive as I can be," she replied. "Maybe you chasing after him scared him away permanently," she added hopefully.

"Maybe, but in the meantime, I've asked Dallas to make sure we do extra patrols by your house each night and he agreed to do so. I wish we could put somebody on you full-time, but that's just not feasible with our manpower issues."

"I understand that," she replied. "I like the part where you said he might eventually turn his attention to somebody else, although I wouldn't wish this on any other woman. It's so creepy to know somebody is watching you and leaving you things you don't want. At least I've got good locks on my doors." She picked up her drink and took another long sip. "If and when this creep reveals himself to me, I swear I'm going to punch him right in the face."

He laughed. "I would hate to have to arrest you, Bailey."

"Hmm, I might like you putting me in handcuffs," she replied teasingly.

His eyes darkened and lit with a fire that shot a flame into the very pit of her stomach. She leaned forward, her heart suddenly racing with a sweet and fiery anticipation. "Kiss me, Benjamin," she said softly. "Please, kiss me."

Chapter 8

She didn't have to ask him again. He scooted closer to her, drew her into his arms and then took her mouth with his. Oh, the man could kiss. His lips were wonderfully soft, yet masterful, and being in his arms felt like being home.

She was the one who deepened the kiss, dipping her tongue in to dance with his as the flames inside her burned hotter. She leaned into him closer and his arms tightened around her.

This is what she'd thought about all evening while they'd been eating. She had fantasized about kissing him again and being held in his big, strong arms. Now that it was happening, her heart sang with joy.

The kiss continued to build in intensity as his hands moved up and down her back in slow, sweet caresses. She wanted more. The need for more of him grew deep inside her.

His lips left hers and slowly slid down her throat in nipping, teasing kisses. She was more than half-breathless as electric currents flooded through her veins.

"Bailey, you drive me absolutely crazy," he whispered, his voice slightly deeper than usual.

"You drive me absolutely crazy, too," she replied.

He took her mouth with his once again in a fiery kiss

that sent her half out of her mind. She had never wanted a man as much as she wanted him. She wanted him naked in her bed and against her body. She wanted to feel his warm skin against hers. She wanted to be as intimate with him as a woman could be with a man. No matter what happened in the future, she wanted to make love with Benjamin right now.

She finally leaned back from him. "Come to my room with me, Benjamin. Please, come and make love to me."

She saw the start of a protest in his beautiful eyes before he spoke. "Bailey, I don't think…" he began.

"Don't you want me?" she asked.

"Of course, I do, more than you know, but…"

"Shh." She placed her index finger against his mouth. "Don't think, Benjamin. Don't think and just be in this wonderful moment with me." She got to her feet and held a hand out to him. He hesitated only a moment and then he stood and took hold of her hand.

They were both silent as she led him up the stairs and into her bedroom, where the lamp on her bedside table created a soft glow. Once there, he gathered her back into his arms and kissed her once again.

The flames between them were still there, hotter than ever. As their kissing continued, she began to unbutton her blouse. Once it was fully undone, she shrugged it off her shoulders and it fell to the floor behind her.

In turn, he pulled off his polo, exposing his beautiful, broad chest to her view. She took off her earrings and put them on the nightstand, then turned out the lamp. Then the fire between them quickly exploded and they both finished undressing in a frenzy, finally sliding into her pale pink sheets.

He took her back into his arms and she loved the feel of his warm, naked skin against her own. Their kisses became frantic, filled with a hungry need and passion.

His mouth left hers and he kissed the sensitive skin just behind her ears, making her grateful she'd taken off her earrings. She wanted to melt into his warm, smooth skin and never be found. She had never felt this incredible kind of need before.

His hands cupped her breasts for only a few moments before his mouth moved down to lick first one erect nipple and then the other. Electric currents raced through her, from her breasts and into the very center of her. He teased and tormented her breasts until she thought she'd go absolutely mad.

At the same time one of his hands slid slowly down her stomach, caressing down to the place where all her nerve endings met. She gasped and moaned his name as his fingers began to move against her.

"You're so beautiful, Bailey," he whispered.

"So are you," she replied mindlessly as the tension inside her rose higher and higher. He quickened his finger dance against her and suddenly she was there…soaring and unraveling as her climax crashed within her. She clung to him and cried out his name.

Once the exhilarating wave had passed, and despite her still gasping for air, she reached down to encircle his hardness with her hand. He was fully aroused and just feeling him pulse with life in her grasp awakened a new hunger inside her.

He allowed her to caress him for only a few moments before he rose up and positioned himself between her hips.

He slowly eased into her and she gripped the side of his hips to urge him in deeper.

He completely filled her up inside and the feeling was beyond wonderful. His gaze held hers intently, visible from the hall light that spilled into the room. He then groaned her name and began to move against her. Slowly at first, he stroked in and out of her.

The sensations inside her were overwhelming as his lips sought hers once again. When the kiss ended, he pumped into her harder and faster. She welcomed him, raising her legs behind his back and clinging to him as the tension inside her rose higher.

The waves of pleasure came faster and faster, and suddenly she was there once again, spiraling out of control as another powerful orgasm gripped her.

As she began to crash back down to earth, he climaxed, as well. When it was done, he collapsed to the side of her, and for several minutes they remained that way as they each tried to catch their breath. It was at that moment she realized she was madly and desperately in love with him.

Benjamin stood in the guest bathroom down the hallway from Bailey's bedroom and stared at his reflection in the mirror. "Dammit, man," he said aloud with self-disgust. This wasn't supposed to have happened. This was the very last thing he'd wanted to happen between them.

With the scent of her still clinging to his skin, all kinds of regrets swept through him. Oh, making love with her had been beyond wonderful. He'd half imagined it in his head, but nothing had prepared him for the heart-stopping act of actually making love with her.

She'd been so passionate and giving and had stirred a

passion deep inside him he'd never, ever felt before in his life. Damn the fact that he hadn't stopped things, that he hadn't just kissed her good-night and left it at that. Damn the fact that he hadn't been stronger than his own desire for her.

One of the reasons he'd insisted they go the pizza place and eat in public in the first place was to prevent any kind of intimate physical contact between them. He should have known coming inside with her for a nightcap was a bad idea. He'd set himself up for failure by coming into her house. And he'd failed miserably.

He sluiced cold water over his face and then got dressed in his clothes, which he'd plucked up off the floor on his way out of her bedroom.

Okay. What was done was done and he couldn't go back and change it. However, he could never, ever repeat this mistake with her again. What he needed to do now was see her a few more times and then begin to distance himself from her. It was what was best for both of them.

He'd made love to her, but he certainly hadn't proposed to her. He'd made no promises about any future with her and before he left to go home tonight, he needed her to understand that.

He left the bathroom and realized she was no longer in her bedroom. "Bailey?" he called out.

"I'm down here." Her voice came from the lower level. He went downstairs and found her seated in the corner of the sofa. She had pulled on a pink robe over what appeared to be a pink nightgown. Her short hair was slightly tousled, her lips appeared pink and slightly swollen and she looked absolutely beyond gorgeous.

"Benjamin," she said with a soft smile and patted the

sofa next to her. "That was positively wonderful. I can't tell you how much I loved being in your arms."

He sank down and looked at her somberly. "It was wonderful," he replied. "But, Bailey, it shouldn't have happened."

She frowned. "But it was what we both wanted, wasn't it?"

"In that moment, yes. But I should have had better control over things…over myself. We didn't even have protected sex."

"If you're worried about me, I haven't been with anyone for a very long time and I'm on the pill," she replied.

He frowned. "Okay, but I just need you to understand that I'm not in a position to make you promises about any kind of a future," he said.

She shifted positions on the sofa and moved her arms across her chest. "Benjamin, I swear, you think way too much. We are just two consenting adults who slept together. I certainly don't expect anything from you, except maybe to repeat this again soon," she said with a naughty smile.

Her words set him somewhat at ease. Maybe he had overthought everything. Still, he was determined that this wouldn't happen again in the future. There was no reason for it to happen again.

"I wanted to ask you to spend the night with me, but I know tomorrow is your day off and you probably have a lot of things you need to do before going to your parents' house for your family dinner. I knew if I asked you, you'd probably say no," she added.

"You're right, I would have said no." The last thing he'd want to do was fall asleep with her in his arms because he would like it too much and it would just make things even more complicated between them than they already were.

Thirty minutes later, when he was in his car and driving home, he knew it was time to stop seeing her. He was getting in too deep with her. Initially, he'd worried about hurting her, but the truth was his heart was the one that would hurt when she was no longer in his life.

Still, you didn't stop seeing a woman after making love with her. That certainly wasn't the right thing to do and he would never do something like that to Bailey.

So he would see her a few more times and then stop seeing her. A wave of depression swept through him at the very thought of not having her to talk to and to laugh with anymore. She had been the welcome lightness in his life that he'd desperately needed.

He called her the next day and asked her to dinner at the café on Monday evening. She readily agreed and he hated how much he was looking forward to it. Dammit, he'd never felt so out of control when it came to a woman before.

Sunday afternoon he drove out to his family's farm-house for an early dinner with his parents, his sister and her husband and their kids. The Sunday gathering was a long-standing tradition and Benjamin always had Sundays off unless something popped up that needed his attention at work. Or in the case of last weekend, when he'd taken Bailey out to dinner on Sunday.

The farmhouse where he'd grown up was a rambling three-bedroom ranch style. Benjamin's father, Johnny, had worked hard all his life as a farmer on the land. Benjamin's mother, Marie, had spent her life as a loving support to her husband and her children.

Benjamin had a lot of wonderful memories from growing up on the farm. He'd loved sitting on the back porch and watching lightning bugs dance in the yard while they all ate homemade ice cream or a piece of freshly baked pie.

There had been snowy days when the four of them had built snowmen, had snow fights and made snow angels. They'd gone apple picking together and shared picnics, among so many other things.

His parents had worked hard to instill a strong sense of family. Although there had been times growing up when the last thing he'd wanted to do was spend time with his parents, he could now appreciate those family times.

He pulled up and parked next to Lori and her husband's car. The minute he entered the house, he was attacked by his sister's children.

"Uncle Benjy," five-year-old Amelia squealed and hit him midcenter for a hug. He pretended to be knocked off his feet and fell backward on the floor.

That set Amelia into a giggling fit. Three-year-old Aaron crawled on top of him and pulled on his nose. Benjamin pretended to sneeze and then made other noises with his mouth that had the two little ones giggling with delight. He absolutely adored Lori's children.

"Ah, I should have known my brother had arrived by the noise coming out of this room," his sister said as she stood in the threshold between the living room and the kitchen.

Lori was a pretty woman with light brown hair and blue eyes. Her husband, Charlie Statler, was a good guy who was also a farmer working on their own land.

"Kids, leave Uncle Benjy alone, and Benjamin, get up off the floor and stop tormenting my children," she said teasingly.

"Ha, they're tormenting me instead of the other way

around," he protested with a laugh. "Okay, kids." Benjamin got to his feet. "Uncle Benjy needs to go talk to the grown-ups now."

"And you two come with me, it's almost time to eat," Lori said to her children. She picked up Aaron and put him on one hip and then grabbed Amelia's hand and led them into the kitchen.

Benjamin followed behind and entered the large airy kitchen where the table was set for five and a toddler and high chair were present. "Hi, Ma," Benjamin said and walked over to the stove where his mother was pulling a large tray of chicken breasts out of the oven. He leaned in and gave her a quick kiss on the cheek. "Need some help with that?" he asked.

"No, I've got it. Go sit down with the other men," she replied. "You know how I am about men in my kitchen."

"Right," Benjamin responded. She'd never wanted help in the kitchen. She only allowed Lori to help out occasionally.

Benjamin's dad sat at the head of the table with Charlie seated on one side of him. Benjamin sat across the table and down one from his brother-in-law, leaving the other chair next to his father waiting for his mother.

The kids were wrangled into their chairs, and ten minutes later the food was on the table and they'd all begun to eat. Besides the baked chicken, there was a bowl of noodles, seasoned green beans that were from their garden and homemade yeasty rolls. There was also a red gelatin mold with applesauce in it.

Meals when they were all together usually involved a form of controlled chaos as Lori fed the two children while trying to feed herself. Benjamin tried to help her out, encouraging the kids to eat their green beans as they slurped up the noodles.

As they ate, and in between the children's needs, they all talked about the week that had just passed. Johnny and Charlie spoke about farming issues and the preparations already being made for the winter and then the conversation turned to the latest murder.

"Is Buddy riding Dallas's back about a solve?" Johnny asked, referring to Buddy Lyons, the town mayor.

"No. Actually, he's been surprisingly very supportive so far. He knows we're all doing everything possible that we can to catch the killer."

"Poor Bailey, I can't imagine walking into my place of business and finding a dead body sitting there," Lori said and visibly shuddered.

"Yeah, it was pretty rough on her," Benjamin replied.

"The word on the streets is that you and Bailey have gotten pretty close." Lori gave him a knowing grin. "In fact, that same rumor mill said you skipped out on us last Sunday to have dinner with her at the café."

"Is that true?" his mother asked. "Are you seeing her… dating her? From what I've heard, Bailey is a lovely young woman."

"Yeah, we've been hanging out together a bit, but it's nothing serious," he replied.

"It's never anything serious with you, Benjamin. You aren't getting any younger, son," Johnny said. "Surely you don't want to be all alone for the rest of your life. You need to find a good woman and get married."

"Of course, I don't want to spend the rest of my life all alone, but I can't help it that I haven't met the perfect woman for me yet," Benjamin protested. Except that he had and yet he knew it would never work out with her.

They finished the meal and after the cleanup Lori and her family left while Benjamin hung around for a little while longer, especially since he'd missed last Sunday's family meal.

"Benjamin, why don't you come out to the front porch and sit with me for a while," his mother suggested after his father left the table and turned on the television in the next room.

"Sure," he agreed.

Minutes later the two were seated in the wicker chairs on the front porch. "How are you really doing, son?" Marie's blue eyes searched his face. She was still a beautiful woman with salt-and-pepper hair and delicate features.

"I'm doing okay," he replied.

"I worry about you, Benjamin. I know how much weight these murders have put on your shoulders and how much you take your work to heart."

"Dallas is the one who is really taking the brunt of it."

"But I know you and how deeply you care about what you do," she continued.

"Really, Mom. I'm okay." He smiled at her in an effort to reassure her.

"I do wish you had somebody special in your life," she said.

"I know…maybe someday I will," he said. "What I need most right now is for you to stop worrying about me because I'm doing just fine."

She laughed. "Don't you know? That's my job as a mother—to worry about my children until the day I die."

"I love you, Mom."

"I love you, too, son."

He got up from the chair. "And on that note, it's time for me to get out of here." His mother also stood and he gave her a quick hug. "Tell Dad I said goodbye and I'll check in with him later in the week."

"You take care of yourself, Benjamin. And take care of that beautiful heart of yours," she advised.

He walked out to his car, got in and then headed home. As he drove, his mother's words played and replayed in his mind. *Take care of that beautiful heart of yours*. That's what he was trying to do and that was ultimately the reason he needed to stop seeing Bailey.

Chapter 9

After making love with Benjamin, Bailey was torn about what she needed to do where he was concerned. She was more than crazy about him. She had fallen in love with him and she hadn't felt this way in years. In fact, she'd never felt this depth of love for a man before.

She'd always been able to easily walk away from the men she dated, especially knowing what she did about herself. *You're not normal. You're selfish and not right.* All the things that Adam had said to her when he'd broken up with her years ago flew around and around in her head as she drove to her mother's house on Sunday afternoon.

She'd called earlier and told her mother she was bringing over some things from the bakery as a treat. What she really wanted was some advice from her mother. She also needed to confess the reason she had relationship issues. It was past time she had that conversation with her mother. Maybe Angela would be able to give her some concrete advice.

As she pulled into the driveway and parked, intense nerves tightened her stomach. Her throat threatened to close up with dreadful anxiety. Surely, she shouldn't be so nervous about talking candidly with her own mother.

She grabbed the pink-and-white-striped box from the

bakery that was on her passenger seat and then left the car and headed for the front door. "Hello?" she called as she stepped into the house.

"In the kitchen," her mom replied. "Ah, you're just in time," she said as Bailey walked in. "The coffee just finished making. Have a seat and I'll pour us each a cup."

Bailey sank down at the table. "Have you had a good day so far?" she asked. As usual, Angela looked impeccable today. She was clad in a blue-flowered blouse that pulled out the blue of her eyes, and navy slacks. Her ash-colored hair was perfectly coiffed and dainty blue earrings completed her look. Her mother waited to answer until she had the two cups of fresh brew on the table, along with two small plates. "I've had a lovely day so far. I slept in a little bit and then watched videos on jewelry-making. I figured I'd do a little research before I actually started the process for myself."

"That sounds like a smart thing to do," Bailey replied.

"And how has your day been so far?" Angela asked.

"Not too bad," Bailey responded.

"Now, tell me, what is the special occasion that has you bringing me goodies from the bakery?"

"Can't I just do something nice for you without it being a special occasion?" Bailey asked.

"Of course, and I'm eager to see what you brought me from the bakery."

Bailey untied the white ribbon across the top and opened the box to display the strawberry bars that she knew her mother loved. "Oh, what a lovely treat," Angela exclaimed. She immediately took two of the bars and placed them on the little plate in front of her. Bailey took one for herself as nerves once again tightened her chest and made her feel slightly sick.

Angela took a bite and then sipped her coffee, her gaze direct on Bailey over the rim of the cup. She lowered the cup, but kept her gaze focused on her daughter. "So tell me why you're really here? What do you need? A loan? You know I'm not made of money, especially since I retired. Or do you want to borrow something? A dress or maybe a blouse of mine?"

"Of course not. You should know by now I'm financially solid. The salon is doing very well and I've never had to borrow money from you," Bailey replied. "And let's be honest, we don't exactly share the same fashion sense." She drew in a deep breath. "Actually, I need some advice from you."

"Advice about what?" Her mother eyed her curiously.

"I'm sure you've probably heard through the grapevine that I've been seeing a lot of Benjamin Cooper lately."

"Yes, I have heard that through the grapevine. I've also heard he's a good, solid man, although I'm sure his job has been quite difficult lately."

"It's been very difficult for everyone in law enforcement right now," Bailey agreed. "Are you going to the town meeting this Wednesday evening?"

"Yes, I'm planning on attending, but you didn't come by here to get my advice on whether I should attend the meeting or not. So what advice do you need from me?" Angela eyed her curiously.

Bailey drew in a deep breath and then released it. "Mom, it's finally happened. I'm in love. I have fallen madly in love with Benjamin." It was the first time she'd said those words aloud and they sang in her heart, but also caused a shaft of pain to rush through her as she thought of ending things with him.

"Well, that's wonderful. Do you know if he feels the same way about you?" Angela asked.

"I'm not sure. He hasn't said the words to me, but I know he cares about me a lot." She was sure she'd seen love shining from his eyes when he gazed at her. She was positive she'd tasted love in his lips when he kissed her. Yes, she believed in the depth of her heart that he was in love with her, too.

"So then what's the problem?" Her mother took another bite of her strawberry bar.

Bailey once again drew in a deep breath and released it before answering. This was the moment of truth. It was past time she told her mother her secret. "Mom, I don't want to have children," she blurted out.

Her mother's eyes widened. "Whatever do you mean? Bailey, you're being silly. Of course, you want children," Angela scoffed. "Every woman wants children."

"Not me. Mom, I've given it a lot of thought, but I just don't have that maternal feeling. I've never had it. Most of my friends have had babies and seeing them hasn't moved me or given me the feeling that I couldn't wait to have one of my own. I just don't want any of my own."

"Bailey, you're being absolutely ridiculous." Angela frowned at her. "Maybe you need to see a therapist about this. It's just not normal to not want children."

Those words stabbed a sharp sword through Bailey's heart. *You aren't normal.* "I love my life just the way it is. Isn't it better not to have children than to have them and then somehow resent them?" Bailey asked. "Mom, I'm fulfilled by my career and by my life the way I'm living it right now. My life is full enough already."

"You know what your problem is, Bailey? You're very

selfish. Only a selfish woman wouldn't want to have children." Her mother leaned back in her chair and crossed her arms. "You know, I could have decided not to have you after your father left me, but I wanted a baby."

Bailey shook her head. "And I just don't want any babies."

Angela's nose thinned as she blew out an exasperated sigh. "I know I certainly did nothing in your upbringing to warrant you feeling this way. Well, this certainly explains why you haven't married yet," she continued. "Most men want children. It's important to them to have a family. No man would want you knowing this about you. So what possible advice could you want from me?"

Bailey wasn't sure why she'd thought it would be a good idea to come here and bare her heart to her mother. So far Angela had told her she wasn't normal and she was selfish, repeating the same things Adam had said to her so long ago. She supposed unconditional love from a mother wasn't a given when it came to somebody like Angela.

"I guess I was just wondering if you thought it was wrong of me to keep seeing Benjamin without telling him where I stand on the children issue," Bailey said.

"Well, of course, it's wrong. Bailey, he has an absolute right to know this about you. I can't believe you haven't told him already. You shouldn't tie up his heart any longer. He deserves to move on from you and find a woman who isn't so self-absorbed and will give him the family he probably wants."

"But we haven't had any talks about the future yet. It's not like we're planning on getting married next week. Everything has been kept pretty casual so far." There was no way she intended to tell her mother that they'd already made love.

"I still think you should have the conversation with him immediately, although I suppose there's always a possibility that you'll change your mind about having children."

"Mother, I'm thirty-four years old. I know myself pretty well by now. Trust me, I'm not going to change my mind about it," Bailey said.

"Then you'll wind up a bitter old woman and will be all alone for the rest of your life," her mother replied.

Bailey left soon after that. She drove around for about an hour, tears chasing down her cheeks as she played and replayed the conversation in her head.

You aren't normal. You're selfish. Maybe you need to see a therapist. The words went around and around in her head as sobs escaped her.

Had Adam been right about her after all? Was her mother right about her? Was it selfishness that made her not want children? Was it some sort of a weird abnormality? Was it really so wrong for a woman to know instinctively…intellectually that she didn't want to have any kids?

She finally found herself pulling up in front of Joe and Lizzy's place. She swiped the tears from her face and drew in several deep breaths to get her broken emotions under control.

She'd never told Lizzy her feelings about children, although Lizzy had talked often about her desire to have children. Bailey's mother's words had hurt her horribly and she just wanted—just needed—to talk to her best friend right now.

She got out of her car, walked to the door and then knocked. Lizzy answered. "Hey, Bailey," she said with a smile.

To Bailey's surprise, she burst into tears. "Oh, honey,

what's going on?" Lizzy instantly put an arm around her shoulder and pulled her into the living room and to the sofa. Bailey collapsed there with Lizzy by her side. "Bailey, what's going on? Why are you crying? Did Benjamin break up with you?"

Bailey shook her head and tried to pull herself together as quickly as possible. "Where are Joe and Emily?" she asked, not wanting them to walk into the room and find her such a blubbery mess.

"They went into town. It's just us two here. Now, talk to me," Lizzy insisted. "What's going on?"

Bailey drew in a deep breath and expelled it slowly. "I just left my mother's place and she really hurt my feelings."

"This isn't something new, Bailey," Lizzy said softly. "Your mother has hurt your feelings many times in the past."

"I know, but she was way worse today. I went over to talk to her because I was hoping to get some advice from her and then I told her something that really set her off. It's something about me that really nobody knows, not even you."

Bailey's chest tightened. If she told Lizzy her secret, would her best friend also tell her she wasn't normal? That she was selfish? Would she not want to be friends with Bailey anymore?

"What is it, Bailey? Do you want to tell me?"

"Oh, Lizzy, it's been a secret of mine forever and I'm so afraid you'll hate me once I tell you."

Lizzy pulled Bailey's hand into hers and squeezed. "There is absolutely nothing you can tell me that would make me hate you, Bailey."

Bailey drew in a deep breath and it slowly shuddered

out of her. "Lizzy... I don't want to have children," she finally blurted out.

"And?" Lizzy looked at her with confusion.

"And nothing. That's it—that's my big secret. According to my mother that makes me not normal and selfish."
Tears once again blurred Bailey's eyes. "She told me I need
a therapist."

"Well, that's all utterly ridiculous. Motherhood isn't for
everyone," Lizzy replied.

Bailey straightened up and stared at her friend. "So you
don't think I'm abnormal or selfish?"

"I think you're very smart to know that about yourself
before you bring any children into the world. Bailey, if you
were selfish, I wouldn't be friends with you. I'm sorry your
mother said those hateful things to you because they simply
aren't true. They're nothing but small-minded nonsense."

"But Adam said those same kinds of things to me when
I told him I didn't want children," Bailey admitted. "He
told me that when he broke up with me."

"Adam was a total jerk who wanted to own you. He
wanted nothing more than to keep you pregnant and bare-
foot in the kitchen. You were really lucky to be rid of him."
Lizzy looked at her curiously. "So what advice did you
want from your mother?"

"I wanted to know how to handle this situation with
Benjamin. Do I owe it to him to tell him this about myself
now or can I wait?"

"Really, Bailey, only you can answer that question,"
Lizzy said. "The two of you haven't talked about children yet?"

Bailey shook her head. "It's just never come up in our
conversations. We really haven't talked about any kind of a

future together at all. But I'm in love with him, Lizzy, and I'm afraid he won't want to see me anymore if he knows I don't want children."

"Maybe he doesn't want children, either," Lizzy replied.

Bailey frowned thoughtfully. "I don't know. I do know he absolutely adores his little niece and nephew, which makes me think he'd want some children of his own."

Emotion pressed tight against her chest once again. "Oh, Lizzy, I've never allowed myself to fall in love before because I knew this part of me was probably a game-changer for the men I dated. But somehow, Benjamin got beneath all my defenses. So the way I see it is I either sacrifice my own wishes for a man or I wind up alone. And I just can't sacrifice who I am and what I want in my life."

"Then talk to him, Bailey. If you think your relationship is at the place where you need clarity about this, then just have the conversation with him. That's the only advice I can give you," Lizzy said.

"And you don't think any less of me because I don't want kids?" Bailey asked with uncertainty.

"Of course not. I admire you for knowing what is right for you. Besides, from what I hear, more and more women are choosing not to have children. Part of it is the economy right now, but women are also being fulfilled by their careers, or travel, or hobbies, or whatever. You are certainly not alone."

"But I feel so all alone," Bailey replied mournfully.

Lizzy leaned over and gave her a big hug. "You aren't alone, girlfriend. You've always got me," she said as she released her.

"Thanks, Lizzy. I appreciate your friendship more than you'll ever know." Bailey got up from the sofa, utterly drained by the emotional afternoon. "And now, I think I'll just go home, get into bed and pull the covers up over my head."

Lizzy laughed and also stood. "You'll be okay, Bailey. No matter what happens with Benjamin, or what your mother says to you, you're going to be just fine."

Bailey headed for the front door with Lizzy at her heels. "Call me, Bailey, or just come by. You know I'm always here for you."

Bailey smiled. "I know, and I really appreciate it."

Bailey left the house, then got back in her car and headed home. There was no question that talking to Lizzy had made her feel better, but it also hadn't solved anything. She still didn't know what she was going to do about Benjamin.

She saw it when she pulled into her driveway. The brown teddy bear on her porch was twice the size of the last one. She pulled into her garage and parked, then watched to make sure the door shut behind her.

Once inside the house she went directly to the front door, opened it and grabbed the bear. She looked around the area and thankfully saw nobody lurking about. But what bothered her was the fact that somebody had to have been watching her to know she'd left the house and it was safe to leave the bear without risking his identity.

Her first thought was to call Benjamin, but what could he do now, after-the-fact? At least nobody had broken into her house or done anything scary like that. It was the same old thing...a gift she didn't want from somebody she didn't want to know.

There was an envelope stapled to the bear's paw. She ripped it off and opened it. *You are going to be mine for-*

ever very, very soon. She tossed the note on her coffee table and then threw the bear across the room. Finally, she sank down on her sofa and began to cry once again, this time with a combination of fear and heartache.

This note definitely sounded more threatening than the others. Did this mean he was escalating? Was he getting ready to make a move on her? What kind of a move?

Who was it that was stalking her? It was terrifying to know that somebody was watching her. It was even more terrifying to think that the person had some sort of a deadly obsession with her.

She thought about calling the police to make a report of it, but she knew there wasn't much of anything they could do about it. Even if they caught him red-handed on her property, he probably wouldn't be charged with much. He'd probably be charged with trespassing and given a warning to stop leaving her things. She had no idea what it took to have somebody actually charged with stalking. Would the legal system see the notes as threats?

The sobs ripped from the very depths of her. She had a stalker and she was afraid. And she had a man she loved desperately and she had a definite feeling she was going to lose him.

On Monday evening, Benjamin dressed casually for his dinner at the café with Bailey. Along with his jeans, he pulled on a silver polo-style shirt and called it good.

They'd made plans for him to pick her up at six. It was still a bit early for him to leave. He sank down on the sofa and as always, when his mind was empty for just a moment, it filled with thoughts of Bailey.

He'd always been so careful, so cautious, when it came

to his relationships with women. But somehow, Bailey had barged into his heart with her warm, big smiles and her obvious zest for life. She'd sneaked under his defenses with her full-bodied laughter, sharp wit and intelligence.

Then there was the way she kissed him and the way she felt in his arms. Making love to her had stirred him to the very depths of his soul. There was nothing he'd like more than to make love with her again and again, but, of course, he couldn't allow that to happen.

When it was time for him to go pick her up, he couldn't help the little edge of excitement that filled him. There was no question that he enjoyed her company immensely. She was a welcomed respite from the frustrations that plagued him at work.

But in his heart, he knew she was much more than that to him. He would enjoy her company just as much when his job became easy again.

The Scarecrow Killer remained elusive and he was picking off young women one by one without making any mistakes. The button was their only clue and if he realized he'd lost it, he'd probably throw away the shirt it came from. Then the button would be worthless in their investigation.

They'd spent the day running on a damn hamster wheel, checking and rechecking all the murders, throwing out suppositions that had no real merit.

They combed the internet for sites that sold straw hats and frayed jeans, but had no real way to check sales. There were hundreds of sites that sold straw hats and none that sold frayed jeans, but who knew what might have been available for sale when. It had been an exhausting day, but now that he was on his way to pick up Bailey, a burst of new energy filled him.

He pulled into her driveway and, as usual, she immediately ran out toward his car. And, as usual, she looked positively lovely.

She was clad in a royal blue dress with a silver belt that showcased her slender waist and her shapely breasts. The short length of the dress displayed her shapely legs. Big, silver earrings danced on her ears, and the smile she wore cast a deep warmth inside him.

She slid into his passenger seat, bringing with her the wonderful scent of hers that half-dizzied his senses. "Hi."

He grinned at her. "Hi yourself," he replied. He backed out of the driveway. "Are you hungry?"

"Starving. I spent the whole day trying to get the supplies in my garage in order and so I skipped lunch," she explained.

"Then I hope the café has enough food for you," he said teasingly.

"Ha ha, you're a funny man," she replied. "You know I eat like a little bird."

"Ha ha, you're a funny woman."

They both laughed at their own silliness. It took only minutes to get to the café. He parked, and together, they got out of his car. It was another beautiful evening. The sky was clear and it was a bit cooler than it had been. September was gone and Halloween was just around the corner.

"Winter is going to be here before we know it," she said as they walked toward the café's front door.

"Ugh, don't remind me. I'm definitely not a big fan of winter," he replied.

"That makes two of us. I hate the cold and the snow makes business slow down, as getting nails done isn't a necessity when the streets are slick. Although I do love a white Christmas, but I just want it for that one day."

He laughed. "It rarely happens that way."

"I know, but I can wish," she replied.

There weren't many people in the café on Monday nights so they easily found a booth. She opened a menu and began to look at the offerings. He already knew he was going to have the bacon cheeseburger with fries on the side.

"Seeing anything exciting?" he asked.

"Several things. For a change I'm really not in the mood for the usual burger and fries, but I am thinking of having the special."

"And what is the special on Monday nights?" he asked.

"Spaghetti with meat sauce, garlic toast and a house salad."

"Sounds good, but I'm going to stick with my burger," he replied.

At that moment, their waitress arrived and took their orders. "So how were your days off?" he asked once they were alone again.

She frowned. "Kind of a mixed bag. Like I told you before, I worked in my garage all day today and yesterday I had a difficult visit with my mother and then stopped by Lizzy and Joe's place." A flash of pain swept quickly across her features.

"You want to talk about your visit with your mom?" he asked, hating to see the sadness in the depths of her beautiful eyes. If she needed to talk about it, he certainly wanted her to know he was available to listen.

She smiled. "No thanks. It was just kind of the usual bash-on-Bailey party. I've gotten used to it by now."

But she wasn't used to it. Benjamin knew from the pain

he'd momentarily seen in her eyes that she definitely had been hurt by her mother. Personally, he couldn't imagine such a thing. Mothers were supposed to be a child's biggest champion, weren't they?

"Anything else new in your world since last time I talked to you?" he asked.

Once again, a dark shadow filled her eyes. "Yes, but I don't want to talk about it right now. What about you? Anything new in your life?"

"Not really. I had dinner with my parents and my sister's family yesterday." He couldn't help but smile. "My niece and nephew decided to start calling me Uncle Benjy poo-poo head, much to my sister's dismay."

She laughed. "And what did you do to earn such an esteemed title?"

"I might have made some noises with my mouth while I was wrestling with them," he admitted.

"Bad Uncle Benjy," she replied. She looked down at the table and then gazed up at him once again.

"What?" he asked. She looked like she wanted to say something else.

She shook her head and smiled at him. At that moment, the waitress arrived not only with their drinks, but also with their orders.

"I know you were off work yesterday, but tell me about your day today," she said as they began to eat.

"There's not much to tell. The Scarecrow Killer case is still stalled. We spent the day going over and over things, and then this afternoon we spun our wheels to check out a tip that came in. Unfortunately, the tip was wrong and so it was just another total waste of our time."

"I'm sure you all are beyond frustration," she replied.

"Definitely." He watched with interest as she twirled a bite of spaghetti on her fork and then neatly popped it into her mouth. "You look like an expert eating that pasta. If I was eating it, I'd have it all over my chin and probably down the front of my shirt, as well."

She laughed once again. "The spaghetti twirl was taught to me by my mother when I was about eight years old. She wanted me to know the proper way to eat it so I wouldn't embarrass her if I ordered it when we ate out in public."

"I've never ordered the spaghetti here. Is it good?"

"Delicious," she replied. "You want me to twirl you a forkful?"

"Sure, if you don't mind sharing," he said. "I wouldn't mind a taste of it."

She smiled at him. "I never mind sharing with you." She neatly got the spaghetti on the fork and then they both leaned forward so he could eat it from her. It was just a simple, quick bite, but as she looked into his eyes, it became something far more intimate.

"What do you think?" she asked.

I think I want to kiss you, right here and right now in the middle of the café, his brain whispered, but, of course, he said none of that aloud. "It's good," he responded. "But I'll stick to my burgers."

They continued their small talk as they ate. As always, it was easy with her. He felt so very comfortable with her except for one issue.

He wanted her again. She was definitely deep in his blood now and as he sat across from her the memories of their lovemaking filled him with a wild hunger to repeat it.

"You've gotten very quiet," she said when they were halfway through the meal.

"I guess I'm just focusing on eating this burger," he replied. He couldn't tell her he was focused on her lush lips or the way the top of her breasts peeked out of the scoop-necked dress. He couldn't exactly tell her his head was filled with images of her naked in his arms.

She grinned. "I swear, we need to widen your horizon when it comes to food, otherwise you're going to become a burger."

He laughed. "Hey, leave my burgers and me alone. Besides, you love burgers, too."

"That, I do," she agreed. "Have you had a Big Jolly's burger?"

"Oh, yeah, that's my favorite go-to for lunch when I'm on duty," he replied.

The rest of the meal passed with more banter between them. He loved teasing her and hearing her witty comebacks. She would be the perfect woman for him if he was open to a serious relationship.

They talked about where they'd like to travel to. "I'd love to visit New York City," she said.

"I wouldn't mind that, but I'd also like to see the Grand Canyon and some of the desert area. I'd also like to see Niagara Falls."

"Both of those places are supposed to be pretty spectacular," she replied. "Most of the places I'd like to visit are right here in the United States. I really don't care about traveling abroad."

"I agree. There's enough in the US to visit without going to other countries," he said.

They finished their meals and then left the restaurant. "Benjamin, can you please come into my place when we get there? There's something I want to show you," she said when they were almost to her house. "It's important," she added.

He was reluctant to go into her house, especially since he'd been on sexual sizzle the whole night with her. But there was a serious tone in her voice that made him realize he probably needed to go inside.

"I can do that," he agreed as he pulled into her driveway.

They got out of the car and as always, when they walked to the front door, his gaze swept the area. Seeing nothing amiss, he waited for her to unlock her door and then he followed her inside.

He saw it immediately—a big, brown teddy bear sitting in the chair in the living room. "I assume that's a new gift and you didn't buy it for yourself."

"Yes and no," she replied. "It was on my porch yesterday afternoon when I got home from Lizzy's place." She sank down on the sofa. "Here's the note that came with it." She pointed to a small envelope on the coffee table.

He sat next to her and reached for the envelope. He carefully took the note out and read it aloud. "'You are going to be mine forever very, very soon.'" He looked back up at Bailey. Her blue eyes simmered with uncertainty and what appeared to be more than a touch of fear.

"The 'very, very soon' is what bothers me the most," she said. "I mean, what does that mean? Is this guy going to abduct me off the street tomorrow? When is very soon? Is it tomorrow…? The next day or a week from now…when?"

Benjamin took her hands in his. Hers were cold and trembled slightly in his. "Honey, don't get yourself too worked up. I think if this person really wanted to harm you, he would have done it already and he wouldn't give you a note warning you that it was coming. Maybe this just means he's about to reveal his identity to you. Maybe he believes he's won you over with his gifts and notes."

Although he was somewhat concerned about this note, he would say anything he could to take the fear out of her beautiful eyes. The bottom line was he didn't know just how seriously he should take all of this, and even if he did take it seriously, then what could he do about it?

Thankfully, her hands had warmed in his. "I hadn't thought about that," she said slowly. "It would be wonderful if he did finally reveal himself to me." She leaned forward and kissed him on the lips. It was a short, sweet kiss. "Thank you, Benjamin, for always being there for me."

Her eyes lit with a flame that had nothing to do with uncertainty or fear and he felt the sear clean down in his very soul. She leaned forward again and he couldn't help his desire...his need to kiss her long and deep. And just that quickly he was completely lost in her.

"Stay the night with me, Benjamin," she whispered once the kiss ended. "I've been so on edge lately and I always feel so safe with you. Please stay with me for this one night." Her eyes pleaded with him and he couldn't deny her. Dammit, he couldn't deny himself.

He knew he was making yet another big mistake with her. He knew they were going to make love again, but he swore this would be the very last time. Then he would have to find the perfect time to stop seeing her.

Chapter 10

Bailey awakened and slowly opened her eyes. It must be early, as dawn's light wasn't yet peeking into her bedroom window. The first thing that came into her consciousness was the fact that Benjamin was spooned closely around her back. He made a perfect big spoon to her little spoon.

His breath warmed the back of her neck and his scent surrounded her. Oh, she felt so safe, so wonderful in the shelter of his body. She closed her eyes once again and savored the feel of his naked skin against her own.

They had made love again last night and it had been just as amazing as the first time. It also left her more confused than ever on where they were with their relationship. Were they just good friends with benefits? Or were they working toward something more serious? But it couldn't be serious.

She was just so confused. She knew how she felt about him, but she didn't know exactly how he felt about her. He wasn't talking about a future with her. In all the time they'd spent together, he hadn't mentioned anything except the next time they'd see each other. Yet here he was in her bed after the two of them had made love for the second time.

If they could just remain friends with benefits then maybe she'd never have to tell him about her little secret. It would be the perfect world for her. She'd have his wonderful companionship and his beautiful lovemaking in her life without having to worry about any real future with him.

Even as she told herself that would make her very happy, she knew deep down in her soul it wouldn't. She wanted a wedding. She had always wanted to be a bride and she needed the full commitment that something like a marriage would bring to her. That was what she'd always dreamed of.

As far as she could see it, this was a lose-lose situation all the way around and eventually she was going to get her heart broken. She couldn't help the deep sigh that escaped her and at that moment he stirred against her.

He slowly pulled his arm from around her waist and slid back from her. It was obvious he was trying to get up without awakening her. "Good morning," she said to let him know she was already awake.

"Good morning to you," he replied. He rose up and kissed her naked shoulder. "Do you know what time it is?"

She looked at the clock on her nightstand. "It's a little after six, early enough that I can make us some breakfast before we start our days."

"Bailey, that isn't necessary," he protested.

She turned to look at him, barely able to make out his features in the semidarkness of the room. "It's not necessary, but it's something I'd like to do. Are you afraid to eat my cooking?"

"Bring it on, woman," he replied with a laugh and they both got out of bed.

Ten minutes later she was in her nightgown and a robe and in the kitchen frying up some bacon. The fresh coffee was dripping into the carafe and Benjamin was in her shower. He was taking one here so that all he'd have to do when he left here was go home, change into his uniform and then go in for his eight-o'clock shift.

Since she had no appointments until eleven today, she'd called Naomi and asked her to open up shop at the usual time and take care of things until Bailey showed up. So she had more time to get ready for work than he did.

She was just taking the crispy bacon strips out of the skillet when he walked into the kitchen. He brought with him the scents of fresh soap and shampoo and clean-smelling male. He was dressed in the same clothes he'd had on the night before, and he looked wonderfully handsome.

"Have a seat and I'll pour you a cup of coffee," she said.

"Wow, a full-service restaurant," he responded humorously as he sat in one of the chairs at the table.

She laughed and set the cup of fresh brew in front of him. "How do you like your eggs?"

"How ever you want to make them," he replied.

"Then I'm making it easy. You're getting them scrambled with cheese." She got the eggs out of the refrigerator, along with the milk and a bag of shredded cheese.

"That sounds good to me." He took a sip of his coffee. "How did you sleep last night?"

She smiled at him. "Very well. What about you?"

"I definitely slept well. You make a nice, warm little spoon."

She laughed, pleasantly surprised by how their minds worked alike. "And you make a wonderful big spoon." She scrambled the egg mixture and then poured it into the awaiting skillet. Once it was cooking, she pressed the bread down to toast.

By the time she had the meal on the table, the sun had risen over the horizon and filled her kitchen with a golden light. They made small talk as they ate, chatting about the forecast for some stormy weather over the next couple of days and she shared with him how much she hated thunderstorms.

"I remember when I was five or six there was a terrible thunderstorm one night and I got so scared. I ran into my mother's bedroom, hoping she would let me crawl into bed with her, but that didn't happen. Instead, she told me to stop being so ridiculous about something that couldn't hurt me. She called me a big baby and then she sent me back to my room." Bailey released a deep sigh and then smiled. "To this day I'm still afraid of something that can't hurt me. I absolutely hate thunder."

"I'm so sorry you are afraid of it. To be honest, it's never bothered me. Maybe it's because when I was young, my mother told me that thunder was actually the angels up in heaven taking a break from their heavenly duties and enjoying a game of bowling."

"Oh, that's a nice vision to have. I'll try to keep that in mind the next time it storms," she replied.

It wasn't long before they were finished eating. He insisted on helping her with the cleanup and then it was time for him to go.

They walked into the living room, where the teddy bear still sat in the chair and the note was in its envelope on the coffee table. Just that quickly, a wave of apprehension swept through her.

"Do you have a plastic bag?" he asked. "I just need one big enough to hold this envelope. I want to take it in and see if we can pull some fingerprints off it."

She went back into the kitchen and grabbed a quart-size baggie from the box in a drawer, then hurried back into the living room. "Can you hold it open for me?" he asked. She held the bag open while he picked up the envelope by its very top and then dropped it into the bag.

"You know my fingerprints are on it," she said.

"And mine, but we'll check it to see if there are any others on it."

"It would be wonderful if you could get his prints off it and we could finally identify him," she said.

He smiled at her. "Yes, it would be wonderful." He reached out and ran his finger down the side of her face. She turned her face into his caress. She so loved his touch.

"I'd love to see you without the edge of apprehension in your eyes." He dropped his hand back to his side. "And I assume you want me to take away the teddy bear."

"Yes, please—destroy it like I assume you did the last one," she replied.

"Actually, I didn't destroy it. I have it in the trunk of my patrol car so if I ever have a traumatized child on my hands, I can give it to them. Every officer tries to keep some stuffed animals on hand for that very purpose."

"Oh, that's so nice," she said. "Then I'd love it if you use the bears for that purpose."

"Okay, then it's time for me to get out of here and go home to get ready for my shift." He grabbed the bear from the chair and she walked with him to the front door. Once there, he leaned in to kiss her. It was a sweet, quick kiss that warmed her from head to toe. "I'll call you later," he said.

"Have a good day and catch a lot of bad guys," she said.

He laughed. "That's always the plan. And you paint pretty nails today and try not to worry too much about things."

She watched as his car pulled out of her driveway and

disappeared up the street. She closed the door and locked it, and then headed upstairs for a shower.

This morning it seemed as if they were a married couple, eating breakfast together before they parted ways to go to work for the day. It had felt so right and she desperately wished it would be like this every morning.

The truth was, she wished she was married to Benjamin and they could build new dreams together. They could travel together to all the places they had talked about, or maybe get a puppy to raise together. She wanted to fix him breakfast every morning and sleep in his arms every night.

You're not normal. You're selfish You need therapy.

The words crashed over and over again in her head as she got beneath the warm shower spray. Why should she expect Benjamin to love her when she believed her own mother didn't really love her?

It was almost time. He had worked so hard for the past few months preparing things for her. The isolated house was all ready for her. He'd worked diligently to make it a place where she would feel comfortable and be at home.

She would never have to work in the nail salon again. Being his spiritual bride would be enough to fulfill her. Once she got comfortable with their arrangement it would all fall into place.

He'd left all the gifts and notes to make her see the absolute depth of his love for her. He'd wanted her to know that he was thinking about her all the time.

Without a doubt, he knew she was the perfect woman for him and eventually she would see that he was the perfect man for her. It would probably take some time for her to adjust to everything, but he had all the time in the world for her. And once he made his final move, she would have all the time in the world for him.

Just sitting in his living room right now and thinking about what was to come with her stirred a wealth of sweet anticipation and happiness inside him.

It was just a matter of timing now. He needed to find the perfect time and place to take her away and get her into the home where they could live together without outside voices and opinions intruding.

He frowned as he thought of the cop whom she'd been spending a lot of time with. Maybe Benjamin Cooper thought he was the perfect man for her, but Benjamin couldn't be more wrong.

She obviously didn't know what was best for her right now, but he did. The time he'd had with her had been all too brief, but that was going to be rectified very soon.

Oh, he couldn't wait to have her all to himself. He couldn't wait to make her realize they belonged together forever.

Benjamin called Bailey on Monday evening and made arrangements to bring Chinese takeout to her house for dinner on Friday night. There was a new Chinese place in town and several of the men at the station had raved about it, so he'd decided to give it a try.

Bailey had told him she liked sweet-and-sour chicken, but he'd make his mind up on what to order for himself when he went into the place and looked at their complete menu.

Normally, he wouldn't want to be alone with her in her house, but this was not going to be a normal date. He'd have dinner with her and then he intended to break things off with her.

It was past time for it to happen, even though the thought of it broke his heart. He was deeply in love with her and he knew with certainty she was in love with him. It didn't matter that the specific words hadn't been spoken between them, since the sentiment, the emotion, was there between them every time they were together.

But he had to let her go. She needed to find a real man who would fulfill all her dreams. And he just wasn't that man. He'd never be that man. He'd been selfish in seeing her for as long as he had.

Even now, as he sat on patrol, his heart ached at the very thought of not having her in his life anymore. She'd brought such happiness to him. She'd brought laughter and passion, and there would be an aching void in him for a very long time to come when she was gone.

The worst part of it was he knew he was going to hurt her and that was the last thing he'd ever wanted to do. But it couldn't be avoided any longer.

He'd fingerprinted the envelope and note that had been left for her and unfortunately there had been nothing. He had also fingerprinted the box of candy that had been behind the tree on the night he'd chased the culprit. There had been no prints on it, either. Apparently, whoever had left it for her was smart enough to wear gloves.

He wished like hell he could discover who was behind it all and take away the fear he knew she felt before he broke things off with her, but that probably wasn't going to happen.

As he watched the traffic from where he was parked, just off Main Street, Celeste drove by. Celeste. He hadn't thought anything about the woman since Bailey had told him the divorcée had come into Bailey's salon to try to put her off him and then later when he'd run into her at the grocery store.

Celeste. Her name now thundered in his head. Was it possible she could be behind the gifts and notes to Bailey? Was it possible she was hoping Bailey would be excited about a new man in her life and that Bailey would break things off with Benjamin?

He thought about the night he'd chased the person lurking behind the tree. He'd just assumed it was a man, but could it have been a woman? Was it possible it could have been Celeste? Physically, he supposed it could be possible. But surely, it was a crazy idea.

He stewed about it until lunchtime, when he grabbed a burger and fries at Big Jolly's for himself and the same for Dallas. When he got back to the station, he and his boss went to the break room to eat their lunch and it was then that he brought up the Celeste question.

"So what do you think? Is it too far-fetched of an idea to think that Celeste might be behind the gifts and the notes to Bailey?" Benjamin asked his friend and then popped a fry into his mouth.

Dallas frowned thoughtfully. "I wouldn't have even thought about her if you hadn't brought her up. But to be honest, I wouldn't put anything past Celeste. I've always thought she had more than a little crazy inside her. Have you checked with the florists to see if anyone has ordered the flowers Bailey has received?"

"I checked and it's a negative. I also checked with the drugstore that sells the kind of candy she got. Again, the answer was no. I'm thinking whoever it is must be ordering the bears and the other stuff off the internet."

"Celeste would certainly know how to order things off the internet. Those fancy clothes she wears certainly don't come from the dress shop in Millsville," Dallas replied.

"I'm sure you're right about that," Benjamin agreed.

"I suppose you could question her, but I'm also sure Celeste has the art of lying down to a fine science," Dallas said.

"I imagine you're right about that, too," Benjamin said.

For the next few minutes, the two men ate in silence. "If Celeste is behind all this, then what would be her endgame?" Benjamin asked.

"I imagine she's hoping either you'll break up with Bailey or Bailey will break up with you and then you'll find yourself back in Celeste's arms." Dallas grinned at him. "This is what you get for being such a hot stud of a bachelor in town. You are the endgame for Celeste."

Benjamin released a dry laugh. "Under no circumstances would I ever go back to dating Celeste." He hesitated just a moment and then added, "Although this Friday night I'm breaking things off with Bailey."

Dallas looked at him in surprise. "Why? I thought things were really going good with you and her. I've got to be honest, buddy, I've never seen you as happy as you've been since you've been seeing her."

"Things have been going great with her, but you know my feelings about marriage. And it's not fair for me to keep seeing Bailey and deepening our relationship knowing it's never going to go to the next logical step."

Dallas shook his head. "I swear, I've never understood

your aversion to marriage. Don't you want to have somebody special in your life forever?"

"Nah, that's really never been for me. I'm good with dating casually, but I know in the end I'm meant to be alone. Bailey and I have gotten in too deep with each other and I need to break it off with her before she gets hurt."

"I imagine she's going to be hurt, anyway," Dallas replied soberly.

"Yeah, I know and I hate that. But better I do it now than after we've spent even more time together." The mere thought of hurting Bailey caused a crashing pain inside him.

Why had he let their relationship go on for so long? After the second or third date, why hadn't he stopped seeing her then? Before they'd made love…before things had gotten so—so complicated.

The answer was he'd been utterly enchanted by her. He'd enjoyed each and every moment in her company. The answer was he'd fallen deeply in love with her and he kept wanting to see her one more time…and one more time again. And Friday night he would walk away from her and from that love for good.

He now released a deep sigh and wadded up his fast-food wrappers. "Guess I'll hit the streets again, unless anything else comes up."

"And let's hope like hell nothing else comes up," Dallas replied. "Unless it's a valid tip on the Scarecrow Killer." The two men rose from the table and disposed of their trash in the nearby trash can. "In case you need me, I'll be in my office for the rest of the afternoon."

"Copy," Benjamin replied.

Minutes later, Benjamin was back in his car, driving up

and down the streets to check for any trouble. He knew in which homes law enforcement had been before due to domestic violence and where an underage chronic shoplifter lived with his wealthy parents.

Benjamin pretty much knew everyone who lived in town and most of the farmers who lived on the outskirts of town. But he didn't know where the Scarecrow Killer lived. And he couldn't imagine one of the neighbors he knew who probably smiled at him and passed the time with him harboring such a deep, evil darkness inside him.

Where was this murderer? Where did he live? He knew with certainty the killer would strike again and all he could hope for was that the man got sloppy and left behind a fingerprint or something else that would finally get him behind bars.

If that didn't happen and the man continued to kill, then eventually there would be no more blond-haired blue-eyed women left in town, and that included Bailey.

His heart clenched tight. It was bad enough that he was going to hurt Bailey on Friday night, but the thought of her being one of the Scarecrow Killer's victims drove him absolutely crazy.

The hours slowly crept by and all that was in his heart was the dread of Friday night. He fought the desire to call her, just to hear her voice and to see how her day had been.

Each time he drove down Main Street and passed her salon, he wanted to stop his car and go inside, just to see her pretty face and her beautiful smile.

On Wednesday night when he got off duty and after the town meeting was over, he parked his car down the street from her house. It was a dark night with storm clouds gathering overhead. The forecast was for thunderstorms tonight and then again on Thursday night.

As he gazed toward her house, he looked for any movement in or around her property. It just made him feel better to sit here for a couple of hours and watch over her place. Unfortunately, he couldn't stay here all night as he was on duty in the morning. Once again, he wished they had a bigger department, so that somebody could sit on Bailey's place all through the hours of the night.

As a rumble of thunder sounded in the distance, he remembered her telling him how afraid she was of the sound. God, he wished he could go inside her house and get in bed with her. He wanted to hold her while it stormed overhead.

He wished he could comfort her like nobody else ever had. But he couldn't go in. He couldn't give her any more false hope that he would continue in a relationship with her.

While he dreaded what he had to do on Friday night, he also couldn't wait to get it over with. The anxiety of what was to come was eating him up inside. He was finding it difficult to concentrate on anything else. Finally, at midnight, when a torrential rain began to fall, he headed home.

Thursday night found him parked in the same place, watching her house as again storm clouds darkened the sky overhead. He really wasn't sure why he was here other than these nights were his long goodbye to her.

Every minute he sat in his patrol car down the block from her house, he spent the time going over each and every moment he'd spent with her. Every minute he sat there, he grieved deeply for the loss of her.

Tomorrow night it would be over, but memories of their time together would haunt him for many years to come.

When raindrops began to fall, it felt as if the sky was weeping the tears that pressed tight and hot against his eyes.

Tomorrow night it would be all over and he knew he would never be the same again.

Chapter 11

Bailey couldn't wait to see Benjamin on Friday night. The hours of each day dragged by as she gave manicures and pedicures and listened to the gossip of her clients, all while anticipating spending more time with him. She would never be able to get enough time with him. She would always want more.

The days were gray and dreary and Wednesday night she'd suffered through the thunderstorms, alone as usual and by hiding her head under her bed pillow.

Thursday morning, she awakened a little cranky from not getting enough sleep the night before due to the thunderstorms. She wasn't thrilled that the same weather was forecast for later that night, too.

She spent most of the day battling with herself about having the serious talk with Benjamin, the one she knew she needed to have with him. It was time—past time—that he knew who she really was. It was past time that she let him decide if she could be enough for him without the addition of a family.

It was about four thirty in the afternoon when Letta Lee and her good friend Mabel Treadway came in for their appointments. The two older women were the last appointments of the day. Bailey got them both in the chairs and their feet soaking in the scented water and then she helped them pick out new nail color.

Naomi began working on Mabel's feet while Bailey started on Letta Lee's. Right now, they were the only clients in the salon. Hopefully, there wouldn't be any walk-ins at this time of the day.

"The local gossip is that you seem to be seeing quite a lot of Benjamin Cooper lately," Letta said. "Do I hear wedding bells finally ringing for you in the near future?"

"Oh, no, we haven't really talked about the future. We're just enjoying each other's company for now," Bailey replied.

"Maybe it's a case of why buy the cow when you can get the milk for free," Mabel said with a side-eye at Bailey.

"Mabel!" Letta said and then tittered.

"I'm just saying," Mabel replied in mock innocence.

"As I said, we're just enjoying each other's company for now," Bailey said, slightly irritated by the whole conversation. She tried to tamp down her crankiness.

"In my day and age, things were certainly different between men and women," Mabel continued. "Marriage and family were the most important things."

"Bailey, whether you think so or not, you're getting fairly old and I can't believe you haven't married and started a family of your own by now," Letta said.

"I'm not that old," Bailey protested with a small laugh that she hoped masked her annoyance.

"All I know is some of the ladies in the gardening club are making bets on when your engagement to Benjamin is going to happen," Letta said. "Half of them are betting before Halloween and the other half are saying it will happen after Halloween."

"Well, it's nice to know I'm the subject of gossip for all you ladies in the gardening club," Bailey replied. "But I wouldn't hold your breath waiting for any engagement between us to ever happen."

Even though she said it lightly, the fact that she knew it would never go further with Benjamin than what they had now, or even less than that, sent a shaft of pain through her.

She had finally decided that tomorrow night she should definitely have the discussion with him. If he was going to break up with her over the children issue then it needed to happen sooner rather than later.

She'd let things go far too long between them and now it was going to hurt badly when he walked away from her. She had allowed him to get far too deep inside her heart, deeper than anyone she'd ever let in before, and he was the one she would never, ever forget when he went away.

The absolute worst thing about it was that he wouldn't go away completely. They would still be residents of the same small town. They would still run into each other from time to time and she knew each time she'd see him, her heart would break all over again.

"The town meeting was just another grim reminder of the awful killer that's living among us," Letta said, pulling Bailey from her thoughts.

"Bailey, aren't you scared going out and about on your own?" Mabel asked.

The town meeting the night before had consisted of Dallas updating the people about the latest murder and him reminding all the women in town to travel together.

She had only seen Benjamin briefly when she'd first gone into town hall as he was on duty and stood with other officers near the podium where Dallas had spoken. When the town meeting was over, the officers had been gone.

"I'm not overly scared, but I'm being as cautious as I can be," Bailey replied to Mabel.

"I'm glad I'm too old to make into a good scarecrow," Letta said.

"That makes two of us," Mabel agreed.

The last thing Bailey wanted to think about was the Scarecrow Killer when she had to go home alone on a dark and stormy night.

At least the conversation changed to the more pleasant matters of the gardening club as the women finished up getting their toenails and then their fingernails done.

"We're putting together a nice fall display for the lobby in town hall. We're hoping to get it up by the first of November," Letta continued.

"I think it's going to be beautiful," Mabel said. "We have so many beautiful fall colors to work with."

"And we hope everyone in town will stop by to see it," Letta added.

"I can't believe that Halloween is just around the corner," Mabel said.

"I hate Halloween," Letta replied. "It's my least favorite holiday of the year. I always keep my shades tightly closed and my porch light off so no little goblins will come to my door."

"I don't know about you, but I find the two of them utterly exhausting," Naomi said when Letta and Mabel finally left the salon.

Bailey laughed. "They can be a lot. Thankfully, we're done for the day." She walked over to the front door and flipped the Open sign to Closed. "I've been half-sleepy and kind of cranky all day."

"Well, you're a true professional because you didn't show your cranky to any of the clients," Naomi said. "And if anything, the last two women should have pushed you over the edge considering they were gossiping about your relationship right in front of you."

Bailey laughed. "All I know is I'm ready to get home and hopefully tonight the thunder will stay quiet tonight so I can get a good night sleep."

"Unfortunately, the forecast isn't in your favor on that. We're supposed to get storms after midnight."

"Maybe they'll pass us by," Bailey said hopefully.

"That would be just fine with me," Naomi replied.

A few minutes later Bailey stepped out of the salon. The air outside was hot and soupy with humidity, a perfect combination to brew up bad weather. It was a little bit odd to be having this kind of weather in October, as usually the stormy season was in the spring. But in the Midwest all bets were off when it came to the weather.

When she got home, she changed into her nightgown and robe, then fixed herself a microwave meal of seasoned chicken and broccoli. After eating, she went into the living room and turned on the television.

She had a few hours before bedtime and so she turned on a movie she'd recorded earlier in the week. Still, even the antics of the romantic comedy couldn't keep her from thinking about the next night.

Benjamin would be here with take-out Chinese and she had to decide if she was going to have "the talk" with him. If history meant anything then they would probably eat and then wind up in her bed.

Should she talk to him before that happened? Or did she want one more night in his arms and she'd talk to him after they made love and before he went home? She knew what she really wanted. She wanted Benjamin in her life forever and always, but that probably wasn't going to happen.

She'd seen the way his eyes lit up when he'd talked about his niece and nephew. He obviously loved children and she refused to compromise on the fact that she didn't want to have babies.

She couldn't give in on what she believed was best for herself. The salon was her baby and it not only required a lot of her time, but it also fulfilled her. She'd like to do a little traveling or explore a hobby. Did that mean she was selfish? Was it wrong to know what was best for herself?

She hadn't heard from her mother since she'd gone to the farmhouse to share her secret and ask for advice. She knew the silence from Angela was a punishment for Bailey's choice in life. There was no question that she was hurt by her mother's lack of support. But there was nothing she could do about it. The only real time she'd felt her mother's full support was when Bailey had decided to move out of the farmhouse and make her own way.

When the movie was halfway over, she stopped it. She'd watch it another night when she wasn't so distracted by her own thoughts. Instead, she turned on a half-hour comedy show and once that was over, even though it was relatively early, she decided to call it a night.

She got up off the sofa and walked over to the front window. She moved the curtains aside and peered outside. She was relieved that there was nothing on the front porch and there didn't appear to be anyone in the area. She let the curtain fall back into place, double-checked to make sure her front door was locked and then headed upstairs.

Once there, she went into the bathroom and washed her face and then brushed her teeth. She hung her robe on the hook on the back of the door and then headed for her bed. She was absolutely exhausted.

As her mattress enveloped her, her thoughts once again went to the man she loved. Wouldn't it be wonderful if she told him she didn't want children and he admitted he didn't want them, either? Then there would be nothing standing between them as their relationship deepened.

Then there would be the real possibility of an engagement happening between them. Then she would have a wonderful life loving and being loved by Benjamin.

She drifted off to sleep and into sweet dreams of Benjamin. She was back in his arms and they were laughing together, and then they were making slow, sweet love. But then the dreams changed. Benjamin disappeared and suddenly it was raining little teddy bears. She was outside and running for some sort of cover as the bears hit her in the head and glanced off her shoulders.

There was a loud boom and she shot straight up. Wildly, she looked around the room. It took a moment for her to orient herself as to what was happening. She was in her bed and there were no teddy bears. It had only been a dream... a very unsettling dream.

She settled back against her pillow at the same time a flash of lightning rent the darkness of the room. It was followed quickly by a loud boom of thunder. She realized that was probably what had awakened her.

She squeezed her eyes tightly closed and then opened them once again. At least if she saw the lightning, she would know to expect the thunder. The storm appeared to be right on top of her, as the lightning came over and over again, along with the deep roars of the thunder.

It can't hurt me, she told herself. *It's loud, but it can't hurt me*. She tried to think about it the way Benjamin had told her. It was just a band of angels taking the night off and enjoying bowling.

It couldn't last all night. Surely, the storm would move away fairly quickly. Another flash of lightning illuminated the room and then she saw him. A man wearing a ski mask and dark clothing stood in the threshold of her room.

She screamed as sheer terror exploded in her veins. Any sleepiness she felt disappeared beneath her wild fear. With a deep sob, she grabbed the lamp off her nightstand and threw it toward him. She didn't know if it hit him or not. She quickly rolled to the opposite side of her bed and dropped down to the floor.

She crouched there as her brain frantically struggled to work. Oh, God, this had to be her stalker. Who was he? The answer to that question didn't really matter now. He was here, in her bedroom, in the middle of the storm, and he wanted to make her his forever. Her heart thundered inside her as sheer terror shot through her veins.

The room was in utter darkness between the lightning flashes and so for a moment she didn't know where the man was, but she sensed he was close to her…far too close. If she could just make it to the bathroom, she could close the door and lock herself inside.

What did he want? Why was he in her house? Of course, she knew the answers to those questions. He wanted her. How had he gotten inside? What did he intend to do to her?

Wild questions flew through her head as she tried to crawl as silently as possible toward the bathroom.

She couldn't believe this was actually happening. She swallowed against the deep sobs of fear that threatened to burst out of her. Rain pelted at the window, making it impossible for her to hear him. She had to get away. Dear God, she somehow had to get away from him.

She was almost to the bathroom door when he grabbed one of her legs by the ankle. She flipped over on her back and kicked at him, screaming once again as she tried to fight him off.

"Who are you?" she screeched as she kicked at him with all her might. Lightning flashed and the thunder boomed overhead, further adding to her terror.

She managed to kick him hard in the groin. His hand slipped off her leg and he groaned. She scrabbled forward and was halfway through the bathroom door when she felt the tiny pinprick in her thigh.

Oh, God, what had he done to her? She continued to kick at him, but before long she began to feel woozy. Her head swam and she knew she was in deep trouble.

Sleepy…she was so sleepy. "What do you want?" Her words were slurred.

"You."

The single word was punctuated by a loud crash of thunder and Bailey knew no more as a deep, darkness descended.

Friday morning, Benjamin woke up with a huge ball of dread sitting tight and heavy in his chest. As he dressed for work, he thought about the night to come. It would be one of the most heartbreaking nights of his life. Saying goodbye to Bailey would be the most difficult thing he'd ever do in his life. But it had to be done.

Once again, he was on regular patrol today since nothing was happening with the Scarecrow Killer case. The mood in the police station was grim. They knew the killer would strike again soon and right now there was absolutely nothing they could do to stop him.

Dallas and the others on the task force continued to go over the murders that had occurred, looking for something, anything, that might prove useful. But other than the button, which they suspected had come off a man's shirt, there was nothing. The killer was extremely organized and wasn't making mistakes.

Benjamin checked in at the station and then went out to patrol. As he sat in a spot just off Main Street to watch for speeders, his mind once again went to Bailey and the night to come.

He'd stayed awake half the night thinking about her as it had thundered overhead. He wished he could have been the one to comfort her through the stormy night. The thought of her all alone and afraid had chewed into his very soul.

But he wasn't going to be her hero. He wasn't going to be the one who comforted her when she was afraid. He wasn't going to be the man to enjoy laughing with her or making love to her. He definitely wasn't going to be the man to grow old with her and that was what broke his heart most of all.

After tonight, it would be over. At least he'd gotten a taste of what it felt like to love and be loved. He would always be grateful to her for that. It would be memories of her that warmed him on many a cold, lonely, wintry night.

He'd decided he would never date again. Even the abstract idea of going out with another woman was intensely unappealing. There would be no more dating after Bailey.

He didn't want to play this game anymore of seeing a woman a couple of times and then breaking it off with her. He'd find another way to deal with his loneliness, but it wouldn't be by randomly dating.

It was around eleven when his phone rang. He looked at the caller identification, but didn't recognize the number. "Officer Cooper," he answered.

"Uh, Benjamin… Officer Cooper. It's Naomi—Naomi from the nail salon," she said. "I was just wondering if you'd talked to or seen Bailey this morning?"

"No, neither, although I have plans to see her later for dinner. Why? Is there a problem?" His stomach clenched.

"I don't know…maybe not. She's just usually in the salon by now, but she didn't have any appointments scheduled for this morning."

"Did you try to call her?" he asked.

"I did, but it went directly to voice mail," Naomi replied.

"Maybe it's possible she was kept up by the storms overnight and knowing she had no appointments, she just decided to sleep in," he said.

"I guess that's possible," Naomie agreed. "She just usually calls if she's going to be late. I just got a little worried about her and wanted you to know."

"How about if she doesn't come in by some time this afternoon, you give me a call back," Benjamin replied.

"That sounds good," Naomi said in obvious relief. "Thanks so much."

He tried not to overly worry about the phone call, but given the evidence that she was targeted by somebody, it bothered him enough that he decided to do a quick drive-by of Bailey's house. A few minutes later he pulled up in her driveway, got out of his patrol car and then walked to the front door. He didn't see anything amiss, nothing that would warrant his immediate concern.

He left the porch and headed for the garage. He peered inside the small window in the door and saw her car parked there. He then returned to his car and got back inside.

Bailey was a grown woman, and if she decided to turn off her phone and sleep until noon, then that was her prerogative. The fact that she didn't have any appointments that morning made him believe this was the case. She'd probably been up all night with the storms and was now catching up on her sleep.

He pulled out of her driveway and decided to head to the local convenience store to grab a soda and maybe one of the hot dogs they grilled.

He was pulling into the convenience-store parking lot as a teenager burst out of the door with two eighteen-packs of beer in his arms. He took off running around the side of the building as Benjamin parked and jumped out of his car.

Raymond Smythe, the owner of the store, came flying out of the establishment, cursing and yelling at Benjamin to catch the thief. The kid dropped the beer as he came to a fence. He scrabbled over the top of the fence and dropped down to the other side.

Benjamin didn't bother to follow after him. Instead, he picked up the beer and carried it back around to the front of the store. "Did you catch the little bastard?" Raymond asked angrily.

"Nah, he jumped over the fence. I don't need to chase him down now. We both know who he is," Benjamin replied in disgust. Raymond held open the door for him, and Benjamin carried the beer inside and set it on the counter.

"It's not like he hasn't done this before," Raymond said, anger still lacing his voice. "How many chances does he get before the prosecuting attorney does his job and keeps the kid behind bars for a while? When in the hell will his parents step up to discipline that boy?"

"I wish I had some answers for you, Raymond, but I don't. All I can do is arrest him for shoplifting again and then it's out of my hands," Benjamin replied.

"I know... I know, I don't mean to yell at you. I'm just frustrated as hell," Raymond said. "Times are hard enough without seeing your merchandise walk out the door. I'm for sure pressing charges against him."

"Don't worry, Raymond. I'll go hunt him down now," Benjamin said.

"Thanks, Officer Cooper," Raymond responded.

Minutes later Benjamin was back in his car and headed toward the Kane residence, where sixteen-year-old Bradley Kane would probably be hiding out.

Ida and Emmett Kane lived in one of the biggest houses in Millsville and word was they were one of the wealthiest families in town. Their son, Bradley, was their only child and this wasn't the first time Benjamin had been to their house to arrest the young man.

The kid probably had had enough money in his pocket for the two packs of beer and a dozen other things. But he was underage and so he thought it was okay to just steal the beer he wanted.

He pulled into the driveway of their oversize, two-story home and got out of the car. The house was only about a block away from the convenience store so Bradley should have had time to get here before Benjamin.

He got out of his car, went to the front door and then knocked. Ida Kane answered the door. She was a tall woman with dark hair and green eyes. Those vivid green eyes narrowed as she greeted him. "Officer Cooper," she said stiffly.

"Afternoon, Ida. I'm here for Bradley. I just caught him red-handed stealing beer from the convenience store," Benjamin explained.

Emmett came and stood behind his wife. "Officer Cooper, why do I get the feeling you have a vendetta against my son?"

"I have a vendetta against people who break the law and about fifteen minutes ago Bradley broke the law," Benjamin replied.

"You said this was at the convenience store?" Emmett asked.

"That's right."

"I'll give Raymond a call and make things right with him. I'm sure we can work it out man-to-man. There's no need to arrest my boy again," Emmett insisted.

"I'm sorry, but it doesn't work that way, Emmett. Now, you want to go get Bradley for me?" Benjamin asked.

"He's not here," Ida said, her gaze averted from Benjamin's, which let him know she was lying.

"You're just wasting time because as soon as I see him, he's going to be arrested. It can either happen here in relative privacy or out in the street somewhere," Benjamin said.

The couple hesitated a moment and then Emmett released a deep sigh and turned around. "Come here, son," he shouted. The three of them waited a long minute.

"Bradley, come on out here," Ida shouted angrily.

Bradley was a tall, thin young man. He showed up at the door, not with contrition on his features, but rather a whine waiting to happen. He tied his long, dark hair back with a strip of rawhide and then looked at Benjamim.

"Man, I just wanted a little beer for a party that's happening tonight," Bradley grumbled.

"First of all, you know you're underage and secondly you can't just steal what you want," Benjamin said. "Now, turn around."

"Bradley, don't say another word," Emmett said. "We'll get the lawyer and get you out as soon as we can."

Fifteen minutes later Benjamin was headed to the station with Bradley in his back seat. The kid was sullen and quiet on the ride, but Benjamin didn't feel sorry for the spoiled thief.

If Ida and Emmett didn't draw some boundaries and have Bradley face some serious consequences now, then they were going to have a real problem on their hands once Bradley hit legal age.

It took over an hour to book him in and then he checked in with Dallas before heading out for more patrol work. As he drove through Big Jolley's to get a burger for a late lunch, he wondered if Bailey had finally made her way into the salon.

He hadn't gotten any more calls from Naomi, but it suddenly felt important that he check in and make sure everything was okay and Bailey was in the salon, where she belonged.

Instead of calling, he decided to drive to the salon and check on Bailey. He wouldn't mind confirming with her that they were still on for that night.

He pulled up to the salon and was surprised that her car wasn't there in its usual parking space. An edge of concern shot through him. It was just after two o'clock. Where was Bailey?

Had she decided to take the entire day off work? Certainly, as the owner of the business, she had that right.

He got out of his car and went into the salon, where there were no clients and Naomi was seated in one of the chairs flipping through a magazine.

"Hey, Naomi, have you heard anything from Bailey yet today?"

"No, nothing," she replied as a crease danced across her forehead. "In fact, I was going to give you a call soon to see if you'd heard anything from her."

"No, I haven't. Has she ever done something like this before? Just not shown up?"

"Never," Naomi replied. "And she would never do something like this without calling me."

The edge of anxiety that had brought him into the salon now exploded into full-blown apprehension. "I stopped by her house earlier and saw that her car was in the garage, so I just assumed she might be sleeping in later than usual. But I'm going to head over there to check on her again right now."

Naomi got up from the chair and followed him to the door. "Could you call me and let me know what's going on with her?"

"I'll call you as soon as I know something," he agreed and then he left the salon.

As he headed toward her house, he tried to come up with all the reasons why she wouldn't be in the salon and why she wouldn't have called Naomi to check in. He couldn't come up with a single reason, considering the lateness of the day, and that definitely had him concerned about her.

The first thing he did when he arrived at her house was to peek into the garage. Her car was still there. He then went to her front door and knocked.

When there was no reply, he knocked even harder. "Bailey," he yelled. "Bailey, are you in there?"

Still, there was no response. Dammit, what was going on here? With her car in the garage, where else could she be? He stood on the porch for several long minutes and then decided to look around the house.

God forbid she had gone outside for some reason and had fallen and couldn't get back up. Or for some ungodly reason she'd gone out in the storm last night and been hit by a falling tree branch. God forbid she was lying in the yard, helpless and unable to call for help.

He headed around the corner of the house, where nothing appeared amiss. Thankfully, the gate on her backyard fence wasn't locked so he could head around to the back of the house.

Again, he saw nothing there to give him pause. He looked all around the yard and then exited and went to the last side of the house.

He saw it immediately. A screaming alarm shot through him at the sight of the broken window. The glass was completely gone, leaving a gaping hole big enough for somebody to get through. Oh, God, somebody had gone into her house. With trembling fingers, he called Dallas.

"Dallas… I think she's gone. Somebody broke into her house and I don't know if she's dead inside or if somebody took her away."

"Where are you now?" Dallas asked quickly.

"I'm at her house… I'm at Bailey's."

"Just sit tight, I'll be right there," Dallas said.

"Dallas…hurry." Benjamin's heart crashed painfully in his chest. Something had happened to Bailey and he didn't know if she was dead or alive. Dear God, what had happened to her?

Chapter 12

A headache...pounding at her temples and making her feel half-nauseous. Bailey slowly climbed to consciousness, although she kept her eyes closed against the severe banging in her head.

Was it morning? Did she need to get up and get ready for work? That thought made her open her eyes. She stared around her in utter confusion.

For several minutes she simply looked around her and she couldn't make sense of anything. She was tied to a chair at a table in a kitchen she didn't recognize. It looked kind of like her kitchen, but it wasn't. Where in the hell was she?

Her brain struggled and worked to figure it out. Was this some kind of a strange dream? No, she was definitely awake. Suddenly the events of the night before exploded in her brain. The storm...the man... Oh, God, who was the man who had come into her house? And where was she now?

Her heart pounded with intense fear as she pulled on the ropes that bound her arms and feet to the chair. She had to get up... She needed to get away now—now!

Panic seared through her to her very soul as she tugged and yanked at the ropes, hoping to find some give to them, but there was none. She began to sob in fear as she twisted her wrists first one way and then the other. She only stopped when her wrists burned painfully and she was out of breath.

She gave in to her tears then, sobbing until she felt as if she had no more tears left to cry. She leaned back in the chair, exhausted and afraid.

She assumed she was in a house somewhere, but there didn't seem to be anyone inside with her right now. The place was completely quiet, other than her occasional hiccupping sniffles.

As she once again gazed around the kitchen, a new sense of horror filled her. The room was painted a bright yellow, just like her kitchen in her house. There were colorful roosters hanging on the walls, just like at her place.

Somebody had gone to a lot of trouble to try to re-create Bailey's kitchen here. Why? What did it all mean? The only real difference in this kitchen was that the refrigerator and stove appeared brand-new.

This was too weird for her to comprehend. Why had somebody done this? It scared her as much as anything and she began to pull and tug at the ropes with a renewed fervor.

What was going on here? Who had drugged her and carried her out of her house to this place? And when was that somebody going to return here? And what was he going to do to her?

You are going to be mine forever very, very soon.

As the words to the last note she'd received flew around and around in her head, she began to scream.

When Dallas and a couple of other offices arrived at Bailey's house, Benjamin quickly filled them in on the fact that nobody had seen or heard from Bailey all day and he took them directly to the broken window.

"This gives us cause to go inside the house," Dallas said tersely.

Together they all moved to her front door. To everyone's surprise the door was unlocked. Benjamin was the first one in. As Dallas went to the room that had the broken window, Benjamin began to search the house for Bailey.

His heart thundered in his chest as he went from room to room. She wasn't anyplace on the lower level, so he quickly headed upstairs and directly to her bedroom. It was there he found the signs of a struggle.

Fear shot through his veins as he stared around. The blankets appeared to have been dragged off one side of the bed and one of the bedside lamps appeared to have been thrown or knocked to the floor. What had happened in here? "Dallas," he yelled down the stairs urgently as his heart beat a frantic rhythm. "Up here."

Dallas and Officer Ross Davenport ran up the stairs and into Bailey's bedroom. Dallas looked around with a deep frown. "We need to process this as a crime scene," he said. "Here and the dining room downstairs, where apparently somebody entered the house through that window. I'll call in more men and they can get started. The most important thing we need to investigate is Bailey's disappearance."

"Somebody took her, Dallas," Benjamin said, his heart sick with fear for the woman he loved. "She's been kidnapped. Where can she be? Dammit, I should have taken the notes and gifts she'd received more seriously. Whoever sent her that stuff is behind all this…behind her disappearance. We have to find her. We just have to…"

"Benjamin, calm down," Dallas replied sympathetically.

"You need to hold it together for Bailey. The first thing we need to do is contact her mother and see if she knows anything about any of this." Dallas pulled his phone from his pocket. "I should have her number in my contacts from when she was working for the mayor."

Benjamin's heart pounded so hard in his chest that for a moment he couldn't hear anything else and he could scarcely take a breath. Why hadn't he taken the notes she'd received more seriously? Why hadn't he staked out her house throughout the nights to keep her safe from danger?

Exactly when had she been taken? If he'd stayed outside her house for another hour last night, could he have prevented this from happening? If he'd stayed just another fifteen minutes, would he have seen the person go into her house?

And how much danger was she in? Was she being held somewhere or had the worst already happened and had she been killed? No... No, he couldn't think of that right now. He had to maintain the hope that she was alive no matter where she was.

"Angela," Dallas said into his phone, which was on speaker. "It's Dallas."

"Yes, Dallas." Angela's voice came across the line.

"Have you heard from or seen Bailey today?" Dallas asked.

"No, I haven't. Why? Is she in trouble for something?"

"She hasn't done anything wrong, but we think she's in trouble." Dallas explained the fact that nobody had seen or spoken to Bailey that day and that they believed she had been taken against her will from the house.

"What do you mean she's missing?" Angela asked when

Dallas was finished. "More importantly, what are you doing to find her?"

"We're going to do everything in our power to find her, Angela," Dallas replied. "Did she ever mention to you about her getting love notes and little gifts from somebody?"

"No, she never said anything about that to me. Why?"

Once again Dallas explained what had been going on in Bailey's life.

Benjamin wanted to scream. Minutes were passing by…long minutes that they couldn't get back. Too much time was being wasted. He wanted action right now. They needed to be beating down doors to find her.

They had no idea exactly when she had been taken or how much time they'd already lost. All Benjamin knew for sure was he wanted her found right now. He needed to see her now, alive and well immediately. He couldn't live with any other outcome.

It killed him that while he'd been busy dealing with a petty shoplifter, he could have been out hunting for Bailey. While he'd sat and eaten a hamburger, who knew what she'd been going through?

Dammit, he should have checked things out the first time Naomi had called him. Sheer terror gripped him as he remembered the words from the last note she'd received.

You are going to be mine forever very, very soon.

Now she was gone, but he prayed it wouldn't be forever.

Bailey screamed until she was hoarse and her throat hurt. She fought against the ropes until her wrists were raw and she thought they may be bleeding. Finally, despite her intense fear, drained by all of her exertions, she drifted off to sleep.

She jerked awake some time later and began to cry once again. She'd hoped this all was some sort of a nightmare and everything would be all right when she woke up, but it wasn't. It was real and she didn't know what would happen next.

There was no way she could get out of the ropes. There was no way for her to escape and save herself. She looked over to the window. She couldn't see anything outside, but she assumed it was late afternoon by the cast of the sun.

Did anyone know she was missing? Surely, Naomi would have been concerned when she didn't show up in the salon this morning. Were the police out looking for her? Was Benjamin searching for her?

How could they find her when she didn't even know who had taken her? She knew it was whoever had left the gifts and the notes for her. But who was it?

Looking around the kitchen only freaked her out more. The fact that somebody had gone to so much trouble to try to re-create her kitchen was totally creepy. Damn, who had gone to all this trouble? The same questions kept swirling around and around in her head.

Her heart crashed inside her chest as she heard a door open and close in the direction of what she assumed was the living room of the house. Her nerves screamed in her veins and her heartbeat ramped up as footsteps sounded, coming closer and closer.

A familiar voice rang out… "Honey, I'm home."

She gasped as he came into the kitchen. "Howard," she said in stunned surprise.

Howard Kendall smiled at her. "Hi, darling. Surprised?"

"Howard, what are you doing? Let me go right now. You lied to me," she said. He'd lied to her about it all. He'd said he wasn't behind the gifts and the notes, and she had believed him. Yet it had been him all along. She'd been such a fool to believe him.

"It was a harmless little lie," he replied. He went to the refrigerator and pulled out a package of hamburger and then bent down and took a skillet out of one of the lower cabinets. "I hope you like tacos because that's what's on the menu tonight for dinner."

She stared at him for several long moments. Was he mentally ill? How could he think anything about this was right? "Howard, I don't want to eat dinner with you. I just want to go home. You need to let me go now."

He put the hamburger into the skillet and then turned to face her, another smile curving his mouth. "Bailey, I know this will be a little difficult for you at first, but we belong together and eventually you'll come to realize that. I'm the perfect man for you and I'm all you need."

"Howard, if you care about me at all, then you'll let me go. We can talk about everything once I'm home," she replied, trying to keep her voice calm and even.

"I'm sorry, Bailey, but that's just not going to happen. I know what's best for the both of us and you being here with me is what's for the best."

He turned and once again opened the refrigerator. He pulled out a head of lettuce, a tomato and bagged shredded cheese. She watched him work, her mind still reeling from what he'd just said…by everything he had done.

"Howard, you have to know this isn't right. Untie me and let me go," she said frantically. "Please, let me go," she insisted, her voice rising.

"Just stay calm, Bailey, everything is going to be wonderful," he replied. He took a spatula and stirred the hamburger.

"It will only be wonderful if I'm at home," she responded.

"Honey, this is your home now," he answered.

For several minutes, she simply sat and stared at him, still unable to believe this was all happening.

"I need to use the restroom," she said suddenly. Maybe if he untied her and took her to the bathroom, she might find a way to escape this place. She might find something in the bathroom that would help her get away.

"Of course." He moved the skillet off the burner and then approached where she sat. "I will warn you, Bailey. I need you to behave," he said as he untied the ropes that held her arms. "If you don't behave, there will be consequences that won't make you happy."

She thought about punching him. God, she wanted to hit him, disable him in some way so she could run. But she didn't. She knew she wasn't strong enough to really hurt him and she was afraid of what consequences she might face if she tried anything physical right now. He untied her legs, but kept a length of rope tied around her waist.

He helped her to her feet and she was surprised that she was weak and rather wobbly. Was it because of her fear or because she'd been tied up all day? Or was it the residue of whatever he'd used to drug her the night before?

He led her out of the kitchen, down the hallway and to a door that apparently led to a bathroom. "I'll just be right out here," he said as he dropped his end of the rope and then leaned with his back against the hall wall.

She opened the door and stepped into the bathroom, and instantly a deep wave of sick frustration hit her. The bathroom was completely empty. Instead of a mirror over the sick, a steel plate reflected her image back to her.

The small, high window above the bathtub was boarded up. Still, she ran over to it and tried to pry off the board. But the nails that held it in place must have been long because she couldn't make the board budge.

There was nothing in here to help her. Absolutely nothing. She couldn't get out the window and she couldn't break the mirror in order to get a weapon. The only thing in the room was a roll of toilet paper. New tears burned at her eyes. This was madness...utter madness.

Minutes later, she opened the door and Howard smiled at her once again. She was growing to hate his smile. He was acting as if everything was perfectly normal and it wasn't. There was nothing normal about any of this.

He took her back to the table and then retied her arms and legs to the chair. Once she was secured, he went back to frying the hamburger.

"Are you hungry?" he asked. "I know I am. It will be so nice for us to eat together for breakfasts and dinners. Unfortunately, I won't be here for lunch tomorrow as I'll be at work. But Sunday we can spend all our time together."

"Howard, people will be looking for me. The police will be out searching for me," she replied.

"They're never going to find you," he said with an easy conviction.

"Where is this place?" She knew Howard lived in an apartment in the same complex where Benjamin lived. This was definitely not his apartment.

He looked at her and frowned. "I guess it doesn't hurt for you to know. This place used to be my parents' home. Of course, they moved away years ago and abandoned this house. Nobody will think we're out here. On the outside, the place is a total wreck. The wood is weathered and decayed. The windows are all boarded up and it looks completely deserted. But inside I've worked really hard to make it your dream house."

He was definitely mentally ill. This was way beyond obsession. "Howard, you need some help," she said. "What you're doing isn't right."

"It will all be right in the long run," he insisted airily. "It will just take time and now we have all the time in the world together. You'll come to understand that we belong together."

He chopped up the lettuce and then began to dice up the tomatoes and she wanted to scream. "Unfortunately, I'll be leaving you tonight right after dinner. I have to maintain a certain presence at my apartment until the police clear me from suspicion."

"Why don't you just release me and we'll never talk about this again," she said. "I won't tell anyone about this or about you."

"I went to a lot of trouble to make things right here for you," he responded. "You should be damned grateful for everything I've done for you."

"Well, I'm not grateful," she said angrily. "I hate everything you've done and I hate you for what you're doing to me."

He walked over to her and slapped her hard across the face. She cried out at the blow, hurt by the impact and shocked by the physical abuse.

"You will respect me, Bailey. I love you with all my heart and soul, but I won't stand for any disrespect from you. Now, the tacos will be ready in just a few minutes and we can have a nice meal together."

She remained quiet. It was obvious he wasn't just going to just release her and now she didn't know what to expect from him. Her cheek burned and now she knew he was capable of physical violence.

He apparently had a sick fantasy in his head. All she could do right now was continue to look for a way to escape. All she could really do now was pray that somehow, someway, somebody found her here.

Chapter 13

Within thirty minutes, Dallas had commandeered Bailey's kitchen table as his temporary headquarters. A couple of officers were in the dining room processing the broken window, while others were on the stairs and in Bailey's bedroom to see what they could find there.

Much to Benjamin's surprise, Angela arrived shortly after, obviously very worried about her daughter. It was now dinnertime—the time that Benjamin should have been eating Chinese food with Bailey.

It didn't matter that he had intended to break things off with her. His love for her was thick and rich and his fear for her was like a clawing, savage animal inside him.

"Did Bailey mention anybody she thought might be behind the notes and gifts to her? Anyone from her past?" Dallas asked Benjamin.

Benjamin was seated across the table from Dallas. As much as he wanted every officer out searching for Bailey, he knew they had to be smart with their resources. It would be a waste of time for the men to just head out and scatter with no plan in place.

"She did mention a couple of men. I know she dated RJ for a while and right before we started seeing each other, she had coffee at the café with Ethan Dourty. She also told me she dated Howard Kendall for a while and he continued to want to see her after she broke things off with him. Those are the only three she mentioned to me."

He looked at Dallas with a sense of urgency. "It's got to be one of those three men, Dallas. It's just got to be."

Dallas looked over at Angela, who stood with her back against the refrigerator. "Angela, has Bailey mentioned to you anyone who might have been giving her trouble?"

Angela shook her head, her eyes filled with worry. "No, I didn't even know about the gifts and the notes she got. The only man she ever talked about with me was Benjamin. I wish…" She shook her head and stopped whatever she was about to say. "Just find her…please find her," she finally said desperately.

Dallas looked back at Benjamin. "I know Howard lives in one of the apartments in your complex. I also know RJ and Ethan both live in houses. RJ's place is isolated and on the edge of town. I say we start there."

Benjamin popped up out of his chair. "Okay, then let's go." Finally, some real action. If the tattooed man had taken Bailey…if he'd done anything to harm her, then Benjamin would make sure the man was sorry. He swore before Dallas would be able to get RJ into handcuffs, Benjamin would get in at least one good punch.

As if Dallas knew his frame of mind, he told Benjamin that he would be riding in Dallas's car. Two other officers followed in another patrol car. Four other officers were dispatched to Ethan's house just off Main Street. The rest of the men on duty would remain at Bailey's house, waiting for further instructions.

"I know emotions are running high with you right now,"

Dallas said as they sped toward RJ's house. "But, Benjamin, I need you to remain professional."

"If he's hurt Bailey, then I can't promise anything," Benjamin warned.

"If I can't trust you to keep yourself under control, then I'll assign you to stay back at Bailey's place and not be a part of the search team," Dallas said firmly.

Benjamin stared out the window, willing the car to go faster and faster. Once again, a sense of deep urgency flooded through him. Hopefully, this would be the beginning and the end of their search for her. And hopefully, they would find her alive and well.

Surely, the person who had left her those love notes and gifts wouldn't take her to harm her. From the sound of the notes, the person was in love with her and that was the only thing that kept hope for her alive inside him. Surely, if he loved Bailey, he wouldn't hurt her.

RJ's home was a small ranch set on three or four acres of land that was mostly wooded. There was a detached garage and a large shed. His black pickup truck was parked outside, letting them know the muscled, tattooed man was home.

Dallas and Benjamin got out of their car and the two officers in the other car joined them. "You let me handle this," Dallas said with a pointed look at Benjamin.

The four of them moved to the front door, where Dallas knocked. They waited for a response. When there was no answer, Dallas knocked again, this time harder.

"I'm coming, I'm coming. Give me a damn minute," RJ cried out. After another couple of minutes, RJ opened the door. He looked at Dallas in obvious surprise. "Chief

Calloway. Uh, what's going on?" He gazed at the other officers and then looked back at Dallas.

"When was the last time you saw or spoke to Bailey Troy?" Dallas asked.

RJ frowned. "Bailey? I guess it was at the fall festival. Her tent was next to mine. Why? What's going on?"

"She's missing," Dallas replied succinctly. "Mind if we come in and look around?"

"What do you mean she's missing?" RJ asked in what appeared to be obvious confusion.

"Somebody broke into her house last night and kidnapped her," Benjamin said, unable to contain himself. "So are you going to let us inside?"

RJ looked from Benjamin to Dallas. "And you think I had something to do with this? I would never harm a hair on Bailey's head. I adore that woman," he exclaimed.

Was the man stalling them? Why hadn't he already opened the door to let them inside? Benjamin itched to get in and find out if Bailey was there.

"Do I mind if you come in and invade my privacy? Hell yes," RJ said and then opened the door wider. "But come in and knock yourselves out. I'm offended that any of you would think that I'm capable of such a thing."

He stepped aside and the four officers entered into a small living room. "Check out the bedrooms," Dallas said to the two officers. While they headed down the hallway, Dallas and Benjamin checked the living room and kitchen.

They opened every door and each cabinet. Anywhere that an adult woman could be stashed away, they checked, but found nothing to indicate Bailey had ever been in the house.

They all converged back in the living room. "RJ, we need to check your garage and the shed," Dallas said.

The big man heaved a deep sigh. "Come on then." He grabbed a set of keys off a key holder just inside the front door and then led them out of the house and toward the two outbuildings.

He unlocked the garage door first. Inside were boxes of supplies for RJ's tattoo store. There was little else there and no place to stash a woman. They then moved to the shed, which held a lawn mower and everything necessary for lawn care.

She wasn't here. RJ's had been a bust, a total waste of time. When they were in the car and headed back to Bailey's place, one of the officers who had been dispatched to Ethan Dourty's place called in to report that they had found nothing there to indicate Bailey's presence.

"We'll head on over to Howard's place, although it would be very difficult for him to keep a woman against her will in the apartments," Dallas said.

"Unless he has her bound and gagged." This particular vision of Bailey ripped through Benjamin. He didn't want to think about her being tied up and with duct tape or something else in her mouth to keep her quiet.

And if she wasn't at Howard's place, then where could she be? If none of the three men he knew about had taken her, then who?

Howard had to have her, otherwise every single man in town would be a suspect. It would be a sea of suspects. A deep, breathless anxiety once again pressed tight in Benjamin's chest. He was grateful Dallas didn't talk on the ride to Howard's. Benjamin's fear and apprehension was so great inside him, he had no words.

He fought against tears that burned hot at his eyes. He didn't want to cry now. Tears would mean failure and he wasn't about to admit failure yet.

It seemed to take forever to get to the apartment complex. Darkness had now fallen and the idea of her being somewhere out there alone and afraid tore at his insides.

Benjamin rarely saw the banker as Benjamin lived on one end of the building and Howard lived at the other end. Before they got out of the car, Dallas made a quick call to the landlord to see exactly what apartment number Howard lived in. Once they had that information, they pulled down the complex and parked in front of his place.

Nerves jangled inside Benjamin as he got out of the car. She had to be here, she just had to be. It was the mantra that went around and around in his head as they approached the apartment. He followed behind Dallas and waited impatiently as Dallas knocked on the door.

Howard immediately opened the door and looked at them in surprise. "Chief... Officer Cooper... Uh, what can I do for you all?"

"Do you mind if we come in for a conversation?" Dallas asked.

"Of course not. Please come in." He ushered them into a neat and tidy living room. For a brief moment, Benjamin smelled her...the wonderful spicy scent that stirred him in so many ways. It was there only a moment and then gone. It had to be his imagination and him wanting to believe so badly that she was here someplace.

Dallas sat on the sofa and Benjamin sank down next to him while Howard sat on a chair facing them. "When was the last time you saw or spoke to Bailey?" Dallas asked.

"I haven't seen or spoken to her in weeks," Howard said

with a frown. "Oh, wait, she did call me a little over a week ago to ask me if I was leaving little gifts and notes for her. I told her I didn't know anything about it and that was the extent of us talking with each other. Why? What's going on?"

"We believe Bailey was kidnapped from her home last night," Dallas said.

Howard straightened up in the chair in what appeared to be in genuine shock. "What? Oh, my God, what can I do to help?" He leaned forward in the chair and appeared sincerely stunned at the information.

"Right now, what you can do is let us search this place," Dallas replied.

Howard looked surprised all over again. "You think I had something to do with this? I would never..." Howard's voice trailed off as he stood. "Please, feel free to look around all you want. I would never do anything to harm Bailey and I certainly have nothing to hide."

Dallas and Benjamin checked everywhere in the two-bedroom apartment, but there was nothing to see there. There was no sign that Bailey was there or had ever been there.

As they left the apartment, a soul sickness filled Benjamin. The three men who were the most viable potential suspects had been cleared, so now every man in town was a potential suspect.

Where did they go from here? Where did they even begin? How did they search an entire town for one missing woman? The tiny ray of hope he'd had now threatened to go out. He felt utterly empty inside.

"We'll find her," Dallas said fervently as he pulled back up in her driveway. "I swear we're going to find her, Benjamin."

Once again, Benjamin couldn't speak. Deep emotion ripped at him and the burn of tears pressed heavily against his eyes. Bailey…Bailey. Her name flew around and around in his head…in the very depths of his heart.

When they walked into Bailey's kitchen, Angela looked at all of them and then collapsed into one of the chairs and burst into tears. "Where is she? Oh, dear God, who has her?" She began to weep.

Lizzy Maxwell, who had shown up while Dallas and Benjamin were gone, immediately tried to console the weeping woman. She managed to get Angela up and out of the kitchen chair and led her into the living room, where her sobs were still audible.

Benjamin wanted to fall into a chair and weep as well, but he couldn't. He had to stay strong until Bailey was found. And he could only pray she would still be found alive.

Minutes ticked by, turning into hours. Bailey could tell by looking out the window that night had fallen. She tried once again to get free from the ropes, but she couldn't.

Her cheek still stung and she was still completely shocked that he'd slapped her. While she'd been dating him, she had never seen any red flags that would indicate the man was capable of any violence. But now she knew differently and this new Howard absolutely terrified her.

He'd untied one of her hands so she could eat the tacos with him. However, the last thing she'd wanted to do was eat. But as he talked about how much trouble he'd gone to in making the Mexican food, she knew the best thing for her to do was to take several bites and tell him how wonderful it was. And that was exactly what she had done.

After eating and cleaning up the kitchen, he'd left the house. But that had been hours ago.

When was he coming back here? And what would he expect from her when he got back? The idea of him taking her sexually against her will made her want to throw up. She didn't want him to touch her in any way.

The only man's hands she wanted on her were Benjamin's. She closed her eyes and instantly an image of the man she loved filled her mind. Would she ever see him again? Would she ever feel his big strong arms surrounding her? Would she ever gaze into his beautiful blue eyes or hear his deep laughter again?

His image swam as tears filled her eyes. She'd been missing for hours and hours now, and she feared she would never be found. She'd exist in this strange and sick scenario that Howard had created for the rest of her life...or until the time she ticked him off or he tired of her. And then what would happen? Her blood ran cold. She knew the answer. Then he would have to kill her. There was no way he could just let her go now or in the future.

Why couldn't this all just be a terrible nightmare? Why couldn't she wake up and find herself safe and sound in her own bed?

But this wasn't a nightmare. She wasn't going to just wake up from this. Howard wasn't an imaginary boogeyman. He was the real deal... The monster in the closet... The creature under her bed.

She stared in the direction where he'd come in before with dread coursing through her entire body. How long before he returned? What kind of mood would he be in?

She didn't know how long she'd waited or what time it

was when she finally heard the door open and close. She steeled herself as his footsteps came closer and closer.

"Hello, darling," he said as he came in. "I'm sorry you've had to wait so long for me to return." He threw his car keys on one of the counters and then sank down in the chair at the table across from her.

"It's been quite an exciting evening," he said. "The police showed up at my apartment. I have to say I wasn't surprised since we dated a few times. Anyway, they were out searching for you. Needless to say, they didn't find you in my apartment." He laughed. "I insisted that I would never do anything to harm you and I made sure they knew I'd do anything I could to help them in the search for you. So I'm now completely in the clear. I'm not a suspect."

"Howard, for God's sake, please let me go. If you truly love me at all you'll release me and let me go home. I promise I won't tell anyone about this. I won't mention a word about you. I swear I won't get you into any trouble."

Of course, this was all a big lie. If he did release her the first thing she would do was go to Dallas and tell him all about Howard. The man shouldn't be out on the streets. He was a danger to all the women in town.

He smiled, but the gesture didn't quite reach the cold depths of his dark eyes. "I'm not going to release you and I don't want you asking me again. You're going to learn to love, Bailey. You're going to learn to love me as much as I love you." He stood. "And now, I don't know about you, but I'm completely exhausted. It's time for bed."

Every muscle in her body tensed up and her nerves all screamed. He moved over to her and began to untie her and she had to fight with all her might not to kick him, not to scream and punch him.

But she knew it was a struggle she would lose and it would only make things worse for her. Although she couldn't imagine how things would get any worse. She couldn't fight him. She'd just have to continue to look for an opportunity to escape. Maybe while he slept, she'd be able to slip away and get out of here.

He untied her arms and legs, but she remained tied around the waist with Howard on the other end of the rope. He led her down the hallway and into a bedroom where a pink nightgown and panties were lying across the queen-size bed. The bed was covered with a navy blue spread and the headboard had thick wooden bars that would make it perfect for tying somebody up. An icy chill rushed through her.

Oh God, was that what he had planned for her? Did he intend to tie her to the headboard and then have his way with her? Her stomach twisted and turned as a nausea filled her. She didn't want his hands on her. It would be rape for anything he did would be against her will.

"Go ahead, take the nightwear and we'll go back down to the bathroom, where you can change into it," he said.

She couldn't help the tremble of her body as she grabbed the nightgown and panties off the bed. He led her back to the bathroom she'd been in before and only then did he untie the rope from around her waist.

Once she was alone inside the room, she fought against the need to dry-heave. She couldn't believe this was really happening to her. She couldn't believe that she was actually going to have to get into a bed with him.

She changed into the nightgown, grateful that at least it wasn't too skimpy. But as she thought about what might follow, she felt sick all over again.

She lingered as long as she could in the bathroom, but after several minutes he knocked impatiently on the door. She grabbed the clothing she had just removed and then stepped outside and back into the hallway.

"Ah, Bailey, I knew you'd look lovely in that nightie and I was absolutely right. You look beautiful." He paused a moment and then frowned. "That was a compliment, so what do you say, Bailey?"

"Thank you," she mumbled.

"Good, now let's get situated for the night." Once again, he wrapped the rope around her waist and then tugged her back down the hallway and into the bedroom. He pulled the covers down on one side of the bed and gestured for her to get in.

Once she did, he tied one of her wrists to the bed railing and then her other one, as well. She was forced to lie on her back with her arms up over her head. This position left her utterly vulnerable to him. Once again, nausea rose up inside her, but she swallowed hard against it. The last thing she wanted to do was choke on her own vomit and die that way.

Once she was secure, he stripped down to a pair of boxers. "I know it's been a bit of a stressful day for you, so tonight we'll just get a good night of sleep. But tomorrow night we both should be fully rested and we'll explore our love for each other in a more physical way."

He turned out the overhead light and crawled into the other side of the bed. She remained stiff and still as a statue. Could she really trust that he wasn't going to touch her through the rest of the night?

She hated the way he smelled and the warmth from his body that drifted over to her. She even hated the sound of his breathing. She was afraid to go to sleep and yet longed for the sweet oblivion she knew it might bring.

Please, let somebody find me before he physically wants to share his love with me. Please let somebody find me before tomorrow night comes. That was her mantra as she remained wide-awake and scared.

Chapter 14

Somebody had brought in a couple dozen doughnuts early in the morning. Even the yeasty sweet scent of them nauseated Benjamin after the long and fruitless night. They all had agreed that Bailey probably wasn't being held in the apartment complex. They also agreed that the man who had taken her had to be physically strong.

Dallas delegated the officers to begin a grid search, starting at the south side of town. Three officers would search one side of Main Street and three other men would search the other side. They would be knocking on doors and checking out empty buildings and storefronts.

Benjamin had decided to hang back with Dallas and help guide the search parties. RJ, Howard and Ethan all showed up, eager to help in the search, so Dallas sent an officer with each of them and gave them specific rows of houses to check.

Angela had slept on Bailey's sofa all night. Benjamin had never seen the tough woman as broken as she appeared to be by Bailey's disappearance. Lizzy, along with Naomi and Jaime, had also arrived at the house early that morning, offering to do anything they could to help.

Benjamin was momentarily in a fog of exhaustion, yet his mind kept trying to think of all the places Bailey could be. As the hours crawled by and the search teams checked in again and again with no news, he began to lose any hope that he'd had.

It would take forever for all the homes and businesses in town to be searched. She had been missing all night... possibly for two long nights. The police department was so small and the search area was so big. Benjamin's heart ached with an emptiness that frightened him. He couldn't give up hope yet, not while there was a possibility that she might still be alive. Dammit, they had to find her.

At noon, a knock fell on her door. "I'll get it," Benjamin said, grateful to do something...to do anything. Letta Lee and a half a dozen women from the gardening club stood on the front porch.

"We're here to help," Letta said. She sidestepped Benjamin and entered the living room. She looked over at where Angela and Lizzy were seated on the sofa. "Angela, I'm so sorry this has happened."

"Thank you, Letta," Angela replied and swiped a tissue over her eyes.

"You know we all think the world of Bailey," Letta said.

"I just can't believe this has happened," Angela replied and began to cry once again.

"You need to come on into the kitchen and talk to Dallas," Benjamin said to the older woman.

Letta immediately swept past him and went into the kitchen. "Dallas, we've heard what's happened to Bailey. I'm here with a lot of women from the gardening club and we want to help in the search."

"Letta, I appreciate it, but—" Dallas began.

"Dallas Calloway, don't you dare tell me we're all too old to help out," Letta said.

"I wasn't about to tell you that," Dallas replied. "It's just that we don't know how dangerous this situation might become and so I can't send you all off without an officer and right now all my officers are already out working the streets."

Benjamin didn't volunteer for the job. He'd seen that one of the women was on a walker and another one was on oxygen. As much as he appreciated their desire to help, the truth was they would probably be more of a hindrance.

"If you really want to help, then maybe you could make us all some sandwiches for lunch." Dallas pulled his wallet from his back pocket and got out three or four twenty-dollar bills. "I'm sure the officers would appreciate having something to eat besides doughnuts as they come to check in."

"We can definitely take care of that," Letta said as she picked up the money. "We'll make sandwiches and I'll have Mabel make her good coleslaw and Eileen can put together the pasta salad that everyone raves about whenever we have a potluck dinner."

Letta was still talking about her plans for food as she walked out the front door. "At least I know the men will be fed good this afternoon," Dallas said. Benjamin didn't want to be here that afternoon without Bailey. He had no interest in any food that might be offered. He just needed Bailey. Where could she be?

Dallas leaned back in his chair with a deep frown. "This is like the damned Scarecrow Killer case. I feel like there's something we're missing. I can't believe those notes came from just some random person."

"If not random, then who?" Benjamin asked in deep

frustration. "We already cleared the three men that she'd mentioned to me."

Dallas's frown deepened even more. "What we didn't check was if any of those three men own other property besides where they live." He turned to Officer Ross Davenport, who was in the process of pouring himself a cup of coffee.

"Ross, I need you to head over to city hall and get all the property records for Ethan Dourty, RJ Morgan and Howard Kendall." Dallas looked back at Benjamin. "Maybe it's time that we start at the beginning once again. I should have thought to have these records checked before now."

"Don't beat yourself up," Benjamin said to his friend as Ross left. "I didn't think about any one of them having other property here in town or anyplace else."

Benjamin waited impatiently for Ross to return. He poured himself a cup of coffee and then returned to his seat at the table with Dallas. A map of the town was spread out before Dallas and as officers checked in from various addresses, Dallas marked them through with a red pen.

It didn't take too long before Ross returned. Surprisingly, two of the men had other property. RJ had been left his family's place and Howard had also been left a property when his family had moved out of town.

"I know these two places," Dallas said as he stood. "As far as I know they've both been empty for a very long time. Let's head to RJ's property first. It's not in as bad a shape as Howard's parents' old house is."

Benjamin jumped up, a renewed energy racing through him. How had they overlooked this? They'd apparently had tunnel vision and had possibly believed in the innocence of a person who had lied to their faces.

Minutes later, Dallas and Benjamin were in his car and

two more officers followed behind them as they raced to the property that RJ owned on the southern edge of town.

"Why didn't either of these men mention that they had other property when we questioned them?" Benjamin asked.

"Why would they? It's probably because they didn't even think about it. Both of the homes appear badly weathered and deserted, Howard's worse than RJ's. It's obvious they aren't living in the homes."

"This has got to be it," Benjamin said fervently. "She's got to be in one of these places otherwise I'm afraid we'll never find her and, Dallas, we have to find her."

It didn't matter that Benjamin had intended to break up with Bailey. He needed to see her driving her little red sports car around town. He needed to watch her prance down the street in one of her stylish outfits with her oversize earrings dancing on her ears. He desperately needed to see her happy and vibrant and very much alive.

It took them only a few minutes to arrive at the house that RJ owned and, on the way, Dallas called the officer he'd sent with RJ to search earlier that day. Assured that the bald, muscular man was still out with the lawman, there was no reason to believe anyone would be in the house except Bailey.

The place looked completely deserted, with windows boarded up and spray paint in neon shades adding colorful images and words to the otherwise dark brown house paint.

Benjamin's heart began to pound against his ribs as an enormous rush of adrenaline flooded through his veins. The minute Dallas stopped the car, he jumped out of the passenger side and then impatiently waited for Dallas.

The two officers who had come with them also got out of their car, and together the four of them approached the front door. It didn't appear as if anyone had been inside the house for some time. Spiderwebs hung across the doorway and were destroyed as Dallas kicked open the front door. However, Benjamin knew spiders could spin an intricate web in a matter of hours.

There was no furniture inside and dust covered the floor. There were nests in the corners of the front room where animals had made their home. Benjamin knew she wasn't here. They all knew she wasn't, although they checked all the rooms, anyway.

"Okay, this was a bust," Dallas said once they were all back outside. "Let's head on over to Howard's parents' old place and see what we find there."

Dallas called Officer Andy Edwards to check to see if Howard was still with the search party. He wasn't. Edwards told Dallas that Howard had taken off just a few minutes before, indicating that he needed to go back to his job at the bank before the workday was over.

"We need to hurry," Benjamin said as they headed toward Howard's parents' abandoned home.

"I'm going as fast as I can," Dallas replied tersely as he stepped on the gas.

Had Howard really gone back to the bank to work or was he right now with Bailey? Benjamin leaned forward, straining against his seat belt as if that might make the car go even faster. Howard's old property was on the other side of town from RJ's and each minute they were in the car, they weren't there to check about Bailey.

Were they finally going to find her? Or would this just be another bitter disappointment? Would she be alive or was it already too late for her? Had Howard treated her all right or had his love obsession turned deadly? Was Howard even the guilty party?

The questions flew fast and furious around in his head. Dallas turned right on a side street that saw little traffic. The road was narrow with tree limbs encroaching over the asphalt. After several miles, he made a left on a road that was little more than a dirt path.

"The house is up here on the right," Dallas said as he slowed down.

He turned into a long gravel driveway. The house looked as deserted as RJ's had. The wood had weathered to a bleached gray and the windows were all boarded up. Squirrels played in the trees overhead, adding to the look of complete abandonment.

Benjamin's very last vestige of hope dwindled out of him. All four of them got out and approached the front door. Once again, Benjamin thought he smelled a trace of her in the air. His damn memory was apparently playing tricks on him again.

When they reached the front door, it was locked and the lock looked shiny and new against the old wood. Once again, a wave of adrenaline flooded through Benjamin. Why would anyone want to lock up a place like this? Unless they had something to hide inside.

Dallas threw himself at the door, his broad shoulders leading the way. Once... Twice... And on the third crash, the door frame splintered enough for him to kick the door down.

He stepped inside with Benjamin at his heels and the two men froze. They entered into a living room that looked like Bailey's. It had a black sofa with pink and yellow throw pillows. A bookcase was against one wall and held the same books and knickknacks as the one in Bailey's home.

"What in the hell?" Benjamin said in disbelief.

"Benjamin?" Her voice came from what he assumed was the kitchen. The sound of it shot an electric thrill through his entire body and nearly cast him to his knees. She was alive!

"Bailey?" he shouted as he ran toward the doorway that would take him to her. He was aware of the other officers following closely behind him.

She was tied to a kitchen chair. She had a black eye and blood had dried from an apparent nosebleed. She saw him and began to weep. "Thank God," she cried. "Oh, thank God, you found me."

"Just sit tight, we're going to get you out of here," Benjamin replied. "Somebody call for an ambulance," he yelled as he raced to the kitchen drawers, looking for a knife or anything sharp to cut the ropes that held her. He couldn't even begin to process the injuries to her face. Right now, all he wanted was to free her so he could pull her into his arms.

"He—he's insane," she continued through her sobs. "I—I... He told me he loves me, but I—I think eventually he was going to kill me. I was never going to l-love him...never, no matter how long he held me here."

"Don't cry, honey. You're safe now." Benjamin found a couple of sharp knifes in one of the drawers and he began to cut at the ropes that held her legs while Ross began to saw at the ropes around her arms.

Dallas got on his radio to call for more men. There was a sudden roar of rage as Howard burst into the room. "Stop it," he screamed. "She's mine. You all have no right to be in here. This is my private property. You have no right to take her from me."

Benjamin dropped his knife to the floor and rose to his feet. A simmering rage had been inside him since the moment he'd seen Bailey's face. That rage now exploded.

He rushed at Howard and before the man knew what to expect, Benjamin punched him as hard as he could in his face. Howard reeled backward and howled as his nose began to bleed.

"Benjamin," Dallas yelled. "Leave it now. Bailey needs you."

Benjamin wanted to hit the man again…and again for everything he'd done to Bailey. But reason warred with his rage and as Bailey called out to him, he rushed back to continue to use the knife to free her. Howard was lucky Benjamin didn't use the knife to stab him in his black heart.

"I'm going to sue you all for trespassing and entering my private property without a search warrant," Howard said as Dallas handcuffed him. Blood dripped from his nose. "Then I'm going to sue for police brutality. You saw him, Dallas. You saw your officer hit me."

"I didn't see anything," Dallas replied.

"You can take Bailey now, but she'll come back to me. She'll always come back to me," Howard said confidently.

"Never," Bailey screamed at him. "You'll never have me again. I hate you. Do you hear me, Howard? I hate you."

Howard laughed, the sound of evil with a sense of humor. "Trust me, I'll have her again. Bailey is my soul mate and we belong together."

"Why don't you shut up?" Benjamin said tersely. At that moment, the ropes around Bailey's legs fell to the floor.

"I'll get Howard into the back of my car," Dallas said.

It took only minutes after Dallas took Howard out of the house that Bailey was finally free of all the ropes that had held her.

Benjamin immediately drew her up and into his arms and held her tight as she cried against his chest. Her entire body trembled like a leaf in a windstorm. He stroked her back and whispered into her ear. "You're okay now. You're safe and nobody is ever going to hurt you again."

"H-he thought if he could keep me here long enough, I'd fall in love with him and never want to leave him. But his temper was so scary," she said.

The sound of a siren blared in the air. It suddenly stopped, indicating the ambulance had arrived. He was still holding her when two paramedics came in with a gurney.

"This isn't necessary," she protested as Benjamin gestured for her to lie down.

"You need to go to the hospital and get checked out. Bailey, aside from the physical wounds on your beautiful face, you've been through a terrible trauma. Please, go and let a doctor take a look at you."

She hesitated only a moment and then complied. It didn't take long for the ambulance to carry her away. Dallas came back inside. "I've called in the team to start processing this crime scene. They should all be here shortly, meanwhile I'm heading back to the station to book Howard." He looked at Benjamin. "You're free to head out to the hospital."

"Thanks," Benjamin replied. It was exactly where he wanted to be. He needed to make sure she was really okay, both physically and mentally. He couldn't imagine the horror she must have gone through. Her black eye and the blood on her face had enraged him. The fact that Howard had put hands on her made him want to rip Howard apart.

Before he left, he checked out the whole house. It was shocking, the amount of work that had been done inside, while outside it looked so deserted.

He stopped in the threshold of the master bedroom. His blood ran cold as he saw the ropes that were tied to the headboard. Had she been tied to the bed? Had Howard raped her?

Another rage slammed through him as he drew his hands into fists. Thank God that Dallas had already taken Howard away, otherwise it might have been Benjamin facing charges.

As he drove to the hospital, all he could think of was Bailey and the gratefulness that they had managed to find her before Howard hurt her any more than he already had.

The day had slipped away and night shadows had turned into darkness. Thank God she didn't have to spend another night in that horror of a house.

How sick was it that Howard had attempted to re-create Bailey's home in that house? It had been downright creepy. It was obvious Howard was mentally ill, but Benjamin didn't feel sorry for him.

Howard had certainly known the difference between right and wrong. He'd gone to great lengths to hide his guilt. He'd even met them at his apartment to throw them off him. Benjamin hoped like hell he went to prison for the rest of his life.

By the time he reached the hospital, his thoughts were all on Bailey. He knew she was a fighter and she would hopefully be okay in time. Right now, all he wanted was to be with her, to assure himself that she was really okay. He needed to see her with the blood cleaned off her face. However, he knew the black eye would take some time to heal.

Fatigue tugged at him as he wheeled into the hospital parking lot. It had been a hell of a long twenty-four hours or so. Now that the fear and anxiety were gone, his exhaustion was nearly overwhelming. He parked and got out and then walked toward the emergency entrance.

He went inside and to the desk, where Meri Whittaker, a young attractive woman, sat behind a plexiglass window. As soon as she saw him, she opened the window to greet him.

"Hey, Meri—Bailey Troy was brought in just a little while ago. Could you tell the doctor tending to her that I need to speak with him when he gets a chance?"

"I'll let him know," she replied. She closed the window and then went through a door. She was gone only a few minutes and then she returned to the desk. "He said he'll be out here shortly to speak with you."

"Thank you," he replied and then sat in one of the uncomfortable plastic chairs the room had to offer.

His head whirled with all kinds of thoughts as he waited for the doctor. Had Howard sexually assaulted her? Did she have wounds that hadn't been apparent? Did her body hold the signs of her being beaten? Dear God, he hoped not.

When they'd found her, she'd been wearing a shapeless gray dress that he knew wasn't one of her own. It had obviously been something unattractive that Howard had picked out for her.

It played in his mind that he still needed to end things with her. It was still past time for him to do so.

He was just going to have to pick the right time and it needed to be very soon. He couldn't go on loving her like he did. His heart was already going to be ripped out of his soul when he officially told her goodbye. At least now he knew she was safe. A deep gratefulness for that rushed through him.

He looked up as the outer door whooshed open and Angela came flying in. "Is she okay? Have you heard anything?" she asked frantically.

"No, nothing yet," he replied.

She sank down next to Benjamin and twisted a tissue between her fingers. "There are so many things I need to say to her, so many important things she needs to know. When I thought she was gone…" She let her words drift off.

At that moment Dr. Alexander Erickson entered the room. The doctor was younger than Benjamin, but he was known as a good physician who cared deeply about his patients. Benjamin and Angela both jumped out of their chairs to greet him.

"I've checked her over and other than the black eye and the bloody nose she sustained, she's going to be just fine," he said. "Still, I'm keeping her overnight. She'd been through quite a trauma and I think that's best for her."

"Can we see her?" Benjamin asked.

The doctor frowned. "I've sedated her to help her sleep. How about one of you can go in now and the other can wait until morning."

As much as Benjamin wanted to see her, he could feel Angela's desperate need to see her daughter. "Go on, Angela. I'll come back in the morning," he said.

Angela shot him a look of deep gratitude. "She's in room 107," Dr. Erickson said.

As Angela quickly disappeared down the hallway, Dr. Erickson looked at Benjamin. "I know Dallas is probably going to want to get a statement from her, but all that can wait until morning." He smiled. "She's going to be just fine. Bailey is a strong woman and she'll get through all this."

"Thanks. I'll be back here to see her first thing in the morning," Benjamin said.

He'd desperately wanted to see Bailey tonight, but he wouldn't go against doctor's orders and it was more important that Angela went in to see her daughter.

He checked in with Dallas, who told him they were at Howard's house still processing the scene. But he told Benjamin to go home and get some sleep and come in to the station around nine the next day.

By the time Benjamin got home, his exhaustion tugged on his shoulders and burned at his eyes. But a deep relief also flooded through him. He got out of his clothes, took a quick shower and then got into bed.

Thank God she was safe, but at some point soon he had to break things off with her. No matter how painful it was going to be, it had to be done.

That was his last thought before he fell asleep.

Chapter 15

Bailey relaxed into the hospital bed, just beginning to feel the effects of the sedative that flowed through her IV. A nurse had washed her face, removing all the blood that had been there from her bloody nose. She had an ice pack to use as needed on her black eye and she'd been checked out by the doctor.

They'd allowed her to take a quick shower before she pulled on a hospital gown. Right now, she didn't hurt anywhere too much. She was just grateful to be here and safe with all of Howard's touches on her scrubbed off her skin.

She still couldn't believe everything that had happened. She would have never believed Howard was capable of everything he had done to her. And all in the name of love. That hadn't been love at all. It had been something sick and twisted.

She'd just closed her eyes when she heard her door creak open. She opened her eyes and saw her mother. "Oh, Bailey," she said and hurried to the chair at Bailey's bedside.

Bailey raised the head of her bed and stared as her mother burst into tears. She grabbed Bailey's hand and held tight. "Oh, baby, look at your eye. Look what that animal did to you."

"It's okay now. It doesn't hurt too much," Bailey replied.

"I'm so sorry," Angela said. "Oh, Bailey, I've been so afraid for you."

"Don't cry, I'm safe now, Mom," Bailey said, shocked by her mother's display of emotion. Angela never got emotional about anything.

"I'm just so sorry about so many things. I—I wanted to raise you to be a strong woman. But I realized while you were missing that I never really showed you or told you how very much I love you."

Angela's words were as surprising as finding out Howard had been the one to kidnap her. "It's okay," she said.

"No, it's not okay. I've been too hard on you when I didn't need to be. I took out my bitterness at my life on you. You didn't even share with me about the important things that were going on in your life and I know that's because I didn't make myself available to you. I'm so sorry, Bailey. Can you ever forgive me?"

"Of course, I can… I do. I love you, Mom."

"And I love you, Bailey, and I don't care if you never have children. I just need you to be in my life." She released Bailey's hand, but remained leaning forward in the chair. "I swear things are going to be different from here on out."

"That would be nice," Bailey replied. "Can we talk some more tomorrow? I'm sorry, Mom, but I'm just so tired right now." She could barely keep her eyes open and she was floating on a cloud of well-being.

"Of course." Angela got up from the chair, leaned over and kissed Bailey on the cheek and then she left the room.

These were definitely strange days, when a man who was a respectable banker had kidnapped her in the name of love and her mother had suddenly seen the errors of her ways.

While Bailey was certain Howard would go to prison for a very long time, she wasn't so certain her mother would be able to sustain a new and different relationship with Bailey. Still, her mother's words of love had touched her to the core.

Thoughts of Benjamin filled her head, further warming her. She had hoped to see him, but if he came in now, she wouldn't even be able to have a real conversation with him. She was just too tired. Still, it was his vision that remained in her brain and made her smile with warmth and happiness as she quickly drifted off to sleep.

She awakened early the next morning, feeling surprisingly rested and refreshed. Her black eye throbbed a little, but it was nothing she couldn't handle. She was now eager to see the doctor and go home.

In the meantime, she raised the head of her bed and turned on the television, mostly for the white noise it would provide. Her mind was still filled with everything that had happened to her from the moment she had awakened in the thunderstorm and somebody—Howard—had been in her house. Her stalker had come for her in the storm and nobody had known. So much had happened and she was still trying to process it all.

It wasn't long before the smells of breakfast filled the air and she realized she was starving. All she'd really had to eat since being held against her will was a single taco and that had only been eaten in an effort to appease Howard.

Finally, an older woman she didn't know pushed in a cart to serve Bailey breakfast. There were scrambled eggs and bacon, a cup of fresh fruit, a side of toast, orange juice and coffee.

"Hmm, thank you," Bailey said. "This all looks delicious."

"Hope it tastes as good as it looks," the woman replied and then she was gone.

The first thing Bailey did was pop the top of her coffee so she could take a sip. She was almost finished with the meal when Dr. Erickson came in.

"How's my patient feeling today?" he asked. "I see your shiner is now a beautiful deep purple."

Bailey raised her hand and touched her black eye. "I guess I'm going to have to figure out how to accessorize around it, but other than that, I'm feeling fine and I'm ready to go home."

"I don't see a reason to keep you, so why don't you finish up your breakfast and meanwhile I'll have the nurse draw up your exit papers," he replied.

"Thanks, Dr. Erickson," she said.

"No problem," he replied and then left her room.

She had just finished eating when Dallas and Benjamin came into the room. Benjamin immediately ran to her side. "Bailey, how are you feeling?" His gaze was filled with unmistakable love and it both warmed her yet filled her with sadness, knowing it was a love she couldn't keep.

"I'd like to get an official statement from you," Dallas said. "Are you feeling up to doing that?"

"Absolutely, I'd just as soon put this all behind me as quickly as possible," she replied. Benjamin sat in the chair next to the bed and reached for her hand. She welcomed the warmth and strength that he offered her.

Dallas pulled up another chair and sat. "Tell me the events of the night you were taken from your house," he said. "Start at the very beginning of things."

Just that quickly she was back in it—back in the storm and fighting a masked man. Then she was in a kitchen that looked scarily, creepily like her own. She told Dallas everything that had happened.

"Did anything sexual happen?" he asked when she told him about being tied to the bed.

"Thankfully no, but I believe he would have raped me if I'd been there one more night," she said. She shivered at the very thought of what could have happened...what would have happened.

"How did you get the black eye and bloody nose?" Dallas asked.

"Yesterday morning at breakfast, I made the mistake of telling him I didn't care for sausage links. He punched me so hard and so fast, twice in the face, as he yelled about how ungrateful I was after he'd fixed the sausages for breakfast."

"I wish he was right here right now. I'd beat the hell out of him for hurting you," Benjamin said fiercely.

The interview went on for another twenty minutes or so and then Dallas left while Benjamin stayed behind. "Bailey, I've never been as scared as I was when you went missing," he said.

"Well, it's over now and the doctor is releasing me any minute."

"Do you have a ride home?" he asked.

"No, I was going to call Lizzy and see if she could come get me," Bailey replied.

"Now that I'm here, you don't have to do that. I'll gladly take you home."

Once again, she felt his love for her flooding through her and she knew that today was the day she would tell him goodbye. Within thirty minutes, they were in his car and headed to her house. She still wore the blue-flowered hospital gown as she refused to wear home the gray dress that Howard had her wear.

They didn't talk much on the drive. There would be plenty to say when she invited him in for a talk. Dread pressed tight against her chest with each mile that passed.

"Would you please come inside?" she asked once he pulled up in her driveway. "There's something serious I need to talk to you about."

"Yeah, I need to talk to you about something, too," he replied.

"Can I get you anything?" she asked once they were inside.

"No thanks, I'm fine." He sank down on the sofa.

"Can you excuse me for just a moment, I need to change out of this gown."

"Of course, take your time," he replied.

She ran up the stairs and into her bedroom where she grabbed a pair of jogging pants and a pink T-shirt from a drawer. She quickly changed and then went back downstairs and sat beside him on the sofa.

"Better?" he asked.

"Much better," she replied.

"Okay, you go first, what's on your mind?" His gaze was so soft, so warm on her, and to her surprise she began to cry. "Hey—hey, what's going on, Bailey? Please don't cry." He moved closer to her and began to put an arm around her, but she shrugged him away and cried even harder.

"Oh, Benjamin, I love you so much. I've never loved a man as much as I love you," she said through her tears. "But I've got to let you go. I've already let things go too far with you, but it's time for me to stop seeing you."

He gazed at her in what appeared to be both confusion

and an odd look of relief. Had he just been waiting for her to break it off with him? Had he wanted to stop seeing her, but didn't know how to tell her he no longer wanted to see her?

He frowned. "Can I ask you why?"

She gazed at him through her tears. "You're a good man, Benjamin and you deserve a woman who will love you and give you a family. I'm sure you probably want children, but the truth of the matter is I've kept a big secret from you."

"What secret?" he asked.

She drew in a deep breath. "I don't want kids," she blurted out.

He stared at her for several long moments and then he threw back his head and began to laugh. "Oh, this is so rich," he finally said, amusement lighting up his gorgeous eyes. "Fate definitely has a sense of humor."

She looked at him in utter confusion. "Want to fill me in on what is so funny?"

"I was going to break things off with you today because despite the fact that I love you madly and with all of my heart, I knew I had to let you go so you could have a family." He laughed once again. "Bailey, the truth of the matter is a bad case of mumps when I was twelve left me unable to have children. I can't make babies."

"For real?" she asked, an edge of excitement whirling around inside her as her heart beat a quickened pace.

"For real," he replied. "Is it for real that you don't want children?" He scooted closer to her on the sofa, bringing with him his wonderful scent.

"It's for real," she replied half-breathlessly. Was it possible that fate had brought them together because they truly belonged together? That she could love him and not tell him goodbye?

He reached out and stroked a finger down the side of her face. "Bailey, I love you so very much. I kept telling myself I needed to break things off with you and yet every time I was with you, I couldn't do it."

"Same," she replied. "But, Benjamin, don't you think I'm abnormal or selfish for not wanting children?" Tears once again blurred her vision.

"Of course not," he replied immediately. "I find it highly sexy that you're a strong woman and you know what you want. Bailey, I also know there isn't a selfish bone in your body. If you were abnormal or selfish, I wouldn't love you like I do."

He held her gaze for a long moment. Oh, she could get lost in his beautiful blue eyes. He slid off the sofa and to one knee. "I don't have a ring, but, Bailey, will you marry me? Will you marry me and make me the happiest man in the world?"

"Yes…oh, yes. I'll marry you and I'll be the happiest woman on earth." She bounced up from the sofa and he stood, as well. He pulled her into his arms and for a moment they simply gazed at each other. "Hi," she finally said.

"Hi yourself," he replied and then his lips took hers in a kiss that tasted of love and a deep commitment. It whispered of desire and a happily-ever-after with the man she'd always dreamed of. Finally, and forever, Officer Benjamin Cooper belonged to her.

Epilogue

Chief Dallas Calloway sat at the table in the workroom and stared at the board that held the photos of the murdered victims.

It was just after midnight and he was alone in the station except for one other officer who was manning dispatch and the front desk.

Still, despite the silence that surrounded him, his head wasn't quiet. Rather, the victims screamed in his brain, begging him for justice. They had been screaming in his head since the first victim had been found in Lucas's cornfield.

He now rubbed at his tired eyes. Sleep had been difficult with all the noise in his head and he knew he wasn't functioning at his very best.

What were they missing? Why couldn't they find this man who stabbed women and then trussed them up like scarecrows? What significance did the eyes have to him? Why did he take them and what in God's name did he do with them?

Dallas loved the small town he served and he couldn't stand it that a killer was using it as his personal killing field. And the worst part was he knew a clock was ticking down to another murder.

Somewhere in town, a madman was already plotting

and planning his next kill and there was absolutely nothing Dallas could do to prevent it.

The victims screamed again in his head and more than anything he wanted to give them the justice they deserved. Somehow, some way, he had to find this killer.

The Scarecrow Killer stood at his front window and watched as the sun went down. An excitement roared through his body at the same time the crows cawed in his head.

It was time for another scarecrow to be built. That was the only way he could make the crows go away. The best part was he'd decided whom he'd use as the next one.

Her blond hair and blue eyes were perfect. They were just like *hers*. He was hoping and praying she would be the one to finally stop the noise in his head. If he could just kill her for a final time then maybe it all would end. She'd be dead and wouldn't be able to haunt him anymore.

That was what he wanted and yet he had to admit he liked making the headlines. He liked that he had the whole town afraid. It was what they all deserved. They had never seen him, but they were seeing him now. He had to admit to himself that he liked stabbing his knife in their chests and feeling their warm blood. He liked sewing their mouths closed and taking their eyes out.

Now that he had his next victim picked out, it was just a matter of finding the right time and place to take her. In just a few days another scarecrow would appear. A new burst of excited adrenaline flooded through him as he thought about the fun to come.

* * * * *

Undercover Heist
Rachel Astor

MILLS & BOON

Rachel Astor is equal parts country girl and city dweller who spends an alarming amount of time correcting the word *the*. Rachel has had a lot of jobs (bookseller, real estate agent, 834 assorted admin roles), but none as, *ahem*, interesting as when she waitressed at a bar named after a dog. She is now a *USA TODAY* bestselling author who splits her time between the city, the lake and as many made-up worlds as possible.

Visit the Author Profile page
at millsandboon.com.au.

Dear Reader,

If you love a good heist—the twists, the turns, the adventure, the action—you've landed in the right place.

I came to love the characters in *Undercover Heist* so much while writing, and I hope you come to love them just as much while reading. Ruby Alexander is a brilliant and capable ex-thief who wants nothing more than to put that world behind her. That is until ex-partner Shane Meyers sneaks back into her life and turns that notion—and a few other things—upside down.

It doesn't take long to get the gang together to save their old friend and mentor—once again stealing for all the right reasons, even while everything around them is going terribly wrong...especially those old emotions that Ruby is absolutely, positively *not* supposed to be feeling.

Fun fact: During the writing of *Undercover Heist*, while Ruby and Shane were searching for their happy ending atop a mountain, I got to experience a happy ending (beginning?), too—getting engaged at the top of Sulphur Mountain in Banff National Park.

Thank you so much for reading!

Rachel

Prologue

Max Redfield's eyes became a bit misty as the two most talented students in his current class stood for their bow. The audience roared with appreciation after the story had swept them completely away for one hour and forty-eight minutes. He never tired of watching his actors succeed in stealing the full attention of a rapt audience…the way you could hear a pin drop inside a theater of a thousand, everyone holding their breath to catch each word.

That was *real* power. Sharing time with someone, taking their troubles away, if only for a moment. Getting them off their screens and out of their heads. These days that was almost a miracle.

He sighed a happy sigh, which turned wistful as it drifted off.

If only it was enough. If only the other life didn't call him. The life of excitement, and drama, and all the things that created a great story. Except in the other life, he got to live great stories instead of portraying them. He could never give up the con. He'd tried, of course, and even quit for a few months after Scotland, but the thrill drew him in again and again. He couldn't live without it—it was the one vice he couldn't quite give up.

His two protégés were far too promising. He couldn't let their talents go to waste.

One of two things usually happened after someone with

real talent went through Max's acting school—they headed for Broadway or Hollywood—great contacts to have, especially when they felt indebted to you—or they graduated to a con.

Acting was a highly underrated talent in that world. The art of making people believe could get a person into most places far more effectively than methods other people swore by. At least he thought so. But Max supposed he was old-fashioned.

After the excitement of the evening faded, and the last of the guests and actors departed, Max found himself day-dreaming, trying to think of the perfect story for his star students to tell. This was how he thought of his cons. They were stories—and he relished in finding the perfect role for each actor to play. The ultimate director's high.

Sadly, his stories—his cons—were never quite as elegant as Ash's. Such a waste she left the biz, but Max would have to do his best with the skill he did have.

And so, as he walked home, he thought of stories. Of new ways to deliver a con—but only to those who deserved it, of course. Never innocents. Only real criminals, the kind who used drug money or blood money or the souls of the young and innocent, and with the world in its current state, there was never a shortage of targets. The challenging part, though, was that these were also the kinds of people who tended to be naturally suspicious and more dangerous than the average person.

It was much harder to swindle a swindler.

But sometimes that was the fun part too.

So lost in his thoughts, Max had missed the signs. A noise, easily written off as a feral cat, then a faraway click, escaping on the wind as quickly as it came. A glint of something in the reflection of a window, which might have been anything.

But it had all been something. The noise, a careless foot-step, the click, a gun cocked several yards away and the reflection? The flash of a watch, left on because it wouldn't matter anyway.

Max thought nothing of any of these things.

Until, that was, a heavy hood was pulled over his head, his arms yanked painfully behind his body and cuffed as a vehicle pulled up alongside—a van, judging by the sound of the sliding doors—and whisked him away.

And in that moment, in the black and the speed and the terror, one thought entered his mind—perhaps it wasn't so hard to swindle a swindler, after all.

Chapter 1

Most people didn't always know why they weren't successful, but Shane Meyers knew exactly why he was failing so miserably.

Because he had to.

"Buddy—" his agent said. Shane hated when he called him that—made him think the guy had forgotten his name. Although, Shane thought with a tilt of his head, maybe that wasn't such a bad thing. "—this could have been your big break. *Again*," the agent finished after a dramatic pause. "What happened in there this time?"

Shane let out a long, rehearsed breath. "I don't know, man. I guess I just wasn't feeling the part."

It had been an incredible opportunity. Shane honestly didn't know how Christoph had managed to land him the audition. It would have been a huge role. The lead in a small but potentially significant film. There was no way he'd paid the kind of dues it took to land an audition like that, but something in his film reel had caught the producers' attention.

And then he blew it.

He blew that sucker like a five-year-old blows dandelion wishes, the knowledge that he had no intention of taking the part—even if he had miraculously landed it—solidly planted in the forefront of his mind.

"Not feeling the part?" Christoph was saying, his voice rising to little-girl-squeal-like proportions, though Shane wasn't really paying attention. "Do you know how hard I work to get you the kind of attention you need to become a breakout star? Do you know how many other people would die to have this kind of opportunity?"

"I know, man, and I appreciate it," Shane said, though he was becoming increasingly more interested in the party going on around him than in the conversation. "But I've told you before, I'm not interested in the leading-man roles."

"Shane," Christoph said, exasperated. "That is the whole point of being an actor—to become a star. Get famous and be adored."

Shane rolled his eyes. He wanted to tell Christoph where he could neatly tuck his spiel, but the guy would never understand, no matter how clearly and precisely Shane spoke. Famous and adored was the last thing Shane wanted. Sure, there was a time when he thought those things were important, but none of that held any interest anymore.

To be in the spotlight would ruin everything. Famous would mean he'd be as incognito as a grizzly bear in a fuchsia crop top wandering undetected through a food court. He'd never go unrecognized, which had been essential in his previous line of work.

He would never be able to have the thing he really wanted again. And sure, the thing he really wanted was about as likely to happen as Santa beating the Easter Bunny in a foot race on Boxing Day, but he couldn't take the risk.

He could only take small parts on TV and in movies—the kinds of roles that paid but would never throw him into the spotlight. It was a nice way to live. Gave him the connections that put him in the places he wanted to be. Places like the party he'd been trying to enjoy before his phone had so rudely interrupted him.

His life had become a steady stream of parties, flowing

alcohol, attractive women and flying under the radar. It was what he wanted. Well…as close to what he wanted as he could reasonably expect under the circumstances.

Christoph would never understand Shane's reasons for not aspiring higher. But his acting training had so far helped him keep Christoph's ambitions at bay. "It's not about the fame for me. It's about the craft. The art."

Admittedly, the delivery of that line had not been his best performance.

But Christoph bought it, or at least pretended to. "Whatever you say, buddy. But mark my words—someday, I'm gonna make you a star."

"Great. Looking forward to it," Shane said, trying his best not to hurt himself rolling his eyes too hard.

If there had ever been a cheesier line in the history of the movies, Shane had yet to hear it. But he supposed it was the job of agents to sell dreams, so he could hardly blame the guy. And so far, Shane had been impressed by the things Christoph had done to move his happily mediocre career along, especially considering the utter lack of cooperation from his client.

Shane tucked his phone into his pocket and turned back to the party. He watched a gorgeous brunette in a bathing suit, which left little to be desired, dive gracefully into the pool. *Now this is more like it.* It never ceased to amaze him that in LA it was perfectly normal for swimwear to be right at home in the company of expensive suits…along with everything in between. There was a familiar-looking guy—had Shane worked with him once? Or seen him in something recently?—in board shorts, a hooded sweater and wavy long hair that looked like it hadn't been washed in a while. An attractive woman in a sequined evening gown was sitting on his lap. Only in LA would she be the one fawning all over the guy instead of the other way around.

Shane couldn't help but smile. The inconsistency and oddness of the town were what had drawn him there in the first place. Easier to blend in where anything and everything goes.

He wandered over to the bar, enjoying his life now. Maybe he wasn't 100 percent content, but parties on random Sunday nights—complete with bartenders, waitstaff, caterers and everyone else who made these kinds of events run without a hitch—weren't too shabby. It would be a dream to pull a job at an event like this. So many options for characters to perform.

He pushed the thought from his head. That wasn't his life anymore. No matter how hard it was to stop himself from planning how, exactly, he might get to the painting above the TV. It wasn't the artwork he cared about, it was the thrill of the job, the adrenaline gained from taking the risk.

A voice came from beside him. "It's beautiful, isn't it?"

Shane hadn't heard the woman come up to him. He'd been so lost in his daydream, or rather day-*scheme*, he'd let his guard down. It was nice he was able to do that now. For years he'd been so "on" all the time he'd begun to worry the stress might be affecting his health. Not that he was ever as interested in his health as he was getting to the next thrill.

"Incredible," Shane said, guiding his showstopper smile toward the woman. He knew from experience what this seemed to do to those who'd shown interest in him.

The woman was attractive—auburn hair, great body, a twinkle in her eye suggesting she might like a little mischief almost as much as Shane did.

"Are you an art connoisseur?" she asked.

Shane chuckled. "Not really," he said, turning away from the painting to face her. "I suppose I just like to look at beautiful things."

The woman raised her eyebrows with a little smirk, as if to say "nice play." "Does that line work on all the girls?" she asked.

Shane tilted his head in thought. "Surprisingly, yes," he said, "though I'm not sure if it's the line itself, or the professional delivery."

"Is that your way of subtly letting me know you're some kind of famous actor?" the woman asked.

"Oh, I am very far from famous, but the actor part is accurate." Shane motioned to the bartender to get them two more drinks. "And yes, I suppose I hoped it would impress you in some small, silly way."

She smiled. "Fair enough."

"But let me guess something about you," he said.

The woman looked intrigued and nodded for him to continue.

Shane's heart sped, knowing he was about to enter his area of expertise. He didn't know if it was because he'd studied acting and spent so much time thinking about motivations, or if he was just a natural at it, but he was always able to read people. Well, almost always.

"Well," he began. "I think you have an expectation about what you think I will say, which is that you are an actress."

The woman smiled, her eyes impressed and amused.

"It makes sense. You're at a Hollywood party filled to the brim with actors and actresses, and you certainly have the looks for it. Of course—" he squinted his eyes "—it's clear you have a lot going on behind those intelligent eyes, so you could just as easily be a producer or a director, but I don't think that's quite right either." Shane picked up the drinks from the bar and handed her a fresh glass of the wine she held, taking her almost empty glass and setting it down.

Her eyes sparkled. She was clearly enjoying herself more than she'd expected, which, for someone like Shane, was simply another clue.

"You're here because someone important to you asked you to come, but it's not your usual scene. Perhaps a roommate."

She smiled wider.

"The roommate is an actress, and you love her enough to come to these kinds of parties even though you find them superficial and tedious. You both moved here from the same small town after high school. Her for Hollywood and you for…school, I think," he said.

"Impressive," the woman said, and Shane could tell she wasn't just saying it. He knew he'd gotten it dead right.

But he still had a bit more in his arsenal that he hoped to blow her mind with.

"And I suspect you are a psychology major."

Her eyes widened, her lips parting in surprise. "How did you—"

"Just a lucky guess," Shane said, flashing her his—thankfully less than—famous smile once more.

It wasn't just a lucky guess, of course. It was what Shane did. He read people better than most people read books. She squinted, not quite believing him, but he was nothing if not good at feigning innocence. His boyish charm had gotten him far in life.

"Can you excuse me for a minute?" she asked, starting to walk away. "I'm Isabelle, by the way," she said, "and I'll be right back."

"Shane," he said, shaking her hand. "It's very nice to meet you."

Shane wandered over to the edge of the patio. He'd been in this position more times than he could count. Isabelle would go off to her roommate and let her know she was leaving, then come back and Shane would take her to his place, where they'd finish off the evening enjoying each other's company in various fun and energetic ways.

But he wasn't sure, as he looked out over the gorgeous view of the hills and the ocean beyond, why it didn't feel as exciting as it used to. Maybe it was because he knew he'd never own a view like this one. Then again, with his charm and skills, why would he ever need to? He'd always have plenty of friends in high places who'd let him borrow their views. His thoughts hung a little longer on Isabelle, and how there'd been so many women like her, but nothing that ever stuck.

Not since Ruby.

Maybe he was just bored of everything, since nothing could ever live up to the life he used to have. In fact, when Shane really thought about it—something he tried hard not to do—his life was starting to feel a lot like a psychology major might feel at a Hollywood party.

That it was all a little superficial and tedious.

Ruby Alexander sighed and slammed the enormous book shut, shoving it across the desk. "Flipping comatose sloths!" she said, under her breath.

"Ruby?" Barb said, raising an eyebrow as she poked her head into Ruby's office. "Is everything okay?"

Ruby rubbed her temples. "Yeah. No. I don't know." She shook her head. "It's just…all this red tape. These laws. Some days it feels like everything is working against us."

Barb sat across from Ruby, sighing. "I wish I had words of wisdom to make it better, but unfortunately, this is the work. The art world has a complicated relationship with these governments. The negotiations are always delicate and a lot of the time it's going to be one step forward, two steps back."

Ruby let out a low growl. "But half these people are war criminals."

Barb nodded. "And many of them are all we've got to negotiate with."

Ruby leaned back and gazed out the window. "It all feels so futile. Like nothing we're doing here matters."

"It matters, Ruby," Barb said emphatically. "We're the only support these poor families have to lean on. The only place they can turn."

Ruby nodded even though she knew something Barb didn't. The families whose art was pillaged in various war raids throughout history did have another option. And knowing *that* left her with even more guilt than not being able to do more for these families. She'd left that world behind years ago. It was just…once in a while she wondered if getting out of the heist game had been the right choice.

"Thanks, Barb," Ruby said. "You're right. Sometimes the snail's pace of the whole thing just gets to me."

Barb nodded and stood. "It gets to all of us, hon. It gets to all of us," she said, walking out with a little wave.

Deep down, Ruby knew she'd made the right choice getting out when she did. Things were getting too hot after everything imploded in Scotland. The authorities were starting to close in on the team, and so were some of the dealers trying to sell the black-market pieces. And while a typical art dealer might not be the most terrifying kind of person on earth, the people who protected the shady ones certainly could be.

Still, as she sat in her office day after day pushing paper, she sometimes missed the intrigue, the danger, the pure fun of it.

But she could never go back to that life, to breaking all the rules. She had way too much to lose now. She was a rising star in the legitimate art world, landing her first apprentice curator position at the age of twenty-seven. Over the past three years she'd been working her way up the ladder. After a few incredible recoveries of stolen art, she'd been asked to specialize in helping governments around the world make pacts and agreements to carry out the arduous process of returning stolen art to their rightful owners—ancestors of victims of art raids around the world and throughout history.

And Ruby was becoming a leading expert, able to spot and identify stolen art faster than a high-speed getaway driver.

Of course, her expertise wasn't quite as uncanny as everyone thought. Truth be told, she'd had years of research and hands-on experience, though she couldn't tell anyone about that.

Doing everything through "proper channels" was an exercise in frustration compared to the way she and the team used to work. Still, she was doing good in the world, no matter how slow the process. She helped without having to risk her life or break the law. Without having to always look over her shoulder. It was almost worth the day-to-day slog in the trenches of already found stolen art.

Ruby packed up her things and got ready to head out for the day. She smiled as she strolled down the hall past her colleagues who were also getting ready to leave. Imagine what they would think if they knew about her past, she thought as she waved at Gordon, who would pop his toupee if he had any inkling.

She bet none of them had ever played the part of a damsel in distress inside the mansion of a criminal—a decoy as her team pilfered the man's jewels from right under his nose. Or raided a secret warehouse filled with original artwork stolen in war crimes. And likely none of them had scaled the outside of a thirty-six-story building to retrieve a priceless Ming dynasty vase.

Of course, it wasn't like she could do that anymore either. It wasn't an option, even if she were willing to leave her new world, which she loved, no matter how frustrating. She wasn't equipped anymore. She tried to keep in shape but sitting in front of a computer doing office work for the past three years had made her soft. She worried she'd lost her edge mentally too. She used to be able to peg a criminal's thoughts with shocking accuracy, but she hadn't let her mind go there for a long time.

Ruby stepped out of the museum into a chilly day, the wind sweeping her hair sideways. She pulled her coat tight and walked toward her apartment—another perk of this new life. The museum owned residences nearby for the employees to rent at a discounted rate, and Ruby loved her place—modern and sleek, but with plenty of soft surfaces and artwork to warm the space up.

As Ruby made her way down the street, a strange feeling crawled through her. In her old life, she'd always been on high alert, glancing over her shoulder to make sure no one followed her, but she'd given up the habit a long time ago. Still, sometimes old habits died hard, and she risked a peek back.

Nothing.

But she couldn't shake the sense she was being watched.

She looked again.

If she were being followed, her training was still sharp enough to notice. She shook her head and kept walking, a little faster now, wanting to get home, have a long hot shower and relax with a glass of wine.

Hurrying into her building, Ruby took a final glance back then shrugged, deciding she was being paranoid because she'd been thinking so much about her old life. But that was ages ago, and all that business was a long way behind her. She was grateful for that, though perhaps there was a small pang of nostalgia on the side.

Ruby opened a bottle of cabernet and poured a glass to breathe, then began to undress as she made her way to the bathroom, dropping clothes as she went. It was an old habit, and she felt decadent as she disrobed—a simple luxury, yet it gave her so much pleasure to take those last few steps into the bathroom completely naked. A little jolt of naughty as a throwback to her old life, she supposed.

The shower felt glorious. Another little gift to herself, a ritual to wash the stress of the day down the drain before she indulged in her art, needing to cleanse herself of the traitorous people she helped hunt down before her creative juices could flow.

She wrapped a towel around herself before making her way

back down the hall to retrieve her wine. Halfway to the kitchen she realized something was off and stopped, heart racing. There didn't appear to be an immediate threat, but impossibly, her clothes were no longer scattered on the floor. A sound of a glass clinking came from the kitchen where the clothes she'd discarded sat neatly folded on the counter.

A voice floated from the shadows. "Still doing the same old rituals, I see."

Chapter 2

Shane thought he was prepared to see Ruby after all this time. From the moment their former contact got hold of him, Shane had been warring with himself—one moment filled with dread, and the next, trying to keep his excitement at bay. One glance at Ruby's face—a face he'd believed he'd never see again—was almost more than his wounded heart could take. The fact that she wore nothing but a towel and still looked as good as the day she left—better even—did not help either the dread or the excitement.

Thankfully he had always been the best actor in the room. He reminded himself he was there to play his part and nothing more. Slowing his breath, he tried to calm his heart—the one part of him doing a terrible job at staying in character.

"Jesus, Shane, what the hell are you doing here? How did you find me? And how did you get in?" Ruby's voice rose as the questions poured out of her.

"I think you know the answer to the last question, at least," he said, smirking. "You know I can pretty much break in anywhere I want, anytime I want."

Shane knew the look on her face well. Fuming, with a side of livid.

"Just because you *can* go somewhere, Shane…"

The way she said his name twigged something in him,

made his stomach tighten. He never did handle it well when she was mad at him.

"…doesn't mean you should."

Her eyes still flashed the way they used to, as if her anger lit a flame somewhere deep in her core.

Shane's plan had been to pour himself a glass of wine to match hers and be sitting in the dark recesses of the living room before she got out of the shower. But she'd come out before the plan was fully executed and, as she usually did, caught him a bit off guard.

Good thing he was a master at keeping his cool under pressure.

Of course, there was no greater pressure than the kind only Ruby Alexander could apply.

He continued to pour his glass of wine, slowly, deliberately, then picked up both glasses and sauntered over to Ruby, handing her one. He caught her eye and held it a moment longer than necessary, then turned. "We may as well make ourselves comfortable. You, my friend," he said, catching her eye again as he sat, "are expecting company."

He made himself comfortable, one hand on the back of the couch as he sat, playing the part, acting as if he owned the place.

Ruby, to her credit, played it cool, taking a step toward him. She lowered her hand from the towel, knowing that even a hint that the towel might drop at any moment was enough to throw him off his game.

"I certainly wasn't expecting anything besides a quiet night at home, but since you never bring anything but trouble with you, I guess I should get dressed and prepare for the worst." She took a long sip of her wine and moved to set her glass down on the coffee table. She leaned farther forward than she needed to, affording him a view he tried to resist, but failed.

She caught his eye knowingly and stood up, heading back down the hallway.

He watched her go, his jaw working as if grinding his emotions into submission. As she took the last step into her room, her towel slipped—just a little—and Shane couldn't help but think she did it on purpose to torture him. He leaned back and took a drink, trying not to think about Ruby in there that very moment, letting the towel fall to the floor.

He closed his eyes and breathed, remembering the exquisite torture being around her had always been. Never knowing where he stood, but never being able to walk away either.

Remembering how easy it had seemed for her when she'd finally left.

A knock sounded at the door.

Shane moved to stand, but Ruby was already headed back down the hall, looking as though the couple of minutes in the bedroom had done nothing to ease her anger.

Of course, the anger was completely justified. Especially considering behind that door was the one person Ruby was absolutely not going to want to see.

Having Shane Meyers sitting on her couch as if there was nothing out of the ordinary was making Ruby feel like she had been hit by a toddler on a runaway scooter—dazed, confused and like she'd fielded a solid thwack right to the crotch.

She hadn't seen him in three years, but he was acting as if not a day had gone by. Something about him looked different, though. A little more tense around the jaw. A little shaggier around the edges. A little sexier than she remembered.

Shit.

She got a sense that somehow life had not been kind to Shane in the years since she'd seen him. Perhaps he hadn't landed on his feet in quite the same way she had. The degrees she'd worked for on the side of their…other business…

had been the safety net all those teachers and parental types back in school had warned her she'd better have. She'd never quite bought into those ideas, but school had come easily for her—things tended to be like that when you picked something to study that you were already passionate about. She had to grudgingly admit they'd been right. In her case, at least. She doubted it would have been quite as valuable for people who hadn't ended up with their lives in the kind of massive destruction hers had catapulted into.

Something similar might have helped Shane, though, she mused, noticing a scar above his right eyebrow that hadn't been there before. It was small, but she knew it hadn't been there before, given all the nights she'd stayed up watching him breathe as they lay tangled in bed. But school hadn't come so easily to Shane. Hell, it had been a miracle he'd made it through Max's program… Then again, there was the whole thing about passion. Something Shane never lacked when it came to a job, since playing the part of someone else was his favorite thing in the world to do. Ruby tried very hard never to think about that. Going down the rabbit hole of what had been real and what hadn't could turn into a spiral of doubt, fear and a whole lot of paranoia.

She hated this. Hated feeling shaken in her own damn place, her only sanctuary, and she was pissed he had the nerve—and the ability—to break in even though her security was one of the top systems available. Of course, that had never stopped any of them before, herself included. Still, there was a code people in her former line of work were supposed to stick to.

But frankly, none of that mattered. If she was being honest, her anger was really pointed at herself. She was angry for the way she felt. And the way those feelings snuck up on her in less time than it had taken to say "Be careful with the bloody Rembrandt!" that time in southern Italy. Time should have made it all go away but seeing him again after all these years stirred up…feelings, and that was what *really* pissed her off.

Screw the slightly longer hair, which somehow made him look both more boyish and more mature at the same time. Screw the new, slimmer style of jeans that showed off just how much better he'd been at keeping in performance shape than she had. Screw those hands that looked just as dexterous as ever…and Holy Mother of Pearl, could she remember the way those dexterous hands felt sliding slowly from her hip to her breast as if it were yesterday.

Double shit.

She needed to stop. She moved toward the door, shooting Shane a glare she hoped said, *This is my house and I will open my own damn door, thank you very much.*

Ruby knew the person on the other side of the damn door was likely to be one of three people.

Please be Bug or Max, she silently prayed. *Please be Bug or Max.*

She eased the door open and let out a long, weighty sigh. She wanted so badly to slam the door shut again, especially since she couldn't think of a single reason for this woman to waltz back into her life. But—although she hated herself for it—Ruby was curious. She hated when she couldn't immediately figure out the end game.

Ruby pulled her shoulders back. "Ashlyn," she said, nodding to the woman before her.

"Ruby!" the woman said, as if meeting up with a long-lost friend.

Which of course she was. Long-lost at least, though Ruby would not consider her and Ash friends anymore.

Ruby rolled her eyes and opened the door wider to let Ash in.

The woman looked like she hadn't aged a day, which Ruby found unreasonably annoying. In fact, Ashlyn Greaves looked as though she had grown younger. Ruby wondered if she'd had some work done, though she supposed the relaxed lifestyle of no longer being a criminal was bound to give a person a little pep to their step.

Ash was as put-together as always—pencil skirt, tailored blouse, fabulous coat and perfect accessories, looking as if she'd been professionally styled. Ruby made an attempt to smooth her wrinkled sweatshirt, trying not to think about how she must look—straight out of the shower with the first clothes she grabbed from the heaping pile in her hamper thrown on. Ash had that effect on people. No matter how far you'd come, no matter how respected you were in your field, she had a way of transforming you into your most awkward, uncomfortable, seventh-grade-in-the-change-room self. It was what made her so good at her job. Or used to. Ruby had no idea what Ash had been up to since that night in Scotland.

She tried to push it out of her mind, but seeing Ash brought it back like it was yesterday.

Ruby had felt the job going south and wanted to abort—knew they needed to abort—but it was Ashlyn's call. The plan had worried Ruby from the start. For every other job, the team, without fail, made sure to have three exit strategies. Surprises always came up when pulling off a heist, and contingency plans were the most important piece. Always.

But Ash—the group leader and the strategist—insisted that even though she didn't have a plan C, the score would be worth it and there wouldn't be any surprises.

But surprises were the one thing you could count on.

The team got into the castle, no problem. It was supposed to be vacant. Max and Shane had cased the place for a week straight, and not a single person had come or gone. The family was on vacation off the coast of Morocco and the only security consisted of the nonliving variety. Plenty of cameras, alarms and even a pressure-sensitive floor around the most valuable items, but the team had dealt with all that before. Human interference was always the most volatile kind, and they were confident it wouldn't be a problem.

It was Ash's job to confirm the whereabouts of the family.

But she hadn't been thorough enough.

The teenage daughter had come home from college a few days early for her holiday break, and Kaden had surprised her as he walked into the foyer with a duffel bag full of antiquities.

The family was a paranoid one—most families who collected illegal artifacts were—and they'd had guns stashed everywhere.

The team knew this ahead of time—Bug was always thorough with his recon work—but no one had thought the guns would be a problem. They assured themselves it would be the easiest job they'd ever pulled. Thought they had all the time in the world. When Ruby woke up that morning, she hadn't even been nervous.

What a dazzling fool she'd been.

They'd retrieved everything they went there to steal back, but the cost had been far too high.

The others panicked, but they'd gotten themselves together and succeeded in taking the daughter down. Not to kill her— they tried never to kill people, and certainly not an innocent teenage girl. As innocent as a teenage daughter of an exporter of…let's just say contraband, could be, at least. She'd simply stumbled upon an intruder in her own house. But they had been able to restrain her in a cell in the basement. Even Ruby had to admit that was extraordinarily convenient in the end. They stocked her with plenty of food and water, and only once they were safely out of the country did they alert her family to her whereabouts.

But Ruby hadn't been panicked. Instead, she had been left holding Kaden in her arms as he bled out. It was the exact moment Ruby had decided she was out. Out of the team and out of the lifestyle. She vowed she would never work a con again.

And now, trying to keep her cool as her two ex-partners stood in her living room, she was determined not to let anyone convince her otherwise.

Chapter 3

Shane hadn't realized he'd been holding his breath until he started to feel light-headed. Thankfully the acting classes he'd taken all his life had included breathing exercises, which helped calm him and get back on track.

He wasn't in any sort of character, but he was still playing a part. When he thought about it, he was always playing a part. Then again, wasn't everybody?

Ash sauntered in, removing a pair of expensive-looking gloves and surveying the place.

Ruby did have some nice digs, Shane realized. That museum job of hers must pay pretty well. A whole lot better than the odd acting jobs he'd picked up here and there in the years since the team had disbanded.

Ash looked like she was doing pretty well, too, for that matter.

Shane knew what this little unplanned visit concerned, but Ruby was about to hear it for the first time. Ash knew she could never go to Ruby on her own, not after everything that had happened, but they thought together they might have a chance at convincing her.

"So," Ruby said, grabbing her wine again, probably realizing that with the two of them in her apartment, she was going to need it. "Is anyone going to tell me what the hell is going on?"

Shane had never been so nervous in his life. He didn't get

nervous—that was the whole point. It was what made him better than anyone else at acting, and better than anyone else at the lifestyle. But sitting there, working as hard as he could to appear calm, he realized he didn't like the feeling one bit. But if he and Ash couldn't convince Ruby to make a brief foray back into the world of the wrong side of the law...well, he couldn't think about that.

They needed her. Desperately.

This, he realized, was another feeling he wasn't terribly familiar with, and was even less fond of—desperation. But here they were. A full-on "desperate times calls for desperate measures" situation, sitting in the apartment of a person they'd all sworn never to see again. Ruby had made them promise on their lives.

Given the circumstances, she was being rather...*cordial* was the word coming to Shane's mind. She poured Ash a glass of the cabernet before they all sat down on various minimalist-style furniture pieces around the room, which would have been called stark if not for the decorative items from Ruby's travels around the world. There was even the odd thing he recognized from...well, from before.

They sipped their wine, faster than Shane would have liked. But frankly the tension was thick and the only thing cutting through it was the alcohol. Or the alcohol was making it worse. He couldn't really tell.

"You're looking well," Ash said to Ruby.

Shane couldn't help but notice Ruby stiffen, though to the untrained eye, Ruby was hiding it well. Of course, there wasn't a single untrained eye in the room, so it hardly mattered.

Ash continued as if there was nothing out of the ordinary—just three old friends catching up after a long time apart. Shane would bet his life that Ruby wished it had been much, much longer.

"I'm not surprised you've been doing so well since going

legit. You always did have the best eye of all of us for the pieces," Ash continued, running her finger along an African statue on the bookcase.

Ruby cleared her throat, eyeing Ash like she was afraid she might break something. Not that she didn't have good reason— the last time they were all together, Ash had made the decisions that had broken pretty much everything. The rules, the job... Kaden. In essence, the whole team.

"My team doesn't seem to be complaining," Ruby finally said, a note of "unlike yours" underscoring her words.

Ash let a smirk slide across her lips, almost as if she was finding all this exceedingly amusing. "All the bureaucracy must be frustrating, though, I'd imagine."

Ruby took another sip of her wine, which was already half-gone, anger burning in her expression.

After a moment of seething silence, Ash turned her attention to Shane, making him wish he were anywhere else but in that room. If he didn't already know the reason for the impromptu reunion, he would have been out at the first glance from Ash. But this was too important.

"You, on the other hand, seem to be having a bit of a go with life," Ash continued.

"How nice of you to notice," Shane said, as if it were a compliment.

Truth be told, he'd had nothing but fun in the past few years, living off the spoils of their labors. Sure, they returned artifacts to their rightful owners, but it wasn't like they weren't still paid handsomely. Deals had always been worked out ahead of time for the team's commissions—usually a percentage of what was recovered—and the families were often so happy to get their items back they would throw in a hefty bonus.

Shane had enjoyed suddenly having enough time on his hands to enjoy the money he'd accumulated over the years particularly well. He found days of soaking in the sun on private yachts and drowning in the island club nightlife suited him quite well. Lately, though, it had all been feeling a little empty.

And seeing what Ruby had done with her life in the time since the last job made his lifestyle feel a little shallow. Which was fair enough, he supposed, though he was surprised at the spark of shame he felt. Why the hell shouldn't he use his money whatever damn way he pleased? But the moment *that* thought crept into his mind was the same moment he realized it wasn't the judgment from the others bothering him, it was the judgment he was clearly blanketing on himself. And it was only in that moment he realized he'd been blanketing it on himself all along. Loathing himself for the decadence combined with a healthy dose of idleness. Truly, a case could be made for each of the seven deadly sins having infiltrated his life. Not that he could blame the sins. No, the blame was squarely on him.

"Look, can we just stop with all the niceties and get to the point here?" Ruby said, suddenly out of patience with the song and dance they were all performing.

Ash didn't bother trying to hide her smile this time. "I was wondering when you were going to get jumpy. You always were the first to get impatient with everyone."

"Ash, come on," Shane jumped in. "Getting after each other isn't going to help the situation."

"Which brings me to my point," Ruby said, another sip going down the hatch.

Shane was hard-pressed to believe Ruby was nervous, but the wine swigging was about something. Maybe it was impatience, or maybe it was because she knew exactly why the two of them were sitting in her living room.

"What," she continued, "is the actual situation?"

Ash sighed and set down her glass. "There's a job."

"No," Ruby said, so fast Shane wasn't sure Ash had even finished her sentence.

"If you would just let me finish what I was going to say, I'd like to—"

"I said no," Ruby said, standing and putting her hand up as if to say that was the end of it. "There's no way it's ever going to happen."

"Ruby, just hear her out, please," Shane said.

Ruby shot him a glare. "Hear her out?" she said, her voice rising. "The woman who nearly got us all killed the last time she planned a job for us, and now you just want me to hear her out?"

"I think saying I nearly got everyone killed is a little unfair," Ash said.

"Tell that to Kaden," Ruby fired back.

"Look, I get it. You are angry with me and probably always will be. I've come to terms with that, but just listen to me, please. It's not what you think," Ash said.

Ruby shook her head. "This conversation is over. I don't know why I was even stupid enough to open the door for you." As she spoke, she moved over to the very door she spoke of and put her hand on the knob.

"Ruby." Ash sighed. "It's Max. They have Max."

Ruby's eyes darted from Shane to Ash, then back to Shane again. Then she closed them, a pained expression coming over her face.

Her hand dropped from the doorknob.

"What in the shit do you mean they have Max?" Ruby said, knowing exactly what in the shit they meant, but couldn't stop herself from asking anyway.

"No one has seen him since he left the theater production of his latest graduating class," Shane said.

"How long ago was that?"

"He left late two nights ago. They had all been celebrating after the final show and as far as anyone knows, Max was the last to leave."

Ruby nodded. She remembered Max was usually the last to leave after every show. He always said there was something about the dichotomy between a packed house and an empty theater in a single evening that gave him a sense of balance.

"But he never made it home," Shane finished.

Ruby began to pace. She'd tried to push Max—and all the others—from her mind every time they strayed in there, but she never forgot what an important figure he'd once been in her life. She supposed because her actual father had been largely absent while she was growing up and she'd never had an older, male influence in her life. Or maybe it was just that he'd become a friend. Of course, there was also the fact that he'd given her the first big opportunity she'd ever had in her life.

Without Max, nothing would have been the same.

"We have to get him back," she said, her pacing picking up speed. "This is Max."

"We know," Shane said.

"That's why we're here," Ash added.

"Shit," Ruby spit out, her mind suddenly racing faster than she could keep up. "What do we know?"

"Quite a bit," Ash said, going into her mastermind mode, as the team used to like to call it. Ruby was less than enthusiastic about being reminded that Ash's mastermind mode consisted of pacing as well, which made Ruby sit, though she couldn't keep her leg from jiggling.

"The kidnappers haven't kept it a secret. The moment they had him safely stowed away, I received a text instructing me to check my email."

"I'm assuming you've attempted a trace on the origin?"

"Of course," Ash said, and to her credit, she wasn't even snarky about it.

Had it been Ash questioning Ruby about it, Ruby would have been snarky times a thousand.

"Through the email, we discovered several things. First, we know Max is alive. They've provided proof of life via a video feed on a secured and encoded website."

Ruby stood. "Let me see."

"You can if you want," Shane jumped in, "but we can only assume they're able to track the IP of anyone who logs in, so unless you want these guys to know where you live, we might want to wait until we get somewhere else, or until we can get Bug on board."

Ruby sighed. "Fine. What else do we know?"

Ash tilted her head as if to say, *Could you possibly let me finish before you ask your requisite immeasurable sum of questions?* It took all Ruby had in her not to roll her eyes, since her very reasonable number of questions was usually what saved the team from certain disaster.

She did risk a glance at Shane, who just shrugged and gave her a knowing little smirk that was damned delectable, letting her know they were on the same wavelength. The "yes, Ash is an ogre's buttcrack but we have to humor her for Max's sake" wavelength.

This had to be about Max.

Max, who had taken her under his wing and showed her she had acting chops, at a time she didn't think she had any kind of chops. Hell, she couldn't even afford pork chops back then.

Max, who had been the only father figure she'd ever known, who'd brought her into the fold of his inner circle and made her the star of his show—well, one of the stars—the year she and Shane were set to graduate.

Max, whose inner circle was so much more than just an acting gig at some mostly unknown theater program—it was a real job, out there in the world doing good work. To this day Ruby still believed it had been good work, no matter how illegal most people would have considered it.

Max, who had warned her that love was never a good idea on the job.

And Max, who was the first to console her when that love had gone south and never, ever said, "I told you so."

He'd given her everything back then—her livelihood, his friendship, his acceptance. She'd had to fight for those things with everyone else, but Max just gave them easily and freely.

And he had done the same for Ash and Shane, and countless others along the way. They couldn't just leave him hanging.

Unfortunately, the people pulling Ash's strings must have known all that as well as Ruby did.

"The message was from the same people we used to work for. Max used to be the go-between for the jobs, but now that they have him, they somehow found me," she said, shrugging. "Who knows, maybe Max gave them something on me."

"Did Max even know where you were?" Shane jumped in with a question. And it was a good thing he did, since if he hadn't, Ruby would have called her out about throwing their friend under the bus, and that would have sent Ash over the edge. Ruby paused for a moment to imagine Ash sailing, quite literally, over the edge of a cliff, then spent the next twenty seconds trying to hide the smile attempting to force its way across her face.

"Of course not. When you guys insisted on no contact, I swore to you I would honor that, but Max always did have a way of finding things out," Ash said.

Ruby waved away her comment. "Whatever. Tell us what you know."

Ash looked like she wanted to continue to argue the point, but they all knew their most important resource now was time. "So, these people. They're not necessarily bad people—they do good things in the world—but they're not necessarily good people either. The one thing I do know for sure is that they are reasonable."

"Right," Shane jumped in. "Kidnapping an old man is a super-reasonable thing to do."

Exasperation coated Ash's face, but she did her best to ignore the interruption. "They are reasonable in the sense that they are fair—as I'm sure you well remember, the pay will be generous."

"I don't want their money," Ruby said, "I just want Max back."

"We can figure all that out later," Ash said. "The problem these people are having is they can't find a team they deem good enough to do a particular job. They still have people around the world doing the same kind of work we used to do, but something…special has come up and they don't trust anyone else."

Ruby closed her eyes and shook her head a little. "You know, for the way I can usually see every imaginable outcome to any given situation, I gotta say…being forced back into a life of crime because I was so damn trustworthy was not number one on my list of things I wanted to have happen today."

Chapter 4

If the whole thing hadn't been so disastrous, Shane would have laughed. As it stood, with Max at stake—one of his favorite people in the world, his mentor, for Christ's sake—he was having a hard time not letting the emotions of the situation get to him. Clearly, he'd been out of the practice of compartmentalizing for too long. He used to be so good at it. Then again, when everything in life was going your way, there wasn't a whole hell of a lot to have to shove into a tiny box and lock away on some high dusty shelf somewhere in the back of your brain. He'd filled that shelf right up to the top after Scotland, then kept the door on the memory storage unit locked down—with a little help from a ton of traveling, partying and booze ever since.

When Ash found him and pried the door open again, all the emotions had come oozing out, sitting right on the surface ever since.

Maybe that was why seeing Ruby again made it seem like his whole world was shifting off its axis.

She looked different. Her hair was cut shorter than the bob she used to wear, like she'd started getting the expensive haircuts that looked amazing even straight out of the shower. It suited her, made her edgier, like she was ready to take on anyone and anything. Not that she wasn't always like that, but now she was just…more herself somehow. It wasn't going to be good for the job, though—made her stand out too much.

Of course, she always stood out more than the rest of them, constantly having to use makeup to play down her features, make them more like everyone else's. Especially her lips—which he was trying very hard not to stare at as he watched her talk—shaped almost like a heart. And then there were those piercing gray eyes she hid under brown contacts when they were on the job. Eyes that kept flashing toward him as if looking for some kind of reassurance, of which, of course, he had none to give. He took another swig of wine, wishing it was something a whole lot stronger.

"Even if we agree to do this," Ruby said, "how do we know they're not just going to keep doing it over and over? Snatching one of us in the middle of the most inconvenient time ever and forcing us back into the game?"

"Look," Ash said, sounding impatient, "they've given me their word. They don't know who either of you are, or the rest of the team. They know Max and they know me, that's it. Once we're done with this and have Max back, I'll make sure they can never find either of us again."

"Um," Shane said, "how do you plan to do that?"

Ruby turned to Ash and raised a perfect eyebrow, as if to say, *Yeah, exactly.*

Ash sighed. "When I'm not on the job, I'm unfindable. As for Max…well, he's going to be difficult. Maybe this little kidnapping stint will help convince him. He's going to have to close the school and go into hiding."

"He's never going to do that," Ruby said.

"For you guys, he might," Ash said, knowing Max might not do anything for her anymore, not after Kaden.

Max had felt an unreasonable amount of guilt over the Kaden disaster, since he'd been the one who'd brought him in. Max had brought everyone into the crew—his acting school was an incredible source, but with Kaden, it had been different. Scotland had been his first job. Max had plucked him from his class earlier that month and essentially sent him to his death, and while the rest of the crew hadn't known him very well yet, they'd all known he would have been a star in the business. He had the power to make people around him feel good. Hell, even Shane missed the damn kid and he'd barely known him. Kaden had been one of those guys who just…left a mark on people wherever he went.

Shane put his elbows on his knees and ran his hands through his hair as Ruby let out a long sigh.

"If it wasn't for Max, you wouldn't still be standing in my living room," Ruby said to Ash, spitting the words out like they tasted foul.

"Well, it is for Max," was all Ash said, taking a long drink from her wineglass. "So, are you in or not?"

Ruby glanced from Ash to Shane. "Are you in?" she asked him.

He shrugged one shoulder. "I wouldn't be here if I wasn't. I mean, it's Max, right?"

Ruby's shoulders slumped ever so slightly, then she straightened and turned to Ash. "Yeah, I'm in."

Shane felt a weight lift. He hadn't known if Ruby would agree to do it, even if it were to save Max. As he leaned back in relief, his eyes landed on the master's degree from Columbia she had sitting in a nondescript frame on her bookshelf. He didn't know how she did it. During all those years they were pulling jobs, Ruby had kept at her studies—more than kept at them, excelled at them—and had come out of it all barely breaking a sweat. She'd gone so far in life, a fact that was obvious in everything—the way she looked, the way she acted, hell, even the way they were sitting in this very expensive apartment drinking wine Shane knew was worth more than anything he'd had to drink in the past three years. And she hadn't even known she was expecting company.

There were no two ways about it—Ruby Alexander was so

far out of his league he was pretty sure they weren't even playing the same damn game anymore.

"So, what are we in for?" Ruby asked, what small bit of the
patience she had left waning.

Ash raised her eyebrows. "As you would expect, it's not
going to be easy."

The urge to strike at Ash with some kind of comment about
the word *easy* even leaving her lips flooded through Ruby.
Scotland was supposed to have been easy, then turned out to
be the end of everything. But she couldn't delay this any longer. She had to know what they were up against.

"We've been tasked to steal back an emerald scepter rumored to have once belonged to a Swiss family of high nobil-
ity. It's made of pure gold and is encrusted with three hundred
sixty-eight diamonds, which comprise an ornate cage-like enclosure for the centerpiece—a massive round emerald."

"Value?" Shane asked as he leaned over Ruby's shoulder.

He smelled sweet and fresh—a scent that brought back
way too many memories and made something twinge low in
her stomach.

"There are whispers of a hundred million," Ash said.

"Who did it belong to?" Ruby asked.

"We haven't been told specifically. We can only assume,
based on our previous work with these people, that they hope
to return it to the rightful owners, which more likely than not
is some aristocrat in Switzerland."

The answer was vague. Different from their other jobs with
these people. Normally they laid out specifically what the job
was and who it was for. Ruby had always had the understanding that the people they worked for were a sort of broker—a
go-between—liaising with the team and those families who'd
had their valuables stolen at one time or another throughout history. It was a tricky business given the way history

tended to get skewed and rewritten according to the people in power at any given time. It had always been Ruby's job to confirm all the recovered goods would be going to the legitimate, rightful owners, and being given such imprecise information didn't sit well.

Ash swiped to the next photo on her phone. "The destination we'll be headed to is…remote."

Ruby didn't like the way she said the word *remote*.

"How remote?" Shane asked, clearly thinking the same thing as Ruby.

"About as remote as it gets. Nestled into the top of a mountain. The Swiss Alps, to be precise, on an unnamed peak—the nearest town is Grindelwald."

Ruby let out a long sigh. The top of a damned mountain. That was a new one.

"And security?" Shane asked.

Ash tilted her head. "Pretty much what you'd expect from people paranoid enough to build their complex on the top of a mountain. There are two ways in…helicopter or the large private gondola, which is operated by guards at the top and bottom of the mountain. Once you get to the top, there are additional guards in four perimeter towers."

"These guys are paranoid," Ruby couldn't help but point out.

Of course, she also couldn't help but think that since her team was planning a heist, the intense caution was more than warranted.

Ash nodded. "The main structure itself is massive—almost more like a castle than a modern house. As far as technology, we don't know much, other than to assume it's top-of-the-line."

"Up there, any network would have to be run through satellite," Shane said.

"We're going to need Bug," Ruby added.

"We are," Ash said, an expression crossing her face like she was not particularly happy with that situation.

Not that Ruby could blame her. Ash and Bug had a complicated relationship, considering Bug was completely in love with her. The infatuation may have faded a little after Scotland, but Bug had defended Ash to the end, saying it had all been an accident and couldn't have been avoided. Of course, all of it could have been avoided if they'd all had a little more time to go through all the proper checks and procedures, but there wasn't much sense arguing with Bug. He would defend Ash with his dying breath. The fact that Ash barely gave him the time of day didn't seem to matter.

Ruby's insides coiled up like a not-so-fun little whirlwind. Why were they following this woman again?

Max.

She had to think of Max. And do whatever she could to mitigate the situation. Ruby glanced at Shane, who looked like he was thinking the exact same thing.

If Ash was going to give her vague information, then they'd just have to work harder.

This was not going to be another Scotland.

"Do we need anyone else?" Ruby asked.

"I want to keep the team small. The fewer people who know about this the better," Ash said.

Besides, Ruby thought, there wasn't anyone else, was there?

"These pictures are pretty far away," Shane said. "Couldn't we get in there with a drone or something for some better intel?"

"These were from a drone," Ash said, "which fed these few images to us before it was shot down."

Shane raised an eyebrow. "So, these guys aren't messing around."

"They are not," Ash said, her voice clipped, like she might have been a little annoyed by her precious drone being destroyed. No doubt it had cost an arm and a lung and obtained through some mysterious techno-wizard network, since it would have to be untraceable.

"Doesn't sound like there's a whole lot of good news," Ruby said. "I don't see an 'in' here."

Ash took a deep breath. "These people don't build a place like this for tourists. It's elite. It's remote. And it's damn near impenetrable."

"So, what's the good news?" Ruby asked, sensing Ash was leading to something important.

"The good news is that in three days, they're having a party. And we're going to make sure we're all invited."

Chapter 5

Ash assigned the task of finding Bug to Shane and Ruby, then left before they could argue.

"I guess the longer she can put off that inevitable uncomfortable situation, the better," Shane said.

"Ugh, poor Bug is an awkward mess around the woman," Ruby said.

"I do not get what the draw is," Shane replied, but then again, when Ruby was anywhere in the vicinity, he had a hard time seeing other women, period.

"I don't know," Ruby said. "I think he likes the way she wields power. In his regular life he always needs to be the one calling the shots." She shrugged. "Maybe he likes being bossed around."

Shane made a face. "I do not love the visual that conjures up," he said, a flash of a bedroom scene flitting through his head.

"Ew, stop," Ruby said, apparently reading his mind.

"So, are we doing this now?" he asked.

Ruby let out a long sigh and tipped back the rest of her wine. "I guess we have to," she said, knowing as well as Shane did that Bug was a creature of the night and if they didn't find him before sunup, he'd be in hibernation until this time tomorrow. She glanced down at the clothes she'd thrown on. "But just to be clear, I do not give one rat's ass about how Ash is starting to make this look like a heist. I just want to get in, get Max and get out. That's it."

Shane nodded once. "Sounds good to me."

"Okay, good," Ruby said. "I'm glad we're on the same page. Just let me get changed."

"I think you look great," Shane said, tossing her his most dazzling smile, but Ruby just kept walking, throwing one of her famous eye rolls right back at him.

It was a reaction he was more than used to, and he loved it. Honestly, he loved any reaction he could get out of her. He'd meant it about looking great too. Even standing beside Ash, who was in her heels and fancy little skirt, Ruby outshone her in bare feet and rumpled clothes she'd clearly picked up off the floor or something and thrown on. Tenfold.

Ruby emerged from her room in jeans and a white T-shirt, throwing on an oversize leather jacket and combat boots. Shane marveled at how the woman could pull off pretty much any look. She was damn sexy in anything from her sweatpants to the red evening gown she'd worn on the job in Kosovo that no matter how long he lived, he would never forget.

"Any thoughts on where to start?" she asked, opening the door and motioning for him to go through so she could lock up behind them.

"I was thinking our best bet would be—"

"His sister," Ruby said, saying it with him as he said the last words.

He nodded and they were off, not needing to say more. They both knew where to find her, and Shane briefly wondered if they should be concerned. If they knew where to find Penny Elliot, then so might anyone else. Of course, the man they referred to as Bug—Jacob Elliot—would likely be pegged as an elite hacker about as readily as a still-frozen ice-cream cone might burst forth from Lucifer's butt.

But that was only because the man was a master at hiding in plain sight.

An hour later they were easing into the parking lot of a bar called Twisted Trance, conveniently and purposefully located just outside the outskirts of town. They could have made it in twenty minutes, but Shane had used every evasion trick he knew in case they were being followed.

"What's the play here?" Ruby asked, already appearing to know the answer. She wasn't even trying to hide that she was going to enjoy watching it all go down.

"Obviously I'll do the talking," Shane said, throwing her a side-eye.

Penny had never kept the fact that she was 100.7 percent enamored of Shane a secret. In fact, the next ten minutes were very likely going to prove to be the most uncomfortable ten minutes Shane had experienced in a while. And it wasn't just the fact that the woman liked to flirt—hell, Shane liked to flirt too—but it was the way she flirted. Crawling up all over a guy, which was a tad uncomfortable given her love of weightlifting and tossing drunken bikers out of her bar.

Without even breaking a sweat.

Shane assumed she could do some real physical damage in the bedroom, and *that* was not something he wanted to ever find out for sure.

"It'll be fine, she's a sweetheart," Ruby said, trying to coax him out of the car.

It was a fair point—Penny was a sweetheart—but it wasn't her sweet heart Shane was worried about. It was her biceps that could likely pop the head right off a guy if she ever caught him in a choke hold.

He tilted his head from side to side, cracking his neck. "Okay, let's do this."

Ruby followed, trying—and failing—to hide what could only be categorized as a snicker.

Inside, the bar was...atmospheric. If, by atmospheric, one meant smoky, smelly and dark. Exactly the way a biker bar wanted to be. Just sketchy enough to make anyone too much on the up-and-up turn straight around and peel out of there as fast as the speed limit would allow. It used to be raided by cops on the regular, but they never found anything, likely because they were searching for signs of drugs, prostitution, maybe a little human trafficking.

But none of that was the kind of shady that happened here.

It was genius, really—the absolute last place a law enforcement agency—or anyone else—would ever look for one of the world's most elite hackers.

Even as they headed toward the bar, Shane couldn't see a single sign of tech at all. It had to be there. Bug was the foremost expert in the latest security measures and wasn't about to leave himself exposed, but he did a damn fine job hiding it. There were, however, about thirty uneasy eyes following their every move.

"Well, look what the smitten kitten dragged in," the booming voice said from somewhere in the smoky depths behind the bar.

"Hey, Penny," Shane said, hoping his acting was a lot steadier than his stomach was. "How've you been doing?"

Penny raised one heavy eyebrow. "Doing a lot better now that your fine ass has graced my presence," she said, tilting her head liberally in an attempt to get a better view of said ass.

"Hey, Pen," Ruby said, hoisting herself onto one of the bar stools, looking as comfortable as if she was lounging in her own house. "How about a beer?" She glanced at Shane. "You better get one for him too. And maybe a shot of something. Looks like he could use it."

"He sure does," Penny said, her eyes grazing all the way up him nice and slowly.

Once Penny's gaze turned away to get their drinks, Shane finally found the fortitude to prop himself on the stool beside Ruby.

"You can saunter into the Palace of the High King of Zendovia like you own the place, but this one woman reduces you to a nineteen eighties potluck jelly salad," Ruby teased, just loud enough for him to hear. "You know, all jiggly inside," she finished with a goofy grin.

Shane gave her a glare. "Hilarious."

Penny returned with the drinks. She actually did have a shot of whiskey, which she set in front of Shane with a beer. He might have even been offended if he hadn't needed it so bad, downing it in a flash and enjoying the distracting burn.

"What brings you to our neck of the woods, handsome?" Penny asked, laser focused on Shane, barely paying attention to Ruby, who sipped her beer, quietly enjoying every second of the Squirming Shane Show.

"Oh, you know," Shane said, clearing his throat. Honestly, Penny brought out the worst performances of his life. "Just feeling restless and looking for something to do."

Of course, Penny knew there was precisely one reason Shane and Ruby would ever set foot in Twisted Trance—they were looking for Bug. She also knew it would never happen unless something big was going down. But she was well aware of the drill.

"Well, if you're feeling restless," Penny said, shooting him an actual wink, "I've been known to rid a man of his jitters real quick." She licked her lips, which then spread into a scandalous smile.

Oh, dear god, was about all Shane could think, but he recovered, saying, "I bet you have," and sending his own, somewhat less scandalous, smile her way.

"I get off at two," Penny said, grabbing his coaster and writing on the back. "Call me." She laid down the coaster, with one more wink for good measure.

Blessedly, she headed off to take care of some of her other customers.

Shane got down to the business of drinking his beer, sipping rather more quickly than he needed to, but they'd gotten what they came for and he wanted to get the hell out. They also didn't want to look suspicious, so they needed to make an attempt at finishing their beers. This was a place to drink, not the kind of place people sauntered into, took two sips of a cocktail and went on their merry way.

Mercifully, Ruby was on the same page, and did a damn good job at finishing her beer faster than even he did. He laid thirty bucks on the counter and pocketed the coaster as they headed out the door.

Once they were safely outside, Shane made sure they were alone, then checked what Penny had written, showing the single word to Ruby.

"Barn?" she whispered, but they kept heading for the car.

When they drove in, they'd both noticed the huge, decrepit barn out behind the roadside bar, but hadn't thought much of it—places like this were often remodeled old farmhouses.

They drove back out of the parking lot anyway, not wanting to leave a strange car a regular would recognize as out of place faster than you could say "dive bar."

About a mile up the road, Shane eased the car onto a trail that led toward a cluster of trees, which he pulled behind. It wasn't the best disguise job in the world, but unless someone came down this particular trail, no one would see it until the sun rose.

They ran back off the road, sneaking onto the property from the back, making their way to the barn.

This time it was Shane's turn to ask, "What's the play here?"

But Ruby just shook her head. "There is no play."

Before Shane could stop her, Ruby sauntered right up to the barn and pushed one of the giant doors open with a lot of effort and an alarming amount of noise. He hurried in behind her, heaving the door shut behind him, but before he could even turn all the way around, a light flicked on, and ominous clicks sounded around them.

"Well, I guess we can safely say we've found Bug," Shane said, his eyes darting from one gun barrel to the next to the next.

He followed Ruby's lead and put up his hands.

"I gotta say—" A voice came from somewhere in the back of the barn where Ruby didn't dare glance, since the throng of men and guns pointed at her face were a tad distracting. The voice was punctuated by slow, heavy footsteps. "—this was not the way I saw my night turning out."

The men with guns parted, and Ruby had never been so happy to see a six-foot-two, heavily muscled man with arms covered in tattoos in her life.

"Hey, Bug," she said, rushing forward to clutch him into a big hug.

There was nothing on earth that felt quite like one of Bug's bear hugs, swallowing her like she was the bug and he was the cocoon keeping her safe.

"At ease, my friends," Bug said as he released Ruby and noticed the men still had their aim squarely on Shane.

Ruby wasn't sure if she should be happy or offended that they'd all determined Shane was the one to keep their eyes on.

"I'm going to have to train them better," Bug whispered to Ruby. "You and I both know you're the real danger around here."

Ruby smiled. At least someone appreciated her. "And that's why you're my favorite," Ruby said, leaning up on her tiptoes to give the massive lug a kiss on the cheek.

The men lowered their guns and Shane joined them before Bug started walking toward the back of the barn.

"Let's go to my lair," he said, without a hint of irony.

"Lair?" Ruby couldn't help but ask.

Bug shrugged a heavily muscled shoulder. "Always wanted a lair and now I have one. I feel like it would be a shame to call it something boring like a hangout or, worse, man cave." He gave a little shudder.

"Touché," Shane said as Bug lifted a small, unassuming panel up from the floor and began his descent into it.

Ruby raised an eyebrow at Shane as they followed into the dark space. The idea they could be headed into a trap flitted through her mind briefly, but there were few people she trusted as much as she did Bug. She didn't doubt for a second that Bug had some sort of top-tier security measures in place if someone outside his chosen circle got in, though. And she'd bet her life it was some kind of *Mission Impossible* spy level shit too.

As they landed on the floor below, Ruby had to admit she was a bit disappointed. She wasn't sure what she'd expected, but it hadn't been another barren level of wood walls, wood floor and a single wooden desk slapped right in the middle.

Bug started toward the desk.

"Not quite what I expected," Shane said, sounding both tentative and amused, like one might sound wandering through a carnival funhouse just waiting for something to jump out at them.

"Have a seat," Bug said, motioning to the two seats across from him as he sat in his own chair and fired up the monitor on the desk.

"As far as lairs go, I thought there'd be a little more to—" Ruby started to say, but was cut off by a sudden movement of the floor.

The entire desk, all three chairs and the floor it all sat on started to slowly drop below the rest of the floor, like some sort of giant elevator.

As they continued down, Ruby got her first glimpses of an honest-to-goodness, for-real lair—dozens of screens, banks of computers and a plethora of additional gadgets and machines.

"Right. This is more like it," she finished as the floor came to a gentle halt and a panel slid across the opening above their heads to hide the real lair once again.

With utter satisfaction on his face, Bug spoke. "So, what brings you to my humble abode?"

Shane tilted his head. "How long have you been waiting to be able to see someone's reaction to that little trick?"

Bug's expression slid into a grin. "Since shortly after our last job. It's not like I can invite just anyone down here."

"No, I would think not," Ruby said, her grin almost as wide as Bug's. "This place is amazing."

He nodded his thanks. "But seriously, what's up? I figure it's got to be big if it brought the two of you together on my doorstep."

Ruby's and Shane's expressions turned serious.

"It's Max," Ruby said. "He's been taken."

"When? Where?" Bug asked, getting up from the boring desk and sauntering up to a very different one, the workstation all glass, metal and with stunningly copious amounts of technology.

"We don't know where. We only sort of know a who," Shane said. "The people we all used to work for."

Ruby didn't know what Bug was already typing so furiously away at, but he stopped and spun around on his chair. "Bastards," he said, shaking his head as he turned back around. "Let's start with where he was when he was taken, then."

"Two nights ago, somewhere between the theater and his house," Ruby said.

It never did cease to amaze her the way Bug—this giant, hulking mass of a man—could work a keyboard, his massive fingers whipping over the keys, the tattoos on his forearms a frenzy of movement.

"There he is," Bug said after an astonishingly short amount of time.

Ruby and Shane turned their attention to the large screen on the wall several feet beyond Bug's workstation, where Bug was already pulling up the footage. As the image of Max sauntering down the empty street flickered on, a swell of something—nostalgia, a sense of missing him, fear—washed over her.

Shane made a musing sound. "He looks happy."

Ruby nodded. "Opening night must have gone well," she said, knowing how much Max lived for those nights, where all his hard work paid off through his newest students up on stage. The buzz of the always sold-out crowd, the rush of nerves, the pride so apparent on his face after every performance. Ruby could tell it was all there, dancing behind a glint in Max's eye as he walked along, seemingly without a care in the world.

"Still the last one to leave, I see," Bug said.

"I don't know how many times one man needs to hear that he should change up his routine," Ruby said, frustrated that Max never did heed the warning they'd all given him time and time again.

"Pick a cliché, any cliché," Shane said, with a smirk. "Can't teach an old dog new tricks, perhaps?"

Ruby rolled her eyes, but she knew it was true. It wasn't for any lack of knowledge that Max had been careless—he just didn't seem to think he'd ever be important enough to get in trouble. Strange idea for a man who'd made the better part of his living in crime, but here they were. Maybe Max was just so used to being deep in the shadows of the theater, allowing everyone else to take the spotlight, that he thought the same went for his other life too.

As they watched, Max seemed to tense, so slightly they might not have noticed had they not been waiting for it. Then out of nowhere, a van pulled up and, in a flash, they were beside him, throwing the door open and hauling Max inside before he had a chance to react.

The screen switched from camera to camera as Bug transferred from feed to feed, following the van, while a lump formed in Ruby's throat. A few minutes later, the van found a more remote area of the city, which also meant the street cam feeds ended.

"Shit," Bug said. "They knew where to go."

Ruby nodded. "We gave them the intel back when we used to pull jobs for them."

Shane let out a heavy sigh. "What next?"

Ruby swallowed, willing her throat to return to normal. But they were a hell of a long way from normal.

"Next we go see what Max has been up to for the past three years."

Chapter 6

Shane had forgotten what it was like to be this close to Ruby. Or, more accurately, he'd pushed those memories from existence with a force of will rivaling that of a professional marathon runner.

But now that he was back in her company, he found his fortitude starting to wane. Quickly. Ruby was so much the same as she used to be, but she was different somehow too. She was both softer and stronger, and worse, she smelled like a damned strawberry sundae dipped in moonlight.

Jesus, was he a freakin' poet now? What the hell did "dipped in moonlight" even mean?

The only way he could think of to describe the bloody intoxicating smell, was what it meant.

He let out a long sigh, trying to focus on the road instead of the intense awareness that she was sitting right there. So close all he could think of was dipping strawberries into moonlight, for god's sake.

"What?" she asked, shooting him a quizzical look.

"It's just…surreal being in this place. I never thought any of us would see each other again," he said.

I never thought I'd see you again.

Ruby stared at him, making him shift in his seat, like she could read his mind. She'd always had a way of doing that. Looking at him like she was sure she knew what he was thinking but couldn't decide whether she thought he was a genius or an absolutely atrocious human being.

Her stare always felt like this intense, significant thing, but for all he knew, she might just be trying to figure out what she was going to have for dinner.

Bug pulled the car to a stop a few blocks from their destination. The world felt a little haunted as Shane and Ruby stepped out of the car.

"This is close to where it happened," Bug said, noting the cameras with a tilt of his head.

If they'd been able to hack into the feeds, it was likely whoever had Max could do the same.

"We have to assume we're being watched," Shane said.

They were used to the idea. They'd all trained under Max, after all. The only reason any of them were there was because they'd felt at home in the spotlight—or were at least willing to tolerate it. Shane got the feeling Bug wasn't into being adored but was able to become someone else the way intense acting situations allowed him to do, like it was simply part of the game. Shane, on the other hand, had to admit he loved the adoration. What wasn't to like? Honestly, he couldn't understand what introversion was even about. People had to be kidding themselves, right? For him, life was all about feeling seen. Because, what the hell else was there?

Bug peeled off down an alley while Shane and Ruby kept walking toward Max's place.

"You got us?" Shane said quietly into the comms equipment they'd gotten together at Bug's.

"Loud and clear," Bug replied.

"Let us know when we're good," Ruby said as she slowly eased the gate open in front of Max's house.

The neighborhood was shockingly quiet. Sure, it was the middle of the night, but Shane would have thought someone would be up. Maybe he'd just gotten used to a different kind of nightlife—the kind where a lot of alcohol and loud music were involved. Maybe this was how normal people lived.

"The area has a lot of seniors," Ruby said, which Shane supposed made sense, though he would have felt better if there'd been a TV on in one of the windows.

It was hard to believe every single resident on the block slept so well. It felt like he hadn't had a full night's sleep in decades.

"Shit!" Ruby whisper-yelled as a bright spark lit up the night momentarily.

"What the hell was that?" Shane asked.

But Ruby was already scrambling, whipping something out of her pocket and crouching to the ground, frantically chopping/stabbing/sawing at something down there.

Shane crouched in front of her to get a better look but was shooed away.

"Out of the light, I need to see," Ruby said, as she continued, more frantic by the second.

In his hurry—brought on by the scolding and vehemence in her voice—Shane sort of flung himself backward, landing on his butt. Which might not have been so bad, except Max had his sprinklers on a timer, as evidenced by the giant wet patch thoroughly soaking the ass of his jeans.

Ruby finally stopped hacking and let her shoulders relax.

"What the hell was that?" Bug said, the comms cluing him in to something clearly going down.

"Detonator fuse," Ruby said, her eyes following the wiry line almost directly to where Shane's hand sat.

"Jesus," Shane said, gingerly lifting his hand and leaning away from the explosive. "What if a kid had come in here or something? Or, like, doesn't he have a mailman?"

Ruby leaned in close to the device now that the danger had been neutralized. "It's just firecrackers," she said with a shrug. "Just a warning system."

"Would have been one hell of a warning if my hand had been sitting right on top of it," Shane said, easing himself up to his feet, wiping the back of his jeans even though it was futile.

"Stay alert, guys," Ruby said. "Something's definitely going on here."

"Well. Ho. Lee. Shit," Bug said.

"What?" Shane asked.

"That little welcome warning got me checking a little closer than I normally would—since this is a simple security system—and sure enough, Max has this thing enhanced."

"Enhanced how?" Shane asked.

"Like an innocuous little wire I might not have normally noticed, and just so happens to lead to something a little more intense than a firecracker, how," Bug replied.

"What does Max have himself mixed up in?" Ruby said.

Shane and Ruby made it to the front door, going slow, making sure there weren't any additional fun surprises that would signal the entire neighborhood to their presence.

"In position," Ruby said, scanning the area, the little knife she'd used to cut the fuse still in her hand.

"Give me a second," Bug said.

Hacking a security system never took Bug this long, Shane thought, as he caught Ruby's eye. The look in it didn't make him feel much better.

"Okay, cameras and alarm are disarmed but keep your guard up. This is some old-school stuff he's using here. Manual. A lot of it is unhackable."

"Copy," Shane said, his hand on the doorknob, turning slowly.

He pushed on the door so it would swing open, allowing him to assess the situation before he moved to step inside. Across the house, he could see the back door slowly opening as Bug did the same at the rear of the building.

Almost in unison, two arrows released, whizzing past each

door into the line of fire where a less cautious person would likely be standing had they opened the door and stepped straight in.

Bug let out a low whistle. "That is some real Indiana Jones type shit right there."

The team spent the next hour clearing the house. Gingerly searching for actual, honest-to-god booby traps—disarming them where they could and setting them off while safely out of the way where they couldn't.

"How the hell did he even live in this place?" Shane said, as he searched a desk for hidden dangers.

"I suppose once you know where they all are, it only takes a few minutes to disarm them," Ruby said.

"It's a lot of work every time you come and go from a place," he continued. "I'd hate to have to run back in if I forgot my phone or something."

Ruby smiled, nodding a little. "One thing's for sure. Something was definitely going on with Max. This is not your normal theater director kind of place."

They had all sworn they were getting out of the game, but maybe Max had a harder time letting go than the rest of them. If so, Shane could relate.

Bug was at the back of the house, doing a final sweep for out-of-place electronic equipment such as listening devices, cameras or anything that could potentially blow up in their faces. Literally.

Ruby stuck close to Shane. Or maybe it was Shane sticking close to Ruby. He never could tell. They were always drawn to each other no matter who else was around or what else might be going on.

He watched as she began her search at the desk.

"What do you think we'll find?" Shane asked as he started pulling books off the bookshelf, opening them to see if they had any hidden compartments or loose papers hidden inside.

"Well, I guess we can assume Max was still up to something… less than legitimate," Ruby said, "maybe something similar to what we used to do. Hell, maybe it was *exactly* what we used to do. Max was the one who started us all in the business, after all."

"But he was never the mastermind. Ash was always the one calling the shots."

"Speaking of," Ruby said. "Why the hell are we out here risking our asses and she's off doing who knows what?"

It was the way things usually were. The team out doing the dirty work while Ash was holed up in some undisclosed location being the brains of the operation. Shane was pretty sure she wasn't any smarter than the rest of them, she was just incredibly organized. And truth be told, she wasn't great in the field since her acting left something to be desired. But she'd been one of Max's first students and Max had a soft spot for her. To be fair, Shane hadn't had any misgivings about her role on the team until…well, until he did.

"Oh, you know," Shane said. "She's just off planning a diabolical heist. The usual."

Ruby smiled. The unexpected flip his stomach made caught him off guard. She must have seen something change on his face. She quickly looked away, sorting through some papers on the desk.

They fell into a comfortable silence as they got to work. There was nothing on the bookshelf even hinting at anything out of the ordinary going on in Max's life.

"You got anything over there?" he asked.

"Nothing besides some questionable deductions on his annual tax return and a few cryptic entries in his calendar, although *meet F.P. for lunch* isn't all that damning."

Shane moved from the bookshelf to a small table beside the couch, but it only took about three seconds to determine it held nothing but a couple remotes. He spent some time searching for potential hidden compartments but came up empty.

When the living room was exhausted, Shane moved to the kitchen. He hated searching kitchens. It was rare they ever found anything valuable in a kitchen, and there were just so many damned places to look. But he dove in and started with the freezer. It was honestly weird how often people literally "froze their assets" even though it was one of the oldest tricks on every detective show there was. He supposed people thought they were being clever.

But Max was not one of those people. There was nothing in there but a few microwave meals and a large bottle of vodka.

The fridge was equally uninteresting.

It sounded like Bug was in the room just above, walking slowly and steadily. Everyone had their jobs, and Bug's was tech. Tech in the form of surveillance, tech in the form of communication devices and tech in the form of digital intel. He sighed. What he wouldn't give for an expertly hidden thumb drive right about then.

Ruby had already started on the lower cabinets, so Shane moved to the uppers. It was a tedious routine, but one they'd done a thousand times. It was funny how the movies always made it seem like the day of a heist was the only day that mattered. Of course, Shane supposed, depicting the days upon days of recon would be exceedingly dull.

After a thorough sweep above the cupboards, behind the appliances, and on the floor for any loose linoleum or marks indicating a trap door, they finished in the kitchen and moved on to the main bedroom, which looked like the most used room in the house. It made sense, considering Max spent the majority of his time at the theater.

"Shit," Shane said.

As was their way, Ruby was just coming into the room be-hind him. "What?"

"I think we're in the wrong damn place."

It's odd how some cities have neighborhoods with such a robust night life you'd never find yourself alone on the streets at night, and then there are other neighborhoods that are more like ghost towns after a certain time of day. The Guardian Theater was in one of the ghost town places.

It was a testament to the quality of Max's productions that he never had a hard time filling the place. The Guardian wasn't in a bad neighborhood. In fact, it was in a nice part of town. But it was on the edge of a suburban area, so there weren't a whole lot of people out and about at four in the morning.

The sun would be coming up soon, though, and that would change everything.

"We should hurry," Ruby said.

The last thing they needed was some overcurious early riser who just happened to glance out their window at the beginning of a new day to see three strangers wandering down the street.

Ruby was suddenly very aware of her new hair. She's spent so many years wearing it just past her shoulders in soft waves—like half the female population tended to lean to-ward, which was exactly the point. Once she was out of the business, she could do with it what she wanted, and she may have gone a little over the top. Her current short, edgy cut was rather more…standout-ish than was optimal, given the cur-rent circumstance.

Shane didn't have any particularly stand-out features, other than the fact that he was infuriatingly attractive, which made him the person most people looked at in any room. Add in Bug, a massively muscled, heavily tattooed bald guy, and the trio was not especially incognito.

They'd decided to walk, trying to get a sense of what the

area would have been like for Max on the night he was taken, but Ruby was questioning their choice.

"Yeah, sun'll be up soon," Shane said.

Always the best one with locks, Shane coaxed the back door of the theater open moments later without a sound.

The theater was even more eerily quiet than the street. The smell of the place instantly brought Ruby back to a time when it had felt like home. *Was* a second home, really, considering she'd spent way more time there than she did the shabby two-bedroom she'd shared with Maurine, another theater student, whom she'd lost touch with pretty much immediately after the season's class ended. Max hadn't asked Maurine to stay on for the other type of work once the theater season was over.

Once inside, the three of them lit up the flashlights on their phones, confident no one would see from the street. There were large windows at the front of the theater, but the performance area was closed off from the lobby and they'd come in the backstage entrance.

"I won't be able to do a full sweep," Bug said, "but I'll check for any obvious signs that they were watching Max…or listening in."

Ruby nodded and moved toward the stage, her breath catching when Shane's hand landed on the small of her back. It was a maneuver they'd done a thousand times in dark places. A protective thing, a reassurance that the other was still there with them.

Shane had done it instinctually—an old habit coming back to haunt him. Maybe it was because Ruby stiffened a little, but he jerked his hand away and quietly cleared his throat.

"Sorry," he whispered.

"It's fine," Ruby replied.

But the jolt of energy that shot through her at the heat of his touch made her realize things were very far from fine.

"I'm going to check out the dressing rooms for old times'

sake," Shane said, though Ruby suspected he was giving her some space. Which she desperately needed, but she also hated that he knew it was what she needed.

As Ruby entered Max's office, the door squeaking the way it always had, more of those familiar feelings started to come back.

As far as offices went, Max's was enormous. He loved being surrounded by people—the actors, the crew, even some of his favorites from the audience sometimes. Ruby couldn't count how many times there'd been a full-fledged party going on in that very space.

But there had been quiet times too. The day Max had explained to her and Shane about the other jobs he did, inviting them to join one of his crews. The man could convince anyone of anything. He'd let them know in no uncertain terms it was dangerous work, and it was definitely not on the right side of the law, but he'd convinced them it was the right thing to do. They'd be helping people. Making a difference in the world.

And it had felt right for a long time.

Ruby flicked on the light, realizing she could because there were no windows in the room. She'd never thought it was strange before, but she wondered if it had been on purpose—a precaution Max had planned out. After the booby trap situation at his house, nothing would have surprised her.

Her eyes landed on the lamp standing in the back corner of the room with the crack in its stained-glass shade. The crack that had been her fault. Well, hers and Shane's. Ruby still didn't know who'd stumbled first that night at the tail end of one of Max's famous end-of-the-week parties. She remembered the day itself like it had been five days ago instead of five years, even though she'd had her fair share of the wine Max had provided.

Ruby had wondered how he could afford to buy so much booze and food for everyone, but that was before she knew about his side gig. She thought it would be a onetime thing and should enjoy the opportunity to its fullest.

Just as she was starting to feel the warm buzz, the kind that felt like relaxing into a hot tub on a cool summer night, Shane had sauntered over. They'd met earlier in the week but hadn't talked much, though every time he'd glance in her direction, Ruby could feel something. It might have been one of those "all in her head" kind of somethings, but she didn't think so, and was anxious to find out for sure.

"Hey," he'd said, looking adorably shy, though Ruby couldn't help think he had to be putting his acting on display.

"Um, hey," she'd said back, her brain frantically searching for something interesting to say.

"So, is The Guardian Academy of Dramatic Arts all you'd hoped it would be?" He said it in the cheesiest voice he could muster, which made his question pretty endearing.

She'd smiled, wondering for a moment if his sweet woodsy scent was meant to lull women away from their senses and out of their clothes, because that was the exact effect it was having on her. Her first instinct was to volley some sort of melodramatic answer back, but something about Shane made her want to be more honest. More herself.

"It's exceeding my expectations so far," she'd finally said, the wine confidence she was feeling making the words more suggestive than she'd intended.

But one can't argue with wine confidence so she went with it, letting her eyes take a little stroll down his torso and back up, being way bolder than she should be, especially considering she had to finish out the class with this guy. But when her gaze met his again, he did not seem to mind.

"So, why acting?" she'd asked.

Shane shrugged. "I never could figure out what I wanted to be when I grew up, so I figured, why not everything?"

She nodded. "Choices *are* hard." She grinned.

"Some of them are," he'd said, leaning a bit closer.

"I'm Shane, by the way," he'd said, holding out his hand, though as close as they were standing, the handshake was a bit crowded, to say the least.

Still, she'd taken his hand, enjoying the warmth radiating through her at his touch. "Ruby."

"Like the gem," he'd said, tilting his head. "Makes sense."

She'd given him a grin and rolled her eyes as if he were being very unoriginal even though the truth was, she'd always wished a hot guy would say something like that about her name, though none ever had. Until then.

"I'm afraid I can't come up with something witty to say about your name," she'd said.

"It's what I get for having a boring old name."

"Definitely not boring," she'd said. "It's a good acting name. And it suits you."

"Thanks," he'd said, like it was a question.

She'd smiled. "The real question is, what is the last name to go with it? With that information, I'd be able to tell if you're going to make it as a famous actor."

He'd grinned back, sort of scrunching his face. "I'm not sure I want to know," he said. "What if it's bad news?"

"I don't think it will be bad news," she'd said, her voice becoming flirtier of its own accord, apparently along with her body, which also seemed to be moving of its own accord, leaning in even farther.

He let out a big breath. "Okay, then, it's Meyers. Shane Meyers."

Her eyes lit up. "Ah, very good. Yes, I think that's a fine stage name."

"It's my real name."

She nodded. "Sure, but all that matters is whether people will remember it."

Shane tilted his head in agreement. "Okay, maybe that's true," he'd said. "But I can promise you one thing, Ruby…"

Her eyebrows rose in question.

"It doesn't matter what your last name is," he'd said, the gap between them shrinking even more, "there is no way in hell I'd ever forget you."

His gaze moved from her eyes to her lips, the air between them heavy with that fresh woodsy smell. Ruby was acutely aware of the delicate gap between them—so tenuous, so easy to close. Ruby let herself give in fully to the wine confidence, traveling the final small distance, brushing her lips on his, then drawing away, as if asking a question.

Shane had answered, kissing her back, his hand tracing the curve of her waist, curling around to pull her in. But it was Ruby who'd kept the moment going, her hand climbing up his arm, finding the back of his neck and drawing him closer.

She knew there was a side table somewhere close by. She was sure if she could just think straight for one second, she'd be able to find it, her drink-holding hand searching, only finding thin air as she begged it to please just find the bloody thing already. But feeling more like a passenger in her body rather than in control, she'd stumbled back, taking poor Shane with her, straight into the lamp, a meaningful crack sounding from behind.

They'd frozen midkiss, the lamp snugly lodged between Ruby's head and the wall.

Ruby's eyes had opened wide, like she'd been caught doing something she wasn't supposed to be doing, a giggle escaping her. Shane smiled against her lips, then maneuvered to steady her with one hand, reaching out for the lamp with the other. Ruby had glanced around sheepishly, waiting for the crowd to start heckling them, but it turned out the room had emptied out sometime during their conversation without her noticing. It startled her—made her come back to her senses for a second.

"Just so we're clear," Ruby had said, "I'm not looking for anything serious."

Shane had smiled. "Perfect, I'm not either."

And so it was settled. This...whatever this was...was only going to be for fun. No messy relationship nonsense to worry about.

And that was how it had always stayed...at least in practice.

"Find anything?" Shane's voice jolted Ruby back to the present, making her jump.

She cleared her throat. "Not yet," she said, hurrying over to the desk, hoping he couldn't see the flush heating her cheeks.

Chapter 7

Shane couldn't help but notice what Ruby had been staring at. Their lamp. The lamp that had become their little secret. The reminder of the moment that changed everything. The moment they became inseparable. Until they weren't.

Until everything got so monumentally screwed up it could never be repaired.

No, scratch that. Until *he* monumentally screwed things up so they could never be repaired.

"Hey," Ruby said, rifling through some papers on the desk. "Look at this."

Shane went over to her, acutely aware of how close he was standing. He was careful not to get too much into her space, even though it was all he wanted to do.

"I think we were right that Max might not have been quite as retired as the rest of us," Ruby said, sliding some papers toward him.

It only took a quick glance for Shane to know what he was looking at. Schematics for a large house—a mansion really—with various routes in and out.

"He was doing jobs without us," Shane said, only realizing after he'd said it how sulky his voice sounded. He cleared his throat.

But Ruby just nodded, seemingly not bothered in the slightest. Then again, Shane supposed it was because after Scotland, Ruby appeared to have landed on her feet…and then some. She'd gone completely legit, still able to do the same kind of work, though it had to be challenging with how slow it must all be.

Ruby had moved on to the bottom drawer of Max's desk. "There are dozens of jobs here," she said as she flipped through the papers.

Shane tried not to let the pang of emotion get the better of him.

"What the hell was he up to?" he said, even though it was more than clear by the massive pile of documents.

"The drawer wasn't even locked," Ruby said. "Anyone could have come in here and gone through them."

"I guess the average person might not have known what it all was?" Shane said. "And we never used names on documentation, so the team would be safe."

"Yeah, but what about Max? All this in his possession would be pretty damning if authorities ever came knocking. These jobs go back at least a couple of years. It doesn't make sense."

She had a point. Back when they were still a team and Ash was taking care of this part of the operation, she never hung on to any documents once the jobs were done. She talked about it all the time. "Lose the evidence" was one of her favorite sayings.

"I guess Max doesn't work the same way Ash does," Shane said. "Are you sure the drawer hasn't been jimmied?"

Ruby shook her head. "Not unless they had the key or were good at picking locks. But even if someone had come in here, why would they leave everything? It's not safe for the clients either. Not that their names are in the files, obviously, but it wouldn't take a genius to figure out where all these places are."

Shane nodded, then opened the top drawer on the left side of the desk. "There's one more file," he said, pulling it out and flipping it open.

But Ruby was distracted. Too busy going through the pile on the desk, trying to figure out why on earth Max would be so careless. Back in the day he was never the mastermind, but he wasn't stupid either.

"Shit," Shane said, the contents of the file he was holding starting to sink in. "You're right. He was being surprisingly careless."

"What is it?" Ruby asked, moving in close.

She was so close Shane could smell her shampoo—the same one she'd always used, the damn strawberries. It was also the same one that brought back way too many memories.

"It's our job," Shane said. "The scepter."

"You're kidding," Ruby said, taking the file from his hands.

"And by the looks of things, Max already had a whole lot more figured out than we do."

Ruby flipped through the pages, nodding absently. "He even has the night of the party all laid out. The only thing missing are the names of the operatives."

A low rumble of uneasiness began to swirl deep in Shane's guts. Something was starting to feel a bit off about this job. About Max having all this information. It was a little too handy. "Here's the real question," he said. "If Max had all this planned out and had it pretty much just sitting out in the open for anyone to come along and see it, why the hell didn't the kidnappers take all this with them?"

Ruby stopped flipping, staring at Shane like she was searching for something.

"Because," she said, finding the answer, "they didn't need the specifics of the plans." She shook her head. "These guys don't do the dirty work. They don't need the plans…they need us, the team."

"And Max was the only way to get our attention."

Shane decided he was not a fan of being a pawn in someone else's game. Then another thought struck him. "Bug," he yelled.

A few seconds later, Bug poked his gloriously shiny head

through the door, laptop in hand and a very weird set of goggles with blinking lights over his eyes.

"What in the hell are those?" Shane asked.

Bug shrugged as if he wasn't sure why Shane was questioning him. He shot him a "nothing to see here—so what if I'm sporting a little steampunk tech" look, but just said, "I like to call them Bug's Bug Busters. They find and detect surveillance devices so I can, you know, bust them." Bug appeared exceedingly thrilled to have unveiled his fun little tool, although he seemed prouder of the name than anything.

"Sure," Shane said, "just as I thought."

It was not, in fact, just as he thought—he'd been expecting some long scientific explanation about what the contraptions could do. But, as was his way, Bug defied expectations.

"Anyway, could we bring up the proof-of-life feed?"

Bug started typing away—faster with one hand than Shane could have been even if he'd had three—and moments later, the screen lit up with Max's face. Which, much to Shane's disappointment, was covered with duct tape.

He wasn't entirely surprised. Max did have a talent for being able to speak without pausing in a way that suggested he was simply narrating his stream of consciousness—a bit like those gaming guys who talk nonstop as they play games online for hours. He was probably driving his kidnappers up the wall—a thought that he might have even smiled at, had something else not been glaringly apparent.

"Shit," he said.

Ruby came over and took a spot behind Bug's other shoulder. "Damn."

"What?" Bug asked, though in his defense, Shane thought, maybe he couldn't see the screen well with those ridiculous glasses on.

"They've moved him," he said.

"The background is completely different. It's like he's in a desert or something," Ruby added.

"I'll see if I can pinpoint his new location," Bug said, moving toward the desk so he could set the laptop down and get to some serious work.

But Shane held up his hand. "Don't bother," he said. "By the time you get anything figured out, they will have moved him again."

"How do you know?" Bug asked.

Shane pulled in a deep breath. "Because it's what I would do."

Ruby's hopes plummeted. This whole time she'd been hoping to avoid the con, skip the heist, escape any and all ventures that could potentially jeopardize her new life. She'd spent years cultivating a legitimate career, forging her way into a notoriously challenging field and doing a pretty successful job of it, too, if she did say so herself.

Helping an old friend out of a spot of trouble—okay, more like a giant splotch—was one thing, but pulling a heist was something else completely.

But seeing those plans—where Max had everything laid out so meticulously—and knowing the kidnappers were on the move and likely to remain on the move, made her realize these people would have thought of all that. They would have known Ruby and the team would just want Max back. They'd gotten out of the game a long time ago and didn't seem to have any interest in playing it again. And that was why she knew, beyond any doubt, there would be no getting to Max unless they completed the heist. He was their number one priority and the people who took him would know all the tricks and secrets the team might use to get to him.

Hell, through the years the team had shown the kidnappers their entire playbook.

She let out a long sigh, which Shane picked up on right away.

"You were thinking we would just go rescue Max, easy peasy, right?" he said.

She nodded. "I just… I hate that I have to go back. I promised myself I never would."

"I know," Shane said, and he sounded sincere.

Shane never had a problem with the life of a con, but he'd never made fun of her for wanting to be such a rule-follower either. She closed her eyes and went back to the desk, hoping she could find something, anything that could point them in another direction. Bug headed back out of the room without another word and Shane gave Ruby some space, knowing her moods as well as anyone.

After Scotland, she'd vowed her life of doing things the wrong way was behind her. That breaking any rule of any kind was behind her. It just wasn't worth it. In the end—no matter how good her intentions—everything always went to shit when she broke the rules.

Funny how life always seems to punch you in the face with the same lessons over and over. She should have learned once and for all back in her freshman year of high school. She'd been headed in for her first big final.

"Hey, Jenn," Ruby had said. "All ready for the test?"

Ruby had been nervous but prepared. She was always prepared. Jenn looked a little fidgety, hands squeezing and un-squeezing the binder she held close to her chest. Her gaze was planted squarely on the floor.

"Is everything okay?" Ruby had asked.

She knew Jenn always had trouble with exams. It struck Ruby as unfair that some people were able to take tests no problem, but others struggled, even if they knew the material inside and out. Jenn was one of those people.

And the poor girl looked on the verge of tears.

Jenn shook her head. "I just… I studied so hard, and I know

this stuff, but these tests… It's like my mind goes completely blank the second I step foot through the door."

"It'll be okay," Ruby had said, though she wasn't really sure it would be.

She'd seen Jenn struggle with test after test, and that was just middle school. This time the stakes were even higher—permanent record and everything.

The first tear escaped Jenn's eye as she shook her head. "I don't see how."

Ruby was desperate to help her. Jenn had done so much for her over the years—talked to her when she was too shy to speak to anyone the first day of school all those years ago, taken her camping that one summer in grade three, shown her how to be cooler than she could have ever hoped to be if she'd been left to her own devices.

Ruby had never broken a rule in her life, but suddenly it seemed like the whole system was discriminating against people like Jenn. The way she saw it, she owed Jenn, so she swallowed her fear and decided for once, she was going to be brave. She pulled Jenn aside and spoke to her quietly.

"Look, I know you know the answers, and I also know tests aren't your thing. Maybe you just need a little reassurance. Do you think you could try to forget about the stress of taking the test if you like, had a backup?"

"What do you mean a backup?" Jenn asked.

"Like if you could double-check your answers after you've written them."

Jenn looked dubious. "No way—I'm way too scared to bring in cheat notes. If I get caught my parents would send me to Pittsburgh to live with my grandma. And believe me, Grandma Janice is no joke. My life would be like living with a drill sergeant."

Ruby giggled, picturing Grandma Janice supervising while poor Jenn marched for days on end. "That's not what I meant.

I just meant maybe we could sit beside each other," she whispered. "That way you could glance over—you know…just to make sure you're on the right track."

Jenn tilted her head, thinking. "Maybe that could work," she'd said with a little shrug, still doubtful.

But Ruby was excited. She had a chance to help her friend and she was going to take it. And it wasn't like she was cheating—she knew every answer in the book. But she could still do something to help her friend, right?

As they entered the classroom, everything seemed to go perfectly. There were tons of desks open beside each other and Ruby and Jenn slid into two of them. As the exam began, Ruby tried to answer quickly, to be more efficient for Jenn. Making sure to still look natural, Ruby angled her paper toward Jenn to give her the best chance at being able to see as much as she could.

Everything went smoothly for the first hour or so. Ruby had been so lost in writing the exam she barely noticed anything around her. Every now and again she glanced over at Jenn, who was writing away, not even nervous.

See, she thought to herself, *Jenn knows this stuff.* She just needed a little extra boost of confidence.

Ruby finished soon after and spent some time pretending like she was going over her answers, not ready to give up her role as moral support. In fact, she was feeling pretty proud of the way she'd found a solution to her friend's problem and stuck with her through it.

Just before the bell was supposed to ring, she heard a shuffling from Jenn's general area and glanced over.

Jenn didn't say a peep, but mouthed the words, *Is this right?*

Later, Ruby would wonder what she'd had been thinking. Maybe she'd been finished with the test for so long she'd forgotten what she was even still sitting there for, but whatever the case, she instinctively leaned over to take a peek at her friend's work.

"Ruby Alexander and Jennifer Dales!" a voice came booming from behind them.

Mr. Porter came by and whisked both their test papers off their desks. "To the principal's office...now!"

Jenn looked at Ruby and Ruby looked at Jenn—both with eyes as wide as the gaping chasm of doom opening in Ruby's chest.

"I said now!" Mr. Porter reiterated.

The girls scrambled out of their desks and straight to the principal's office, which was just down the hall. Neither knew what they were supposed to do once inside, so they sat, both too scared to speak.

Soon Principal Chen came out of her office and called Jenn in first.

Ruby had never felt so sick over anything in her entire life, but she reminded herself she was just trying to help a friend. The system was broken, and it wasn't their fault if some people didn't do so well with tests. Surely, she could explain that, and an educator like Principal Chen would have to agree with her.

What felt like hours later, but was probably only twenty minutes, Jenn emerged from the office. She walked straight past Ruby without meeting her eyes and hurried out the door.

The worry train slowly chugging through Ruby's stomach suddenly turned into a runaway locomotive.

"Ruby, come in please," Principal Chen said, motioning her into the office.

She got up and walked slowly, a thousand scenarios playing through her mind. If only she knew what Jenn had said.

Too soon, Ruby was seated across from the principal.

"So, Jenn tells me it was your idea to cheat off her paper," Principal Chen started.

Ruby's mouth slid open in shock. "No... I—"

But the woman held her hand up to stop her. *What was even happening?* There was no way Jenn would have thrown her under the bus like that. They were friends. Friends didn't do that to each other.

"Frankly, it makes no difference whose idea it was," she'd said. "Cheating is cheating, and it cannot happen in this school. You're lucky you have a spotless record thus far."

Ruby nodded vigorously. "Exactly. I always do well on tests. But I think if you look back, you'll find Jenn, like many other students, has trouble with exams no matter how well she knows the material and—"

The hand rose to cut her off again. "The punishment is two weeks' detention, and you should be happy this wasn't a suspension. You will both, of course, receive zeroes on this exam, which will affect your final mark significantly. You can't break the rules and not expect consequences."

The train in Ruby's guts had finally derailed and she'd thought she might be sick. "I didn't even cheat. I was just trying to help…" But her words trailed off. Principal Chen was angrier by the second. "I was just trying to help," Ruby had said again, though she wasn't sure if the words even made it past her lips.

"You're dismissed," Principal Chen said with an air of finality.

Ruby wanted so badly to keep talking, to try to make Principal Chen understand, but as she opened her mouth, a realization washed over her. It didn't matter. Rules were rules and she'd broken them. She might not agree with them completely, but she knew she was supposed to follow them. She was supposed to do the right thing. So she'd done the only thing she could do. She'd closed her mouth back up and walked out of the office, swearing she'd never break another rule as long as she lived.

Of course, that vow didn't last. She'd made the choice to

break the rules for a damn living, for Pete's sake. And then she'd paid the price again with Scotland.

A sick feeling welled in her guts all over again, just like that derailed train all those years ago, and Ruby couldn't help but wonder how high the price was going to be this time.

Chapter 8

"This is kind of the perfect place to headquarter for a job," Shane said, noticing more tech everywhere his eyes fell.

After the theater, the team had gone back to Bug's hideaway to regroup.

The first time he'd entered the underground bunker/war room—or lair, as Bug kept insisting they call it—the sheer expanse and appearance had been almost overwhelming to Shane. His eyes ran along the vast network of wires, which he assumed allowed Bug to enjoy computing power that could give a government organization a run for its money.

Now that Shane was taking a closer look, though, that hadn't been the full story. The place had everything they were going to need, and then some. The tech alone was mind-blowing—Shane couldn't begin to understand what it all did. But on top of all the computer stuff, there was a weapons room, what appeared to be a fully functional crime lab and shelf upon shelf full of gadgets that would have been right at home in a spy museum.

The place legitimately rivaled the Batcave, and Shane conceded that perhaps the place was best referred to as a lair.

"We need to show these to Ash," Shane said, spreading out the plans from Max's place out on a large table in the center of the room.

Bug's face turned gray at the mention of Ash's name.

Shane smiled and slapped his friend on the back. "Don't worry, man, she'd going to love it."

"It's pretty much the coolest place I've ever seen. Really," Ruby added.

Shane would never know why the woman intimidated Bug so much, or why he was so infatuated with her, but to each their own, he supposed. It wasn't like he was immune to feeling sick around a certain team member, who was currently leaning over the table in an incredibly distracting way.

Shane aggressively averted his gaze before something catastrophically embarrassing happened.

Suddenly the room jumped to life. Flashing lights, a death wail of a siren and a computerized voice flooding the air. "Warning! Warning!"

"What the hell is that?" Shane asked, his heart pounding as his mind raced through possible scenarios and checked for exits.

"Don't worry about it," Bug said, "it's just the elevator."

Sure enough, the ceiling above began to descend slowly.

"You don't think that's a little overkill?" Shane asked.

But Bug just shrugged. "I didn't want anyone to get crushed."

Shane's eyes widened. "Is that possible?"

"Only if the pressure-sensitive floor, the movement sensors and the heat signature reader all give out at the same time."

Shane slow-blinked at his friend. "Somehow I don't think that's likely to happen all at once. But hey, I haven't been in an adrenaline-induced coma in a while, so yeah, keep all the flashing lights and ear-fracturing alarms."

Bug smirked as if to say, *Thanks, I think I will.*

Shane was surprised he hadn't witnessed the extreme warning system when he'd been on the elevator, but as the elevator walls moved past the ceiling above, the noises and lights immediately stopped.

The room must be noiseproof, he thought. Which meant

they could be testing explosions down here and the world above would never know. Not that he thought testing explosions in an underground lair was a good idea, but hey, they could if they wanted to.

As Ash and another one of Bug's guys came into view, Bug looked as though he was about to be sick. He was staring at the woman like a lost puppy, though Shane realized he was probably monitoring Ash for her first reaction to the place. No matter how much brilliant work Bug did, none of it seemed to mean anything to him unless it was approved by Ash.

Of course, Ash barely reacted at all—her poker face had always been one of her strengths.

Bug rushed over to the elevator floor to take Ash's hand, assisting her off the single-step platform. Shane caught Ruby rolling her eyes in his periphery, but he thought it was cute, and Ash didn't seem to mind a bit, even flashing a smile Bug's way.

"Thank you, Bug, great place you've got here," Ash said, as she stepped down and took her first scan around. "Very acceptable."

Bug looked like he might faint. "Er, thanks, Ash," he squeaked out.

"Okay," Ash said loudly. "Ruby, you've got the artwork. Find out everything you can. Shane, I need you to verify everything we know about this compound. I need layouts, surrounding area, any obstacles that could get in our way. Bug, you're on security obviously." She clapped her hands twice. "Come on, people, we have a heist to plan."

Bug smiled and jumped into action. "You got it, boss."

This time Ruby rolled her eyes so hard Shane thought she was going to pass out from the strain. Not that she didn't have a point. Ash came storming in and barking orders as if they weren't all already doing exactly what she'd ordered them to, but that was Ash. The woman loved to be in charge. It drove

Ruby nuts, but it didn't bother Shane. The woman was good at what she did and if her ego needed a little stroking along the way, it was an easy trade-off.

So Shane did what he always did. He got back to work.

Ruby had already been researching the scepter and all the other treasures that could potentially show up at the "party," which they all knew was just a code word for black-market auction. The job specified they were only supposed to take the scepter. It seemed like a strange ask, since, according to some sources Ruby reconnected with, there were dozens of other treasures up for auction. But sometimes that was the job. A family only wanted what belonged to them, and they weren't about to claim someone else's stuff.

But Ruby was nothing if not thorough. If they were going to do this thing, she wanted to be as informed as possible. The rumored treasures for this particular "party" included gold, silver, rings, tapestries, jewels, fine china and religious artifacts.

The scepter itself was the star of the show. The gold was of the highest quality and the diamonds were rumored to have come from an uncharted mine somewhere in the Australian outback—an intriguing history in and of itself that Ruby vowed to research more fully when this job was complete. The origin of the magnificent 117-carat emerald crowning the whole thing was unknown.

The last time the scepter was accounted for was hundreds of years ago—it was logged at a Swiss castle. Castello di Siegenthaler had been perched high in the hills, one of three fortresses that once protected the ancient town of Santenal Obli in the Alpine region of Europe. The town no longer existed, but the treasure was well documented if a person knew where to look.

It was Ruby's job to know where to look.

From what Ruby could gather, the three fortresses were

attacked sometime in the fifteenth century, overtaken and raided. The town was completely destroyed, and hundreds of people were killed, including the noble families who lived in the castles. It was a well-planned and well-executed attack. If a few of the people hadn't made a daring escape, eventually making it to the border of Austria, history may never have known about it.

The scepter showed up again briefly just before World War I, where an unnamed Swiss family sent a photograph of it to a museum that was potentially interested in purchasing it. The purchase did not go through, and at last mention the scepter was rumored to have been among the treasure looted by the Nazis during World War II.

No family had ever come forward to claim the scepter when it was found, most likely because those first founding noble families of Santenal Obli were obliterated during the original attack. It was a fascinating piece, and Ruby couldn't help but wonder who the kidnappers' client was. In each of the jobs they'd done back in her con days, Ruby had been assured the clients were fully vetted and authenticated as the rightful owners of each recovered treasure.

Ruby zoomed in on the grainy picture of the scepter to get a better view of the coat of arms. It appeared to show a picturesque valley with a waterfall feeding into a body of water. Something prickled in Ruby, as if she'd seen something similar before, though she couldn't place when or where.

"Ruby?" Ash was saying. And then again, louder, with a snap of her fingers. "Ruby!"

Ruby had been so engrossed in her research she'd barely noticed the team making plans around her. "What?"

"Do you still have your info to get into The Vault?"

"Oh, uh, yeah, I think so. I'll have to double-check, I guess." Ash let out a long, exasperated sigh.

"What?" Ruby asked. "I was out of the game. I was never

supposed to have to need any of this again. You're lucky I didn't destroy everything the minute I left Scotland."

The room fell silent at the mention of their final, failed job.

But the team recovered, as Ash faced them. "I'll work on compiling everything we've found out. In the meantime, you all need to go get your stuff in order. Pack what you need."

"I need to take time off work," Ruby added.

Ash shook her head. "Fine, take time off work if you must," she said, making it sound like work was some kind of ridiculous frivolity Ruby was just killing a bit of time with. "As always, we'll be taking different flights out to avoid any connections between us, and we'll meet in Switzerland. Everyone got it?"

"Sounds good, boss," Bug said.

Ruby really hated when Bug called Ash that. No one was supposed to be the boss of the team, they were all equal partners. But somehow, Ash had become their unofficial leader, something Ruby was not too fond of.

"See you on the other side," Shane said, packing up the papers from the theater, along with printouts of additional research.

Ruby began to save all the information she'd gathered, sending it to a special folder on the computer even though she'd already tucked most of it away in her head. Bug would encrypt everything and keep it ready in case they needed the info during the job. He'd digitize what they'd found at the theater so they'd have it at their fingertips no matter where they were in the world in what they called The Vault.

"Ruby," Ash said in her most stern schoolmarm manner. "You got that?"

Ruby pulled in a slow, fortifying breath. "Yes, Ash, I've got it."

Ash nodded once and turned on her heel, making her way back to the elevator. Bug scrambled behind to accompany her back up to ground level. God forbid the woman had to push a button all by herself.

"I guess she hasn't changed much," Shane said, sidling up beside Ruby as she turned the computer screen off.

His scent drifted past then, and Ruby tried not to think about being even closer to it, nuzzling into his neck…kissing along his jawline.

"Guess not," she said, trying to hide the way her pulse sped up so much she could hardly catch her breath.

After a moment of strange silence—not quite awkward, but certainly not comfortable—Shane straightened. "Well, safe travels," he said.

She nodded, trying to push down the feeling of regret creeping in, telling herself it was because they had to do this job, and definitely not because she had to part ways with Shane so soon after seeing him again. "Yeah, you too."

Three hours later, Ruby was packed and logging in to The Vault. It was essentially a digital safety-deposit box—a highly encrypted space where the team kept and managed their most essential documents. Logging in gave her the same sense of anticipation mixed with dread it always had. She clicked on the icon of the red gem—for Ruby, of course. Inside was her itinerary and digital flight information.

Great. She had to take three flights before she reached her final destination—no doubt the worst travel plans of them all. Ruby guessed Ash had her own private jet and was flying direct. Bug and Shane probably had a couple flights, maybe one domestic and one international, but of course Ruby got stuck flying through Canada and France before finally making it to Switzerland.

At least it would give her time to do more research, she supposed.

It was interesting the job was taking them to Switzerland, right back to the origin of the scepter itself. If Ruby was lucky, maybe she'd have some time to go through local records and see if she could trace the family.

From the outside, people thought her job was boring, but Ruby loved nothing more than digging into lost treasures, to uncover the stories they told.

The only thing left was to pick up her passport and other documentation, and hopefully, enough cash in various currencies to get her to Switzerland comfortably. The process of document retrieval was different every time, and The Vault told her this time she was off to a local waterpark. She wasn't in the mood for a bunch of hyper kids, but she was a professional and she would simply get to work like she always did.

Twenty minutes and thirty dollars to get into the park later, she was standing in front of locker 213 in the change room. She consulted her phone for the five-digit code and punched it in, pretending like she was about to put her bag inside. Once the area was clear of other people, she tucked the small envelope into the bag and made her way back out without encountering too many screaming children.

She arrived at the airport with a renewed sense that this was what was going to help get Max back. She almost felt a jolt of excitement.

Until an aggravatingly familiar and even more aggravatingly handsome face greeted her at her gate.

Chapter 9

She hadn't noticed him yet, and Shane was making the most of his opportunity to watch her unnoticed. A twinge of something squeezed his heart. The way she walked, only half paying attention to where she was going, and half paying attention to whatever bit of research she had on her phone. An untrained observer might have thought she was a little careless…distracted. But Shane knew better. It was part of her cover—what better way to blend in these days than have your attention focused on your phone?

In the hours since he'd last seen her, she'd already changed her hair. Shane didn't know if it was extensions, or a convincing wig, but she was back to her old bob style, a little past her shoulders—the kind of style no one would pay any particular attention to. Sure, she was going to get looks no matter what she did—she was too beautiful to completely fly under the radar—but this was about as incognito as she could get.

As she neared the waiting area at the gate, she glanced up from her phone and Shane gave her a little wave.

He did not particularly love the way the color drained from her face.

"Hey, honey," Shane said, pulling a shocked Ruby into a hug. "Don't worry," he continued quietly into her ear. "I'm not stalking you."

Which obviously made it sound like he was, in fact, stalking her.

He pulled her to a quiet corner with only the slightest bit of resistance. Ruby was probably in a full-on mental war with herself, both desperately wanting to get away from him, but equally curious as to why he was there. At her airport. Taking her flight.

"Ash didn't think you would show up if you knew the plan was you and I posing as a couple traveling together to Switzerland."

Ruby's face stayed neutral. She was always one to stay in character when a job called for it, even in an unexpected conundrum like the one she found herself in. But Shane knew from experience Ruby was far from okay.

She pulled the boarding pass out of Shane's hand, confirming they did, indeed, share a last name. "Why do they even need us to be in disguise for this?" she asked, her eyes darting around. "Presumably the people who took Max already know who all of us are at this point."

Shane tilted his head in agreement. "Maybe, but the people who have the item we are going to retrieve do not."

"I feel like this is a bit overkill," she said.

"It is, but I don't think we're in any position to push back on an abundance of caution…especially after Scotland."

She let out a long sigh. "I guess."

She walked away from Shane without another word and sat on a nearby chair to wait for their boarding call. Shane followed. It was no doubt completely obvious to anyone who might be paying them the least bit of attention that they were not particularly getting along, but Shane figured it wasn't necessarily uncommon for a married couple to do just that—especially when traveling.

"I'm sorry," he said. "This wasn't my idea."

She glanced at him out of the corner of her eye. Shane

wasn't sure if the look she gave him was because she didn't believe him, or if it was because she knew it would never be his call either way.

She let out a low growl. "What the hell is Ash even thinking?"

"Well," Shane said, a small grin forming, "I honestly prefer not to think about that. I imagine it's kind of a flurry of mathematics whipped up into a whirlwind of blueprints and security briefings. Maybe with a hint of commanding power fashion lurking around the edges."

Shane couldn't be sure, but he thought the corner of Ruby's mouth twitched. "She does tend to dress to make an impression," she finally said, her shoulders relaxing.

Shane's relaxed along with hers.

After a beat, he spoke again. "None of this is ideal, obviously, but it's good to see you."

She nodded absently. "All things considered, it's good to see you too. A little discombobulating, but good, I guess."

Shane chuckled. "I suppose I can see how I have that effect on people."

Ruby finally looked at him then. "That's not what I meant. I don't mean *you're* discombobulating, it's just… I don't know, I never thought I'd see you guys again and it's kind of thrown me off, I guess. And the whole thing with Max…" She drifted off, pulling her knee up onto the seat. She turned to face him. "What if we can't get Max back?" she asked, her eyes shimmering.

It was the first note of vulnerability Shane had seen since the moment they reunited back in her apartment, and he had to fight the urge to reach for her.

"We'll get him back," Shane said. "We have to."

"He's done so much for us," Ruby said. "If anything happens—"

Shane shook his head. "We'll get him back. They can't

afford to do anything to him. Max is the only thing keeping us going on this job. If they really want that damned scepter, they can't risk touching a hair on his head. They know we'd be gone in a heartbeat."

She nodded, though she looked far from convinced. "I wish I could check the proof-of-life feed again," she said.

Shane had been wishing the same thing. But for all intents and purposes, they were a couple on vacation—it wouldn't make sense to be traveling around with a bunch of state-of-the-art tech.

Ruby straightened in her seat and pulled back her shoulders. "Okay, we're going to do this. Positive attitude and all that, right?"

"Right."

"But I will tell you one thing. I am going to kick Ash's pencil-skirted ass for giving us all this bloody itinerary."

Shane grinned.

"How about you go up to that young staff member up there and see if we can get an upgrade?" Ruby asked.

He lifted an eyebrow. "I thought we were supposed to be flying under the radar."

She narrowed her eyes, though a glimmer shone through them. "Don't think you can do it, huh?"

"You know very well that is not the issue."

"Uh-huh. Sure," she said, a real honest-to-goodness smile forming.

He worked up the nerve to shove her shoulder with his and for a moment, it almost felt like old times. A fact they both seemed to notice at the same time and the moment devolved back into uncomfortable silence.

"I have an idea," Shane said. "What if we just…didn't make this weird? What if we're just two old friends who know they're reuniting for a short time and won't see each other again after that? It will be great to catch up, do a little work together and then it will be just as great to go our separate ways with nothing but fond memories."

"Just two old friends, hey?" she said, interest showing behind her dark lashes.

He nodded once. "Exactly," even though he couldn't help but think their relationship had never been remotely anything anyone would have ever called just "friendly."

"So, what are we proposing here? Pretending this whole thing isn't weird and uncomfortable and utterly ridiculous?" she asked.

"Yes, that sounds like an excellent plan."

The weird, uncomfortable and utterly ridiculous fact they were even having this conversation was not lost on Ruby. Still, Shane's proposal did seem better than the alternative.

"I suppose it does beat spending the next twenty hours traveling in a smelly cloud of awkwardness," she said.

"It does," Shane said, getting comfortable in his seat, his legs relaxing, one knee falling open to touch hers, causing a little zing to shoot through her.

This was not going to be an easy twenty hours.

She wanted to throttle Ash. Ruby just knew she had some sort of ulterior motive too. Hell, she was probably trying to get Ruby and Shane comfortable again by forcing them to spend a bunch of hours together.

Ruby hated that it was already working. Not that she wanted to be on edge with Shane, but she did not want Ash to have the satisfaction of knowing her plan had worked. Yes, there had been good reasons for her and Shane to be apart, but for now, they were stuck together. There was no reason to make this mission more difficult than it had to be. Working together was going to be key to getting Max back, which was all that

mattered. Even if Ash being right was one of Ruby's least favorite things in the world.

Their first flight was announced, and Ruby and Shane
played their parts the way they needed to. Ruby tried not to
notice how familiar and comfortable Shane's hand felt on the
small of her back as he led her toward the check-in desk, then
tried not to miss it when it was gone. She tried not to notice
the way he fiddled with his passport and sent a smile to the
woman who was checking him in, which was sexier than Ruby
would have liked. And she tried very hard not to notice the
sparkle in the eyes of the woman as she smiled back.

"You want to maybe cool that a little?" Ruby asked as they
made their way down the walkway.

"Cool what?"

"The obvious flirting with the airline staff," Ruby said.
"We're supposed to be acting like we're in love, or whatever."

His eyebrows knitted together in a way that said he didn't
have a clue what she was talking about. Ruby knew Shane
well enough to know it was sincere—he truly didn't know
what he'd done.

Cripes, Ruby thought. That smile—that charming, disarming smile—wasn't even rehearsed. It was just his smile. She
remembered hating it back then, and she hated it now. That
smile for any lucky soul who happened to cross his path in a
day—a cashier, waitstaff, a stranger coming his way down
the street. Of course, if she was being honest with herself, she
didn't hate it. She loved it, as a matter of fact. What she hated
was that he never used that smile on her. The smiles she got
weren't any less beautiful, but still, it was hard not to want all
the smiles to be just for her.

Lord, she was being ridiculous.

"Never mind," she said, giving herself a solid headshake
inside her mind.

Ruby crossed her fingers they would at least have a row to themselves on the plane, ideally with the middle seat empty, but as she approached their row, her hopes began to fall. Of course, she was assigned the middle seat, and of course Shane was going to be snugged up right beside her for the five-hour flight, almost touching her the entire time. Which was about the worst thing that could happen, since Ruby could feel her defenses starting to crumble with each moment she spent with Shane.

She had forgotten how easy things were with him.

Ruby gave the woman sitting in the window seat a smile as she sat down, hoping she wouldn't be much of a talker. Ruby preferred to catch up on sleep or do some quiet contemplating rather than chat nonstop with strangers on a flight. She liked people just fine, but she never did seem to find enough time to just sit and think, which was one of her favorite pastimes. She couldn't understand when people said they hated being alone with their thoughts. How else was anyone supposed to solve problems or come up with new ideas? Those people were almost as strange to Ruby as the ones who said they hated silence.

"Oh, don't you two make a lovely couple," the older woman said as Shane sat—much too close for comfort—in his seat beside Ruby.

Ruby was about to correct the woman, let her know they were not a couple, when Shane reminded her they were supposed to be playing a part by gifting the woman with his flirtatious smile and replying with a gracious thank-you. Ruby shot a quick smile toward her new seatmate, noticing how the woman was flushed. Shane had that effect on women. Ugh.

What Ruby wished they could do, even more than sleeping or getting some good thinking in, was to discuss their next moves. She wanted to know what else had been in Shane's

Vault package. Or compare notes on the other tidbits of info Ash might have conveniently left out of Ruby's Vault. But that would be impossible with the woman so close by.

Unfortunately, sleeping and/or thinking proved to be wildly unsuccessful for two reasons. One, Shane was watching some kind of uproariously hilarious movie. Or at least he thought it was funny. Every time she would get settled enough to close her eyes and begin, Shane would let out another massive laugh, effectively jolting her out of her thoughts. The second problem was, when the movie was finally done, Shane decided to strike up a conversation with their seatmate. He asked her all about her grandkids and hobbies, making it impossible for Ruby to relax.

Ruby couldn't help but think Shane was doing it just to spite her. Sure, he may have just been passing the time on a long and uneventful flight, but how he could be so interested in little Jesse's piano lessons was beyond Ruby.

By the time they were making their final descent, the woman—Rose—was more smitten than a schoolgirl at her favorite boyband concert. And as they deplaned, Shane walked Rose all the way to the exit, stopping only because if he went any farther, he'd have to go through security all over again.

"Quite the charmer," Ruby said, once Shane had returned to find their next gate.

"Got to keep up appearances," he said, his eyes practically sparkling.

"Which appearance is that? The one where you're much more like a trusty shadow than the doting partner you're supposed to be?"

Shane pulled off a flawless performance of mock offense. "What kind of a partner would I be if I didn't take an interest in my fellow travelers?"

"Your fellow female travelers?" Ruby couldn't help but point out.

"Ruby Walters!" Shane spouted, and Ruby had to admit she was impressed he'd even memorized her false name, no pause or anything. "That woman was old enough to be my grandmother, what are you implying?" He grinned wide.

Ruby couldn't help but grin right back. She'd forgotten how fun being with Shane could be, even when they weren't doing anything. "Oh, nothing, dear," she said, knowing he hated being called *dear*, always saying it made him feel like he was ninety-three. But she knew he couldn't do anything about it since they were supposed to be playing the happy couple.

"You know you love it. Who would I even be if I didn't flirt with cute little elderly ladies?"

"I honestly have no idea," Ruby said, smiling, and she meant it.

Shane had more "people person" personality in his pinky finger than Ruby had in her whole body. She hated that she loved the way the twinkle in his eye brightened with their exchange. He was enjoying this.

Then again, so was Ruby.

Oh, no. What was she thinking, trying to flirt with Shane of all people? Although, one might be hard-pressed *not* to flirt with Shane. He was the master at it, bringing out the flirt in most everyone he talked to. Rose had been a prime example.

Their second, and longest, flight was slightly better, since much of it was spent flying over the ocean in the dark. The flight was full again, so no such luck on talking strategy, but at least Ruby thought she could get some peace and quiet and even a little sleep. Quality thinking time was still eluding her, since she was finding it a bit difficult to concentrate on anything besides the way Shane still smelled like a damn forest-scented candle—sweet with just a hint of pine in the morning.

Apparently, she was the only one who was having trouble focusing. By the time they reached elevation, Shane was already peacefully asleep.

Chapter 10

Shane knew how to get people on his side. Sure, their seatmate Rose had been an easy target, but still, he knew how to work situations to his advantage. But no matter how good he was with people, he was still surprised every time Ruby played along.

There were just certain people whom he'd always feel nervous around, no matter how confident he appeared on the outside, and Ruby was one of them. So he closed his eyes when they boarded their last flight, not wanting to jinx the moment.

The Meyerses had always been winners, no doubt about that. It was in their DNA, threaded deep into every cell. Shane had grown up knowing this to the core of his soul, and he never questioned it.

Until, of course, he did.

He would always remember the feeling of inadequacy at the most inopportune moments. Admit to himself there might be certain situations where he didn't quite measure up. He tried to push the thoughts away, to keep his confidence. He'd never have admitted it out loud, but back when he still lived in his hometown and his name commanded respect, he secretly felt like he was just a little better than everybody else.

But that was before Renaye came to town in his senior year. Shane wasn't sure if it was because she was new, or if it was her incredible looks that caught his attention first. He'd had his fair share of girls pay attention to him, and frankly, the girls from his small town were starting to get boring.

Yeah, Shane knew how bad that made him sound, which was why he'd never say it out loud—his mother taught him better than that. But a small town with the same twenty girls in your age range got a little stale after fifteen years of knowing them inside and out. Besides, he'd already kissed all the ones he wanted to, and there was the additional problem of having all their parents know you too.

Small towns. Everyone always all up in your face.

It was a strange place to be—both itching to get out of Dodge the moment you graduated, yet knowing you'd be taken care of—and well—for the rest of your life if you stayed. There was no lack of admiration or people fawning all over you where he grew up.

The Meyers men had always been the ones people in town called troublemakers—but with a wink to go with the word. They were a little too handsome, had a little too much charm and were maybe a little short in the smarts department. But that didn't matter. School was a joke anyway—his family owned half the town and most of the "smart" people relied on them for their jobs.

"Hey," he'd said, waltzing up to this new, gorgeous being, flashing the winning smile that worked every time.

Renaye glanced up from her book, slight annoyance crossing her face, which Shane was surprised didn't go away after she got a good look at him. His smile faltered, just a little.

"I'm Shane. Shane Meyers." He hated that he threw in the last name, just to make sure she really knew who he was. Something about this girl made him feel like he needed all the arsenal he had available to him.

"Renaye," she said, turning her gaze back to her book.

But Shane had been taught well. He knew how to talk to girls. And this one had already given him some insight into her interests. "So, uh, what are you reading?" he asked, expecting her to get excited, to start droning on about ever minuscule plot detail.

His dad had taught him a long time ago that girls wanted to be seen, wanted someone to pay a bit of attention to them. "And that, son, is the fastest way to get what you want," he'd said with a double pump of his beefy eyebrows. Shane had felt a bit of an uneasy twinge when his dad first said it, but over the years, he'd discovered his dad had not been wrong. So he'd mentally prepared himself for the plot onslaught, readying to go into fake listening mode.

"It's the new Suzanne Collins," she'd said.

Shane nodded, waiting for her to continue into her diatribe. But that diatribe never came.

"Oh, yeah? Is it any good?"

The girl actually sighed. "Yeah, I guess."

Okay, this girl was a hard nut to crack. But Shane wasn't one to give up easily. "So, what's it about?"

She'd looked up at him again, kind of squinting since the sun was behind Shane. Maybe that was the problem—maybe she couldn't see him very well.

"Shane?" she'd asked, seeming like she had to dig a little harder than Shane would have liked to remember his name.

"Yeah?" he'd said, flashing the smile again.

"What was the last book you read?"

Shane had made a face. "I don't know. Something in school, I guess."

"And did you finish it? Like read the whole book?"

Shane shrugged. "Doubt it."

Why read a whole book when you could get a girl to give you the lowdown? They loved to do that kind of shit for guys they liked.

She'd nodded. "That's what I thought."

"I guess I'm not that into reading," Shane had said, not thinking much about it.

Reading had never been important. Like yeah, he *could* read, of course, but beyond the bare minimum that helped a person comfortably get by in the world, he didn't see the appeal.

"Well, Shane," Renaye said, "I guess I'm not that into guys who don't read."

She'd said it in a way that made it clear it was the end of the conversation and she had no desire to ever have another.

"Oh, um, okay," Shane said, walking away, wondering what in the hell was wrong with her.

He never tried to talk to her again.

It was his first lesson in reputation. As in, it wasn't going to get you everything you wanted in life, contrary to what his family would have him believe.

It was a lesson Shane was thankful for now. The satisfaction in winning someone over with his own skills—using his own charm, his own intelligence, which he'd finally started to hone after the Renaye incident—was so much greater than just being somebody in some small town in the middle of nowhere.

Shane had gotten a little melancholy, thinking about the past during the final plane ride. He had been thinking of it as they got off the plane and headed to the luggage carousel. He was even still thinking about it the moment he realized something wasn't quite right.

"Hey," he said, moving in close to Ruby's ear. He felt her stiffen, and hoped their audience didn't catch it. "We have company."

The sensation of Shane's breath on her ear raised goose bumps on Ruby's skin. How the man still had that effect on her even with all they'd been through, she'd never understand.

But she didn't have the luxury to think about any of that at the moment. Not if they were being tailed. She turned her full attention to Shane, pivoting to meet his eyes, though she was hoping to get a glimpse of whoever the "company" was in her peripheral, but nothing obvious jumped out at her. Although, she supposed, the tail wouldn't be much of a tail if they'd been obvious. Still, she was trained to know what to look for and was frustrated she couldn't spot them. Or maybe she was just frustrated Shane had spotted them first.

"So, what's the plan?" Ruby said, keeping her voice light so she wouldn't attract suspicion in case the person following could hear.

Shane pulled her into an unexpected hug, one which might have sent her into shock if she wasn't so focused on staying in character. It was a smart move—they'd be able to talk for a minute quietly enough so no one could hear—but Ruby wished it didn't make her feel so…discombobulated.

"We need to figure out if this is one of the guys who have Max, or if it's someone else," Shane said.

"Who else could it possibly be?"

"I don't know. Maybe someone's keeping track of anyone researching the scepter. Maybe our passports got flagged somehow. Maybe I just have a very eager secret admirer," he said, pulling away from the hug with a grin.

Ruby smiled back. "Are you saying it's a woman?" she asked, her eyes darting to the left.

Shane adopted an expression of mock hurt. "Are you saying I couldn't attract the attentions of a male admirer?"

Ruby raised her eyebrows. "Solid point."

The alarms had started for the luggage carousel, and they turned their attention toward it. Shane took the opportunity to speak while the noise was assaulting the air. "We'll just grab our luggage and head for the taxis. I didn't get a good look. Maybe I'm being paranoid."

Ruby squinted her eyes at him, feeling like he was up to something. "Are you going to ditch me?"

Shane looked a little wounded for real this time. "Of course I'm not going to ditch you. I just think our best bet is to lose them as soon as possible. Ideally before we make it out of the airport."

"Fine," Ruby said, realizing Shane was using it as an opportunity to challenge himself.

They'd both been out of the game for a long time. Ruby assumed she was a little rusty—which was confirmed by the fact that she hadn't even spotted the tail—and she could only assume Shane felt the same.

"Like we did in Cairo?" Shane said.

"Should work," Ruby agreed.

They stepped toward the carousel, Shane moving left and Ruby moving more to the right, both jostling their way to the front the way the most obnoxious passengers tended to do. For the plan to work, there had to be a bit of confusion. They had to get separated.

Ruby spotted Shane grabbing his bag first, taking off toward the exit. Ruby hung back a bit, but only for a few moments, snagging her bag off the turnstile at the last possible second, heading in the opposite direction.

Because Shane had taken off first, they assumed the person watching would go after him, but if there was more than a single person, this maneuver was designed to get them apart. It meant Ruby and Shane would be separated, too, but this way they'd regain the upper hand. Take back the element of surprise.

Ruby strolled relatively slowly—the trick was to walk at a different pace than the people around so you could try to pick up on anyone who might be matching your pace. She glanced as surreptitiously as possible into every reflective surface—windows, signs, even the bars of luggage trolleys. But she heard nothing...saw nothing.

Still, she couldn't shake the feeling someone was back there. Maybe it was paranoia from being away from the con game for so long, but back in the day she'd had a sixth sense for these things…and her "Spidey-senses" were tingling. As Ruby neared an almost deserted area of the airport, she snuck into a washroom.

Back at Bug's, they'd all been given special suitcases with handles that came all the way out. The ends of the metal posts were angled, creating a concealed, but highly effective weapon. She hid around the corner of the entrance, heart beating, every sense on high alert.

As the woman on Ruby's tail walked in, she was met with quite a surprise in the form of a headlock and—much to Ruby's astonishment and Bug's credit—a rather effective-looking, bladelike object nestled along her neck.

Chapter 11

Airports are interesting spaces. Some areas are packed with people, and others are ghost towns. Thankfully, Shane knew how to navigate both. The question was, which area to choose? The answer depended on who his pursuer was, of course.

But Shane had no clue who that might be.

By now the person tailing him would know something was up. A couple traveling together doesn't usually just split up. Shane had to assume his follower had at least some idea who he and Ruby were, and their suspicions would be on high alert.

At first, Shane chose to keep to the places with people, following the throng filing out of the baggage area, out toward the area where hotel shuttles, taxis and families waiting in long drive-through lanes congregated in a flurry of activity. But he wasn't about to leave the airport without Ruby. They had plans in place if they got separated—they both knew where to meet and several routes to get there, but Shane didn't think they'd gotten to that point yet. Plan A—a little evasion work, then meet back up near the domestic security gate— was still in place.

Shane weaved through the people, glancing around as if he was a lost tourist, speaking briefly to an airport employee helping people find the right combination of taxis, shuttles and buses for their needs. Shane felt bad for taking up so much of the man's time when there were clearly people needing help more than he did, but he wanted to get another look at his tail and the man had presented the perfect opportunity.

But a good look was not to be had—the guy was competent, intuitive, trained. Shane only got a shadow of a glimpse that told him nothing besides what he already knew. His tail appeared to be a man, and a rather commanding one at that, well-muscled and on the tall side.

Shane thanked the airport employee for all his help and continued his winding route. There were plenty of places he could sneak into if he wanted to confront his pursuer—empty spaces, walkways, between large trucks—but he didn't want to risk it with so many people around.

Shane spotted an entrance propped open with a small brick, an employee smoking a few feet away with his back turned.

Perfect.

Pulling his luggage close to squeeze through, he ducked into the door, hoping the guy smoking would finish quickly, too quickly for his tail to follow, but no such luck—the guy apparently hell-bent on using every last second of his break time.

Inside, Shane found what he was looking for. He was in some kind of secure, employees-only space—dark and extremely quiet. He considered confronting his tail right there, but he knew the employee was bound to stumble upon them if he stayed, so he jogged down the dark corridor. He didn't bother testing door handles for anything that might be unlocked—an enclosed space like a small room would be his last resort. What he needed was a space where he could hide, take his shadow by surprise, but still have at least a few options for exits. He was a good fighter, but by the size and skill of his shadow, he couldn't assume he'd come out on top in a hand-to-hand battle.

The annoying thing was, Shane couldn't figure out why this person would follow him. Even if someone had guessed what they were up to—and that was a big if—the people watching them wanted the team to succeed in their mission. This whole bloody thing was about securing the scepter and trading it for Max. Nothing was making any sense.

Thankfully, his pursuer was moving slowly, knowing Shane could jump out at him from any of the nooks or doorways along the hall, which bought Shane a little time to find the kind of spot he needed. The end of the hall opened into a large room filled with chairs and tables, like some sort of staffroom or cafeteria for employees. It was deserted. A quick survey told Shane there were three exits. He wouldn't get a better opportunity than this to find out what his new friend was up to.

It felt like forever. Shane slid Bug's special handle from his suitcase, readying for anything, though after three long flights, he knew his energy would be less than optimal and hoped whoever this was just wanted to talk. Unfortunately, Shane knew from experience that wasn't often the case.

He ducked behind a serving counter to wait.

And wait.

Seriously, was this guy even following him anymore? Shane was about to come out of his hiding spot and head to the meetup point to find Ruby when he heard the tiniest scrape of a footstep entering into the cafeteria. The man moved with caution, which Shane hoped was a good sign. His pursuer was a thinker, not making sudden moves or charging in like a drunk rhino. Which also meant he was calculating every possible situation, just like Shane was. This was the exact reason Shane had chosen the hiding spot he did—because it was not his first choice... or his second. He always chose the third place he spotted so anyone on his tail would most likely check two other places first, giving Shane the opportunity to surprise them from behind if all went as planned.

Of course, there was no plan for situations like this. A person just had to do the best they could with whatever tools the universe provided them, but Shane was an expert at improv. So when he lost sight of the guy—who, to his dismay, was much bigger than he'd hoped—Shane started to get a little nervous. And when he crept out from behind the counter and the room still seemed empty, he got even more nervous.

But that was nothing compared to the massive shot of adrenaline catapulting through his body when an obviously practiced hand yanked the suitcase handle out of his grip and an equally practiced second arm wrapped neatly, and rather snugly, around Shane's neck, cutting his air off.

It had been a brilliant move—the man had climbed onto the counter, likely knowing that was the precise place Shane would been hiding. A perfect position, with the advantage of the high ground, and one where he could spot Shane no matter which way he came out.

Shane's thoughts raced through a thousand scenarios—most of which did not end well. But he had the kind of mind that moved fast, and he prepared his stance for a counterattack, though he couldn't decide whether to try to flip the guy over his head—something the man would likely see coming a mile away—or duck and hope to catch him off guard. It was also a move that would be expected, but Shane's options were somewhat limited.

"Hey, buddy," Shane's pursuer said, his voice surprisingly jovial.

And with those two words, Shane's entire body relaxed, and he stood, turning to face his pursuer as the man's grip loosened.

Shane let out a long, exhausted and relieved sigh.

"Bug, what the hell are you doing here?"

It was the smell that first caught Ruby's attention. A very expensive, and very familiar, perfume, which she knew a person could only get once a year at the Fête du Jasmin festival in Grasse, France. She let all the air she'd been holding in out in one big whoosh.

"Are you going to get your hands off me, or what?" Ash said, having to choke the words out due to Ruby's expert grip around her neck.

"Ash? What the hell, man?" Ruby said, letting Ash go, adding just a touch more aggression than was strictly necessary.

Ash rolled her eyes. "I am not a man, and we are not in hell."

It only took a moment for Ash to straighten her coat and she was the picture of perfection again. Ruby, on the other hand, with the almost twenty hours of flights behind her, felt like a smashed bag of cow dung. She made a weak attempt at smoothing her hair back into place.

"Feels like hell to me after that excruciating flight itinerary," Ruby said, moving to a sink to splash water on her face. "And seriously, what are you doing here? I assume it's Bug you've got tailing Shane?"

She went to the automatic hand dryer, waiting for Ash to start speaking before letting it do its thing. The exasperation Ruby saw on Ash's face was even more satisfying after sitting on those damned flights and plotting her payback for hours.

When the drying stopped, Ash put a hand on her hip. "Are you done?"

"I think so," Ruby said, examining her hands, where a slight dampness still lingered.

Ash opened her mouth to speak again just when Ruby got the machine going again. It was totally juvenile and ridiculous, but Ruby couldn't help that it was damned funny too.

Still chuckling, Ruby moved her hands away from the dryer. "Sorry, couldn't help it. I'm feeling a little out of sorts after all the travel."

Ash raised an eyebrow. "That couldn't be helped," she said, with a wave of her hand that said she was quite done discussing it.

Ruby inserted the handle back into her suitcase and rolled

it along behind as they left the restroom and headed back up the deserted wing toward the gates.

"So, what happened?" Ruby asked. "And why were you tailing us instead of just meeting us like a normal person?"

"The Vault has been compromised. We were following you in case one of two things were happening. First, to keep some distance in case you and Shane caught yourselves a real tail, and second, in case anyone was watching from afar. We needed to get you somewhere secluded and lose any possible tail. Bug did his thing with his computers and gadgets and couldn't spot anything, but we wanted to be as careful as we could."

"Okay, but what do you mean The Vault has been compromised?"

"Bug discovered some glitches in the system, so he went in and checked out the code, or whatever it is he does," she said, shaking her head as if it was astounding there was something in this world she didn't understand. "In any case, he discovered someone had been in there, so now all our information is compromised—plan A, plan B and plan C are all shot."

"The whole operation is shot?" Ruby asked, panic starting to rise.

Ash shook her head. "Not the operation. We can assume the people who have Max already know most of our plan since it was already laid out by Max, and anything else we've come up with since then we've kept separate. Standard protocol. All they know is our travel itineraries and, well, now our base of operations has been compromised. So I guess that's the third reason we needed to be here when you and Shane arrived."

"So, do we have a plan D?" Ruby asked.

They had reached an area where a few more people were milling around, so Ruby started scanning for things that didn't belong. She trusted Bug and Ash would have spotted anyone who could have been spotted, but there would always be an outside chance someone was simply really, really good and didn't twig any danger vibes.

"We do now," Ash said. "I've called in some favors and secured us a new spot, which…should work."

Ruby decidedly did not like the pause in her sentence. "Please tell me it isn't some run-down warehouse, and all we have to sleep on is a bare concrete floor."

"I'm sure it's a bit better than that," Ash said, though Ruby couldn't help notice she did not seem convinced.

As they neared the domestic flight area where Shane and Ruby were supposed to meet if they got separated, Ruby tried not to be annoyed with the new plan. The whole last flight, all she'd been thinking about was a hot shower and at least a short sleep, and she wasn't sure if that was even going to happen now. But she had to think of Max. She shook her head at how insensitive she was being. The poor guy was locked up. And she knew Max would never complain about any accommodation situation if the tables were turned and he had to help one of them.

As they turned the last corner toward the domestic security area, Ruby found her gaze searching for one thing.

Shane.

Now that it was over, she hated how panicked she'd been when they split up and was surprised to realize it was more because of her worry for Shane than it had been for herself. Surely that must have been because she'd known the pursuers would likely go for him instead of her. Of course, the worry for Shane hadn't stopped after she realized someone was following her, too, but she wasn't going to think about that.

Still, her heart calmed the moment her gaze fell on him. He had his back turned as he talked to Bug, and Ruby took a moment to admire his lean, lanky frame, always relaxed, always confident. She sometimes resented that about him, the confidence. Even though she was successful, she never quite felt like she could find the assuredness he had. She never quite felt worthy in the world, which she knew was linked to the way she so often felt like she was doing something wrong—probably because she had done so much wrong in the past. Broken every rule. In theory, she could justify it, and believed in the end everything she had done had an overall positive effect on the world, but that feeling never left.

Still, even if she might never achieve that kind of swagger for herself, it looked damn good on him.

He turned, gifting Ruby and Ash with *that* smile—the one that, had it been in a cheesy commercial, would have a sparkle graphic and high-pitched ding accompanying it.

"Hey, guys," Shane said, "guess who I found hanging around."

Bug gave Shane a look. "I'm pretty sure I was the one who found you."

"Hey, Bug," Ruby said.

"We should keep moving," Ash said, never one for social niceties.

"And hello to you too," Shane said.

But Ash just kept moving, not a reply to be found inside that tight business skirt of hers.

Ash had rented a car, which Ruby guessed was also a last-minute changeup, since the four of them were squashed in there like it was a clown car. Ruby struggled to avoid accidentally touching her knee to Shane's in the tiny back seat. How in the hell could the guy possibly still smell so good after three damn flights?

Shane, of course, did not seem to be having the same idea about not touching, since he was manspreading all over the place. Either he was doing it on purpose to get inside her head, or he was oblivious to the fact that there was another person in the row with him.

Of course, Ruby knew Shane was rarely oblivious about anything.

But the other scenario didn't make much sense either. When the team split after Scotland, Shane had made sure to let Ruby know he wasn't interested in extending their relationship. He'd apparently always seen it as a sort of coworkers-with-benefits situation. The realization had struck Ruby like a sledgehammer to the face—she'd thought they'd had something that transcended the team, something lasting—but she wasn't about to beg him to be her boyfriend. That kind of humiliation was far worse than the pain of heartbreak.

Nearly an hour later, with nothing but small talk and the clickety-clack of Ash's laptop—the woman was either always busy, or always wanted everyone to think she was busy—they pulled onto a remote trail, leading toward a grove of trees. Beyond the trees was a small yard that must have been incredibly picturesque in the daytime, with a cozy cottage nestled in the center.

Ruby suddenly had thoughts of waking with her coffee to the sounds of jolly songbirds and merriment, having a morning frolic in a meadow of wildflowers, leading up to a lunch of fennel and lemongrass salad, then spending the afternoon leisurely foraging for mushrooms while wearing those trendy yellow wellies. Her evenings spent with huckleberry tea and journaling, her brain abuzz with ideas for the novel she'd always meant to write.

"This doesn't look so bad," Ruby said, though Ash didn't seem convinced.

Ruby should have known the place might not be as bad as she feared. Ash was nothing if not a glutton for luxury, and this quaint little cottage was her idea of roughing it. But after the thoughts of concrete floors Ruby had had, this was heaven.

"As long as there's running water, I'm a happy camper," she said, stepping out of the car.

The air felt fresher than any air she'd ever breathed.

Inside, the cottage was even more enchanting than it was

from the outside. Mostly a creamy white, with wood ceilings, it was brighter than Ruby imagined it would be. The furniture was a mix of rustic antiques, like the adorable kitchen chairs with hearts cut out of the backs, paired with more modern, modular furniture. Ivory cupboards and beige rugs were accented with pops of color in the drapes and pillows—and all of it put together was wildly charming.

Bug made a quick sweep of the place and came back to the kitchen where Ruby had already flopped onto the most comfortable couch she'd ever sat in. Or maybe it was just comfortable compared to an airplane seat and a tiny clown car, but she was grateful nonetheless.

"There are only two bedrooms," Bug announced, as he stepped back into the kitchen/living area.

Ruby's eyes flitted to Shane's, and he caught her gaze. Ruby did not like the way her stomach did a little somersault.

Thankfully, Ash spoke before Ruby or Shane could say anything ridiculous they couldn't take back. "Boys in one, girls in the other," she announced, making it clear there would be no arguments.

"I'll take the couch," Shane said, apparently not wanting to share a queen-size with Bug.

Which meant Ruby had no choice but to bunk with Ash.

"One of the rooms has two small beds," Bug said. "You guys can take that one if you want."

"Fine," Ash said. "I get the shower first."

Of course, Ruby thought, but didn't have the energy to argue.

Ash took her sweet time in the shower and Ruby could barely keep her eyes open, her head nodding toward her chest more than once. Eventually Ash emerged and the guys were good enough to let Ruby have the shower next.

It was one of the most glorious experiences of her life. There was just something about a hot shower after a full day, and then some, of travel, but she kept it short so Bug and Shane could get in there too. She, at least, had some sense of courtesy for other people, even if Ash didn't.

After she was clean and feeling more ready for sleep than she had in a very long time, she flopped into the other single bed in the room where Ash was already snoring like a lumberjack, which was to say, as loud as a chainsaw. But it wouldn't matter, Ruby always packed her earplugs and had no doubt sleep would find her in seconds.

An hour later, her doubt was beginning to show as she continued to stare at the ceiling. By now she knew about forty times over that there were eleven and a half tiles across the ceiling of the room, and about ten and a quarter going the other way. Almost 118 square feet of white, bare, boring tiles. Counting them should have been enough to put her in a slumber for days, but her buzzing brain had other ideas.

It was no use.

The longer she lay there, the more awake she felt, and she knew from experience there was nothing she could do to ever get her any closer to the rest she needed. So she got up, hoping she might find a book or something to help take her mind off everything that had happened and everything that would have to happen to get Max back.

But as she padded out to the living area in her bare feet, she realized she was not alone.

Chapter 12

Shane startled as he heard the back patio door slide open.

"Hey," Ruby said, as she slipped outside. "Couldn't sleep?"

She looked innocent somehow. Vulnerable, with a blanket draped over her shoulders. She was back to short hair. Apparently the bob was a wig, though this style suited her so much better. Shane shook his head. "I think I'm too far past the point of tired. You?"

"Same, I guess," she said, setting the empty glass she'd brought out onto the table and sliding it toward him. "Where'd you find the booze?"

"Back of the cupboard above the fridge. It was a little dusty, but I figured it might help me sleep." He poured her a generous shot of the bourbon.

Ruby nodded. "That's what I'm hoping too."

"It stings a little going down," Shane said, "but definitely warms you up once it hits your stomach."

"Mmm, a cozy bourbon heat in the chilly Swiss countryside," Ruby said, clinking her glass to Shane's.

Shane realized if someone had proposed that exact thing, he would have said it sounded like a good time. If only they weren't in search of a friend in a buttload of danger, it could have been a nice little vacation. Shane took another sip of what was a tad closer to the burning inferno of hell's deepest depths than the cozy sweater warmth he was hoping for, but it was getting the job done. His mind was already starting to relax.

Ruby made a face and let out a little cough as she took her first sip. "Good Lord," she said, peering into her glass as if trying to make out what in the fresh hell was happening in there. "So, how've you been, Shane?" she asked.

They'd spent the past twentysomething hours alone together, but they hadn't really been alone for a single second of it. This was the first time they'd gotten a chance to talk.

"Oh, you know, living the dream," he said, swirling his glass, as if adding a bit of crisp, fresh air might help the burning firestorm situation.

"But how've you really been?" she asked, knowing his first answer had been a cop-out.

He smiled. He'd forgotten what it was like to have someone who knew him—really knew him—to talk to. He shrugged. "I'm good," he said. "I've been traveling a lot, having fun, getting into trouble…you know how it is."

Ruby tilted her head. "I'm not sure I do. I've spent the past three years trying to stay as far away from trouble as I can get."

Shane's smile faltered. "And then I waltzed back into your life."

She looked at him for a long time. "It might not have been so bad if had been just you," she said, taking another quick sip as if to chase the words down.

"I thought you'd never want to see me again," he said, surprised.

"It wasn't you, necessarily. It was the life. I just…couldn't be around any of that anymore."

Shane nodded. "And I feel like I've been chasing after that life, trying to find it again since the moment it was taken away."

Ruby smiled a sad smile. "We're quite a pair," she said, the words thick in her throat.

"We always were," Shane said. "It's just that we used to balance each other out."

"Until we didn't," Ruby said.

"Until we didn't," Shane agreed.

Shane wished he'd never made the mistake of finally taking the bait after Ruby had pushed him away so many times. He pretended it was fine that she didn't want a commitment. That she didn't want to be "pinned down" as she always called it. But Shane had always wanted more and the harder he pushed Ruby for it, the harder she pushed back, the work or her school always more important. Always taking all her time.

After a while, he'd just given up, hoping maybe he'd find what he was looking for somewhere else. At first, he'd even flaunted it in her face, showing up with women when she was around. It was stupid—he was young and wanted to make Ruby jealous, thinking it was what would make her change her mind, but—cue the shock and awe—it had the opposite effect.

He never did find what he was looking for. Only found ways other people weren't Ruby.

They sipped in silence for a while, Shane relishing the burn of the bourbon. It felt good—like a mini punishment for all the things he'd done in the past. Or maybe he was using the heat to burn down the past. Here she was, the one woman he knew he'd never forget—the one he wanted to fix everything with for so long—sitting right in front of him after all this time.

"Ruby," he said, and she glanced up from her glass into his eyes. "I'm sorry for…everything."

She shrugged. "There's nothing to be sorry for. We didn't promise each other anything," she said, with a weak smile.

"But we knew. We both knew there was more to you and I than just a bit of fun," Shane said.

"Maybe," Ruby said. "But that's probably why everything

went down the way it did. With Scotland, maybe it was just… easier to walk away when we had the chance."

Shane sat back heavy in his seat. "After Scotland there was just…nothing anymore."

"There wasn't nothing," Ruby said. "There was finally a life. I should have seen it way before I was forced to, but getting out of that world felt like the start of my real life."

Shane half smiled, gazing off toward a towering mountain range in the distance. "Not for me. Scotland was pretty much the end of my life."

"You can find all that again," Ruby said. "If I can do it, you can too."

Shane shook his head. "I know that life was never for you," he said. "But it was everything I ever wanted. Sure, we weren't exactly on the up-and-up, but we were doing good in the world. It was my only chance to ever do anything important. I have to say, I'm a little bit jealous that you're still out there doing the important work."

Ruby shrugged. "It's a good job, sure. But it's not quite as satisfying as I thought it would be."

Shane raised an eyebrow in question.

"It's just…not particularly efficient. It takes approximately six thousand years to get through all the red tape. Then it's months, if not years, to recover anything. Honestly, it all feels a little useless."

"At least you're trying," Shane said.

Ruby tilted her head, conceding. "Yeah."

They sat in silence until eventually Shane spoke. "It's not that I have a shitty life. It's just… I miss everything. I miss the team, I miss the chase…" He drifted off, not brave enough to say his last words out loud as he thought them.

I miss you.

Ruby was nodding absently. "I miss all that too," she said, her voice soft and clear in the crisp air. "But I hate that we're back here. Back in the con. I feel guilty every second we're here, knowing I'm doing the wrong thing."

"That's where we're different," Shane said, "I love that we're here. Not because Max has been taken, obviously, and yeah, Scotland went bad—I get why we had to stop. But I would love nothing more than to do a thousand more jobs with the team. And with you," he said, finding her eyes.

Ruby's lips parted as if she were about to say something, but instead she lifted her glass, draining the last of her bourbon in a gulp larger than one Shane would be willing to take of the volcanic swill. She barely flinched.

Ruby could feel the burn of the liquor all the way down her throat, into her stomach, and had to fight the urge to cough the fumes still burning her nose.

She wasn't about to admit, especially to Shane, how much she missed working with her old team too. She didn't miss having to watch her back and live in a world where she was paranoid 24/7, but she missed the camaraderie. They used to have so much fun together. Except maybe Ash. But the rest of them had a hell of a lot of fun messing with Ash, which made it almost as good.

The place out in the middle of the Swiss countryside was nothing short of spectacular. It was beautiful, quiet, remote— the absolute perfect place to hide out for a bit. Or forever, Ruby couldn't help but think, wondering for a moment how much real estate in this part of the world might cost.

A breeze found its way into her blanket and a shiver rattled through her.

"You're cold," Shane said, his voice full of concern.

Ruby always used to love and hate the way Shane wanted to take care of her—she hated anyone even implying she was less than completely independent, but she couldn't say attention from someone like Shane wasn't kind of nice sometimes. Of course, in the end, she wasn't the only woman Shane showed attention to. Not even close. Not that they'd made any commitments at the time—she was adamant about that. Neither of them did anything technically wrong, even though they were both hurting each other.

"I'm fine," Ruby said, though she was getting cold, but for whatever reason—some kind of silly pride thing, she supposed—she was reluctant to admit it.

"Well, I'm getting cold," Shane said, gathering up the glasses and bottle of bourbon.

There was a time when his actions would have annoyed Ruby. She knew he was heading inside because she was cold. That, plus the gathering of the items on the table, even her glass, would have sent her into an independence spiral. Maybe she was exhausted, or maybe she had simply mellowed over the past few years, but tonight it all felt kind of chivalrous.

They headed into the cottage, Ruby opening the door since Shane's hands were full.

"Hey, do you remember the last time we ate anything?" he asked, his voice lowering to a whisper.

"I don't think you have to worry about waking the snoring twins," Ruby said, smiling.

Bug's deep snore vibrated through the place, followed almost immediately by Ash's wheezier, but no less noisy, snuffle-snore.

Shane smiled back, shaking his head. "Glad I brought my noise-canceling headphones," Shane said.

"I never thought of that," she said. "I was trying to use earplugs, but some kind of soothing sounds or something might have lulled me to sleep easier."

"I like to throw on a guided meditation sometimes," Shane said, "but my mind wouldn't slow down tonight."

"But back to your question, I think the last time we had

anything was between our second and third flights. The coffee shop at the airport."

"Right. I had a couple doughnuts," he said, "but I'm pretty sure they're long gone by now."

Ruby opened the fridge, which was woefully bare, unless you needed some hot sauce or were interested in a sad little jar of mayonnaise. Shane was already checking out the cupboards, but from the way he was moving from one to the next, he wasn't having much luck either. She started opening cabinets from the opposite side, the situation more and more dire. Eventually they met in the middle, Ruby opening the final cabinet and Shane gasping, both reaching in for a miraculous bag of potato chips, their hands grazing.

"Sorry," Ruby said, glancing Shane's way.

It was the exact moment Shane also glanced Ruby's way, their faces suddenly close. Really close. Time seemed to stop, and Ruby realized their hands were still touching around the bag of chips. Shane's eyes flitted to Ruby's lips—just for a millisecond—but it was enough to make Ruby's breath hitch.

Was he thinking about kissing her? Did she want him to kiss her? Was this the longest moment in the history of the world two people touched hands in a cupboard and stood this close together?

The moment was so strange, yet so familiar.

Shane's head moved ever so slightly, maybe half an inch, but it was enough to get Ruby's heart racing. Her thumb brushed against his, the chip bag crinkling.

Everything slowed, the air growing heavy between them. Her body seemed to forget to perform its most basic duties, like a kind of magic in the little cottage was breathing for her. For them. They were about to break the rules. The past few days had been all about breaking the rules, but this was the one that meant the most. Still, she was having a hard time reminding herself to worry. She was having a hard time getting her brain to do anything.

And then, before she realized what she was doing, her head moved to meet him and his lips were on hers, and they were kissing hungrily...desperately. There was no thought. The world didn't drift away, exactly—more like an impenetrable bubble softly enclosed them, protecting them from the world outside that moment.

Shane's hand found its way to her waist ,and he squeezed, just a little, in a way he'd done so many times. A maneuver so achingly familiar that tears suddenly sprang behind Ruby's eyes—not because she was scared or sad, but because nothing had ever felt so much like home. The feeling was so strong it startled her, a snapshot of a memory so vivid and bright it could have been yesterday, pouring into her mind. Shane bringing her coffee to bed, just the way she liked it... cream, no sugar. A streak of sun slicing over them from the gap between the curtains. His hair an adorable disaster with one un-wrangleable chunk sticking straight out the left side. The smile he reserved just for her. She was able to melt into him until the memory passed, until something more urgent swirled deep inside her.

Her hand moved from the cupboard to his waist and his moved to pull her tighter, his other hand running up the length of her arm to her still-damp hair. He held her head as he grazed her chin, his stubble scraping delightfully up to her ear, then down her neck.

The heat in Ruby's belly intensified as she grasped onto him, trying to catch her breath. The air sucked out of the room as if it were on fire, the little cottage forgetting to breathe too.

And everything fell away. There were no swirling thoughts about the operation or whether she should even be there— there were no ideas about right and wrong at all. No more snapshots of the past. Just Shane and the way his hand was in her hair, making her feel so protected, the other one sliding its way around her body, electricity sparking with every millimeter until it finally came to rest on her lower back, and he pulled her even closer.

And then one thought niggled its way through to her conscious mind—the thought that this was the only place in the world she could completely lose control.

In Shane's arms.

She sighed at the reprieve of it—like a rest from the everyday of life, its frustrations and dark moments. But she also hated this feeling of not being able to follow her own rules, to make her own choices.

In truth, it was why she'd never let him get as close to her as he wanted to.

But the thought flew away, and she fell again. Fell into the oblivion of Shane.

"Oh, shit, sorry." The jarring voice came from out of nowhere.

Ruby jumped back and nearly let out a squeak, but Shane just straightened, reaching again for the bag of chips as if nothing out of the ordinary had been going on.

"Um, just needed a glass of water," Bug said, sheepish, even though it was Ruby and Shane who should have been the guilty-looking party.

"All yours," Shane said, stepping away from the cupboard/ sink area and sitting at the dining table.

He opened the chips and held the bag out to Ruby, who was having a bit more trouble gathering herself than Shane was.

"Thanks, but I think I'm just going to go to bed," she said, suddenly panicked.

How could she have let things get so far? After all the years of trying to build back the broken pieces. Years trying to forget. And the past few days had been one big reminder. She wasn't sure she could survive losing everything all over again.

She could never let it happen again. She had to keep her distance.

Chapter 13

Shane didn't know what time he finally fell asleep, but it had been late. Way too late considering the pressure they'd be under today, but it wasn't like he could just turn his brain off. Thoughts of Ruby swirled—the way her hair felt under his hand, the way she'd leaned into him, so familiar, her skin cool from the night air contrasting against the warmth of her lips.

He wondered if it had all been a dream, but his lips were slightly raw. It had been real. She had been real, and he couldn't stop the smile that crept across his face.

He'd thought of Ruby so many times over the years. She was the one he compared all the others to, so often wondering if he'd ever get to see her again, and if it would live up to all the times he'd imagined having her back in his arms.

It had, and so much more.

But now it was early. Way too damn early. And someone was up in the kitchen, not making the slightest effort to keep the noise down. How anyone even found anything in the cupboards to prepare was beyond him, but soon the scent of coffee began to call to him, and he cracked one eye open.

The noise instigator was Ash, as bright and chipper and put-together as ever. A bit maddening, since it had partially been her snoring that had kept him up—he couldn't imagine what it must have been like for Ruby right inside the room with her.

He closed his eyes and rolled over, not quite ready to let go of the feeling, trying his damnedest to memorize every second of last night's encounter. The way Ruby looked as she came outside to the way she shot back the last of her bourbon…the way the bourbon lingered in their kiss.

Then it was Bug's turn to waltz into the room. "Bless the gods," he said, rummaging around. Shane heard him pouring coffee, his body panicking that he wasn't going to get any, and so he roused himself to a seated position, rubbing his face, wishing his eyes didn't feel like they would never fully open again. He needed that coffee badly, and he was ready to fight anyone who got in his way.

"Well, good morning, Sunshine," Bug said, chuckling a little. "Looks like the couch was about as comfortable as the lumpy bed in there."

"Oh, yeah," Shane said. "It seemed real hard to sleep what with you snoring like a pack of passed-out sailors."

"It really was quite something," Ash piped in.

Shane gaped at her. "Seriously? You were worse than he was."

"Very funny," Ash said, giving him a look. "I do not snore."

Shane stared at her. "You believe that, don't you?"

"Of course," Ash said, waving her hand like it was the end of the conversation.

Which made Shane chuckle. "Have you seriously never had a partner tell you you're like a freight train rumbling through a nitroglycerine plant?"

Ash tilted her head. "No, I have not."

He and Bug chuckled a bit, but then Bug's expression turned to worry. Like he was concerned he might offend her…or maybe he was worried for her—maybe she'd never had someone get close enough for that. Which frustrated Shane a bit, considering Bug would have been that person and more if Ash would ever lower whatever soaring standards she must have in order to give the guy a chance.

The silence had grown awkward by the time Ruby padded out of the bedroom in her usual uniform of the wrinkled T-shirt and shorts she liked to sleep in. He thought of the first time he saw her all those years ago in Max's office. He remembered thinking that her features were a mix of contradictions. An extraordinary mix of things that should have never been paired together—the dark brows and light eyes, the angled nose with the soft, rounded lips. Unique. Interesting. The most beautiful thing he'd ever seen.

She still was.

Though, Shane noticed, trying to hide his smirk, the new haircut did not do well with sleep—especially the restless kind of sleep Shane assumed she had. Not for the same reason as him, of course, but because they had such a massive day ahead of them. It was a good thing Ruby had the wig to wear, he thought, because he wasn't sure how that hair would ever be tamed again.

"What's going on?" Ruby asked, sensing the tension in the room.

"Nothing," Bug said, obviously not wanting to bring up Ash's sore spot all over again. "We're all just tired, that's all."

"I guarantee not one of you is as tired as I am. Please tell me there's coffee left," Ruby said, to which Ash just rolled her eyes.

Shane grabbed the coffeepot and held it out as Ruby found a mug. She caught his eye and smiled, which made Shane forget to watch what he was doing and nearly overflowed her cup. He smiled sheepishly, feeling nervous all of a sudden.

He got to work making a new pot, figuring they'd all need at least a second cup. Ruby cleared her throat and sat. Bug was looking ridiculous trying to pretend he wasn't sneaking glimpses of Ash every five seconds. Not that Shane could talk, since he was pretty much doing the same thing to Ruby. Which then made him feel like he was a useless fool, back in high school in his nothing hometown, trying to impress the cool new girl in school.

"We're going to have to get food on the way," Ash said. "With the last-minute change to the plan, we didn't have time to get stocked up here. Hopefully I'll have a chance to get a few things if we end up staying here again tonight."

"If we stay here tonight?" Ruby asked, with a heavy emphasis on the word *if.*

"I thought we were all out of alternate plans."

Ash shrugged. "We are, but we were before we found this place too."

Out of nowhere, a clunk sounded somewhere in the vicinity of the front door, making everyone jump.

The team leaped into defense mode, all moving at once.

"What the hell was that?" Ruby asked.

"Could have been a bird hitting a window or something," Bug said.

But Shane had a feeling it wasn't a bird. The noise was a deeper *thunk* than a bird hitting glass and was too convenient coming from the front porch. He moved toward the door, pulling a gun from the back of his pants, not entirely loving the way Ruby looked at him like she was disappointed. He knew she hated guns, but in this business, you'd have to be reckless not to have one nearby.

He eased over to the door and pushed the curtains on the tiny window aside just enough to peek outside. Nothing. He grabbed the knob, turning slowly, cracking it open half an inch. There was nothing there. But as he went to close the door again, his gaze landed on a small, flat package sitting neatly on the welcome mat. He thrust the door open, quickly and efficiently checking one way and then the next, his training kicking in.

After a quick circuit around the house, Shane going one

way and Bug the other, they determined that if someone had been there, they were long gone.

"There were no footsteps in the snow," Shane said, coming back into the cottage.

Ruby and Ash had already taken the package to the table.

"Could have been a drone," Bug said.

"Wouldn't we have heard if a drone flew overhead to drop it?" Ruby asked.

"Not necessarily," Bug said. "Some of the new tech has made some drones almost noiseless."

"That's...disturbing," Ruby said.

But Bug just tilted his head. "Or rather convenient. How do you think I get most of my surveillance footage?"

"Exactly. Disturbing," Ruby said, smiling to let him know she wasn't judging.

In a situation like the one the team was in, they all knew they had to use every advantage.

"Let me get some equipment to take a look at that. It could be dangerous," Bug said. Returning to the room a few moments later, Bug scanned the package with various techy gadgets. "No dangerous chemicals detected," he said, "and there's nothing electronic inside. Should be relatively safe."

Ash picked it up and gingerly opened it, the entire team holding their breath.

She pulled out several photographs and started leafing through, letting out a long sigh as she did. "Well, so much for staying here again tonight."

"What is it?" Ruby asked, pulling the pile from Ash's hands. "Shit," she said as she flipped, then handed them to Shane.

The pictures showed the four of them in the airport, taken some time in the minute or so from the time they met up to when they got in the car. The next one showed an aerial shot of the car driving down a long, deserted road. Then the cot-

tage. The next photo was a night shot of the backyard sometime when Shane and Ruby had been drinking out on the patio.

The final shot was the real kicker.

Somehow the drone had flown low enough to get a shot
of him and Ruby through the window. A twinge of panic ran
through Shane, but it wasn't quite as strong as the twinge of
desire that hit Shane hard, witnessing him and Ruby fully
making out like that.

"Well, I guess we know why everything feels so awkward
this morning," Ash said.

"We need to check on Max," Ruby said, pacing across the
kitchen floor.

"We need to get out of here," Ash said.

Shane shook his head. "They've clearly known we've been
here since the moment we stepped foot in the place. If they
were going to do something to us, they would have done it
by now."

"Bug, could you please pull up the feed of Max?" Ruby
said, trying with everything in her to keep calm.

Bug grabbed a laptop from his room and sat at the table,
bringing up the page.

Max looked tired, thin and had a small gash over his right
eyebrow, but he was alive. Although the feed had no sound,
he appeared to be giving his captors hell the way he was wag-
ging his finger as he gave them a piece of his mind. Ruby
smiled. She'd only had that finger-wag pointed at her a couple of times, but there was nothing Max was more known for.
And he always wagged with love—except maybe in the case
of these jackasses who were keeping him locked up. Which
made Ruby smile even more.

But her smile faded. "They know who we are," she said.

A thick silence fell over the room. Back at Ruby's apartment, Ash had assured them these people had no idea who

they were. They could contact Ash, but Ruby, Shane and Bug were safe.

Ruby's stomach churned. Through all of this, the most important thing had been to stay off the radar—especially now with her job at the museum. "Bug?" she said. "How likely is it that they've figured out who we are?"

Bug looked angry, and like he didn't want to answer her. "High," he said. "There's no way people who have the kind of tech we've been seeing don't have some kind of facial recognition. They probably had us cased in three minutes."

"Shit," Shane spat out, turning away.

"Now can we get out of here?" Ash said, checking the closest window.

"Are you kidding right now?" Ruby asked. "We just find out our identities have been compromised—my whole world is blowing up—and you just want to get back at it?"

Ash blew out a long breath. "I'm sorry, okay? They never tried to find out who the people on the team were before. They never cared as long as the job got done. I didn't think anything would be different this time around."

"Everything *is* different this time around, though," Ruby said. "I have a life this time around. They've stooped to kidnapping this time around. And don't even get me started on how none of us have any trust in you this time around. Not after Scotland."

Ash looked like she'd been slapped. Ruby almost felt bad, but the truth was Ash had failed them all on that job. And now Ruby felt twice as much pressure because of it.

She had to make sure she was doing her job, plus make sure Ash was doing hers too.

She had to have the team's back, but she had to have her own now too.

She had to think of every possible scenario before it happened so they wouldn't be surprised.

Ruby glanced at the photos spread out on the table, her eyes landing on the one of her and Shane in the kitchen.

She had to keep her damned head in the game more than ever.

Shane stepped over to her, but she put her hand up. She couldn't risk him touching her when she was feeling like this. Hell, she couldn't risk him touching her at all. What had she been thinking last night? This wasn't about putting things back the way they used to be; this was about getting in, getting out, getting Max and getting on with her life.

And that was not going to happen if she got tangled up in Shane all over again.

Shane put his hands down and took a step back, hurt crossing over his features. But he recovered quickly. "This sucks— I get that. And I know I don't have as much to lose as you or Bug do, but these guys know us now. The information is out, and there's nothing we can do about it."

Ruby knew everything he said was true, but her mind still whirled, hoping, praying, to find a way she could go back to believing her life was still hers. She was supposed to be able to go back when this was all done and not have to worry about looking over her shoulder.

But there was no going back from this.

"Fine. Let's get the hell out of here," she said.

They all went to pack up—not that they'd had much of a chance to unpack. Five minutes later they were headed to the car.

"Not to be the voice of doom or anything," Bug said, "but I think we have to assume we're going to be followed no matter where we go. I can ditch our tail if we can get back into a city, but I guess my question is, do we need to?"

"What do you mean?" Ruby asked.

"Do we need to ditch the tail? Because they already know most of our plans, so…does it matter if they're watching us?"

Ruby didn't like the thought of anyone watching her in any scenario, but she could see his point.

"I don't like the idea of a potential curveball," Ash said.

"I don't think any of us do," Shane said, "but we're on a time crunch and the more time we spend dealing with this thing that might not even be a threat, the less time we have to prepare for the actual job."

"But why send the photos?" Ash asked. "We would have never known they were watching."

"Maybe they want us to know they're watching," Ruby said, the idea coiling uneasily up her spine.

"Why?" Shane wondered. But no one had an answer for him.

They got in the car and drove off, no one saying a word for a long time. Snow had started to fall in light, fluffy flakes, and Ruby concentrated on the countryside. Even the views along the highway were stunning, mountains in the not so far distance, green peeking out here and there from the snowy wonderland.

If, after all this, she had to go into hiding, she wondered what life would be like living there. But no matter how beautiful her surroundings, the thought of having to hide away from everything she'd worked so hard for was painful. She'd finally found a place in life where she was comfortable. Where she was happy.

The snow fell harder.

Ash interrupted her thoughts, deciding it was time to get to work. "Okay, we all know the drill. Shane and Ruby, you're going in as waitstaff. Bug has already taken care of getting you on the list and they'll be expecting you. Bug's going to run surveillance and security remotely. We're hoping we can get close enough with a van without raising any suspicions, but you know what to do if we can't get away with it."

Bug nodded once and mumbled something under his breath.

Ruby could only imagine what kind of awkward position

Ash was willing to put Bug into. Once she had him waiting down a sewer shaft for hours so he could get a wireless feed into an exclusive apartment building in Chicago.

Of course, Ash never put herself into any danger. She was always off parked in front of some safe house or coffee shop somewhere, ready to rattle off instructions while the rest of them put themselves on the line.

It suddenly hit Ruby that Max wasn't going to be with them on this one. He was always in the thick of it with Ruby and Shane—sometimes as hired help at an event, but more often as one of the guests, able to pull off any persona. He had an indistinct coloring about him and was able to pull off any character—from a Middle Eastern business tycoon to royalty from an obscure island off the coast of the Mediterranean…hell, he'd once even pulled off posing as a high-powered rancher from Texas.

Ruby smiled, recalling how hard it was not to break character that time, what with his thick, twangy accent and hat that made him look much smaller than he was.

But her smile slowly faded as she remembered that the stakes had never been so high.

Chapter 14

The sky was ominous. Shane had hoped the storm the weather station was calling for would hold off for a few more hours, but that had been wishful thinking. As he got out of the car a few blocks from his destination, the snow covered him in an instant.

He let out a long sigh.

This was going to make things much more complicated. At least he was going to be indoors, he thought, hoping all would go as planned and there would be no need for some of the contingency plans.

He arrived at the temp agency a few minutes before Ruby. They needed to get to the event space as soon as possible, and people on staff would arrive hours before the guests. Shane and the team had spent the rest of the drive into the city going over the plan approximately four hundred and seventeen times. To be honest, Shane had found the whole thing a little excruciating. He knew how to do this—it was the one thing he was good at, and most of his part was usually improvised anyway. He was the one who caused distractions where distractions were needed. He was the one who charmed when charming was called for. He was the one who watched the room to make sure everything went the way it was supposed to. And to do whatever it took to fix it if something didn't.

The plan was simple, though of course it wouldn't be easy.

Get in, snatch the scepter, get out. And deal with about sixty-eight layers of security while they were at it. Easy peasy.

Ruby had the harder job, even though she'd disagree. She was the one who had to keep to the shadows, be invisible. Shane didn't think he could be invisible if he tried. And honestly, he didn't know how someone who looked like Ruby could ever fly under the radar either, but she got away with it every time. That was real acting. Not making eye contact. Not leaving a single memory in her wake. Just another unimportant person that witnesses would never be able to recall enough to give a good description. Ruby always said everything about her was average, but to Shane she was the least average person on the planet. She was everything, and he kicked himself every day for ever agreeing to keep things strictly casual with her.

He hated himself even more that he let her believe anyone else could ever measure up.

And last night with the bourbon, and the cottage, and the kiss, it had all felt like coming home again, even though he'd never stepped foot in the place before. He had a suspicion it wouldn't matter where in the world he was, Ruby would always be that home for him.

But she was past all that now. She had her new job, her new fancy apartment, her new life. And Shane didn't fit into that world. Still, the kiss meant there still had to be something there, didn't it?

But he didn't have time to think about it. He owed it to Max to focus on what he needed to focus on—to do what he did best and get his friend back.

He gave the woman checking the workers in his best smile. "Bryce Hudson," he said.

The woman's eyes sparkled. "An American," she said, looking him up and down. "Something tells me you're going to be a hit."

Shane was decent at accents, but he hadn't had as much

time to prepare as he would have liked. Normally he'd get to a country ahead of time and soak in as much language as he could, but with the time constraints, he decided to go with his regular accent. Besides, it was his job to stand out, and having a different accent than everyone else made it even easier.

"I try my best to provide great service," he said, his smile never faltering.

"I bet you do," the woman said suggestively.

Shane stood and smiled a bit longer, the woman just appreciating him for a while. It didn't make him uncomfortable, the way women sometimes acted around him, but he couldn't say he enjoyed it either. It was simply one of the tools in his arsenal that made him good at this. Finally, he cleared his throat. "So, uh, what now?"

The woman blinked as if coming back to the present. "Right." She consulted her list and checked his name off, running her pen along the page. "Server, okay, perfect. Head to the back room and find yourself a uniform. The servers are pretty simple, dark pants." She leaned back and took a good long look at his crotch. "Yup, those will do," she said, nodding. "Guess this isn't your first go around," she said appreciatively.

"No, ma'am, definitely not," he said, trying to seem appreciative right back.

"Okay, so find yourself a white collared shirt and an apron and wait with the others in the big room at the end of the hall."

"Sounds great, and thanks for all your help," he said, shooting her a wink for good measure.

"Oh, you are most certainly welcome," she said, turning to watch him walk away.

He turned to her once more and chuckled a little, acting like he loved the attention she was shooting his way. Thankfully another person showed up to check in and Shane could get on with his mission.

Once he was in the new shirt and fitting in nicely with the

rest of the waitstaff, he leaned against the wall to wait. Several people filed in, one after the other, but Shane kept his eyes open for just one.

He checked his watch. It wasn't like Ruby to be running this late. Or late at all, really. Inwardly, he groaned. If she didn't make it, he was not about to go on this job without her. She was the one everything depended upon. Sure, they all had their parts to play, but without Ruby, the job couldn't go on.

Beginning to pace, Shane checked his watch once more. Soon, the woman who had checked him in came into the room.

"Five minutes, everyone. And make sure you're put-together. This is an incredibly particular clientele, and they will notice if even a hair is out of place."

A few people moved to mirrors set up around the room, smoothing hair and straightening collars, while Shane wondered when he should call it. There was no way he was going if Ruby didn't make it. He paced a couple minutes more and decided he needed to make a break for it. Would it be easiest to fake being sick, or simply try to find a way to sneak out?

More importantly, where the hell was Ruby? he wondered, his stomach starting to feel out of sorts.

If he was going to do this, it had to be now, before the woman came back and wrangled him onto the bus transporting them to their destination.

He started to move.

Suddenly, a woman stepped in front of him, stopping him in his tracks.

"Oh, sorry," the woman said, looking into his eyes in a weirdly meaningful way.

Something about her voice tried to twig something in Shane's brain, but he couldn't quite place what it was.

"No problem," Shane said, about to move around her when he realized. "Oh, hey," he said, shocked at how different she looked.

Ruby had always been the master of disguise in their little group, but she had outdone herself this time. Shane had to give the black-haired, dark-lipsticked, glasses-wearing beauty one more glance to confirm it was her.

"Hey," she said back, pushing her glasses a little farther up the bridge of her nose.

"Wow," he said quietly, giving her a nod of approval and moving back into the room.

She nodded at him, more than a little amused.

Ruby hadn't been sure if she'd fly under the radar the way she wanted to, but the moment she spotted Shane, she knew. He had no idea who she was. And if he, the person who probably knew her best in the world, didn't know right away—a thought that caught her a bit off guard—nobody else would have a clue. The people watching them would likely figure it out soon enough, but if there was even a chance she could keep the element of surprise, she was going to damn well try to take it.

She boarded the bus along with the rest of the staff hired to work the party—everyone from kitchen staff, to wait-staff, to guys who must be additional security. She spent most of the bus ride trying to memorize each person and figure out how much of a threat they could potentially be, though she was very careful not to make eye contact. She knew how to not get noticed, and avoiding eye contact was rule number one.

Ruby used several tactics to disguise herself. She left her hair just a little messy, not enough to stand out, obviously, or to garner the attention of the managers, but just enough to look less put-together. Baggier clothes were another tool she used, but not too baggy—just enough that nothing hugged her figure, to give the appearance of "nothing to see here." She'd gone a little different with her makeup than she normally would, the dark lipstick and smoky eyes more likely to draw attention, not in a sexy Hollywood siren sort of way, but more like a mainstream goth if there was such a thing.

The overall effect was a sort of non-sexy, not quite girl next door. Just an "average, everyday nice person" kind of thing.

After she'd checked in, she kept to the edges of the room and didn't make any moves to try to talk to anyone…until, that was, it looked like Shane was about to bolt.

She loved the little thrill that had surged through her, realizing Shane didn't know she was there. The way he'd been pacing made her wonder, but she hadn't known for sure until she saw the recognition dawning in his eyes and she had to work hard not to break character and laugh, or, you know, gloat. But they were on the move now and she couldn't risk eye contact with Shane again.

They traveled by bus for several miles to the base of an unnamed mountain. On the ride, they'd been told to not ask questions, not bother the guests and well, basically, not talk to anyone. Once they arrived at the base, a large group was already there waiting. Ruby pulled the collar of her jacket up higher on her neck, thankful the wig she wore was helping keep her warm. The snow that had been falling in beautiful large flakes had turned icier, with smaller flakes driving through the wind. As they waited, guards searched through everyone's bags.

What seemed like hours later, though according to her watch had only been forty minutes, Ruby was grateful to finally enter the capsule that would transport them up the mountainside. She thought she'd been prepared for the gondola ride, but she had never been on one, and had never been a fan of heights. With the increasing winds, she was in for a bit more than she bargained for. At least she wasn't the only one who looked nervous as the large capsule that about fifteen of them were trapped in swayed slightly one way and then the other, jolting a bit whenever they crossed a support pole. At least Shane wasn't on the same gondola—he'd left on the one that departed about fifteen minutes before hers.

The woman seated beside her began to turn a little green around the edges and Ruby prayed she could keep it together until they got to the top. She couldn't imagine having to finish the ride after someone had lost their lunch in the small enclosure.

Ruby had never been so relieved to exit a space in her life, sucking in big gulps of air as her feet hit solid ground again.

Taking her first glance around the grounds, Ruby wondered how rich the people who owned it were. She'd been in plenty of mansions and grand houses before, but this place was next level. Straight ahead, an enormous building made mostly of glass loomed above, several stories high. She couldn't help but think it didn't have a whole lot of privacy. Of course, when you lived at the top of a mountain where the only ways in were a secure gondola or maybe a helicopter, privacy probably wasn't much of an issue.

Ruby did not like that their potential exits were so limited, but the views from the top of the mountain were perhaps more spectacular than anything she'd ever witnessed. She'd been in mountains before, but never this high up. Three-hundred-and-sixty-degree views of snow-capped mountains with nothing but trees and nature to hold her attention. Far below a river weaved lazily through the base of the mountains as if saying, *Whatever, dude, you just stand there, I'm happy to go around—I've got all the time in the world.* Despite all the things going on, Ruby found herself smiling, trying to take it all in.

Shivering and ducking her head against the wind, she began to move toward the house, but only got a few steps before a large man stopped her.

"Where do you think you're going?" he asked.

"Um, to the house to help get the place ready for the party," Ruby said, unsure why she had caught the man's attention— something she had decidedly not wanted to do.

"No, you wait."

Ruby stepped back into the group to wait for whatever was supposed to come next. At least she wasn't the only confused one, as the waitstaff in her group all glanced at each other for guidance, which of course no one had.

Soon another vehicle pulled up, smaller than a bus, with large tracks on it instead of wheels. Ruby wondered if the thing had climbed all the way up the mountain, or if it had come by some sort of giant military helicopter or something, causing her to wonder again just who these people were. The extravagance she'd seen on other jobs was starting to pale in comparison.

"Where are we going?" someone in the group asked as the machine jostled them along to their new destination.

A trickle of worry danced through Ruby's stomach. Wherever they were headed had not been on the blueprints of the complex. She'd memorized every outbuilding on there and they'd already left each of them behind. As they moved along the bumpy trail, small buildings—security huts—came into view every hundred meters or so. She could practically feel the rest of the group around her starting to wonder what the hell they had gotten themselves into. It was something she knew because she was feeling the exact same thing.

Finally, they came to another, more typical building, a single story, though the glass theme continued with large windows on three sides. When in Rome, Ruby supposed, or more accurately, when on a remote mountaintop. Her mind whirred with contingency plans, though there had been no discussion as to what they might do if the event was held in a location they knew nothing about.

But it wasn't like they could just back away. Max's life was at stake…and since the people holding him knew who they all were now, all of theirs were too.

Chapter 15

"How you doin', Bug?" Shane asked quietly.

The comms Bug had come up with were state-of-the-art, fitting into Shane's ear like one of those new hearing aids you could hardly see when a person was wearing it. With the thing buried so far in his ear, he had no idea how the team could hear him clearly without any muffling, but he could hear the rest of them as if they were right inside his head—which, he supposed, they kind of were—so he assumed they could hear him just as well.

"Oh, you know, just hanging around," Bug answered.

Shane could hear the wind that must have been swirling around Bug, who was apparently—and quite literally—hanging off the side of the mountain as they spoke. Bug was an experienced climber, but Shane couldn't begin to fathom how he'd gotten all his climbing equipment up there, let alone all the tech he'd need to hack into the security system and keep the team safe.

Of course, true to form, Bug already had the team fully connected to each other and was well on his way to breaking into the top-of-the-line security system.

There wasn't a whole lot for Shane to do at that moment and he felt a little guilty about it. His job—watching and waiting—always seemed a little lame compared to what the others were always doing. Sure, the team used to tell him he was the only person who could do what he did, but still, he kind of felt like a useless ball of, like, lint or something. Pretty lint, maybe, lint from a set of silky, shimmery sheets, but still lint. But he was a professional, and he had a job to do, even if he wondered whether his job even mattered much.

He fed Ash as much information as he could about the exits in the place, obvious and not so obvious places where they could potentially make an escape. As he spoke quietly, making sure no one spotted him talking to himself, he'd shoot the odd smile to some of the other waitstaff. He'd instinctively always known that making as many friends as possible—on a heist as much as in real life—was a good way to magically find additional contingency plans in case things went wrong. He was the "shit! things are going south" guy. The guy they hoped never to use but who was there if they needed them.

Fortunately—or perhaps unfortunately for Shane—the crew was careful, organized and practiced, so his talents did not often come into play.

"Figuring out everything okay, new guy?" a woman asked, sidling up to him.

Shane had been so focused on making sure he hadn't missed any potential exit points, he'd barely seen her coming until she was right in front of him.

"Oh, uh, yeah, I think so, thanks," he said, hopefully dazzling her with the smile he shot her way.

She smiled back. "You seem a little distracted there," the woman said. "Something on your mind? Fight with the girlfriend, perhaps?"

Shane was used to this kind of questioning. The not-so-subtle information dig, fishing to see if he was taken. His smile went from dazzling to a bit more playful. "No girlfriend at the moment," he said.

The girl arched one eyebrow. "Boyfriend?"

He chuckled a little. "No significant other of any kind," he clarified.

"Aw, sad," she said, not sounding at all like she thought it was sad as she slid a finger up his arm. "We'll have to see if we can do something about that."

He made his eyes dance as she turned to get back to work, well practiced at keeping a person interested without making any promises. His job wasn't just to get one person willing to help if need be, but ideally, all of them.

He got back to his own work—he'd been tasked with helping to set up the tables—and he laid down another set of cutlery as he continued to scope the place.

"Three large skylights could become a factor," he said once he was confident no one was close enough to hear.

"Got it," came Ash's voice over the comms.

Ash was stationed somewhere outside too. But Shane knew better than to think she'd be even close to hanging off the edge of a cliff. More likely, she'd found an unused vehicle or outbuilding to run operations from. He chuckled to himself, wondering if she was tucked into some snowplow or tractor somewhere.

"Okay, so I'm thinking our best window to grab the target is sometime during the auction. As of now, we don't know where they're holding the auction items, so we're going to have to play this by ear a little bit," Ash continued.

A sigh came over the comms. Ruby. She did not like to play anything by ear, always wanting to plan things out and take every possible outcome into consideration. Shane, on the other hand, started to get excited, his stomach even fluttering a little. This was where he shone—in the realm of the unknown. The realm where anything was possible. He had to fight the smile that wanted to slip across his face.

Shane could also practically hear the eye roll Ash was no doubt performing.

"Anyway," Ash continued, "our best bet will likely be immediately after the item is auctioned off and is leaving the stage. There will be plenty of security around the scepter, but a lot of them will be focused on other items as well. Ruby, Shane, see what you can find out about where the stage is going to be, and any potential routes the auction items will take on and off the stage."

"Got it," Shane said, still placing silverware.

The hardest part of a job was waiting for opportunities, or more accurately, keeping your cover while waiting for opportunities. But he continued to work until all the tables were set, his eyes scanning the room nonstop, waiting for anything that might be a clue as to where this whole thing was going to go down.

It turned out, in the end, it was pretty easy to spot when part of the crew set up a podium at the front of the room. It was an obvious place for the auction to be held, the view out the windows spectacular—though Shane wasn't sure how spectacular it would be once it got dark—but it was the place Shane had been most hoping it wouldn't be held. First, because he assumed that was the very window—and cliff—Bug was probably hanging off. Having an entire room full of people staring in that direction all night was not the best scenario. And second, because there was only one way to and from that area of the room—a single door off to the side.

He needed to see what was behind that door.

Luckily, the woman who'd checked him in hours ago was standing near the staging area. He thought it might be a good idea to remind her of his existence.

"How's everything going, boss?" he asked, shooting her his trademark dazzle.

She turned, a slight expression of annoyance crossing her face—until she saw who was talking, that was.

"Oh, hey," she said, her eyes brightening. "It's, uh, good, I think," she said, though she looked a little nervous.

"Is there anything I can do to help?" Shane asked. "You look kinda stressed."

She let out a long breath. "Well, I'm always stressed during a job, but this…well, this is a really big job."

"I kind of figured," Shane said, with a crooked smile. "Can't say as I've been to too many parties on the top of a mountain."

"And that's why everything has to be perfect." She started glancing around the room again, searching for any tiny thing potentially out of place.

"I get it," Shane said. "But don't worry. I can tell by the way you run things that this night is going to be spectacular."

She focused her attention back on him, giving him another once-over like she'd done back at the check-in table. "You know, I think I'd like you to cover these tables at the front," she said, motioning to a few tables nearby—the ones closest to the stage. "It couldn't hurt for everyone to get a good look at you."

"Oh, brother," a voice said deep inside his ear through the comms unit, and he fought the urge to say something back.

"Of course, anything you need, boss," he said. "I won't let you down."

Something crashed across the room, and she rushed off, but Shane had gotten what he needed. Being stationed at the front of the room would get him close to the auction, which meant being close to the scepter.

And close to the mysterious door that it would exit through.

Ruby watched as Shane flirted with every girl in the room—and a few of the guys too. The man was nothing if not a charmer. She kind of hated that she fell for his charms just as much as everyone else—hell, probably more—but the thing was, she knew him so much better than any of these people and, to be honest, he was so much more than just charm.

But she was angry with herself about last night. She could never let anything like that happen again. When this was all over, she could hopefully get back to her life, her real life, and leave it all behind. Shane would never leave the life behind.

He always said it was the only thing he was good at, even if Ruby knew better. Shane could do anything he wanted—it was just…the only thing he ever wanted was for things to go back to the way they were. Back to the con life.

Come on, Ruby, focus, she scolded herself. She was acting like some ridiculous kid with a schoolgirl crush. She hadn't even done this when she and Shane were dating, but something felt different now. Maybe she'd just been lonely the last few years.

That had to be it, she thought, happy she'd figured it out. Now she could get on with the matter at hand.

Find a way through that damned door at the side of the room. The team had to find out what was back there before the auction started or they'd have no chance. They needed to know what exits were beyond the door and come up with some kind of plan.

"I'm in the system," Bug said over the comms.

Finally. Ruby wasn't sure if it was because he was hanging off the side of a cliff, the fact that he hadn't been on the job for years or that security had been that hard to crack, but it had taken Bug way longer than usual to get in.

Not that it mattered. They were in now and could get down to some real work.

"Anything on the door at the front of the room?" Ruby asked, tucking a piece of hair behind her ear and covering her mouth to prevent her conversation being seen by a nearby staff member.

"Give me a sec," Bug said, with lightning-fast keystrokes tapping lightly in the background.

Ruby busied herself straightening a napkin here, or moving a water glass a fraction of an inch there.

"Shit," Bug finally said. "There's nothing on the plans. The door doesn't even exist in in the system."

"What does that mean?" Ruby wondered.

"It means they have all the priceless artifacts stowed away

in a place that doesn't exist and has no security. At least no security that ties into this system."

"So, there must be a separate security system."

Bug made a musing sound. "Smart," he said. "But not good for us."

"We need to find out what's behind that door," Ash said, her voice even more grating from practically right inside Ruby's brain.

She glanced over to see if Shane had any chance of getting near the door, but he was currently surrounded by not one, but three of the female waitstaff, apparently on some kind of break. There was a *lot* of giggling going on. She suppressed the urge to look toward the heavens. She couldn't be mad—he was doing what he was supposed to be doing. It was just that sometimes she wished she didn't have to watch it.

She focused on the view behind Shane, the miles and miles of sky, the enormous old trees, the pristine snow practically begging for someone to jump into it. Ruby wondered if that could potentially start a massive avalanche, which made her think of Bug out there on the mountainside, vulnerable and likely not having the best time of his life.

The least she could do was find a damn way through that door.

And then she saw it.

A tiny, but distinct smudge on the wall of glass. A small, single smudge, as if someone had touched the glass lightly, not with their whole hand, but just a light swipe of the tip of their finger. But it was enough to give Ruby an idea.

She headed back to the kitchen area, and in a back closet, found what she needed, then headed back toward the podium area.

"Just what do you think you're doing?" Madeline, the woman in charge of the staff, asked.

"Oh, sorry, I just noticed a smudge over there," she said,

pointing to the offending mark, "and thought I should give these windows a once-over." She held up the glass cleaner and paper towel as confirmation.

"Right," Madeline said. "Good catch." She nodded toward the windows, essentially giving her permission to go ahead with the task.

Ruby silently thanked whoever had been careless enough to leave the mark, starting at the far end of the window wall away from the door. She wanted a little time to blend into the background. When a person first starts doing something new, people take notice. But once you've been doing it for a few minutes, people tend to forget you're even there.

She polished away, moving closer and closer to the door, making sure to obliterate the offending smudge along the way. As she neared the door, she began to glance behind her, getting a sense of where everyone was and what they were doing. With the room pretty much ready to go, there were only a few people left in the room. Most of the staff had been given last-minute tasks in the kitchen and at the back of the building, where guests would be arriving soon.

Ruby was not going to get a better chance.

She slipped through the door, as confidently as she could. If she was going to get caught, she wanted to be able to play it off as a mistake. The good old, "oh, sorry, thought this might be the bathroom" trick, but there was no one behind the door. In fact, there wasn't a whole lot of anything behind the door besides a long, seemingly endless hallway.

"I'm in," Ruby said quietly, her whisper echoing off the walls of the dimly lit space.

"What do you see?" Bug asked.

"Nothing really. A hallway."

"Go down it if you can," he said, but Ruby was already well on her way.

Her footsteps echoed as she walked, a sense of urgency

and unease drifting through the air. At the end of the hall was another door, just as nondescript and ordinary as the one at the other end.

"It's another door," she whispered.

"Be careful," Bug said.

Ruby took a second to still her breath and steel her nerves. She hated going into things this unprepared. But she slipped the door open anyway.

And there was…nothing there. Just a cubicle of a room with large metal doors on the other side.

"It's an elevator," Ruby said. "And it looks like it only goes down."

"Do not go into that elevator," Ash said, her "do as I say" voice coming into full effect.

But she didn't have to say it. There were a lot of things Ruby was willing to do—risks that were worth it once you calculated out the potential outcomes. But jumping into an elevator and getting essentially swallowed into the depths of the earth with, likely, a bunch of highly trained security people on the other end, was not a risk she was willing to take.

She was pretty sure she couldn't just play it off as a search for the loo.

"I'll see what I can dig up," Bug said over the comms as Ruby did the only thing she could do.

Turned around and went back the way she'd come.

She made it about halfway when a sound made the hair on her arms stand up. A whirring, much like the sound an elevator might make.

She began to move a little faster, though she was nervous about making too much noise.

Just as she neared the door back to the event hall, a tiny ding sounded.

But she smiled—she was going to make it.

But the smile faded at warp speed when the door just a few feet ahead of her began to creak open.

Ruby frantically glanced around, but her glance only confirmed what she already knew.

There was nowhere to run, and definitely nowhere to hide.

Chapter 16

"Holy hell, Shane!" Ruby whisper-yelled.

Shane marveled at the way Ruby could look as angry as she did, yet was obviously also relieved. She frantically motioned for him to go back to the event area, then stormed past him as she reentered the large room.

"What the hell are you doing?" she whispered in a rather non-gentle manner over the comms.

Shane pretended to adjust a couple plates on the nearest table. "I just wanted to make sure you were okay," he replied quietly.

"I was perfectly fine until you opened that door and gave me a heart attack!"

"Sorry," Shane said, making sure his back was to Ruby before he smirked.

It was one of those moments when you absolutely couldn't laugh. But remembering the expression on Ruby's face as she spotted him, all deer in the headlights, it took every ounce of theater training he'd had not to fall apart.

A moment later, staff began to stream in from the kitchen area, led by the supervisor.

"Everyone get ready," the woman yelled, clapping her hands. "I've just been notified that guests are starting to arrive. These people are the elite of the elite, so tonight you must serve like you've never served before. They are used to luxury and the absolute best service, and it is time to rise to the challenge!"

Shane couldn't help but be impressed by the way she delivered her speech—the pep talk giving him a little surge of adrenaline, like he was about to perform a feat like no other.

"Due to the remote location, and the weather not fully cooperating, guests will arrive slowly, so it's up to us to keep them happy. Keep the drinks and hors d'oeuvres flowing at all times. Do what you can to enchant them, and let's make this the most unforgettable night of their lives."

Okay, maybe the use of the word *enchant* was a bit over the top, Shane thought, but he admired her passion. He could certainly see why she'd been hired for the event.

Shane grabbed a tray of champagne and took his position at the edge of the room.

Ash's voice came through his earpiece. "Well, team, we were hoping we'd be able to snag the target item once it left the stage after the auction, but with what Ruby just found out, that is going to be much more difficult than we'd anticipated. Essentially, if the scepter is not intercepted before it goes back through that door, the layout of the hallway—with a single way in and a single exit out—means we won't have a chance. Bottom line, we need to do this inside the auction room, so prepare for plan E."

Shane pulled in a fortifying breath. This was not how the team usually worked. They were a behind-the-scenes kind of crew—usually getting in and out and being long gone before anyone was the wiser. Plan E meant a lot more risk.

There was a small flurry of activity as two couples entered at the back of the room. The women shed their expensive fur coats. Shane hoped they were faux fur, but with this particular crowd, he had his doubts.

The sun was just beginning to set, casting a rosy hue across the snowy landscape, shades of pink breaking through the clouds as if it were a special effect created for the occasion.

Shane wondered if people with this kind of money might be able to do that.

But none of the people arriving even noticed. Maybe they saw spectacular sights every day, or maybe since they were surrounded by it at all times, they'd become immune to beauty.

The men were dressed in tuxedos and the women in fancy evening gowns, some sparkly, some shimmery, but all impeccable, like they'd been custom-made. Shane's fingers began to itch with all the jewels walking around the room. He imagined some of them were likely the kind of item the team would go after—valuable and illicit. Ruby's head must be exploding, her mind on fire, trying to pinpoint where some of the items belonged, which was most certainly not on the necks, wrists and ears of people in this room.

He tried to relax, but mostly he tried not to be obvious about the fact that he was watching Ruby like a hawk. Plan E meant he needed to run interference if anyone got in the way of her next steps. And judging by the way their supervisor had suddenly taken notice of Ruby, whose food tray was almost empty—an absolute no-no for the event—it was time to move.

He plastered on his most charming smile and beelined for the boss lady.

"Anything last-minute that needs to be done?" Shane asked, easing in front of the woman, blocking her view of Ruby.

He knew Ruby would pounce on the moment and be invisible within seconds, but he had to hold this woman's attention for at least that long, or things would get a lot trickier.

The woman blinked, startled that someone had just pretty much bounded in front of her, an angry expression flitting across her face, though fading when she noticed who it was.

"Ah, Bryce, right?"

"That's right, boss," he said, making his eyes light up like he was delighted she remembered his name.

"I think everything's under control for now," she said, tilting her head so she could gaze at him more suggestively. "But after this is all over, I wouldn't say no to a little help…relaxing." She grazed a finger along his forearm.

Shane pretended to be shocked, then smiled wider. "That sounds intriguing," he lied, wanting nothing more than to get back to work now that he had done his job with the boss lady.

"Just keep up the good work," she said, kind of peeking behind him. "Hey, did you see where that girl went?"

"What girl?"

"The kind of mousy one with the emo sort of style. Dark lipstick never looks very good on people with pale skin," she finished off, unnecessarily.

Shane shrugged. "Sorry, I don't think I've seen her," he said.

Shane headed back toward the front of the room smirking a little, since he could say it with 100 percent confidence: the boss lady was not going to see a mousy emo girl again today.

Ruby grabbed her bag out of the locker at the back end of the kitchen and headed to the lobby area. The waitstaff were not supposed to use the washrooms in this area, but if anyone questioned her on the way in, she was going to say she was inspecting them for cleanliness.

No one would be questioning her on the way out.

She made her way to the stall at the farthest end of the room and began rummaging through her bag. She used a premoistened makeup remover on her lips to get rid of the dark, almost black lipstick. Then she applied a more muted red color that made her more mainstream than the goth situation she'd had going on, maybe made her even a little sexy. Her lightly smoky eyes would work as they were, and as soon as she took off the dark glasses and dark wig and tousled her own short, brown hair, she looked very different from when she'd walked in.

Underneath the usual gum, lip glosses, wallet, phone, etc., Ruby pulled the small tab revealing the bag's false bottom. It was only about an inch and a half of space, but it was enough for what she needed. She pulled out a shimmery, slinky slip dress in some kind of magical material that didn't wrinkle, shrugging out of the white shirt and black pants she'd been wearing as a member of the staff. She slipped the dress over her head, clicked the four-inch stiletto heels onto her convertible shoes, which she'd previously been wearing as flats, and stuffed all her gear into the small backpack. She listened for a few moments to make sure the bathroom was empty, then exited the stall, tossing the bag into the trash, carrying only a small silk pouch with her lipstick and phone inside. If she needed proof of identity, anything she'd need could be found on the phone.

Ruby liked to be as prepared as possible for any job, always researching as much as she could find on collections and targets, and then researching some more, but her work before a job was nothing compared to Bug's. For every contingency plan, Bug had to do a ton of legwork. Honestly, she wasn't sure where he found time to sleep.

For this, plan E, Bug had set Ruby up with an entirely new identity—Gabrielle Le Croix, an art dealer with a reputation for getting her clients what they wanted…even if that meant going through less than proper channels. It wasn't a real reputation, of course. But when Bug did a job, he didn't half-ass it. Gabrielle was fully set up with months' worth of social media posts, a full website, misinformation planted on the dark web—which was where her reputation preceded her—as well as identity documents and banking information.

It was just one plan out of several, for one member of the team. Each of them had several identities they'd had to memorize since they didn't know which plan Ash would eventually decide to use. And Bug had to do all that setup.

"Ready," she said quietly into her comms.

"The room is almost full," came Shane's voice in reply.

It was time to move. With her new disguise, Ruby was posing as a guest at the party—it was too risky to have both her and Shane waiting the tables at the front of the room.

As the guests filed in, Shane made sure a seat at the table closest to the stage would remain free. Ruby never could understand how he did it—she would certainly never be able to—but Shane always got the job done. If he said he could do something, which, incidentally, almost always required convincing people of things, it would happen without fail. It was one of the things she admired most about him—the ability to charm someone even if they knew you were charming them, which somehow made them respect him more. It was what he had done to her.

"The auction's set to begin in ten," Ash said in Ruby's ear.

Ruby stepped from the restroom as if she'd been there all along, and strolled into the auction room as if she was always meant to be there and didn't have a care in the world.

She did, of course, have a lot of cares in the world, but this was what their training with Max had been all about. Becoming someone else, if only for a short period of time.

In the background, Ruby's brain was going a mile a minute, taking in every face, noting details of clothes, seating arrangements…who was mingling with who. She didn't recognize any faces but knew it was inevitable that some of their names had come across her desk, either in her legitimate position at the museum, or before.

These were people who were not on the up-and-up. Or, if they were, they didn't have an issue with obtaining things through means that were not on the up-and-up. These were not good people. They were people who took advantage of others. People who made their living on tricks and schemes. They were crooks and scoundrels.

And as she walked straight to the front of the room, Ruby knew she had to be the most cunning of them all.

Chapter 17

It didn't matter how many times he'd seen Ruby enter a room, the sight of her always took his breath away. And that was when she *wasn't* dressed in a sexy formal evening gown, looking like she just walked out of the pages of *Vogue*. And okay, he hadn't read a whole lot of *Vogue* lately, but if the women in those pages looked anything like Ruby did in that moment, it was no wonder the magazine was still popular after all these years.

She'd gone back to the short hair, which shouldn't have been as sexy as it was, but the way it guided his eyes down to her bare shoulders, to the soft angles of her collarbone, nearly undid him. She so rarely wore clothes that showed off her body, but as she sauntered in—radiant, sultry, confident—the dress she wore clung to her body in a way that made Shane feel like he was seeing her for the first time all over again.

He wasn't supposed to stare. He wasn't supposed to draw attention to himself in any way. And most importantly, he wasn't supposed to draw attention to Ruby, but he was having a hard time keeping his eyes to himself. A quick glance around the room told him he wasn't the only one with greedy eyes, though, so he hoped he hadn't appeared too obvious.

He had to admit, he felt his ego blowing up a little, remembering he'd recently had his lips on those sultry ones that every man in the room—and probably plenty of women—wanted to feel under theirs.

"Okay, steady, people," Ash said over comms, as if she could read Shane's mind.

He blinked back to the task at hand—none of this was going to work if Ruby didn't get the seat she needed at the front of the room. He straightened the place setting at the last empty chair at the table at the front—the one he'd been carefully ensuring stayed empty by blocking it whenever a solo person was eyeing it up. He'd even snaked a half-empty glass of wine from one of the other guests, giving her a fresh one, of course, and set the lipstick-stained glass at the seat to make it look as if it was taken.

He whisked the wineglass away, leaving a pristine, untouched space for Ruby, turning away from the table as she approached as if he'd never been there at all. She sat without skipping a beat as if it had been her seat all along. And with the way she was oozing confidence, nobody would have dared question her.

For a while, Shane did the job he was hired—or rather, set up in a computer system by Bug—to do. He had three tables assigned to him—the staff plentiful enough to ensure the guests were well taken care of—and he was good at serving them. Smiling and flirting a little when the moment called for it, and being as invisible as possible when it didn't. He took Ruby's drink order, but besides that, kept an especially low profile at her table.

There wasn't a whole lot of chitchat at Ruby's table, but Shane did overhear her introduce herself as Gabrielle Le Croix, an alias he hadn't heard before. Bug must have gone all out, burning the midnight oil to set up the profiles for the job. Which, given the short amount of time they'd had to prepare, must have been exhausting. He thought about him out there on the side of the mountain.

"How you doin', Bug?" he asked.

"Oh, you know, just getting the job done," he said, his voice much more cheerful than Shane's would have been in the same situation, that was for sure.

"You always do, man," Shane said quietly.

"The auction should start in less than five." Ash's voice came into his ear, and he picked up his pace to deliver the last of his drinks.

Boss lady had been adamant that every person had a full drink when the auction began—they were still going to give the guests what they wanted as the auction proceeded, but they wanted as few disruptions as possible. Nothing was more annoying than bidding on a priceless item you'd been coveting for years while trying to peek around a server. Or at least that was what the boss lady would have them imagine.

Soon, movement began near the front of the room as a few people began to file through the door at the side of the staging area—the one where Ruby had taken the long stroll to the dead-end elevator. The hall of no return, as Shane had begun calling it in his mind.

He moved to the side of the room, not far from the door.

"The scepter won't be up for a while. It's one of the premiere items in the catalog, so it's likely to be auctioned near the end of the night," Ash said.

Shane settled in to wait, ready to move only when someone at one of his tables needed a drink cleared or a new one brought to them. Otherwise, he was doing his best to be invisible, though he couldn't help but notice boss lady was definitely shooting him a glance every now and then. If the heist didn't go down as planned for whatever reason, he was going to have a lot of backpedaling to get out of his implied after-evening plans with her.

"The first item up for bids is a portrait of…" the auctioneer began at the front of the room, though Shane tuned him out pretty fast.

The evening passed without a hitch other than Shane taking a few sneak peeks at Ruby, confident everyone's attention would be mostly on the auction area. Just like Ruby's was, who appeared rapt with interest as each new thing up for grabs rolled out. Truthfully, she was likely legitimately intrigued by each piece up for sale, no doubt knowing everything about each item as if it were her job to know. Which, he supposed, it was. He wondered what kind of intel she was tucking away in that big brain of hers to take back to her job at the museum.

His heart sank at the thought. After all this was done, everyone would go back to their normal lives and Shane would be left right back where he'd been. Unhappy and bored.

He shook his head at himself. He had a good life, more than good. Privileged, really, and he felt like a jackass for feeling sorry for himself, but he just didn't know how much more of all that he could take. His life had just felt so…purposeless since the team had disbanded after Scotland.

And for the first time in years, even though the situation with Max was terrifying, he finally felt like himself again.

He just wished it could stay this way forever.

The next auction item was wheeled into the room and the place fell silent.

The scepter…casting a spell over the room. People held their breath. Mouths dropped open slightly. Hearts forgot to beat.

Until the auctioneer quietly, almost reverently, cleared his throat, giving a few details about the scepter in a whispery voice.

Even Shane was impressed. The scepter was larger than he imagined, though he didn't know if it was actually larger than what he'd thought, or if it just somehow commanded all the attention in the room.

"Let's begin," the auctioneer said, and a flurry of activity began.

It was clear this was the item everyone was interested in. Of course it was. Why wouldn't the job get another step more complicated? Everything about this job had been as if they were honey and complications were flies.

The bidding was almost as fast and furious as Shane's increasing heart rate, as he waited for his signal. If they didn't hurry and make a move, they would lose their window, and with the bidding easing past sixty million, they couldn't possibly have much longer.

He glanced at Ruby, who was starting to look concerned, clearly thinking the same thing.

And then the room went black.

Without missing a beat, Shane moved toward the front of the room, the rest of the people still looking around, wondering what was going on. Shane ignored them all and headed for Ruby, who was headed for the scepter, but not as fast as the guard who'd been standing much closer to it than she had.

But the team had anticipated this.

Shane ran to the man, who, with lightning-fast reflexes, had secured the scepter into its case and was already turning toward the door he'd brought the scepter in from.

The door of no return.

But Ruby had one arm around the strap of the cylindrical case, fighting him for it with everything she had in her. The man looked incredibly strong, but distracted by Ruby, he'd left his back wide-open for attack. Shane pulled him into a sleeper hold, pulling him gently to the floor as his world went black. The guard wouldn't be out for long, but with any luck, the team would be long gone before he woke up.

Shane watched as Ruby was already on the move toward their planned exit—through the kitchen—then suddenly stopped, her eyes going wide as people began to stream from their exit point.

Rather serious people with guns.

A few women screamed and people began to get up from their tables, fleeing toward the main entrance to the hall.

"What the hell?" Shane heard Ruby say over comms, though she was already turning around, heading back toward him, surprisingly fast in her fancy heels.

The team had contingency plans prepared, of course, and Shane moved to exit strategy number two—the one near the back on the south wall. But no matter what plan they decided to change to, his job was always the same. Protect the target. In this plan, it was his job to clear a path though the panicking crowd for Ruby and the scepter. But the target—the scepter—was not his focus. It never was.

His real mission would always be to protect Ruby.

They'd only made it a few steps before he realized people with guns were streaming in from the back door as well.

Thoughts flew through Shane's head, so fast it almost made him dizzy. Who were these guys? What if the people with guns were the good guys? Some kind of raid or something? But what would that mean for the team? And worse, what would it mean for Max? There were no other exits besides the main one already fully crowed with panicked auction guests.

The whole scene took only a moment to survey and Shane realized they only had one option left.

And it was an option he decidedly did not like.

The door of no return.

Ruby knew even before Shane tilted his head to signal her, they had no choice. They had to go through the one door they absolutely could not go through. To do so was to head directly into the belly of the beast, and they didn't even know what that beast might do when they got there.

But they went for it anyway. If they could get through, and by some miracle, there wasn't anyone directly on the other side, they might be able to buy themselves a few seconds to formulate a plan. Not that the team had been able to formulate a plan in the hour or so since they found out about the surprise door, but still, desperate measures and all that.

Maybe they'd get lucky.

Not that Ruby believed in luck. She believed in having a plan, in knowing every possible outcome, in not taking uncalculated risks.

But she ran anyway, fueled by instinct and desperation, a combination she hated relying on. Shane was maybe the only thing keeping her levelheaded. If anyone could find their way out of a situation like this, it was him. He was the king of improv. The one who figured ways out of impossible situations. And as she flung open the door they weren't supposed to go through, she was heartened to see that the dim hallway was empty. With any luck it would stay that way.

Then again, there was the whole not believing in luck conundrum.

Still, the empty hall had stoked her hopes, if only a little, and as she ran, she slipped the canvas handle of the scepter case over her head and began scanning for ways out that she might have missed before. Maybe a vent, a drain in the floor…anything.

Shane was still back at the door. "It has a lock!" he yelled, and Ruby's hope rose even higher. It wouldn't keep an army of guys with guns out for long, but it might buy them another few seconds.

As Shane moved toward her, Ruby took a moment to remove the heels from her convertible shoes again—they were the universe's gift to heel-wearers—knowing the next few minutes could come down to a foot race, and if that were to happen, she needed as much help as she could get.

Shane reached her, breathing almost as hard as she was, and placed his forehead on hers, holding on to her arms, instantly calming her. "We're going to figure this out," he said.

And somehow Ruby found the courage to believe him. "Okay, let's go," she said, and they both ran toward the door where Ruby had found the elevator earlier.

It was the only choice they had, so for the moment, it was a no-brainer.

"Maybe there won't be too many of them," Shane said.

"Yeah, maybe," Ruby replied, though she knew it was wishful thinking.

Moments later, a new noise echoed in the long hallway as footsteps began pounding from the direction they were headed. Someone—or by the sound of it, several someones—must have been alerted and were headed straight toward them.

On instinct, Ruby and Shane turned around, running back toward the door that led to the auction. It was pointless, Ruby knew—there was nothing good waiting on the other side for them—but they did it anyway, completely out of options once again.

In a few more steps, the auction door burst open as the people on the other side finally busted through the lock.

Ruby and Shane halted to a dead stop, clutching each other. .The people on either side of them stopped as well, the space becoming eerily quiet.

For a moment no one moved. Ruby didn't dare to even breathe.

As they stood like statues, even the air stilled in anticipation of what was to come. Ruby and Shane were out of options, simply waiting for the people on either side to close in. It's strange what goes through a person's mind in situations like that. Scenarios should have been playing through Ruby's mind...options, contingencies, desperate choices. But in that moment, when every one of those scenarios had already been exhausted, everything calmed. For just a second, she was so incredibly present. More present and aware than perhaps she'd ever been—the massive glass wall before her providing the most spectacular and surreal view she might ever see in her lifetime.

A large clearing with massive, snow-dusted trees and mountain peaks in the background, the clouds parting just enough to showcase the moon hanging huge above, casting its light onto the snow and creating millions of tiny sparkles, like she was standing in front of a sea of jewels. Ruby blinked—once, twice, an intense calm settling deep into her bones.

And then, the world exploded.

Well, the glass wall in front of her anyway.

Ruby ducked as Shane leaped on top of her, shielding her with his body as glass rained down.

The word *run!* invaded her head as Ruby glanced up and saw a sight that made a tiny ray of hope burst into a big, shining sun ball of it.

Ash—her arms outstretched to either side, guns in each hand, shooting in either direction.

Ruby had zero time to think, only able to react as she ran out into the open air of the night, Shane alongside her.

Ash paused her firing just long enough to let them pass, then what seemed like a thousand shots rang out, though Ruby wasn't sure if they were only from Ash's gun, or if they were from the other people too. So she just ran harder, her only thought to get away.

Unfortunately, that getaway was heading straight toward the cliff's edge of a damn mountain.

But she kept running, Shane a bit ahead of her, though he was not leaving her behind. The world grew darker, the light from the building receding as they neared the edge.

Just before she was about to go over, Ruby risked one glance back toward the building. It was lit up like a beacon in the dark and her stomach seized as she caught one last, horrific sight.

Ash. Standing in the hall she and Shane had just vacated.

Ash. Pummeled by bullets from either side, her body convulsing with shot after shot.

Ruby choked on a scream as she jumped over the edge.

Chapter 18

The ground slipped away from Shane's feet. Where once it was solid underneath him, now there was only air. Thoughts that slip through one's mind when confronted with an impossible situation can be a strange thing, such as wondering if he looked like one of those cartoon characters who hang in the air for a moment until they realize they're about to fall. Because that was sort of what it felt like. The ground beneath his feet, then what seemed like a legitimate moment of hang time before he began to plummet into the darkness.

Shane didn't even know when to expect the landing. It felt both like a long time and no time at all before he felt the impact, the landing at odds with itself, too, feeling both unbelievably hard, yet somehow strangely soft. When he blinked his eyes open, he was buried almost completely in snow.

Digging his way out, he couldn't see Ruby anywhere. But then a groan, both inside his ear and somewhere off to his right reached him. He ran toward the spot, where Ruby was beginning to climb her way out. He reached for her and pulled her the rest of the way, realizing she must be freezing in her tiny dress.

"Hey, guys," a voice said, in echo, like Ruby's groan had been.

Shane turned where only a few yards away stood Bug, grinning like the cat that ate the canary. "How's it going?"

Shane couldn't help but grin back. "Oh, you know, just dropping in for a chat."

Bug chuckled. "Wanna get out of here?" he asked, motioning to the three snowmobiles he had waiting.

During the hours Shane and Ruby had spent setting up inside, and before he'd hacked into security, Bug had been running snowmobiles up the mountain with Ash. First, bringing two sleds up, then taking one back down together to retrieve the third.

His equipment was already packed up and he was ready to go.

"Hell yes," Shane said, moving toward the nearest sled.

"Wait," Bug said, a note of worry slipping into his voice. "Where's Ash?"

Shane glanced back up the mountainside, only realizing then that she hadn't jumped behind them. He glanced at Ruby, but the expression on her face did not make him feel better.

"Guys," Bug said again, his voice sounding panicked and angry all of a sudden.

But then a sound came over the comms. Someone clearing their throat. "I'm right behind you."

Ash.

Relief flooded over Bug's face. "We're not going without you," he said.

"You get that scepter the hell out of here now. That's an order," she said, though something didn't sound quite right with her voice.

"I said I'm right behind you. Go, go, go!"

There was a pause while the three of them stood on that mountain in the dead of night. It felt like one of those moments where if you didn't make the right choice, life would never be the same. Although, Shane thought, maybe life was never going to be the same either way.

He glanced at Ruby, who had tears in her eyes, and he knew. It was too late for Ash.

Shane swallowed the giant lump trying to choke off his breath.

Ruby wasn't facing Bug, so there might still be a chance.

"Well, you heard the woman," he said, his voice overcompensating, sounding more cheerful than he'd meant for it to. "Time to go."

They didn't have time for much besides stepping into heavy winter boots and shrugging into the large parkas Bug had waiting for them. Ruby looked a bit ridiculous in her evening gown and parka, but she must have been grateful to have a little protection from the cold.

Shane climbed onto the closest sled and Ruby climbed on behind him so they could leave the last sled for Ash.

"Come on, man," Shane said, starting up the engine. "You have to lead us. We don't know the way down."

Bug stood for a moment, but then noises above them—yelling…more gunshots—seemed to shock him into a decision. "Yeah, okay, we're going, boss," he said.

"Good," said Ash. "I'll be right there," and Shane knew it would be the last time he would hear her voice.

Bug revved his machine and took off down the hill, slowly at first, and then picking up speed as the mountain began to flatten out a little.

If the situation hadn't been so terrible, Shane would have had a lot of fun on that sled. The untouched snow, the crisp air, the gorgeous woman hanging on tightly to his sides. The beauty of that place on that night almost took his breath away, but he also couldn't stop thinking about Ash, and how the hell they were going to get Bug to safety.

If the people at the top of the mountain had sleds of their own, the tracks they left as they went would lead the bad guys, and their guns, straight to them.

Once at the bottom of the mountain, the team drove the

snowmobiles the final few miles through the valley, all the way to their car, which was waiting on the edge of the city.

"Where the hell is she? She should have caught up to us by now," Bug said, his eyes straining through the darkness toward the direction they'd come.

Shane got off his snowmobile and removed his helmet. "Bug, I don't think she's coming."

The look that flashed in Bug's eyes was pure anger, a hatred Shane didn't think Bug had in him. He moved toward Shane like he was about to hit him.

"Bug!" Ruby yelled, sort of jumping in front of Shane.

Bug could have pushed Ruby to the side without much effort but seeing her made something change behind his eyes. He was still angry, but now there was a fear there too. And then his face crumpled completely. "What do you mean you don't think she's coming?" His voice was pitched higher than normal, as he fought the rage and desperation inside him.

Then Bug turned and faced out toward the mountains again. "We have to go back," he said, a few tears breaking free.

"Bug," Ruby said, moving around to stand in front of him. "She's gone. I'm so sorry, but she's gone. I saw it. There's no way she could have survived."

Bug glanced between Ruby and Shane. "And you assholes let me leave?"

His fist balled up again and he started to pace.

"I'm sorry, Bug," Ruby said again. "There was nothing any of us could do—if there was, we would have done it. She... she sacrificed herself to save us. To save Max," she finished, her voice trailing to a whisper.

Bug broke down then, and they both guided him into the back seat of the car. Ruby climbed in beside him, turning to Shane. "We have to get out of here."

She was right. The snowmobile tracks led directly to the car. The plan had been to ditch the machines there and once in the car, their tracks would blend in with the thousands of others on the street. The team knew they were still being tracked by the people who had Max, but that wasn't their concern at the moment. The real concern was the group from the auction, wanting their precious item back.

They had to find a safe place to go.

But Ash had been the only one who knew what the plan was.

"Just get off the street," Ruby said. "Find a hotel or something. I have cash in my suitcase."

Thank goodness they had their luggage, Ruby thought. She was definitely done wearing slinky evening gowns for a while. The giant snow boots could go too—they were fine for plowing across the side of a mountain, but were a bit much for regular city activity. She rummaged in her case for some pants, socks and shoes, all while keeping one arm around Bug.

Shane drove for a long time. Thankfully, the city was relatively large and should be easy to get lost in, at least for a little while to give them a chance to regroup. In movies and on TV, people are always headed to seedy little motels to hide, but that wasn't the best way to get lost in a sea of people. A person wanted to go to a regular old motel where any family would stay if they wanted to remain unnoticed. The people working in low-end places were always on edge, sizing people up as they approached—always vigilant for their own safety. But the people working in some random Holiday Inn in the suburbs rarely had to think about anything like that, which made them less suspicious, and more likely to forget they even had an interaction with you.

Still, to be on the safe side, Ruby made Shane go in and get a room so they could lie low and figure out their next move, while she and Bug stayed in the car. Using his key card at a back entrance, Ruby and Bug snuck in without anyone the wiser, and the people at the front desk thought Shane was just like any other solo businessman in town for the night.

For a while, Ruby and Shane left Bug alone with his grief. Ruby couldn't imagine what it must be like to lose someone you cared so much about without ever having told them your real feelings. She glanced at Shane. Her feelings were a lot more than she'd ever told him about, too, but she was going to have to live with the fact that it was going to stay that way.

She closed her eyes, centering herself. They had to get the scepter to the people who had Max and get Max back. They owed at least that much to Ash.

She approached Bug cautiously. He'd been staring at the same spot on the wall for the past twenty minutes. Ruby wasn't sure if he'd even blinked.

"Bug?" she said, her voice soothing. "I know you don't want to think about this right now, but do you know anything about what the next steps were supposed to be? Do you know how we're supposed to get Max back?"

Bug turned his head and his glossed-over eyes took a moment to focus on her. "Next steps?"

"Yeah, like was there a meeting place where we were supposed to swap the scepter for Max?"

He blinked. "Oh, I don't know," he said, turning his head back to the wall, looking like he was thinking hard. "She never told me," he finished, his voice cracking a little.

Ruby had hoped he might elaborate, but Bug fell silent again.

She went over to Shane on the other side of the room. It wasn't a large room, so Bug would be able to hear them talking, but Ruby didn't think he was paying attention to them. There was too much going on in his mind.

"What do we do?" Shane asked. "Why the hell didn't she tell any of us what the exchange detail were?"

Ruby shrugged. "Was there ever a job where you knew

any of those details? I sure as hell never knew anything like that. The exchanges were always done after the fact, after you and I had already done our jobs and were on our way home."

Shane ran his hands through his hair. "How did we not see that this could happen?"

Ruby was surprised she'd never thought of it either. Ash had always just been so...reliable. She never imagined Ash, of all people, getting hurt during a job. She certainly hadn't imagined her ever storming in with guns blazing either, though. It was so unlike her. Which sparked a whole new pang of guilt inside Ruby. She didn't think Ash would ever be the one to sacrifice herself, but she was willing to do it for Max. God... Max. How were they ever going to tell him?

Well, she realized, they sure as heck weren't going to tell him anything if they didn't get him back.

"Bug?" Ruby said, moving back across the room. "What about The Vault? Do you think the info would be in there? Can you get access to Ash's Vault?"

He shook his head. "I designed it so no one could access it, not even me. All of your Vaults are like that. Unless..." He trailed off, his gaze going back to the wall.

"Unless what, Bug?"

Bug shook his head a little, blinking again. "I might be able to if I can get to her secured network at her place."

"Her place? Like her house?"

Bug nodded absently, only half paying attention to the conversation.

"I think we should wait here. We know these guys are watching us. They must know we have the scepter. If we can't get to them, they'll come to us, won't they?"

"Maybe," Ruby said, a new idea forming. "We need to check on Max. We had to be careful about it before, right? Because we were worried they would find us too easily, so why don't we just do that?"

"Yes!" Shane said, already pulling his laptop out of his bag.

Bug didn't seem to be paying attention at all.

Shane typed in the web address, the hotel Wi-Fi taking forever to load the live feed.

And then finally, there he was on the screen. Max looked a whole lot less feisty than the last time they'd checked in on him, but he didn't look any worse for the wear. Other than the fact that he looked exhausted, Ruby thought. Then again, she imagined she didn't seem too chipper at the moment either.

"He looks miserable," she said.

"I think we all look miserable right now," Shane said. "At least he's still alive." Realizing what he'd said, Shane glanced to Bug. "I'm sorry, man, I didn't mean to be insensitive."

Bug glanced up and sort of half smiled. "I'm glad he's still alive too. I mean, if they didn't mess with the feed, that is."

"Mess with the feed?" Ruby asked.

Bug tilted his head. "In theory, they could have filmed him before and could be running the feed in a loop."

Ruby's eyes grew wide, which Bug noticed, coming a bit more back to himself instead of lost in his thoughts and grief.

"But there's no reason they would want to. We still have what they want—for them, nothing has changed."

Ruby's stomach knotted, hating that these people were getting what they wanted while their entire team was being ripped apart.

"Is there a way to check to make sure?" Shane asked.

"Probably," Bug said, struggling to ease himself to a standing position.

He moved toward the computer and sat down hard in the chair, like his body had grown twelve times heavier in the past few hours. But then he just sat there, staring.

Ruby was beginning to wonder if he was searching the feed itself for clues, until he finally spoke.

"I know where this is."

Ruby searched the room on the screen. Max was sitting on a sofa that could be any old regular sofa that might be in anyone's house. The place was decorated minimally—a few books on the coffee table, a lamp in the corner, a couple prints of insignias on the walls. Nothing that would make the place particularly stand out.

"Where is it?" she asked.

"It's Ash's place."

So many thoughts whirled through Ruby's mind. She wondered if Ash had information on the team filed away at her house, including their identities. Was she going to have to upend her life and move, go into hiding and start all over again? Was this always going to be the meeting place, or were these people trying to mess with their heads?

There was only one thing she knew for sure—they were headed back home.

Chapter 19

Shane, Ruby and Bug had one big problem.

The scepter.

"It's not like we can just carry a massive, stolen scepter through airport security with no one batting an eye," Shane pointed out.

"What about disguising it in some kind of case? Like maybe a guitar case or something."

Bug was shaking his head. "Airport security is designed to pick up on things like that. Even if we had the time to construct something that might have a chance at working, it's still taking a huge risk."

"Is there any way to get fake documentation to get it through?" Bug asked.

This time it was Ruby's turn to shake her head. "It's almost impossible to get anything to appear authentic without help from a world-class forger, and something like that would take time. Plus, there's a good chance the scepter is already in antiquities databases. The people who work customs at airports are trained to spot these things."

"Whatever we do, time is definitely not something we have to spare," Shane said.

"Ugh, this is so frustrating," Ruby said. "I never even considered we'd have to find a way to get this thing back home. I thought we'd make the trade for Max somewhere over here."

She began to pace. Shane didn't know what was going on

inside that magnificent mind of hers, but he could tell she was worried, and if she was worried, they all needed to be worried. Bug was a computer and tech genius, but strategy had never been his thing. Ruby, on the other hand, could give Ash a run for her money any day, and Shane sometimes wondered if Scotland would have turned out very differently had Ruby been in charge.

But then, she stopped pacing, which worried Shane even more.

He went to her, putting his hands on her arms, just below her shoulders. It had taken everything he'd had in him not to react to her, not to focus only on her when they'd been in character, but now they were back to being themselves, and Shane was tired of pretending.

She stiffened, but didn't move away.

"Talk to me, what are you thinking?" he asked.

"I don't know what I'm thinking," she said. "A million things, and none of them feel like the right choice. Every possible scenario ends up with someone getting hurt."

"Just…stop thinking about the scepter for a second." He tried to pull her into a hug, but she pushed him away.

"This can't happen again," she said.

Bug shifted his position on the edge of the bed. Shane had almost forgotten he was there. Christ, here he was trying to get closer to Ruby right after the poor guy had just lost the love of his life. Not to mention that love was also a good friend of his too.

God, he was a selfish asshole. It was just that having this time with Ruby again had made him realize one thing. Nothing mattered without her.

He gently pulled Ruby out into the hall. "Can we please talk about this?" he asked.

She closed her eyes and tilted her head upward. "There's nothing to talk about, Shane."

"Ruby, last night—"

"Please," she whispered. "We can't go there."

"Why the hell not? What's stopping us?"

Ruby shook her head, like she was struggling with what to say. "I just… We have other things to figure out," she said.

Shane's shoulders fell. She didn't even want to talk about them—about the two of them being together again.

A woman came out of a room down the hall and shot them a strange expression. Shane supposed they did look a little out of sorts, after being chased down a mountain and all.

Shane smiled at the woman, who gave them a wide berth as she passed.

"I won't be able to think about anything else until this is taken care of," Ruby said, quieter.

"It will be fine. I'll carry it through the airport and—"

Ruby cut him off. "Don't be stupid. You know that isn't an option."

"If we can just hide it somehow, put it in a case like you said…"

She was shaking her head more now. "No." Ruby finally looked up at him then. "It wouldn't work. No crew in the world would take that chance. The likelihood of getting caught is like, 95 percent, and the consequences of getting caught means game over. Whoever is holding that thing will be put away for years."

"Maybe it's worth it for Max," he said.

"If we get caught, it's over for Max." Ruby still shook her head, like the whole situation was just impossible.

Which, he supposed, it was.

"Can you take care of the flights home? Just get us on a plane first thing in the morning. I'll be back in a couple hours."

"What do you mean you'll be back in a couple hours? It's the middle of the night."

"It's not even midnight," she said, as if that made it any better.

"Exactly," Shane said.

"I'm fine," she said. "It'll be fine."

She grabbed the scepter on her way out.

"What are you doing with that?" he asked.

"I'm taking care of our problem," she said, and walked away.

Shane wanted nothing more than to follow, but he knew if he did, it would just delay whatever it was she was going to do. He knew he would never stop her. Once Ruby put her mind to something, there was no holding her back.

Shane had a feeling whatever it was she was about to do, it was the only chance they had.

He also had a feeling it was a very bad decision.

Ruby purchased a burner phone to check in on a couple of old friends in the area.

An hour later, she was seated across a diner booth from Jessica Weber, a colleague who worked for a renowned national museum in Zurich. They'd never met in person, but Jessica had been instrumental in a few of Ruby's overseas transactions with her job.

Jessica was taller than Ruby had imagined, although it was a bit challenging to tell height from a small profile picture on the internet. She'd been incredibly helpful to Ruby over the years and Ruby hoped she could trust Jessica to do what needed to be done as quietly as possible.

"I'm so sorry to have to meet at such an inconvenient hour," Ruby said.

Jessica waved the comment away. "It's fine. So much of my job is working with museums and galleries all over the world—I'm used to working all hours of the day," she said, her smile warm and friendly.

"Thanks so much for meeting me."

"Of course, it's great to finally meet you in person. And I must say, you certainly have my interest piqued."

Ruby took a deep breath, gathering courage for what she was about to propose. If anything went wrong here—if Ruby had miscalculated, and Jessica wasn't the ally Ruby hoped she would be—the whole thing could be over, and Max might be gone forever.

She let out the breath slowly, stalling. "I have a favor to ask."

"Of course," Jessica said, as if it were no big deal.

Except the favor *was* going to be a very big deal, potentially landing the two of them in hot water. There wasn't much question Ruby would be in hot water after all this was over, but she hoped she wouldn't take Jessica down with her.

"I need to get an artifact back to the States."

Jessica shrugged. "Sure, easy. I can fill out the paperwork and ship it out in the morning," she said, though curiosity crossed her face, like she wasn't sure why they might be meeting at a diner in the middle of the night for something so insignificant.

Ruby cleared her throat. "So, the thing is, it's not just any artifact. I've…uh…" Ruby wasn't sure how to word the next part. "I've recovered a stolen artifact, and, well, there could potentially be some controversy over how it was obtained."

Jessica began to nod. "Well, since you've invited me down here at this hour, I'm going to go ahead and assume there might be some…fudging that needs to be done with the documents?" She raised an eyebrow, though Ruby couldn't tell if it was one of those intrigued "ooh, this is interesting" eyebrow raises, or more of a scolding, looking down on her kind of a situation.

Ruby was suddenly starting to worry about the decision to contact Jessica. She barely knew the woman and had called her based on nothing but instinct. And maybe a little desperation.

"Maybe this wasn't such a good idea," Ruby said.

Jessica put a hand up to stop her. "I know we don't know each other well, but I'm honored you trust me. I'm going to need a whole lot more information before I agree to do this, but I'm willing to hear you out."

Ruby relaxed her shoulders a bit. "Thank you," she said. "And just know I wouldn't be here if it weren't a potentially life-or-death situation."

Jessica leaned forward a bit. "Are you in some sort of danger?"

Ruby shook her head. "I don't think so—at least not yet. But someone who is very important to me is, and this is the only way to get him back."

Jessica nodded as if it all made perfect sense. Which it absolutely didn't, but she'd obviously seen a thing or two in her day.

Ruby started in on the story about the auction. She didn't tell Jessica every detail behind what the team had to do to get the scepter, or why, but Jessica was a smart woman. She understood if Ruby didn't give her certain details, it was out of protection for her.

"Can I see what it is?" Jessica asked, and Ruby handed over the case without question.

Jessica opened the end of the case and pulled the scepter partially out, her eyes going wide. "This is quite the find," she said.

Ruby wasn't sure if Jessica knew the full history of the scepter, or if she could simply see the value from the jewels and gold, but she closed the case back up, giving a quick glance behind her.

"You can see why I wanted to find someone I trusted and who knows how to handle this particular type of item," Ruby said.

Jessica nodded. "I'll do it," she said.

"Really?" Ruby asked. "It's a big ask."

"It is," Jessica said, "and I also know you're the one putting your neck on the line for this. My part it simply filling out a few forms based on information you've given me and having an artifact sent overseas. In my job, this is what happens every day."

"There are risks, though," Ruby said.

Jessica nodded. "There are. And I'm willing to stick my neck out a little for someone who has helped me so much over the past few years. But I'm also going to mitigate my risk. I'll put down on the paperwork what you've told me. I don't know how the artifact came into your hands, and so I will simply leave that part out. If I'm questioned about it later, I'll explain just that—that I don't know."

"They could say you didn't do your due diligence," Ruby said, not sure why she was playing the devil's advocate.

"They could, and I'll simply say that wasn't the important part of our meeting. I believe an artifact like this needs to be back on the record books, and the true owners deserve to be found. It's my position that retrieving these types of items back from…less than legitimate sources is far more important than specifically how they were retrieved in the first place. My integrity wouldn't allow me to let the piece get lost to history yet again."

Ruby's whole body relaxed. "I knew you were the right person to call. That's exactly how I feel too."

Chapter 20

Shane was uncharacteristically anxious as he went through airport security, even though he was doing nothing wrong. Other than, you know, using a false passport—but he'd done that a hundred times over the years and not once had he been this nervous.

Maybe he was just on edge in general.

Things had been...tense with Ruby ever since she left to go on her secret errand in the middle of the night, and she still hadn't let him know what she'd done with the scepter. She'd come back and fallen into a deep sleep. Thankfully, Bug had also gotten a few hours of sleep, albeit restless, but sleep had eluded Shane. There was just too much to think about, though if he was being honest with himself, most of those thoughts centered around Ruby.

Even in that moment, it felt like they were miles apart, though they couldn't be sitting much closer together than they were—side by side in the economy section of an airplane.

"We won't have the, um, thing back right away," Ruby said, surprising Shane. She'd hardly talked to him all morning. "And we can't get Max back without it."

Shane nodded. "They must know we wouldn't have been able to bring it through when we came back."

"That's what I keep thinking about. Why would they want to do the trade back home? It doesn't make any sense."

"Unless the people who want it live there," Shane said. "Maybe that's the whole reason behind all this. It might have been much easier just to buy it at the auction if they wanted it that badly. These people don't strike me as being hard up for cash."

Ruby was the one nodding now. Shane could tell her thoughts were flowing fast. "What if they... Shit," she finished, looking a little wild.

"What if they what?" Shane asked. "Wait, what did you do to get it sent back?"

"Nothing, it's fine. Don't worry about it," she said, though Shane did not think it was fine at all.

If there wasn't anything to worry about, Ruby would just tell them how she was getting the scepter back. The fact that she wasn't was making Shane more uneasy by the second.

"We'll still have to go to Ash's place," Ruby said, more to herself than Shane, but Shane was going to take every opportunity to keep her talking.

Maybe he could figure out what was going on before it all blew up in their faces.

"Of course, we have to," he said. "It's the last place we know they had Max."

"Yeah," Ruby agreed, "but he won't be there anymore. We were too far away, they've had too long to move him."

"Probably, but I'm still going to hope."

"Even if he was still there, we don't have the scep—" She cleared her throat. "We don't have the thing to trade."

Shane leaned back into his seat and sighed. "You're thinking this was all set up from the beginning, aren't you?"

"It had crossed my mind," Ruby said.

"Ash would never do that to us." Shane leaned his head out into the aisle to make sure Bug wasn't listening to their conversation.

Ruby shrugged. "It wouldn't really have been *us*, though, would it? Just me."

Shane shook his head. "Unless…"

"What?" Ruby asked.

"Unless she wanted to get the team back together. She knew she'd never be able to convince you, but if you lost all your other opportunities, then maybe."

"I guess she didn't know me as well as she hoped she did, then," Ruby said. "I would never go back to that life. Never."

"Was it really so bad?" Shane asked.

"Yes."

They sat in silence for a long time. Shane was hurt Ruby thought of their old life—the only part of his life worth anything—as something she regretted. As something bad.

And yeah, Shane got that they were doing things that weren't on the right side of the law, but in the end, they were on the side of what was right.

"Look," Ruby finally said, her voice softer. "I'm not saying it was all bad. Obviously, there was a lot of good that came out of those days. But I'm sorry, I could never go back."

"I understand," Shane said, "I do. But so much of it was incredible—the excitement, the adventure…you."

He swore Ruby's neck turned a little red.

Her voice was still quiet. "All of that stuff was good…great, even. But my anxiety about getting caught just grew and grew until it consumed me. I could never go back again. These last few days have only confirmed it."

"I'm sorry," Shane said, though he wasn't sure what, exactly, he was sorry for.

It just felt like he was responsible for some part of it.

She shook her head a little, as if to say, *Don't be sorry*, but the conversation drifted off. There was so much to say, but Shane couldn't seem to find a way to say any of it.

Because of the time difference, it was still early afternoon when they landed, though Shane couldn't remember the last time he'd been so tired. It was a huge inconvenience, especially considering how much he traveled, but he'd never been able to sleep on a plane. He was happy Ruby didn't suffer from the same condition, but her tiny snores only flooded his thoughts with memories of lying side by side with her through the rest of the flight.

After landing, the three of them went straight from the airport to Ash's condo.

Shane was surprised when they pulled up to the building. It was just a normal apartment-style building in an average part of town. He'd always imagined Ash living the high life in some luxury place in the trendiest part of town, and this was just…so plain.

No fancy shops on the bottom floor, no doorman to greet them, just a regular old buzzer and lock on the door. It was the perfect place to hide in plain sight—he just never thought Ash would settle for something so ordinary. The building was on a fairly busy street, so the trio moved around to the back.

Bug checked for security cameras before Shane made quick work of the lock on the back door.

"There's probably more to this place than meets the eye," Bug said. "I wish I'd paid more attention the last time I was here."

"Why were you here?" Shane couldn't help but ask.

It was a question he'd been wondering since the moment they'd seen the feed and Bug recognized the place.

"Ash reached out to me about a year ago. Had me do a little freelance work for her."

Shane raised an eyebrow. "Was she still in the business?"

Bug shrugged. "I didn't ask a lot of questions. Just got in, did the work and got out."

Shane knew better than to push. Bug was a professional. He

wasn't about to spill Ash's secrets, even if she wasn't around anymore to be upset.

Bug led the way upstairs. More surprises. The condo wasn't even on the top floor. Then again, it wouldn't have been keeping with the hiding-in-plain-sight thing if it had been. Every person in the building would know who lived on the top floor, and Ash certainly wouldn't have wanted to be in that spotlight. Shane began to wonder if this was just a shell apartment Ash got mail sent to or something. He just couldn't picture her there. She was more of an "own her own private island hideaway" sort of person.

Shane put his lockpicking skills to work once again when they reached her door. "Heads up, everyone, we know they've been here. Could still be here."

He turned the knob and pushed the door.

As expected, the place was deserted.

Once inside, they split up, Bug heading off doing his techy thing, and Ruby headed straight for the art hanging on the walls. Shane had never seen her do that before, but considering their former occupation, maybe Ash had some particularly interesting pieces.

Shane went for a den area off the main living area. If Ash had worked out of this place, this was where she would have had her office. There was a laptop on the desk, but Shane thought that was best left for Bug. He began to sift through the few papers next to the computer.

It didn't take long before he found something he knew was from the kidnappers. The reason he knew this was because it had his name on it. It had Ruby and Bug's name on it too. But it didn't have Ash's.

Which meant they knew she was gone. It wasn't surprising, but it made Shane angry. Max's captors were watching them and he hated it. Worse, it felt like they were messing with them.

"Guys!" he yelled.

Ruby and Bug came to the doorway.

"I found something," he said, and turned the page around for them to see.

Saturday, 2 p.m.—
Market Square Beside the Church

"Well, that seems pretty clear," Ruby said, immediately thinking back to the last time she'd been in the market square.

Her mind was already running through scenarios about what could happen given how crowded the area would be that time in the afternoon on the market's busiest day. It was a smart place for the exchange with so many variables in play. Her brain wouldn't stop running through the possibilities until she'd exhausted each and every one at least three times.

"I'll scope the place out before we meet tomorrow," Bug said. "Make sure there are no surprises."

Ruby nodded. "Okay, good. Thank you," she said, though she knew there was no way to plan for every potential surprise that could be thrown their way.

"I'll get the scepter back. Let's meet up at Bug's place before we go," Ruby said.

"I can come with you," Shane said.

Ruby's heart gave a little tug, but she shook her head. "I need to do this on my own."

"Ruby," he said, frustrated. "You don't always have to do everything on your own."

She smiled a sad smile. "I know," she said, even though she wasn't sure if she believed it. "But I have to do this one on my own. Trying to sneak you in with me would make it a thousand times harder."

He tilted his head in confusion, but thankfully didn't question her.

Ruby went home, showered and changed into her best work

suit—a gray striped pantsuit that always made her feel like she belonged in the world-renowned museum. She was unstoppable in that suit.

At least she hoped she'd be.

She arrived at work after the place closed. With any luck, most of the employees would have gone home and the ones who hadn't would just think she was working late. They'd all know her face, though hopefully they wouldn't know she was supposed to be on vacation.

She paused at the top of the steps before she made her way in. This was the moment when everything was about to change. After she walked through those doors, there would be no going back.

But she knew she was going to do it anyway. She owed that much, at least, to Max.

She took a deep breath and used her key card to unlock the door and let herself in.

Her heels clicked more loudly than seemed possible in the quiet of the building. On Fridays, everyone was so ready for the weekend they usually sprinted out of there after work. Tomorrow the place would be bustling with museumgoers again, but for now, the place was a ghost town.

She made her way to the basement—the most secure area of the building, where the most valuable items that weren't on current display were stored.

"Hey, Dave," she said as she approached the man on duty at the secure locker.

Ruby knew he'd be there. Dave was always there after hours—the place manned by trained security 24/7.

"Ruby! I haven't seen you in ages. You burning the midnight oil today?" Dave smiled. He was an easy guy to like, and she suddenly wondered if she would see him again. "What can I do for you?" he asked.

"There should have been a high-priority package sent from

Zurich in my name," she said. "I was hoping to do some pre-
liminary screening of it before I left for the weekend."

Dave started typing into the computer. "Yup, looks like it
just got here this afternoon," he said.

He rolled his office chair back and went down one of the
shelf-lined halls to retrieve the scepter.

Ruby held her breath until he slid the package under the
cage window. "Key card and punch code, please. You know
the drill," he said, winking.

"I sure do," Ruby said, hating that his day was going to
become a lot more hellish later on, and that it would be her
fault. "See you in a bit."

"I'll be here," he said, turning his focus back to his book
and giving her a little salute.

Ruby went to her office and pulled her gym bag out of her
small closet, emptying its contents onto the closet floor, closing the door behind her. Footsteps made their way down the
hallway toward her office, and she scrambled to shove the
scepter and bag under her desk.

"Ruby! What are you doing here?" Barb, her boss, asked,
poking her head around the door.

"Hey!" Ruby said, a bit too enthusiastically. *Dial it down*,
she scolded herself. *You're supposed to be a professional.*
"Yeah, just got back a bit early and thought I'd come in and
see if there were any emergencies or quick to-dos to tackle,
so Monday wouldn't be such a nightmare." She made a goofy
face that was supposed to convey that Mondays after vacation
were almost not worth going on vacation for.

"You do have quite a bit piled up there." Barb motioned
to the pile of papers, mail and a few packages, then shooting
her a goofy face back, which warmed Ruby's heart. "That
one looks fun," she said, pointing to a large box on the pile.

Ruby nodded. "I think I'll leave it until Monday," Ruby
said. "It'll give me something to look forward to."

"Smart," Barb said, turning to leave. "Have a good week-end." She raised her hand in a wave as she walked away.

It struck Ruby that over the past three years, Barb had become more than just her boss. She had become a friend. Ruby was going to miss the after-work drinks on paydays, the Monday-morning catch-ups about the weekend, the two-hour chats in the middle of the day about whatever scandal was going on in the world of priceless artifacts.

Ruby was going to miss this whole life, really.

She carefully packed her gym bag with a very specific item not meant for the gym and walked out of the museum for the last time.

Chapter 21

Shane spent the next morning staked out on the roof of a building across the street from the meeting point at the market square. After the sleepless flight, his body had finally given out; he'd drifted off early, which meant he woke up early too. The restlessness kicked in quickly, since he knew what they had to do later that day.

"Be prepared for anything" had always been the team's motto, which Shane used to hate—he was the one whom they depended on in case they needed to improvise, after all. But after Scotland, he'd come around to the idea.

And so, instead of pacing around his rental place, he went to check things out. Scope the area for potential hazards and find areas they could potentially use for contingencies in case things didn't go according to plan.

When he arrived, the place had been quiet—a single car rolling through the square in the entire first hour of his stake-out. But soon, city workers came to cordon off the street and vendors started to set up their wares. Folks were unpacking boxes of homemade jellies and jams alongside artists with dozens of canvases, and booths filled with graphic T-shirts popped up beside farm-fresh produce. The street was a bustle of activity and Shane began to get overwhelmed with all the variables at play.

He slowed his breathing. There was no way their small team

would be able to account for every possibility, so it was no use trying to determine how it would all go down. Ruby was better at that sort of thinking, and Shane had to focus on what he did best. Trust his instincts. They had never failed him before.

Other than Scotland.

He still didn't know how he hadn't seen it coming. The girl, the daughter who'd come home from college, had been such a surprise. Ash had been so sure no one would be home. Still, he should have felt a presence…should have heard something sooner. By the time he heard the gun being cocked, it was too late. She was already shooting. He would never forget the look in her eyes—the fear.

Focus, Shane.

He wasn't going to do anyone on the team any good if he couldn't stop thinking about how he wished everything had gone differently that horrible day three years ago.

Shane made his way to ground level and tried to blend in with the rest of the people at the market. The busiest time— midmorning—had already come and gone as he'd watched from above, and now the crowd thinned for the lunch hour, but it would pick up again soon enough, just in time to make things more complicated for the exchange.

He waited until a bench freed up, then sat to wait. To watch.

Forty minutes later, Bug sat down heavily beside him. There was no point in trying to hide that they were working together anymore. The people who had Max had been onto them since the beginning.

The thought sparked…something in Shane's brain, though he wasn't sure what bothered him exactly, or what it might mean. There was just…a weirdness about it all.

He shook the thought from his head. He was just being paranoid.

"How are you doing, man?" Shane asked.

"Not great," Bug said.

Bug had always been a man of few words, and Shane got the feeling he was going to be a man of even fewer words for a while. Ash had meant so much to Bug, and Shane couldn't imagine what it must be like for him. He wasn't sure what was worse—stumbling into the love of your life and taking it for granted like Shane had with Ruby, or pining after someone for years but being too scared to do anything about it.

"I'm so sorry," Shane said again.

"I know," Bug replied, the words pained but heartfelt, like he did understand Shane wanted to help him but didn't know how.

A short while later, Shane spotted Ruby coming up the block, the now familiar scepter case slung over her shoulder. He watched as she approached, glancing in every direction, but appearing completely natural as she did it. To the outside world, she could have been carrying anything in the case— a rolled up canvas, or perhaps some blueprints for an architect she was interning for. No one would have guessed she was sauntering along with a priceless artifact. She appeared relaxed, calm, not suspicious in the slightest, and Shane was the only one who noticed she was on high alert.

"Hey," she said, smiling as she approached, hugging both Shane and Bug as they stood to greet her as if they were any old friends meeting for lunch or a drink.

"Good to see you," Shane said, loudly enough for the people in the vicinity to hear.

It was a perfect spot for the trio to meet. Anywhere else, one or all of them may have stood out, but in a trendy neighborhood where everyone was trying their hardest to put on a persona of some sort, a biker dude, a guy who could easily blend in with a Hollywood crowd, and a small woman dressed plainly with sunglasses and a ball cap didn't stand out as much as a person might think.

They chatted as if they hadn't seen each other in years—

maybe old high school friends having a mini-reunion—until two o'clock neared and Ruby said quietly, "Heads up, guys, we're getting close to the time."

They continued to make small talk, each one of them facing a different direction, watching closely past each other as the tension rose by the second.

Shane tried not to check his watch constantly, but it was a struggle. It was like time had slowed with the anticipation, like he could feel each individual millisecond tick by.

"I've got someone coming this way up the alley," Ruby said quietly.

Shane glanced to his right, where, sure enough, a shadowy figure was making their way toward the group. "I see him," he said.

Bug visibly stiffened, his training not working as well as it should be. It was always harder to stay in character when your emotions were humming so close to the surface.

"Hey, guys," the stranger said as if he approached, clapping Bug's shoulder as if they were all old friends.

Shane had to hand it to the guy, blending right into the ruse they had going, confirming they'd been watching them for a while.

Ruby gripped tighter to the strap of the case.

"Ready to head out?" the man asked.

Shane cleared his throat, plastering on a smile. "Where are we headed?"

"It's just through the alley," the man said, not missing a beat.

Shane, Ruby and Bug glanced at each other, questioning. None of them loved that they were about to be led down a secluded alleyway, but what choice did they have?

"Great!" Shane finally said, his acting slipping a little with his overenthusiasm, as the three of them followed the stranger into the unknown.

* * *

Ruby didn't want to call attention to the case on her back, but she couldn't stop checking the strap every twenty seconds or so to make sure it was still there. The scepter was relatively heavy, and she would have noticed if it suddenly wasn't there, but she was having a little trouble controlling her impulses. There was so much at stake. They'd already lost one member of the team, and Ruby wasn't sure if she'd be able to handle it if they lost Max too.

Thankfully, she had Shane in front of her and Bug at her back, both protecting the case just as intently as she was.

Near the end of the alley, the guy made a surprise move toward a door at the back of the church.

"Really? The church?" Shane said, as the man ushered them through.

The guy shrugged, surprisingly congenial about the whole exchange. "As good a place as any," he said, grinning.

Ruby hated entering dark spaces. The precious seconds it took for eyes to adjust felt like a lifetime in a dangerous situation. The best advantage was always knowing what was going to happen, and making sure the people on the other side of the equation didn't.

Ruby hated being on the wrong side of the equation.

The man led them up a steep set of stairs and into the large congregation area. It was strangely eerie walking through an empty church, different from other gathering spaces with its pews, hymnbooks and pulpit up at the front. But perhaps most strange was the way the stained glass windows reaching to the high ceiling bathed them in multicolored light, making the moment seem even more surreal.

He led them out of the main area toward another doorway, opening it to reveal a small room—perhaps the place where the minister waited until it was time to start the service.

And in the middle of that small room was Max, tied to a chair and gagged, but alive, though his head was tilted downward as if he was trying to sleep.

Ruby's heart leaped and she tried to rush to him. "Max!"

"Not so fast," the man who'd led them there said, putting his arm out to stop Ruby from charging in.

"The case?" he said, raising an eyebrow, almost as if he thought it was mildly amusing that she'd forgotten.

Ruby pulled the strap over her head and practically shoved the thing in his hands.

As if coming out of a dream, Max raised his head slowly as Ruby rushed to him, Shane and Bug following close behind.

At first Max looked confused, like he hadn't expected anyone to come for him, let alone his former students and coconspirators. But he blinked out of his confusion and his eyes went wide, almost as if he was scared—like he didn't want them there.

And then there were footsteps, coming from just outside the same doorway the three of them had just come through. Heels—high heels—clicking on the tile floor.

And there was something familiar about the cadence of the walk that made Ruby's stomach seize.

Shane was working on Max's restraints, and Bug worked to untie the cloth wrapped around his mouth. As the fabric loosened its grip, three desperate words escaped from their mentor's mouth. "It's a trap—"

Still crouching, Ruby had just enough time to twist and face the doorway as a person she thought she'd never see again came into crystal clear view, framed in the center of the ornate doorway as if she'd designed her reveal to be as dramatic as possible.

Ash.

And the look on her face, so satisfied—a smirk of knowing she'd outsmarted them all alongside a sparkle of pity behind her eyes, no doubt thinking they were a bunch of gullible door-knobs. The man, who had already opened the case and was in the process of pulling out the scepter, handed Ash the case.

Thoughts whirled through Ruby's head. She'd felt all along something had been off, but she'd never imagined her old teammate, a person she'd been so close with, would do this to her. And yeah, maybe she and Ash hadn't always seen eye to eye, and she could accept that maybe she'd be less than loyal to her, but to Shane and Max? And especially Bug?

A strangled, shocked sound escaped from behind her as Bug began to understand what had happened. Ruby couldn't bear to look at his face. He deserved privacy in that dagger-to-the-heart moment.

Ruby wanted to lunge at her. She'd never been prone to physical violence, but something about the smug expression on Ash's face sent her into a rage like she'd never felt before.

But all she could do was whisper, "Why?"

Ash tilted her smug head to somehow look even smugger and began to pace in front of the two guys she had holding guns on them.

Ruby knew Shane was already trying to work out how he was going to take the two of them down so they could get to Ash, but since it was exceedingly risky to go after guys with guns already pointed at them, she also knew he wasn't going to come up with anything.

Ash no doubt knew it, too, just sauntering around like she'd won the damned lottery. If, you know, the lottery had been rigged and she was the mastermind of it all who liked to toot her own horn.

"Well," Ash said, drawing the word out as if to make sure everyone was listening, "turns out the scepter belongs to me."

Ruby squinted her eyes. "It was stolen from a family in Switzerland in World War I."

Ash nodded. "Exactly. My family."

Ruby knew there had been something familiar about the prints of insignias in Ash's apartment. The crest on the scepter was so similar... Of course, all family crests looked a bit the same, but still, Ruby was a professional. She knew something about them was off. She just hadn't put the pieces together.

How could I have missed that?

"If the scepter belonged to your family all along, why didn't you just go through the proper channels?" Shane asked.

"The scepter was already on the black market," Ash said, as if they were missing a few brain cells. "It was about to be sold again to some new unknown person. I'd finally just found it. I couldn't risk it going underground, to possibly never see it again."

Ash pulled the scepter farther out, the jewels glinting in the light of the room. Her gaze seemed almost hungry, as if she was about to swallow the damned thing.

"So, you used us to do your dirty work," Ruby said.

"Well, at first I thought I only needed Shane and Bug," she said, shooting Bug a wink.

The poor guy looked like he was trying to fight tears. He still hadn't said a word since the moment Ash had strolled in, still alive. Ruby admired his restraint. Or maybe it was simply shock.

"But then there was the question of getting it home," Ash continued. "I knew it would be impossible to smuggle it into the country. And that's when I realized Ruby had the perfect way to do it for me."

Acid rose in Ruby's throat.

"Of course, asking you to give up your entire career wasn't going to work, so that's when I came up with the idea of getting Max involved too."

Ruby breathed hard through her nostrils, trying not to yank the scepter right out of Ash's hands and whack her over the head with it. Unfortunately, there was the small issue of the two dudes with guns who looked like they were hoping for a reason, any reason, to use them.

"Ruby?" Shane asked, still confused, but Ruby knew the pieces would fall into place soon enough. "What did you do?"

But Ash waved his words away. "Don't worry your pretty little head about it, Shane. In a few minutes, none of this is going to matter anyway."

She walked toward the door, turning back one final time with a sigh. "I'm going to miss you guys and all your antics." She smiled and walked out, her heels clicking along the tile floor.

The two guys backed out of the room behind her, and a series of locks clicked with finality on the other side.

Ruby tried the door, even though she knew it was pointless, and as expected, it was locked tight.

"Oh, my protégés," Max said, in awe that the three of them were there, but with an edge of guilt that they were now in the same situation as he was.

"Are you okay, Max?" Shane asked, looking him over to make sure he didn't have any injuries.

Max waved his concern away. "I'm fine, I'm fine. I'm just sorry to have gotten all of you into this mess."

"Max, this is not your fault," Ruby said, only then noticing Bug pacing behind Max, like he was getting ready to punch something. "Bug?" she asked, her voice tentative and quiet.

And then Bug balled his fists and let out a loud, growling scream, as if trying to rid himself of the rage building inside. Ruby had never seen him lose his cool before, and frankly, it was a bit frightening, though she knew he would never do anything to hurt any of them.

He took a breath, blowing it slowly out his mouth. "How could she?" he asked no one in particular, the hurt thick in his voice.

Ruby's heart cracked in two, watching her friend try to process that this woman, their partner and friend, the person he'd thought he loved for so long, had become something he could have never understood. Someone who let her people believe she was dead, all the while setting them up for a massive fall.

She'd played them all.

But most of all, she'd played Bug. Ruby couldn't help but wonder just how far Ash had gone to get inside Bug's head, to make him trust her and, as it turned out, do her dirty work for her.

"Oh, Bug," Max said, sounding like his heart was breaking too.

Still shaking his head in disbelief, Bug straightened, and suddenly he looked a whole lot better than he had since the moment he learned of Ash's "death." Ruby supposed finding out the woman you loved was not, in fact, dead would do that to a person. Especially when said person had suddenly become your enemy and a new fire was lit. A fire of anger and vengeance.

Ruby wasn't sure if she wanted to see what Bug would do fueled on vengeance, but she supposed it was better than watching her friend's heart break over and over the way hearts do with grief.

"Do you know?" Bug asked, turning his attention to Max. "Do you know why she did this?"

Max shook his head. "She couldn't figure out any other way, I suppose," he said.

"But why us?" Shane asked. "How could she double-cross the people who've had her back all these years?"

Max cleared his throat. "From the way she talked to those men, and to me after I'd been captured, she didn't seem to feel we'd had her back at all. She talked about how we had abandoned her after Scotland. How we all blamed her for everything."

"Because it was her fault," Ruby couldn't help but spit out.

A pained expression crossed Bug's face. "Sorry, Bug," Ruby said.

She couldn't imagine the array of emotions storming inside him.

"No," he said, his voice gruff. "I used to think it was unfair so much of the blame for Scotland fell onto Ash, but I'm starting to see more clearly." He shook his head, as if he couldn't believe he'd ever been so fooled. "We need to get that scepter back. We need to find her and make sure she never does this to anyone else," he finished.

"Don't worry about the scepter right now," Ruby said. "We have more important things to worry about, like how the hell we're supposed to get out of here."

As they talked, Shane moved across the room to check the windows. "Locked," he said, though even if they weren't, Ruby wasn't sure what the plan would have been. Judging from the number of stairs they'd climbed to get into the church, the drop would not be something they'd want to risk. Broken bones were decidedly not at the top of her wish list.

"Max, you've been here the longest," Ruby said. "Have you figured a way out yet?"

She was hopeful he had a plan but just couldn't execute it since he was being watched, not to mention tied to a chair.

"I thought about the windows…if there was a balcony or a drain pipe to shimmy down or something, but as you can imagine, I haven't had much opportunity to check."

Ruby nodded, and Shane was already climbing onto a chair to look outside, no doubt hoping for a miracle. "There's nothing like that out here," he said, "and the drop is worse than I thought."

Ruby let out a long, slow breath. "There has to be another way."

As she was saying it, Bug began to sniff the air. "Does anyone else smell that?" he asked, at about the same moment Ruby noticed the smoke beginning to slither its way under the door.

Chapter 22

Shane was still reeling at the idea that all this had been a setup. He and Ash had never been bosom buddies or anything, but he'd always considered her a friend. And he'd never been double-crossed by a friend before. His instincts were usually better.

But people changed, he supposed.

These were the types of moments when Shane was at his best. When things were starting to look dire, with no solution in sight.

Clearly, they couldn't go through the main door. Not only was it locked, but they'd be running toward Ash, who Shane could only assume was getting her feet wet in this new, and alarming, hobby of arson.

The windows were clearly out—especially for someone Max's age. He was in pretty good shape, but the fact that he'd been toted around and kept captive for the past several days would not help.

Bug was at a second doorway on the other side of the room, but he shook his head. "Locked tight from the outside."

It made sense, of course. They had been holding Max captive here, after all, but still, even if Ash needed that scepter so badly, did she want the rest of the team to die? He and Ruby were one thing, he supposed, but Max...who'd given her the opportunity for this life in the first place, and Bug? Shane had always thought they'd been close…the guy must be devastated. Not that he looked it in the moment, suddenly far more focused on finding a way out than lamenting his current status of betrayal.

Shane pulled out his phone. Maybe if they could get the fire department there fast enough, the windows would become an option. After trying his call three times, it became clear that Ash and her new crew had set up a cell phone jammer, rendering all their phones useless.

"Calls won't go through," Shane said. "They must have them blocked. Bug, is there any way to reverse a jammer?"

Bug shook his head. "Not without finding the physical jammer, and I highly doubt it's in here."

The rest of the team exhausted the options they'd been pursuing. Ruby ripped a large curtain right off the wall and was shoving it under the door to slow the smoke, but it was only a matter of time before the fire made its way into the room.

They gathered near the back of the room as far away from the danger as possible, but Max let out a weak cough and reminded everyone they did not have a hell of a lot of time.

Shane glanced desperately around the room, hoping for a miracle idea.

"The ducts?" Ruby asked, pointing to a large return air vent in the ceiling.

Bug shook his head. "You only see that in movies. In real life the vents usually aren't strong enough to hold a person's weight, not to mention we wouldn't get very far. We'd go about twenty feet at most before running into a damper or tight corner or some other kind of obstruction."

But Bug's words got Shane's mind moving in a new direction, the thoughts circling through his mind in fast, jerky sequences.

"In movies you always see people crawling around in the

ducts for a long time, right? But what if we only needed to go a short distance?"

"Sure, but there might not be another fresh air return in this area of the building," Bug said.

"Okay, but you also said it might not hold a person's weight, which means in theory it's a very lightweight material," Shane said.

Bug nodded, starting to catch on.

Shane was already moving toward the vent, pulling the chair Max had been tied to underneath it. He pulled out his utility knife, which had about a million gadgets one might need in almost any sort of pinch, including when you needed a screwdriver. He began to remove the vent cover as quickly as he could, trying to ignore the smoke filtering in faster by the second.

He dropped the grate to the floor and Bug came over to give him a boost up into the opening. It was a bit of a feat trying to wriggle his way up there, and he could only hope the last person who had to make the trek would figure out something to get them closer to the duct than Max's chair, but this could work. The duct was definitely large enough for Shane to crawl through, but, as expected, made a rather alarming groaning sound as he inched forward, his full weight putting the flimsy metal under way more strain than it was designed for. But it held, at least for the moment.

Inside the duct, it was slightly smoky, but most of it seemed to be coming from the same direction as he was, which meant hopefully he'd be heading away from the fire.

Shane began to move more quickly, hoping if he moved fast, he wouldn't put too much strain on any one joint or weak spot long enough for it to give out. He crawled until he thought he was far enough away from the room. Once he got to the next joint in the ductwork, he started to push on it. It let out some groans of protest but didn't want to give.

"Of course," Shane grumbled to himself as he inched his way farther until his feet were close to the joint.

He started to kick, as the stubborn material continued to hold. But then, the groaning turned into an even more alarming noise—a horrid metal-on-metal screech that would have normally signaled disaster, but in that moment, was music to Shane's ears.

"Shane?" Max's voice reached him.

It was as if Max was yelling from somewhere far away, not from just twenty feet or so.

"One minute," Shane yelled, his foot finally breaking through the stubborn metal—then promptly getting caught between the two pieces now ripped apart at the seams. As he lay on his stomach, he used his other foot to free the first foot, and continued kicking, until a substantial hole had formed. He shimmied back so he could use his hands to continue working the duct apart. Soon he could see the room below was dark and small, but it wasn't filled with smoke. As Shane's eyes adjusted, he could just make out the outline of a door, light coming in underneath.

He continued to push on the metal until it resembled a can, peeled open to reveal the contents.

The room below was a storage or janitor's closet. Shane tried to think ahead, realizing if he jumped down into the room, he might not have a way back out if he was locked in there too.

But what else could he do? He decided he had to take the chance.

"I found a closet of some sort," he yelled back through the duct. "I'm going in."

No doubt the team would realize as quickly as he did that if there wasn't a way out of this room, they were out of options.

Shane wriggled his legs and body through, lowering until

his hands were hanging above his body. He let go, dropping the few final feet to the ground.

The place was dark, and it took a moment for Shane to get his bearings, but he quickly found the door and grabbed for the knob.

Locked.

His stomach gave a little jolt before he realized that even though it was locked, most doors locked from the inside. He felt for the locking mechanism and turned it with a small click, the door swinging brilliantly open.

There was definitely some smoke in the hallway, but if they hurried, they might have a chance.

Shane worked up his loudest yelling voice, worried now that he was out of the duct, his voice might not carry back to the others. "We're good to go!" he yelled.

His words were met with silence.

"Guys! We have a way out. Get your asses over here!"

He waited a moment, listening for something…anything. Shane flicked on the light in the closet, and after blinking for a moment, searched for something he could stand on that would be high enough to get him back up into the duct, but all he could see was a five-gallon pail that might get his fingertips to make their way back to the hole, but he wasn't sure how he'd be able to pull himself back up.

"Ruby! Max! Bug!" he yelled one more time, still scrambling to find more things to get himself higher.

"Dude," a voice said.

It was so quiet, so calm compared to the yelling he'd been doing that it was almost startling.

"Enough with the yelling, we're here," Ruby said, popping her head over the opening and shooting Shane her best grin, promptly causing Shane's stomach to give a little jolt for an entirely different reason.

"Well, get down here then," Shane said, grinning back.

Ruby shimmied over the hole until her legs could get through, then lowered the rest of her body down. It was an excellent opportunity for Shane to help her, grabbing her legs as she descended. Once he had her, she let go and he lowered her gently to the floor—her descent much more graceful than his foray into the closet had been.

Max was next, maneuvering over the opening in the duct with a bit more difficulty than Ruby'd had. Although Shane couldn't help but think it wasn't so much "a bit more" difficulty as it was "a whole helluva lot" of difficulty.

He glanced at Ruby, whose face held as much concern as Shane was feeling, as smoke began to billow through the duct.

Mercifully, Max's legs finally appeared through the hole and he started to lower himself down, though he must have been weak from his time in captivity, and lost his grip before falling the last few feet.

But Shane had quick reflexes and managed to sort of half grab him, and half get his own body under Max's to cushion the fall. The result was a mess of limbs and muffled cries, but zero injuries besides maybe a bruise or two. Probably mostly on Shane.

Which was a gloriously small price to pay than what the alternative could have been in the situation, Shane decided.

Bug struggled his way through the hole—his shoulders much bulkier than anyone else's, and his cough much more pronounced, since he'd spent more time in the smoke than the others.

But they were all there, and they were free.

At least free of the locked room. The rest of the church was still a question mark.

Shane led the way down the hall away from the fire. He had no idea where they were headed, but it wasn't like they were going to go back the way they'd come. A building like this—one meant for the public—would have several exits for the exact purpose of fire safety.

At the end of the hall, a set of double doors led them to a stairwell. Shane led the team down, and as he turned on the landing, a sign came into view with perhaps the most beautiful word in the English language.

Exit.

He pushed through the door and immediately a high-pitched wail sounded, the exit having been rigged with an alarm. But the air was crisp and cool, and tasted delicious, like the essence of life itself.

He made it about three steps before he realized several guns were pointed directly at his head.

He sighed. "Really? This again?"

Like Shane, Ruby was getting sick of people pointing guns at her. These weren't the same people, of course, but the feeling was pretty similar no matter who was doing the pointing.

The good news was, they found out their lives were not in nearly as much danger as they had been in the church.

The bad thing was, this time they were being taken into custody for questioning.

She supposed it should have been more surprising, but Ruby had thought so much about this moment, about getting caught, it almost seemed like an inevitable conclusion to her story.

Her thoughts jolted ahead the way they always did, picturing the monotony of her life from that moment on. She wondered who she'd have to make friends with in prison for protection. But most of all, she felt a deep sense of loss when they put Shane in the back of a police cruiser, watching until he'd been driven around the corner and out of sight.

She wondered if it would be the last time she saw him.

And then she was the one being led into a police cruiser

and driven to the station, assuming Bug and Max were close behind.

They kept Ruby waiting for what seemed like hours, though time worked differently when you're locked inside a room with nothing besides your uncooperative thoughts to keep you company.

Eventually, a man and woman sauntered into the room like there was nothing out of the ordinary—just chillin' with my coffee, nothing to see here.

The worst part was, they didn't even offer her a cup.

Maybe she didn't deserve coffee anymore, Ruby thought. If they knew even half the laws she'd broken…well, they had every right to lock her up and throw away the key.

The duo sat, the man dropping a thick file onto the table.

The woman took a long swig of her coffee before she spoke. "This is Anover," she said, pointing to her partner. "And I'm Mills. Care to fill us in on your part in all this?"

"My part in what?" Ruby asked. She wasn't trying to be difficult; she was simply trying to gauge how much they knew.

The corner of Mills's lip curled up a bit. "Oh, you know, the breaking and entering of a church, the little matter of the arson of said church…the heist of a certain priceless piece of history?"

The detective's eyebrow rose at the end of her sentence and Ruby realized they knew everything and there was no point in lying.

Of course, she opened her mouth and lied her face off anyway.

"I planned the whole thing," she said. "I was working with another woman to get the scepter and then was too blind to see she was double-crossing me the whole time."

"Really?" Mills said.

Ruby nodded. "Really."

For the next fifteen minutes, Ruby went into detail about

Ash and the heist, careful to keep Shane and Bug out of it. She mentioned Max's role, but said he was innocent of any wrongdoing—he had just been a pawn.

The detectives listened quietly. The man, Anover, took notes while Mills stared at Ruby, almost unblinking.

Finally, Mills cleared her throat. "I gotta say, that is the most popular story I've heard all day." She turned to her partner. "Seems to be a bit of a theme, don't you think?"

He nodded.

"Sorry?" Ruby asked.

"Well, it's just that the whole lot of you seem bound and determined to take all of the blame and make damn sure everyone else looks as innocent as a baby bunny in the springtime."

Ruby swallowed.

Mills narrowed her eyes. "Your story wasn't quite as good as your boyfriend's, though."

Ruby narrowed her eyes right back. "I don't have a boyfriend."

"You could have fooled me, the way both of you talk all swoony about each other."

"I do not talk swoony," Ruby said, working her jaw.

"I wouldn't have pegged it either, but here we are."

Ruby huffed, crossing her arms. "Just…don't listen to what he says. He can't be trusted."

Mills chuckled a little. "First you try to convince me Shane Meyers is as trustworthy as a kindergarten teacher, and now you're telling me he can't be trusted." She turned to her partner again. "You know, I'm inclined to believe the one who's not changing his story so much."

"I'm not changing my story. I'm just saying my story is the truth."

"Ah, the truth," the detective said. "You know what they say about the truth. There's your truth, my truth and then what actually happened."

"What I just told you is what actually happened," Ruby said.

Mills tipped her head back and forth, as if thinking. "I don't doubt everything you've told me is the truth. It's just that I don't believe for a second that it's the whole truth."

Chapter 23

Shane had given his all with the story he told the authorities, selling it as if he was hoping to get an Oscar. He explained what went down, of course, but he might have gone a bit off script with the ending. Specifically, the part where Ruby sent the scepter back to her museum. In his version of the story, he'd held a gun on her and forced her to ship it using her credentials. It hadn't been her idea at all. He was the one who was working with Ash.

Ruby was going to lay into him if he ever saw her again, but that was a small price to pay to make sure she could keep the life she'd worked so hard for. He was more than willing to trade his freedom for hers.

He just didn't know what was taking so long for them to haul him away.

Shane hated to wait. When given too much time to think, his brain tended to be like an unattended toddler in a kitchen—messy and dangerous.

Eventually, the two detectives—Mills and Anover—returned.

"You're free to go," Mills said, holding the door open so Shane could simply walk out.

"Wait, what?" Shane said, panic starting to rise in his chest.

"I mean, you can sit here longer if you want," Mills said, "but it's not like we're the Ritz here. We aren't going to bring you room service."

"But what changed? I told you, I'm guilty."

"Yeah, yeah, yeah," Mills said. "You're all guilty. I get it." She turned to Anover. "Weird bunch of friends, if you ask me," she finished under her breath.

Shane tried to formulate a coherent thought. "But—"

Mills held up a hand to stop him, clearly impatient. "We caught Ashlyn Greaves and have been questioning her for the past hour."

"What? How?" Shane asked.

Mills sighed as if she didn't have the time or the patience to deal with his questions but was resigning herself to the idea that he wasn't going to leave until he heard the full story. She sat heavy in one of the chairs across from Shane, and Anover followed suit as if he was her shadow.

"At approximately four fifteen this afternoon, Ashlyn Greaves was apprehended by authorities as she was boarding a Greyhound destined for Florida."

Shane blinked. The thought of Ash on a public bus, let alone one to Florida, which would have taken, like, thirty hours, did not compute. Although it wasn't like she could get the scepter on a plane. But why not a car?

Maybe she figured the bus would be the last place anyone would search.

"Florida?" he finally asked when his brain started to focus again.

Mills nodded. "She purchased a property under an assumed name down there. A place to lie low until she could coordinate the sale of the scepter."

"She was going to *sell* the scepter?" Shane asked, dumbfounded. "I thought she wanted it so bad because it was a precious family heirloom."

"Oddly enough," Mills said. "It did once belong to her family—generations back, of course. But Ms. Greaves had no interest in sharing her find with her family. She'd been estranged from them for over a decade. The scepter had been a story told from generation to generation, but no one ever thought it could be retrieved."

"Except Ash, apparently," Shane chimed in.

Mills nodded. "When she did somehow find it, she had no intention of ever sharing the spoils with anyone."

Shane stared at Mills, unable to comprehend what must have been going through Ash's head. A thought struck him. "If it was under an assumed name, how did you know about this place in Florida?"

Mills half smiled. "Your friend… Mr. Elliot," she said, "had an enormous amount of intel on Ms. Greaves—it seems he had a bit of an infatuation with her—and, well, after the way she double-crossed all of you, he was willing to give the info up."

"Bug?" Shane was shocked he'd revealed anything to the authorities, including that he was able to find out almost anything about anyone. He must have been seriously pissed at Ash—not that Shane could blame him. He was more than a bit miffed at her himself. "He's not going to be in trouble, is he?"

Mills shook her head. "His retrieval of the information on Ms. Greaves certainly did not follow the proper legal channels, but after agreeing to use his…skills on a few cases for us, we've agreed to let that slide."

Oh, man, Shane thought. Bug was going to hate that, but he supposed it would all be behind him soon enough. Plus, it must have felt damn good to turn her in after the devastation she'd rained down on him.

"And you were able to get Ash to talk?" Shane asked.

Mills shrugged. "We don't think she'll be too hard to crack, but for now, we're accepting Mr. Elliot's and Max Redfield's accounts of the story, which actually match, and are the only ones that make sense. Yours and Ms. Alexander's are a little too far-fetched," she said, almost rolling her eyes.

Shane only had one question left. "So, Ruby's free to go too?"

"We have a few more questions for Ms. Alexander," Mills said, her voice serious.

"But she didn't do anything—"

Again, Mills cut him off by holding up her hand. "What Ms. Alexander did, she did of her own accord. We won't be pressing criminal charges against her, but she will have to answer to her workplace over the things she's done."

Shane slumped further into his seat.

"But mostly," Mills continued, getting up from her seat, followed by the ever-silent Anover, "what we'd like to figure out is how Ashlyn Greaves was caught trying to smuggle a so-called priceless artifact that was, in fact, a counterfeit."

Ruby could have had six thousand guesses as to who the next person who strolled into her interrogation room would be, but she wouldn't have been successful.

"Barb?" she asked, gawking at her boss from the museum.

"Hey, Ruby," Barb said, like she didn't have a care in the world. In fact, she sounded practically jovial.

"How… Why…" Ruby said, struggling to form a thought, let alone a sentence. "What?" she asked, her forehead crinkling.

Barb chuckled a little. "Good to see you too," she said, sitting across the table from Ruby.

"What are you doing here?" Ruby asked.

She knew she'd be let go from the museum, but she didn't think Barb would have to come all the way down here to tell her. Frankly, she thought the authorities would be the one telling Barb that Ruby wouldn't be at work Monday morning.

"Heard you were having a little trouble with these fine folks down here at the station," she explained.

Not that it was much of an explanation.

"And I thought I'd come down to see what I could do."

"How did you even know I was here?" Ruby asked.

A smirk twitched at the corner of Barb's mouth before they were interrupted with Max poking his head into the doorway. Ruby's whole body relaxed in relief. At least Max was being set free. That was something, at least.

"I heard you were in here," he said. "Thought I'd come by and say thanks."

Max was so sweet, Ruby thought and opened her mouth to say as much, but promptly shut it when Barb's chair scraped back and she headed for Max. As Barb embraced him in a big hug, Ruby realized Max hadn't been talking to her at all. For the second time in a matter of seconds, she was struck silent.

Silent, and so very, very confused.

When they finished greeting each other, both Max and Barb came to sit in front of Ruby. Ruby's brain always wanted to work every question out as soon as possible, but in that moment, it had given up. There was no way she could explain any of this.

"I hear we have you to thank for saving our Max, here," Barb said, squeezing Max's hand that had been resting on the table.

Our Max?

Barb's eyes sparkled with secrets and mischief as she turned to Max. "This is even more fun than I thought it would be," she said, bouncing a little in her seat.

Max smiled. "You better tell the poor girl what's going on before her head explodes from trying to figure it out."

"Right," Barb said, though she sounded like she wanted to draw it out even longer. "Well, I guess I should start by saying I know a lot more about your past than you think I do."

Ruby's stomach clenched with that same old feeling. The one where she was terrified someone she knew had found out who she really was.

A flood of shame washed over her.

"I didn't mean to deceive you," Ruby said. "I just wanted

so badly to do something with my life that was good, for once. I...I guess I wanted a future."

"Ruby," Barb said, her voice kind, "you haven't done anything wrong. I mean, I know you and Max and the team didn't always do things within the strict confines of the law, but trust me when I say you did it for the right reasons. For the overall good of the people you were helping."

Ruby shook her head, her gaze focused on her lap, unable to look Barb in the eye. "It wasn't right..."

Barb shrugged. "Maybe it wasn't, or maybe it was," she said. "But in the end, your intention was to help people and fix what had gone so, so wrong. And that's a noble cause." She cleared her throat. "It took me a long time to realize that, too, but I think I'm finally there."

Ruby's eyes snapped up.

Barb smiled. "As you've no doubt guessed, Max and I are old friends. Well, Max was my mentor, really."

Ruby looked from Max, who appeared to be enjoying himself to no end, then to Barb, and back to Max again. "You were one of his students."

"One of my best," Max confirmed.

"And you got out," Ruby said.

Barb tilted her head. "Sort of," she said. "Though Max and I have never stopped collaborating."

Ruby's eyebrows pinched together.

"I've been working on a project for several years now, trying to find the right people to help me...expedite some of the work we do at the museum, along with other partner museums around the world."

"I'm not sure I understand," Ruby said. "Why are you telling me this?"

"Because I'm hoping you'll agree to work with me on the project."

"Um," Ruby said, gazing around. "I'm not sure if you noticed, but I'm about to be arrested and likely put away for a very long time."

"You are not about to be arrested," Barb said. "In fact, the people who have spent the better part of the day questioning you are partners in the project. Folks in law enforcement who are going to help us speed the process of finding stolen antiquities and getting them back where they belong."

"It's just like what we used to do, Ruby," Max chimed in. "Except this time, it will all be aboveboard."

Something sparked in Ruby, though she wasn't sure she could trust it.

"We've been given the go-ahead to assemble our task force—funded in part by the museum. Though, thanks to Max and his various teams, several rather grateful families whose stolen items have been returned over the past decades are more than happy to show their appreciation with monetary investments as well."

Ruby shook her head. "I'm sorry. The people who have been given back their heirlooms are funding some kind of task force?"

"Precisely," Max said. "They want to see justice for even more families, and frankly, so do we. And we're hoping you'll agree to help us. The work will still be dangerous—as you may have noticed, I have several…precautions at my house—but something tells me that sort of thing isn't going to stop any of my former students."

"And you'd be able to keep your credentials with the museum intact," Barb said. "If, at any time, you decide the task force isn't for you anymore, you'll have your job back at the museum."

Ruby was speechless. She rarely let herself admit it, but she missed so much about her old life. Once a person lived with that kind of adventure—the travel, the adrenaline, the satisfaction of having families immediately reunited with their priceless heirlooms—it was hard to let it go.

"You'd be helping people the way we used to," Max said, "except you'd never have to feel like you were doing something wrong."

Ruby hadn't even realized she was nodding until Barb said, "So, does that mean you'll join us?"

"What?" Ruby asked, as if snapping out of a daydream. She looked at Barb, her boss and friend, then to Max, someone she cared for so much, but who was from an entirely different world.

The whole scene in front of her was jarring, but Ruby decided she could live with her two worlds colliding.

"Yeah," she said. "I'm in. Absolutely, I'm in."

"Great! I think that pretty much takes care of business," Barb said, getting up and holding her hand out for Ruby.

It was a weirdly formal gesture for someone she'd grown so close to, but Ruby had to admit, when she shook Barb's hand, it felt like the start of a new chapter.

Barb turned to go, but paused at the door. "Oh, there was one more thing," she said. "The little matter of a priceless scepter I found abandoned under your desk at work?" She raised an eyebrow.

Ruby smiled, a bit sheepish. "Oh, that." She cleared her throat. "I may have gotten an old friend of mine to whip up a counterfeit. Something about the whole job just felt...off. I never did know what felt wrong, but I thought maybe I'd try to pull one over on the bad guys—with the real one safe at work for backup in case they figured it out."

"At the risk of your job," Barb said.

Ruby nodded. "I wouldn't be able to live with myself if we didn't get Max back...or if the scepter got into the wrong hands."

"I'd love to know how you did it," Barb said.

Ruby shrugged. "I have an artist friend who specializes in reproductions," she said. "Before I had the real scepter sent back to the museum, I had my contact, Jessica, do a full 3D scan of the scepter. It's amazing what my friend Jerome can do with a few good photo renderings and computer-generated specs."

It had been a risky move. If the people who had Max even suspected the scepter wasn't the real deal, they could have killed Max, plus the rest of the team. Ruby had mitigated the risk, knowing they'd have to be an expert to tell the difference between the real deal and the fake scepter. Still, she felt bad for putting Max in that position.

But Max was beaming. "You can never be too prepared."

"Great job," Barb said as she turned to leave again. "See you Monday morning, Ruby."

And Ruby wasn't sure she'd ever heard five better words in her life.

Chapter 24

Ruby couldn't wait to fall into bed and sleep half the weekend away, but there was one thing she needed to do first.

Get the travel filth, the fire soot and the police station grime off her.

She threw her keys onto the console table near her door and began to strip her clothes off, dropping each item on the floor on her way down the hall to her bathroom.

She made the shower hot—hot tub–style hot—and scrubbed the last few days away.

She could hardly believe all the things that had happened, but most of all she couldn't believe she still had her job at the museum. Well, a different job within the museum, she supposed— one that would give her everything she wanted.

Almost.

There was still one big question mark, but she couldn't think about him. If she did, she'd never get the sleep she needed.

She wrapped a towel around herself before making her way back down the hall. Halfway to the kitchen she realized something was off and stopped, heart racing. There didn't appear to be an immediate threat, but impossibly, her clothes were no longer scattered on the floor. A sound of a glass clinking came from the kitchen where the clothes she'd discarded sat neatly folded on the counter.

A voice floated from the shadows. "Still doing the same old rituals, I see."

This time she met his smirk. "And just how did you get in?" she asked, accepting the wine he'd poured for her, but before she could drink, he raised his glass. "What are we toasting?" Ruby asked, her voice sultry, playing along.

"I'm hoping we're toasting to working together again," Shane said.

Ruby raised an eyebrow. "Ah, they talked to you, did they?"

Shane grinned. "When they told me you'd have to answer for the scepter being counterfeit, I thought I was going to lose it. My mind started trying to come up with something, anything, I could say to get you out of trouble with the museum. Some way you could keep your job. Thankfully, they put me out of my misery pretty quickly and told me about the task force." He chuckled. "Or maybe they just couldn't bear listening to my absolute bullshit one more time."

"You always did try to be my protector," Ruby said.

A strange, restless feeling shimmered through Ruby, who was torn between annoyance that he thought she couldn't take care of herself and a weird thrill that he wanted to be her rescuer. It was uncomfortable, like her insides itched. Suddenly she knew what it was.

Vulnerability.

An idea that scared her way more than any jump off a dark mountain could.

"I guess I was hoping that someday, just once, you'd let me," Shane said.

Ruby was scared. No longer worried about losing the life she'd built for herself, but of losing a life from before.

"Shane, I—"

He shook his head. "You don't have to say anything. This doesn't have to be anything. We can just have right now."

"That's not what I want," Ruby replied.

The hurt that moved over his face nearly broke her heart.

"No, I mean…" She sighed, then looked him in the eye.

"I mean I don't want it to be just right now. I want it to be… something else. Something longer."

"But you always said you never wanted serious," Shane said, his eyes questioning. Hopeful?

Ruby's head swam with every moment she'd ever been here. Every time she'd been close to saying what she felt, then chickened out, made up excuses. Even now, everything in her screamed to take it back, to keep things light, stay on the surface. Real feelings could too easily go wrong. Could break a person.

But then…hadn't she already felt broken? Felt like she was missing a piece of herself?

"Shane," she said, tears prickling. "I never really wanted that. Not with you. I just…" She glanced away. "I wanted things to be easy. You wanted things to be easy. What we did for work, it was so dangerous, always felt so impermanent. Anything could have changed at any moment. Everything did change in a single moment. It didn't make sense for either of us to get tied up in a relationship."

"Except you were the one thing that always made the world make sense," Shane said, his voice quiet. Serious.

She looked up at him, the tears threatening to spill over. "I think I finally know that now."

"So, you're on board with working together again? The way we used to?"

Ruby put her wine down and took a step closer to Shane. "I'm on board with a lot more than that."

She felt breathless with the admission. Before the words had tumbled out, she wasn't even sure if she'd be able to say them, but in the end, it was easy. Probably because she'd never been so sure of anything in her life.

"For real this time?" Shane asked.

"For real this time."

Shane set his glass beside Ruby's and closed the remainder of the space between them as his gentle hands lifted her face and he kissed her deeply. There was no desperation in it this time, only certainty.

Every cell in Ruby's body sparked, every flutter of emotion racing straight to the surface of her skin, prickling each nerve ending with sensation. Delightful little prickles of heat, electricity, light.

Her hands found the back of his neck, curling up into his hair, and she only had one thought. That this felt right. Nothing in that moment could have made her feel like anything she was doing could be wrong.

Shane kissed down her neck and Ruby sighed with relief and desire, the tingling dancing even brighter between her thighs.

She pulled his head back to hers, kissing harder—almost frantic.

He kissed her back just as hard. Heat swelled inside Ruby—the kind of heat she hadn't felt in a very long time. She needed a moment for air, the sensations almost too much to handle, and she took a step back, keeping her gaze locked on his. She smiled and reached for the place where she'd tucked her towel into itself.

Shane followed her lead, starting to unbutton his shirt as she let the towel fall to the floor.

Shane flung his shirt to the ground and moved his hands to his belt, then stopped. He didn't smile. He didn't say a word. He just looked.

Emboldened, Ruby reached for her wine and took a long sip as Shane fumbled with his clothes, every sparked sensation burning brighter as his eyes roamed over her.

Nothing in Ruby's life had ever felt this right. This necessary.

Shane came out of his trance and rid himself of his clothes by the time Ruby had carefully made her way backward to the couch, wine still in hand. She sipped as Shane moved toward her. Muscled shoulders leading to a lean chest and torso. His legs holding their own, too, though she didn't quite get past the erection that most certainly did not disappoint. Shane took the final steps toward her, keeping the slightest gap between them, looking into her eyes, silently asking if she was sure.

And my god, was she sure. There was a familiarity to the moment, like coming home, but it was all new, too, the desire somehow more intense than it had ever been.

Shane took the wineglass from her and set it on the side table, while every cell in Ruby's body screamed that if she didn't close the distance in the next few seconds, they might never forgive her.

She arched, her chest grazing his, his lips finding her throat. As she leaned back, waves of heat flooded her, frantic, alive— senses spiraling out of control. Shane's lips explored, tasting his way past her collarbone, slowly working their way to the sensitive nerves of her nipple, instantly igniting a fuse straight down her center. He took his time, swirling…savoring, as the invisible fuse burned brighter and hotter, inching closer to sparks, fire, explosions.

Shane lifted her then, setting her gently on the top edge of the couch as he traced the invisible thread farther down, past her chest, toward her belly button. Mercifully, he did not stop there, searching for the fuse's final destination, and she spread her legs, letting her head fall back, as if opening her-self to the universe, but more importantly, to the man below.

He grabbed her hips and closed his mouth over her, his ex-pert tongue stroking, caressing…then sucking with a gentle pressure until she could barely hold herself up any longer, the blaze building to combustible levels, until she couldn't hold it inside any longer and cried out with an explosion unrivaled by any she'd experienced before.

After some luxurious moments allowing herself to revel in

the satisfaction, Shane holding her tight, always her protector, Ruby gathered enough composure to slide down the back of the couch, and Shane laid her gently across it. They began again slowly, a kiss here, a soft touch there.

Ruby's body had always responded to Shane's. His lips, his arms, the muscles down his torso. Her body had not forgotten. Only screamed at her that it had been too long since she'd been here with Shane. Since she'd come home.

They'd found their way back to each other and Ruby wondered how she could have allowed the part of her that fought this to win. To be without for so many years.

And Shane treated her like she was his home too. Treasured, valued…loved.

Their slow kisses and soft touches soon turned more urgent, Shane setting a faster pace as Ruby helped him find the way to his own, much-deserved explosion.

Afterward, they lay quiet for a long while, Shane stroking her shoulder as she rested on his chest, and Ruby found that her thoughts had calmed. She'd forgotten being with Shane used to do that. Made her feel less…out of control.

"I can't believe everything that's happened," Shane said eventually. "I feel like we get to have our old life back."

A familiar twinge shot through Ruby at the thought of going back to that life, to that world. The old combination of excitement mixed with a heavy dose of dread…but then she remembered she could push those feelings of dread away.

"Not our old life," she said. "The old life never quite felt right. Like we couldn't quite fit all the right pieces together."

Shane made a musing sound. "So maybe it's like we get to have all the best pieces of our old life back."

Ruby nodded. "Plus some new, very interesting pieces," she said, draping her arm across his chest.

A sense of contentment washed over her then, an unfamiliar feeling that she couldn't quite place.

"Some very interesting new pieces," Shane agreed.

"And this time they all fit together," Ruby said, suddenly realizing exactly what the sensation was.

A falling into place of the pieces. A completion.

A life she knew could never be flawless—nothing was, not even the most precious piece of art—but this life, with this man in her arms, was about as close as she could imagine to perfect.

* * * * *

Romantic Suspense

Danger. Passion. Drama.

Available Next Month

Colton's Blizzard Hideout Deborah Fletcher Mello
Threats In The Deep Addison Fox

....

Cold Case Secrets Kimberly Van Meter
Escape From Devil's Den Bonnie Vanak

....

LOVE INSPIRED
Crime Scene Secrets Maggie K. Black
Wilderness Witness Survival Connie Queen
Larger Print

....

LOVE INSPIRED
Danger On The Peaks Rebecca Hopewell
Texas Ranch Cold Case Virginia Vaughan
Larger Print

....

LOVE INSPIRED
Baby On The Run Hope White
Colorado Mountain Kidnapping Cate Nolan
Larger Print

6 brand new stories each month

Romantic Suspense

Danger. Passion. Drama.

MILLS & BOON

Keep reading for an excerpt of a new title
from the Special Edition series,
TAMING A HEARTBREAKER by Brenda Jackson

Prologue

Sloan and Leslie Outlaw's wedding...

"Sloan definitely likes kissing you, girlfriend."

Leslie Outlaw couldn't help but smile at her best friend's whispered words. "And I love kissing him."

She'd married the man she loved, and she'd had her best friend Carmen Golan at her side. Leslie followed her friend's gaze now and saw just where it had landed—right on Redford St. James, who was being corralled by the photographer as Sloan took pictures with his best man and groomsmen.

Unease stirred Leslie's insides at her friend's obvious interest.

Leslie had known Redford for as long as she'd known Sloan, since she'd met both guys the same day on the university's campus over ten years ago. Redford had been known then as a heartbreaker. According to Sloan, Redford hadn't changed. If anything, he'd gotten worse.

"Carmen, I need to warn you about Redford," Leslie said, hoping it wasn't too late. She'd noted last night at the rehearsal how taken her best friend had been with Redford. She'd hoped she was mistaken.

"I know all about him, Leslie, so you don't need to warn me. However, you might want to put a bug in Sloan's ear to warn Redford about me."

Leslie lifted a brow. "Why?"

A wide smile covered Carmen's face. "Because Redford

St. James is the man I intend to marry. Your hubby is on his way over here. I will see you at the reception."

Leslie watched Carmen walk toward Redford. Marry? Redford? She had a feeling her best friend was biting off more than she could chew. Redford was not the marrying kind. He'd made that clear when he'd said no woman would ever tame him.

Chapter One

Two years later...

Redford St. James froze, with his wineglass midway to his lips, when he saw the woman walk into the wedding reception for Jaxon and Nadia Ravnell. Frowning, he immediately turned to the man by his side, Sloan Outlaw. During their college days at the University of Alaska at Anchorage, Sloan, Redford, and another close friend, Tyler Underwood, had been thick as thieves, and still were.

Redford had been known as the "king of quickies." He would make out with women any place or any time. Storage rooms, empty classrooms or closets, beneath the stairs, dressing rooms …he'd used them all. He had the uncanny ability to scope out a room and figure out just where a couple could spend time for pleasure. He still had that skill and used it every chance he got.

Although he, Sloan and Tyler now lived in different cities in Alaska, they still found the time to get together a couple of times a year. Doing so wasn't as easy as it used to be since both Tyler and Sloan were married with a child each. Tyler had a son and Sloan a daughter.

"Why didn't you tell me Carmen Golan was invited to this wedding?"

Sloan glanced over at Redford and rolled his eyes. "Just

like you didn't tell me Leslie had been invited to Tyler and Keosha's wedding three years ago?"

Redford frowned. "Don't play with me, Sloan. You should have known Leslie would be invited, since she and Keosha were friends in college. In this case, I wasn't aware Carmen knew Jaxon or Nadia."

Sloan took a sip of his wine before saying, "The Outlaws and Westmorelands consider themselves one big happy family, and that includes outside cousins, in-laws and close friends. Since Carmen is Leslie's best friend, of course she would know them." Sloan then studied his friend closely. "Why does Carmen being here bother you, Redford? If I recall, when I put that bug in your ear after my wedding, that she'd said she intended to one day become your wife, you laughed it off. Has that changed?"

"Of course, that hasn't changed."

"You're sure?" Sloan asked. "It seems to me that over the past two years, whenever the two of you cross paths, you try like hell to avoid her. Most recently, at Cassidy's christening a few months ago." Cassidy was Sloan and Leslie's daughter. Redford was one of her godfathers, and Carmen was her godmother.

"No woman can change my ways. I don't ever intend to marry. Who does she think she is, anyway? She doesn't even know me like that. If she did, then she would know my only interest in her at your wedding was getting her to the nearest empty coat closet. The nerve of her, thinking she can change me."

"And since you know she can't change you, why worry about it?"

"I'm not worrying."

"If you say so," Sloan countered.

Redford's frown deepened. "I do say so. You of all people should know that I'll never fall in love again."

Before Sloan could respond, his sister Charm walked up and said the photographer wanted to take a photo of Jaxon with his Outlaw cousins.

When Sloan walked off, leaving Redford alone, he took a sip of his wine as he looked across the room at Carmen again. Sloan's words had hit a nerve. He *wasn't* worried. Then why had he been avoiding her for the past two years? Doing so hadn't been easy since he was one of Sloan's best friends and she was Leslie's, and both were godparents to Cassidy. Whenever they were in the same space, he made it a point to not be in her presence for long.

He could clearly recall the day he'd first seen Carmen at Sloan and Leslie's wedding rehearsal two years ago. He would admit that he'd been intensely attracted to her from the first. It was a deep-in-the-gut awareness. Something he had never experienced before. He hadn't wasted any time adding her to his "must do" list. He'd even flirted shamelessly after they'd been introduced, with every intention of making out with her before the weekend ended.

Then he'd gotten wind of her bold claim that he was the man she intended to marry. Like hell! That had wiped out all his plans. He was unapologetically a womanizer, and no woman alive would change that.

Carmen wasn't the first woman to try, nor would she be the first to fail. Granted she was beautiful. Hell, he'd even say she was "knock-you-in-the-balls" gorgeous, but he'd dated beautiful women before. If he'd seen one, he'd seen them all, and in the bedroom they were all the same.

Then why was he letting Carmen Golan get to him? Why would heat flood his insides whenever he saw her, making him aware of every single thing about her? Why was there this strong kinetic pull between them? It was sexual chemistry so powerful that, at times, it took his breath away.

Over the years, he'd tried convincing himself his lust for

her would fade. So far it hadn't. And rather recently, whenever he saw her, it had gotten so bad he had to fight like hell to retain his common sense.

Although Sloan had given him that warning two years ago, Carmen hadn't acted on anything. Was she waiting for what she thought would be the right time to catch him at a weak moment? If that was her strategy then he had news for her. It wouldn't happen. If anything, he would catch *her* unawares first, just to prove he was way out of her league…thanks to Candy Porter.

Contrary to her first name, he'd discovered there hadn't been anything sweet about Candy. At seventeen, she had taught him a hard lesson. Mainly, to never give your heart to a woman. Candy and her parents had moved to Skagway the summer before their last year of high school. By the end of the summer, she had been his steady girlfriend, the one he planned to marry after he finished college. Those plans ended the night of their high school senior prom.

Less than an hour after they'd arrived, she told him she needed to go to the ladies' room. When she hadn't returned in a timely manner, he had gotten worried since she hadn't been feeling well. He had gone looking for her, and when a couple of girls said she wasn't in the ladies' room, he and the two concerned girls had walked outside and around the building to find her, hoping she was alright.

Not only had they found her, they'd found her with the town's bad boy, Sherman Sharpe. Both of them in the backseat of Sherman's car making out like horny rabbits. The pair hadn't even had the decency to roll up the car's window so their moans, grunts and screams couldn't be heard.

Needless to say, news of Candy and Sherman's backseat romp quickly got around. By the following morning, every household in Skagway, Alaska, had heard about it. She had tried to explain, offer an excuse, but as far as he'd been concerned, there was nothing a woman could say when caught with another man between her legs.

Heartbroken and hurt, Redford hadn't wasted any time leaving Skagway for Anchorage to begin college that summer, instead of waiting for fall. That's when he vowed to never give his heart to another woman ever again.

That had been nearly nineteen years ago, and he'd kept the promise he'd made to himself. At thirty-six, he guarded his heart like it was made of solid gold and refused to let any woman get close. He kept all his hookups impersonal. One-and-done was the name of his game. No woman slept in his bed, and he never spent the entire night in theirs. He refused to wake up with any woman in his arms.

Redford knew Carmen was his total opposite. He'd heard she was one of those people who saw the bright side of everything, always positive and agreeable. On top of that, she was a hopeless romantic. A woman who truly believed in love, marriage and all that bull crap. According to Sloan, she'd honestly gotten it in her head that she and Redford were actual soulmates. Well, he had news for her, he was no woman's soulmate.

When his wineglass was empty, he snagged another from the tray of a passing waiter. When he glanced back over at Carmen, he saw she was staring at him, and dammit to hell, like a deer caught in headlights, he stared back. Why was he feeling this degree of lust that she stirred within him so effortlessly?

There wasn't a time when she didn't look stunning. Today was no exception. There was just something alluring about her. Something that made his breath wobble whenever he stared at her for too long.

He blamed it on the beauty of her cocoa-colored skin, her almond-shaped light brown eyes, the gracefulness of her high cheekbones, her tempting pair of lips, and the mass of dark brown hair that fell past her shoulders.

Every muscle in his body tightened as he continued to look

at her, checking her out in full detail. His gaze scanned over her curvaceous and statuesque body. The shimmering blue dress she wore hugged her curves and complemented a gorgeous pair of legs. The bodice pushed up her breasts in a way that made his mouth water.

"Now you were saying," Sloan said, returning and immediately snagging Redford's attention.

"I was saying that maybe I should accommodate Carmen."

That sounded like a pretty damn good idea, considering the current fix his body was in.

"Meaning what?" Sloan asked.

A smile widened across Redford's lips. "Meaning, I think I will add her back to my 'must do' list. Maybe it's time she discovers I am a man who can't be tamed."

Sloan frowned. "Do I need to warn you that Carmen is Leslie's best friend?"

"No, but I would assume, given my reputation, that Leslie has warned Carmen about me. It's not my fault if she didn't take the warning. Now, if you will excuse me, I think I'll head over to the buffet table."

He then walked off. At least for now, he would take care of one appetite, and he intended to take care of the other before the night was over.

"I wish you and Redford would stop trying to out-stare each other, Carmen," Leslie Outlaw leaned over to whisper to her best friend.

Carmen Golan broke eye contact with Redford to glance at Leslie and couldn't help the smile that spread across her lips. "Hey, what can I say? He looks so darn good in a suit."

Leslie rolled her eyes. "Need I remind you that you've seen him in a suit before. Numerous times."

"Redford wore a tux at your wedding, Leslie, and he looked

good then, too. Better than good. He looked scrumptious." Carmen watched him again. He definitely looked delicious now.

She knew he was in his late thirties. He often projected a keen sense of professionalism, as well as a high degree of intelligence far beyond his years. But then there were other times when it seemed the main thing on his agenda was a conquest. Namely, seducing a woman.

Carmen knew all about his reputation as a heartbreaker of the worst kind. She'd witnessed how he would check out women at various events, seeking out his next victim. He had checked her out the same way, the first time they'd met.

She'd also seen the way women checked him out, too and definitely understood why they fell for him when he was so darn handsome. His dark eyes, coffee-colored skin, chiseled and bearded chin, hawkish nose, and close-to-the-scalp haircut, were certainly a draw.

Then there was his height. Carmen was convinced he was at least six foot three with a masculine build of broad shoulders, muscular arms and a rock-hard chest. Whenever he walked, feminine eyes followed. According to Leslie, although he made Anchorage his home, his family lived in Skagway and were part of the Tlingits, the largest Native Alaskan tribe.

Since their initial meeting two years ago, he'd kept his distance and she knew the reason why. She'd deliberately let it be known that she planned to marry him one day, making sure he heard about her plans well in advance. And upon hearing them, he'd begun avoiding her.

"Granted, it's obvious there's strong sexual chemistry between you and Redford," Leslie said, interrupting Carmen's thoughts. "Sexual chemistry isn't everything. At least you've given up the notion of trying to tame him. I'm glad about that. You had me worried there for a while."

Carmen broke eye contact with Redford and looked at Leslie. "Nothing has changed, Leslie. I'm convinced that for me it was love at first sight. Redford is still the man I intend to marry."

Leslie looked surprised. "But you haven't mentioned him in months. And at Cassidy's christening you didn't appear to pay him any attention."

Carmen grinned. "I've taken the position with Redford that I refuse to be like those other women who are always fawning over him. Women he sees as nothing more than sex mates. Redford St. James has to earn his right to my bed. When he does, it will be because he's ready to accept what I have to give."

"Which is?"

"Love in its truest form."

Leslie rolled her eyes. "I've known Redford a lot longer than you have, and I know how he operates. I love him like a brother, but get real, Carmen. He has plenty of experience when it comes to seducing women. You, on the other hand, have no experience when it comes to taming a man. Zilch."

"I believe in love, Leslie, and I have more than enough to give," Carmen said softly.

"I believe you, but the person you're trying to give it to has to want it in return. I don't know Redford's story, but there is one. And it's one neither Redford, Sloan nor Tyler ever talks about. I believe it has to do with a woman who hurt him in the past, and it's a pain he hasn't gotten over."

"Then I can help him get over it," Carmen replied.

Leslie released a deep sigh. "Not sure that you can, Carmen. Redford may not ever be ready to accept love from you or any woman. You have a good heart and see the good in everyone. You give everyone the benefit of the doubt, even those who don't deserve it. I think you're making a mistake in thinking Redford will change for you."

Carmen heard what Leslie was saying and could see the worried look in her eyes. It was the same look she'd given her two years ago when Carmen had declared that one day she would marry Redford. She understood Leslie's concern, but for some reason, Carmen believed that even with Redford's reputation as a heartbreaker, he would one day see her as more than a sex mate. He would realize she was his soulmate.

"I'm thirty-two and can take care of myself, Leslie."

"When it comes to a man like Redford, I'm not sure you can, Carmen."

Carmen shrugged. "I've dated men like Redford before. Men who only want one thing from a woman. I intend to be the exception and not the norm." Determined to change the subject, she said, "I love June weddings, don't you?"

The look in Leslie's eyes let Carmen know she knew what she'd deliberately done and would go along with her. "Yes, and Denver's weather was perfect today," Leslie said.

"Nadia looked beautiful. This is the first wedding I've ever attended where the bride wore a black wedding dress."

"Same for me, and she looked simply gorgeous. It was Jaxon's mom's wedding dress, and she offered it to Nadia for her special day."

Nadia not only looked beautiful but radiant walking down that aisle on her brother-in-law Dillon Westmoreland's arm. Both the wedding and reception had been held at Westmoreland House, the massive multipurpose family center that Dillon, the oldest of the Denver Westmorelands, had built on his three-hundred-acre property. The building could hold up to five hundred people easily and was used for special occasions, family events and get-togethers.

Carmen glanced around the huge, beautifully decorated room and noticed the man she had been introduced to earlier that day, Matthew Caulder. He'd discovered just last year that he was related to the Westmoreland triplets, Casey, Cole and Clint. It seemed the biological father Matthew hadn't known was the triplets' uncle, the legendary rodeo star and horse trainer, Sid Roberts.

It seemed that she and Redford weren't the only ones exchanging intense glances today. "You've been so busy watching me and Redford stare each other down, have you missed how Matthew Caulder keeps staring at Iris Michaels?" Carmen leaned in to whisper to Leslie.

Leslie followed her gaze to where Matthew stood talking to a bunch of the Westmoreland men. Iris was Pam Westmoreland's best friend. Pam was Nadia's sister and was married to Dillon. "No, I hadn't noticed, but I do now. Matthew is divorced, and Iris, who owns a PR firm in Los Angeles, is a widow. I understand her husband was a stuntman in Hollywood and was killed while working on a major film a number of years ago. I hope she reciprocates Matthew's interest. She deserves happiness."

Carmen frowned. "What about me? Don't I deserve happiness, too?"

"Yes, but like I told you, I'm not sure you'll find it with Redford, Carmen, and I don't want to see you get hurt."

"And like I told you, I can take care of myself."

At that moment, the party planner announced the father-daughter dance, and Dillon stood in again for Nadia's deceased father. While all eyes were on them, Carmen glanced back over at Redford. As if he'd felt her gaze, he tilted his head to look at her, his eyes unwavering and deeply penetrating.

Like she'd told Leslie, she didn't intend to be just another notch on Redford's bedpost. Their sexual chemistry had been there from the first. It was there now, simmering between them. He couldn't avoid her forever, and no matter what he thought, she truly believed they were meant to be together. She had time, patience and a belief in what was meant to be.

She would not pursue him. When the time was right, he would pursue her. She totally understood Leslie's concern but Carmen believed people could change. Even Redford. His two best friends were married with families. She had to believe that eventually he would want the same thing for himself.

Was he starting to want it now? Was that why he'd been staring tonight after two years of ignoring her? Her heart beat wildly at the thought.

When everyone began clapping, she broke eye contact with Redford and saw that the dance between Nadia and Dillon had ended. Now the first dance between Jaxon and Nadia would start. As tempted as she was, she refused to look back at Redford, although she felt his eyes on her. The heat from his gaze stirred all parts of her.

When the dance ended, Jaxon leaned into Nadia for a kiss, which elicited claps, cheers, and whistles. As the wedding planner invited others to the dance floor and the live band began to perform, Jaxon and Nadia were still kissing.

Carmen smiled, feeling the love between the couple. She wanted the same thing for herself. A man who would love her, respect her, be by her side and share his life with her. He would have no problem kissing her in front of everyone, proclaiming she was his and his only. He would be someone who would never break her heart or trample her pride.

How could she think Redford St. James capable of giving her all those things when he was unable to keep his pants zipped? Was she wrong in thinking he could change? She wanted to believe that the same love and happiness her sister Chandra shared with her husband Rutledge, the same love Leslie shared with Sloan, and Nadia shared with Jaxon, could be hers. Even her parents, retired college professors now living in Cape Town, were still in love.

People teased her about wearing rose-colored glasses, but when you were surrounded by so much love, affection and togetherness, you couldn't help but believe in happily ever after. She was convinced that everyone had a soulmate. That special person meant for them.

Unable to fight temptation any longer, she glanced back at Redford. His eyes were still on her and that stirring returned. He smiled and her heart missed a beat.

Then her breath caught in her throat as he began walking toward her.

NEW RELEASE

BESTSELLING AUTHOR

DELORES FOSSEN

Even a real-life hero needs a little healing sometimes…

After being injured during a routine test, Air Force pilot
Blue Donnelly must come to terms with what his future
holds if he can no longer fly, and whether that future
includes a beautiful horse whisperer who turns his life
upside down.

In stores and online June 2024.

Subscribe and fall in love with a Mills & Boon series today!

You'll be among the first to read stories delivered to your door monthly and enjoy great savings.

MILLS & BOON

JOIN US

Sign up to our newsletter to stay up to date with...

- Exclusive member discount codes
- Competitions
- New release book information
- All the latest news on your favourite authors

Plus...
get $10 off your first order.
What's not to love?

Sign up at **millsandboon.com.au/newsletter**